VISION QUEST

Na-qu, na-qu, na-qu . . . the syllables and beat of the drum seemed to match the stroke of wide wings so dark they shone, flashed like a mirror in the sun. They were bearing her high and away, into the great cave of the sky, and the feeling was so restful, despite this residual giddyness and slight nausea, that she kept her eyes closed. She no longer tried to understand the words but heard them like the songs of birds – pure yearning or celebration or lament – or the moaning of branches in a breeze . . . Tolek was nothing but a yellow, grinning skull over the drum, but his striking hands seemed to trace fire over the pale disk of stretched skin. Tatka was another skull, nearer, simpering at her, and in its eye sockets the same fire flickered. Everything else was vanishing into the darkness, actually moving away, it seemed to her . . . They were sinking into the earth and catching fire at the same time . . .

GH00724535

About the author

Will Baker lives on a small farm in California's North Coast Mountains. He is the author of *Backward: an Essay on Indians, Time and Photography* and *Mountain Blood* (winner of the 1985 Associated Writing Programs for nonfiction). He has also written several novels – including the acclaimed *Shadow Hunter* and *Star Beast* – and two collections of short stories. He is married and has three children.

The Raven Bride

Will Baker

NEW ENGLISH LIBRARY
Hodder and Stoughton

First published in 1998 by Hodder and Stoughton

First published in paperback in 1998 by Hodder and Stoughton
A division of Hodder Headline PLC

A New English Library paperback

10 9 8 7 6 5 4 3 2 1

British Library Cataloguing in Publication Data
A CIP catalogue record for this title is available from the
British Library.

ISBN 0 340 65776 6

Printed and bound in Great Britain by
Clays Ltd, St Ives PLC

Hodder and Stoughton
A Division of Hodder Headline PLC
338 Euston Road
London NW1 3BH

For Malinda, Kate, Carole, Dru, Annie, Louise, Marian, Wendy, Karen, Rachel, Susan, Frances, Aunt Gayle, and Aunty Marie

'Here the human race is now being tested to see what it has become in the present and what can be expected of it in the future.'

– Valentin Rasputin, *Siberia on Fire*

'The young ladies bloom like roses, the wild game flies about the streets and comes to meet the hunter of its own accord. An inordinately large amount of champagne is drunk. The caviar is marvelous.'

– Fyodor Dostoyevsky, *The House of the Dead*

'Nature is bare to the point of ugliness . . . In summer, a river, in winter, snow. That's all nature offers here.'

– Josef Stalin, *Works*

'At 40 degrees below zero all things living retire into their lairs and nests. The sun shines brightly, the frosty air is crisp, and the whole world seems to have died out. Only now and then does a fat raven fly past.'

– Yuri Semyonov, *The Conquest of Siberia*

CHAPTER ONE

Satchi Kutznetsova observed caution approaching the parking
shed at this last station, just at timberline. More than once she
had pulled up in bad weather and nearly run over reindeer
huddled under the roofed port. Once it was a snow fox with her
half-grown kits, and once – her most heart-stopping moment – a
great white bear.

She drove a Sno-Klaw, a Japanese engine in a Norwegian-
designed body, which was the smallest snow cat on the market.
It could – theoretically – carry four persons and pull a utility
sled. That time, wheeling around the drift in front of the shed,
she had nudged the bear's hind quarters before she could brake
to a stop. She would never forget the sudden apparition, looming
above her windscreen. The black lump of nose peeling away from
yellow daggers of incisors and a red cave of throat. Then, immense
as he was, he was gone in half a dozen long, fluid bounds.

She had sat for a long time at the wheel. I could bearly stop, she
thought in English, and giggled hysterically. When her fright waned
she knew another excitement. These big whites were very rare now,
and she had heard of no sightings this far south and inland, though
of course the browns, the Siberian giants, were still occasionally a
nuisance for miners or loggers in remote camps. And here was not
only a sighting, but almost a touching, and she felt pride in her
good luck. Her father would be impressed.

Many animals were on the move now, away from the storms
lashing in from the Sea of Okhotsk, and it was Satchi's busiest
time. Every station had to be switched over from solar to wind
or autotimed generator, batteries had to be replaced, and also
scrolls, tapes, and ration kits. Various instruments and the radio
would need checking.

This afternoon she would only take a few readings, update the log, and talk to her father on the radio. By then it would be dark and she would melt ice in a pot on the two-burner stove, drop in a frozen packet of food, and begin her long evening of reading and dreaming and planning, while the wind muttered and whooped outside, pummeling the tiny, insulated unit until it vibrated like a struck gong. The storm had been a full-scale blizzard only two days ago, and scattered squalls were still going through.

She loved this season most of all. Almost every week she hopped on jitney planes into places like Suksukan or Galimy, then drove the Sno-Klaw overland to the stations. The tundra was frozen now and there was enough snow to fill ruts and gullies, so in good weather she could travel swiftly. There was often extra time, so she took along her books and notes, and between chores nibbled at some new text. Once she was snowed in for five days, and then her studies, her gorging on words, grew wearisome. Then it was too much of a good thing. Another charming English phrase. Like ice cream on a polar expedition, her old teacher had explained.

She parked and secured the Sno-Klaw, but before turning to unload the trailer-sled she approached the fuel tanks against the rear wall of the port. Plenty in the natural gas unit, but there was a scrim of frost over the gasoline gauge, and when she breathed it away the needle showed less than an eighth, a reading confirmed by her thump on the tank. She hissed between her teeth in irritation. Whoever brought in the last supply tractor must have peered into the port, seen the first gauge, and promptly driven away. Russian efficiency.

She would have to call for a special fuel drop. What was left in the storage tank, plus her onboard reserve, might not be enough to get her over the ridge. She decided to put off unloading the trailer until morning; there would be plenty of time, perhaps a whole extra day, if the resupply flight was late. The idea transformed her irritation into a pulse of pleasure. She would have extra time, unexpected time, to read and think and dream.

She hurried through the airlock and got the lights on and the wall heater going. The mouse droppings on the table were old; she knew the reason, having glanced at the thermometer on the way in. Almost forty below freezing. Possibly a new record for mid-October. Records were made to be broken. One of the clichés

Kenny had taught her. Was there a record, she wondered, for early mouse hibernation?

That was the sort of thing her father and Kenny argued about, in a stiff, polite, awkward way. Kenny would dredge up articles through his computer at the company offices. Then her father would point out that the life cycles of Alaskan mice differed significantly from those of Siberian species. Kenny would reply that without data no comparison was possible, and her father would note with undisguised acidity that without comparison, no data was meaningful. And so on.

Satchi would be reduced to the role of arbitrator and translator, as usual. In this case she would no doubt remember her mother, whose people told many funny stories about Mouse-woman and her children. Such tales wouldn't work on her father and Kenny, of course. She would have to divert them to cards or the television, hoping they would not simply play with grim, false enthusiasm, or fall into a new dispute over whether American media exploited and corrupted the youth of the whole world (as her father believed fervently). Sometimes both would turn to cabbages propped in front of the screen, watching football matches or old Western movies, which were apparently somehow exempt from Doctor Kutznetsov's theory of electronic imperialism.

Thinking of Kenny, she felt a warm, furtive pang. Her only teacher for certain words. *Naughty*. She laughed to herself, squirmed out of her parka and hung it by the door. The heater had erased the flags of frost made by her breathing, and after she put a blue ghost of flame under the pot of ice, the plain, small room seemed almost cozy. She removed her mother's old ivory clip, carved to depict a crane in flight, and the full meter of her hair shook down, perfectly straight and mirror-bright as a crow's back.

A naughty girl, he had called her. She had understood *knotty*, and agreed. Twisted, complicated, not easy. She had been flattered, then puzzled. *Yeah, come on, be a naughty girl . . .* Did he mean argue politics again? Or chess? No, he seemed to mean only *Get down here now and . . . you know . . .*

Then she had been angry. Their first serious quarrel, in fact. She was not a girl, but a grown woman, only two years younger than he was and almost a Doctor of Letters. It wasn't what he wanted that offended her, but his leering manner. *He* was the child, in most things. Thoughtless, impetuous, easily hurt. A giant boy. Most of the Americans she had met – the scientists, foresters, surveyors and workers – were children. Kids. Their word for a young goat. Curious and greedy and rowdy and foolish, climbing over everything . . .

The pang came again, heating her cheeks. That energy could also be exciting and delightful, a little dangerous. Glowing yellow eyes and hairy flanks. Something rank and insatiable. For beneath his amiable, innocent manner, Kenny had some of the spirit and appetite of the naked old god with horns and a flute.

She had been amused and charmed by his eager pursuit, and together they had played out a fantasy of reckless, clandestine love. The tiny cedar box containing pellets of pungent, dark tar or vials of exhilarating frost-white powder. The three-day rendezvous in a fine hotel in Vladivostok. She knew naughty now, learned with this overgrown, captious boy, and freely admitted she liked it very much. Of course he had been naughty too, done interesting and delightful things to her. That was another American proverb: *It takes two to tangle*.

The water was thundering in the pot, blowing off steam. She took out a frozen dinner, a gray quadrangle of steak with smaller blocks of corn and potato, and dropped the plastic envelope into the pot, wincing. These awful resurrected meals were the one serious drawback of her work. You had to be half-starved and still they made you gag. Sometimes Kenny brought her tinned ham or salted nuts or fresh fruit from his commissary. More wonderful, forbidden things. In her pack right now were two fresh Algerian oranges, a gift before he left for a week to cruise a tract of spruce north of Irkutsk.

Forbidden things. That was another, more serious flaw in their arrangement. They could not be obvious about their liaison, primarily because Kenny and her father were, effectively, professional adversaries. Doctor Kutznetsov worked for the Environmental Review division of the Bureau of Resource Development in Magadan, which theoretically monitored the timber-cutting of Dixie Pacific, the huge American company for whom Kenny was an Environmental Engineeer.

Her father had always lived in a state of delicate balance, Satchi thought. A brilliant scientist who survived in his tiny office and laboratory by performing invisible drudgery, testing and recording the most basic information. Yet he had shrewdly contrived to get that information to a few international learned societies, some with influence on the trade policies of advanced nations with interests in the new Russia. His work was just visible enough to make it troublesome for his enemies in Resource Development to get rid of him.

Satchi had become part of that work. When she returned from the university, her father had grown too busy and infirm to oversee these remote ecological stations in the vast Kolyma watershed, and she had joyfully taken over the job. It was a *sub rosa* employment, tolerated because Doctor Kutznetsov was a senior scientist, and because his superiors had no funds for an extra salary, so her modest stipend was processed as a travel expense paid directly to her father.

Still, she was connected to the Bureau unofficially. A serious, public romance with a young timber executive would be embarrassing, would carry a faint aroma of scandal. People might recall the reason why the elder Kutznetsov's career had never prospered: his marriage in mid-life to Satchi's mother, a young local beauty with no political connections, the daughter of a Cossack and a Koryak woman from the Taigonos. That marriage ended when Satchi was eleven and her mother died of cancer, and a cruel rumor hinted the Doctor was responsible, because he had given his wife over to native healers at the end. Any revival of such rumors would not only hurt her father deeply; it might even force him into retirement, and his work was all he had.

For his part, Kenny could not comfortably invite her to the company dances or parties, or take her on a tour of his lab or give her his pass to the commissary. A flirtation, a 'fling' – another word Satchi loved – was acceptable. But if his superiors believed he was seriously courting the daughter of a government regulatory officer, they would not be happy. He might even be quietly transferred back to the main office in Irkutsk.

So they pretended to be casual. A casual passion. They were in love, but could not afford to show it. She and her father avoided discussing Kenny. She and Kenny avoided discussing the future. It was an uneasy situation, yet she understood that it suited all of them. Pretense, as the Doctor himself often said, was after all the foundation of Russian society.

She had unzipped her bag and set aside her dictionaries and references, and the new novel still in its mailing pouch. Her fingers itched to unseal the packet, but she selected instead a pad and pen in order to jot down quick readings she could later transfer to the log. Her father had taught her to secure the information from delicate instruments as soon as possible, because sometimes one's arrival itself – the change in temperature and humidity in the room, the little shocks of closing doors – could precipitate a malfunction or skew a reading.

She frowned, noting the uneven and extreme oscillation in barometric pressures and daily temperatures. Ten years ago, according to Doctor Kutznetsov, such swings would have indicated a faulty transistor or relay. Highs and lows eighty degrees apart simply meant an equipment malfunction. Now you couldn't be sure. All these instruments, she sometimes thought, actually brought greater uncertainty.

The seismograph had recorded what were surely illegally low planes. The timber executives on a lark, ordering their pilots after wolf or bear as shooting practice. Her frown tightened, then twisted into a wry smile. Buttholes. One of her most favorite words from Kenny. A term at once obscene and ridiculous, just like those company men with their meaty faces and silly shirts. They were asses – fools, nincompoops, oafs, buffoons – and they were holes. Empty, nothing men – zeroes. In a hotel restaurant in Yakutsk one of them had leered at her, whispering loudly and drunkenly over and over: *Chickee-chickee-chickee! Chickee-chickee-chickee!* She and her father had left. The waiter had apologized, cringing, but only on their way out. He was afraid of losing his tip, the hard dollar everyone was scrambling for.

Her smile faded. She tried, and failed, not to think about Kenny among these men, these buttholes, following their orders, laughing and drinking with them. He hated it himself, he said, but it was part of the job. His only chance to influence policy, to save a few more cranes or a little tract of trees near a traditional village. She wondered, suddenly, if he ever considered the reverse influence – how being part of a high risk industry, with its mighty harvest machines and fleet of sawmill ships, was attractive to him?

An abrasive, insistent beep came now from the battery bin. Satchi let out a long breath of irritation. She would have to start the generator and recharge. The solar panels had not, apparently, been producing as they should. She hurried to the stove and saw that her dinner had thawed and swollen inside the plastic shell. She fished it out with tongs from a drawer, burning her fingers on the pot lid, and draped it over a platter.

Damn, *damn*! She hated the mechanical purr of the generator, after looking forward all day to silence or the atonal flute concert of the wind. It would take an hour, perhaps two, to give her the proper margin of stored power. Some of the instruments would not yield dependable readings without a perfectly steady current. She would wait to call her father, in case she had trouble with the generator. He could take apart these antique motors in his sleep, or, more to the point, over the phone, using her fingers.

She ate her gray meal with the fortitude of a soldier in a bunker. The disturbing image of Kenny, a drink in his hand and head thrown back for a hearty laugh, would not leave her. There was no reason for it. She knew it was more likely that he, too, was eating field rations, possibly in the cockpit of a cruise plane bouncing through updrafts and shear winds. He went with the surveyors to the most scattered, stunted, far edge of the taiga, landing often in snowfields to measure and collect.

She was jealous, sometimes, because he came back with live specimens: an ermine or fledgling hawk, and once a fox kit, which they had tried to keep. Her father told them it would die. Of loneliness, he added. Kenny had rolled his eyes and smiled patronizingly, but the Doctor was right, at least about the kit's not surviving.

From the beginning, the three of them had argued. When Satchi brought Kenny home for the first time, they were stiff and suspicious for no more than an hour, and then the combat erupted, and ever since it had been passionate and uncompromising. Her father would sit beside the brass samovar and puff on his pipe, trying to look sagacious and amused, his English dictionary in his lap for reinforcement. Kenny would begin with a comradely handshake, his big-toothed grin. But before long the two of them would be gesturing and stomping about the room, scattering tobacco and sugar over the Turkoman carpets.

Kenny might claim recklessly that the fauna of the region were not declining 'significantly'. He was proud of his restocking and inoculation programs, the nesting sites he had succeeded in protecting. In the heat of exchange he would go further, claiming the new fast harvesting techniques were minimizing impact. She and her father had stared at each other, dumbfounded. They had seen the consequences of these techniques. It was her father's job, after all, to visit the cuts, to verify compliance with habitat regulations, and the first time he had taken Satchi along, the sight had stunned her.

A hissing, sizzling sound, a curl of smoke, and a tree would groan and topple into the snow. Then another and another, the laser-harvester swiveling slowly and steadily, mowing down the dense wall of green, while behind the swath came the chippers. These squat, big-tracked machines snapped up the trees, stripped off their needles, swallowed them with a grinding belch, and spat a hail of chips into the cribs they towed behind themselves. A gang of falcons circled above the smouldering stumps, feeding on the mice and hares dislodged by the harvesters.

It may *look* devastating, Kenny would admit wearily, but the machines get in and get out so quickly that trauma is local and minimal; the animals can begin adjusting immediately to a new set of perimeter conditions. If there is a problem, some unexpected pop drop, we can mitigate right away, redesign the operation. We monitor very closely.

You do not monitor pain, her father had said. You do not calculate the result of training falcons to sniff the ass of ugly machines. Satchi had laughed at that, and Kenny went red in the face. *You* drive an ugly machine to an inspection site, and so do I, he retorted. Satchi drives one to the stations to make your rounds for you. We all drive them.

Her father was deeply angry then, to be reminded that he had drafted his daughter to fulfill his duties. It was the real canker in his soul – the shame of being old and overworked, dependent on his child – who, he knew, yearned to be at Cambridge pursuing her own studies, her beloved books, whether or not there was any use or profit in them. Kenny saw the shame beneath the Doctor's rage and apologized immediately; and then they were all embarrassed and forgiving and sad.

Satchi knew her lover secretly agonized. In his previous assignment, he told her, he had opposed the pulp plantations in the tropics. He had in fact testified at the World Bank hearings on the issue. Here in the taiga the rate of the cut also disturbed him, and the elimination of sub-species before there was time to study them. She had seen him grieve, beneath his cool scientific demeanor, over the kit fox that had been so dear to her.

And yet . . . She could not seem to shake her uncomfortable speculations. Her father and Kenny argued and upset themselves, both of them claiming they had no choice, had to do what they had to do, could only rarely and in small ways influence things for the better. Sometimes they collaborated, through very slight, guarded hints, in a trading of slices of territory to establish a corridor or delay a rotation. It was necessary to watch and wait, her father was forever telling her, *pozhivyom-uvidim*. For what, she had asked him a few weeks ago. For what? Christ to return? Armageddon? Death? Your pension?

This flash of bitterness and disgust had startled them both. Perhaps it was true that she resented being stuck in this far, frozen province, handmaid to an old man's duty of penance, or redemption, or whatever it was that drove her father to stay in service to an agency that merely kept records now – records no one bothered to review. An agency that hardly seemed aware, after twenty-five years, of his existence. At this very moment she could have been in a cozy, cheerful room near a great university, reading and translating all day, visiting museums and libraries, having tea with other scholars, hearing the wonderful slur of English vowels, like a run of brass horns.

She gave a guilty start. She was being selfish again. This was a fantasy that always left her feeling furtive, since her father and Kenny were notably absent from the imagined galleries and teas. She got up, admonishing herself sternly, and rinsed off the plate, glass, and silverware, then slipped on her parka and gloves.

The unheated cubicle of the generator compartment was reached through an insulated door. In the harsh overhead light her breath became again a visible phantom, and she saw a film of frost forming already on the bright chrome of the air cleaner. The cold, the darkness, and the wind were always at work against you, she thought. They never broke down and they never gave up.

Fortunately the motor caught on the fourth try, cleared its throat, and settled into a steady drone. There was enough fuel for the night, and tomorrow she would convert the system to the wind generator. She hoped for no more than a breeze, and temperatures above zero by midmorning, so she could handle her tools without gloves. She would, she decided, wait until all that was done, before calling her father.

Back in the living area, she unwrapped the book. For an hour or so, at least, she hoped to immerse herself, to ignore the throb of the generator and the moan of the night wind, to slide away from the uneasy thoughts that had been dogging her. A good novel should do that – take one away, into the past or future. Or perhaps both. Her own proposed dissertation topic was the old novel of the future, a genre the English had practically invented. *Utopia* – an idea first embodied by Sir Thomas More. Swift, Butler, Wells, Huxley, Orwell, Burgess, Carter – she had read these masters, as well as dozens of hacks and scribblers with nothing in common but a wish to see deeply into the waiting abyss.

It intrigued her that this author was already dead, his actual world gone thirty years ago, while his imagined one lay a century beyond. The volume before her was an intriguing hybrid of the sensational and the elaborately prophetic, and it would amuse her, she thought, to chart how the guesses of this dead grandfather were alternately prescient and ridiculous.

A lurid enough cover – one featuring a dark force encroaching on beings aflame with passion and energy, but wearing very little else. A whole dissertation could be done on the covers of this kind of story. She heard the generator hiccup, and looked away from the book. It was black now outside, the moon not yet risen. She underwent a tremor of exhilaration, with an underlying thread of . . . of what? An anticipation with a faint, strange spice. Almost sinful. She laughed. A knotty naughtiness.

The feeling was just below her heart, above her bowels. *Novel*, she had fantasized as a young student, had to be related to *navel*. A center, a birth, a promise that generations could link one to another, always. Or perhaps *nivel*, from the French: a new level, a higher plane, a creative structuring of things . . . but of course that had been only a fancy too.

Fancy. The Americans made it a bad word. Something light and silly. Too much frill and flounce. It was the frill and flounce of a thought, precisely, that always interested her. *Fantasy* was perhaps closer. The buttholes, drinking and guffawing, wouldn't like that one either, she would guess. Afraid of ghosts. Fantasms. She ran one hand into the long dark mass of her hair, lifted it high and let it cascade again down her back. She sighed. Beginning again, trying to get centered, find a new level. She flipped to the first chapter and started reading.

> Craig Turnbull's theory of the split-second began with
> a glimpse of a beautiful woman. She was asleep under an
> umbrella beside a still, deep pool. He saw her from the
> hotel bar, and – just like that – entered a dream . . .

The generator missed again, and yet again, coughed and recovered. She sat up, listening hard. Was there a new rhythm in the pistons, a throb of strain or developing friction? She waited, but the motor ran even and untroubled. Sediment, probably, settled to the bottom of the gas tank. She bit back into the paragraph and ate her way steadily through the first three chapters in an hour. She emerged to yawn, and then sigh. The thing was classic trash. Young scientist falls in love and begins to question the nature of time. Plans a clever electronic fabrication of micro-relativity. Narrative clap-trap.

The building creaked in a surge of wind. The generator was old, she knew. Her father said the stations in their region received the worst second-hand equipment. No one in Moscow cared, he believed, what data they filed. Nothing mattered, as long as the convoys of chip trucks moved from the interior to the docks at Magadan, and the hard dollars came in.

Clap-trap. More native poetry. English had such a concealed profusion of childish rimes. Hush-hush. Higgledy-piggledy. Bow-wow. Wishy-washy. Ting-a-ling. The light over the page dimmed slightly, only for a half-second. A zig-zag.

She swore softly, then recovered the ivory clip and wrapped and stuffed and pinned her black hair into a compact mass. She stood up, took a flashlight from its bracket, and strode to the insulated door. The generator room had warmed slightly, but its lone small window was still coated on the inside with frost. She examined the gauges. Temperature and oil pressure good. Three-quarters of a tank of fuel. The system was charging. She was listening to the valves when she heard – she thought she heard – something outside.

She went to the window, used her thumbnail to scrape away a patch of frost. A half-moon had just cleared the horizon, shining under hurrying clouds and casting long shadows from a scatter of stunted, skeletal alder trees. The snow was a pale darkness that blew and sifted around and over mounds of itself. Nothing.

The motor died suddenly. There was no gasping or spacing out of explosions, no death rattle; only a high ping and then the pumping and hissing of pure compression, fading swiftly to silence. Again the lights dimmed, and this time did not recover.

'Shit!' Satchi clenched her teeth. An instant before she could turn away from the window she heard a definite scraping on the metal skin of the building. She flicked on the flashlight, sent its long beam out the window, sweeping back and forth. Whatever it was was directly under the window, out of range –

The bear stood up then into the glare of the electric torch. The great head with its small eyes was not a foot away from her own, the dull black scimitars of its claws hooked over the lower sill. An instant later its breath blasted a new star of frost on the pane, as Satchi jerked back, the flashlight bouncing and skittering over the floor, a scream caught in her throat.

CHAPTER TWO

T ime had completely lost its shape, the only light coming now from the blue ghosts of flame behind the glass port of the stove. The wind had wiped away the moon, driving the snow in a horizontal lash, buffeting the building until it shuddered. Satchi had difficulty believing her watch, which told her that only thirty minutes had elapsed since the bear began its attack, since she had been a casual reader sipping tea, a long winter's eve ahead of her.

She had made a bad mistake, after slamming the door to the generator room and rushing to unlock the emergency cabinet. She dug out the compressed air cartridge with the siren-horn and took from her pack the old Makarov and its clip. She was very frightened when the bear began to rip at the metal skin of the wall, but she had not panicked. She remembered both the instructions in the safety manual and her father's lectures.

The siren-horn almost always worked, but it was designed for use outside, or through an open door or window. Also, her father had emphasized, one should not do anything before locating the animal visually, assessing its intentions. So she loaded the Makarov and waited. Three or four minutes of snuffling and scratching were followed by a ghastly screech, a panel of metal rending apart, and – just as she triggered the canister – a sizzling pop. At the same time all the lights in the station went out.

In the sudden, spangled dark, the ear-splitting whoop of the siren filled her skull entirely and left her paralyzed. The noise seemed unbearable, and she flung the canister away, toward the insulated door to the generator room, but the siren went on and on, fading only gradually at first, then grinding abruptly into silence. She realized she had left the flashlight on the floor of the generator room, and the spare was in the Sno-Klaw's trailer. She would be able to fire only at sounds, if the bear began to rip at the door between them.

But there was only the keening of the wind, the rasp of snow on the metal skin of the building. At last she could hear her own breathing, and began to think in minute, painful stages. Her mistake was in not using those first precious minutes to activate the radio. The bear had obviously wrenched off the wall panel at the precise point where the conduit from the storage batteries conveyed cable to the main cabin. She had never heard of such an attack before, never imagined that a bear and blizzard could so simply, in a matter of a few minutes, cut her off entirely from her familiar world.

Everything depended, then, on the Sno-Klaw, which could get her at least within range of a base depot as soon as it was daylight – assuming the storm cleared up and did not worsen. She tried to remember the forecast from the morning, and could not. The siren might have frightened the animal away, but she could not be sure. A bear would wait for hours at a rapid when salmon were running, motionless and coiled for one lightning lunge; and it was the season for final, intense feeding.

She wished fervently that Kenny were with her. Her eyes filled with tears of frustration and yearning; she wanted to ask if there had been other incidents like this, if bears ever went mad, if there had been some abrupt decline in the seal population in this region . . . All at once she had a ridiculous thought. This was the bear she had routed the year before, come back to punish her, come to take her away from Kenny and her father and so punish them too . . . *Daba'sh sdachi*. But for what? The lack of seals?

She had without thinking crept closer to the blue flame of the gas stove. Not because she was cold, but only to have a source of light near. The gun in her hands was heavy and black as a chunk of the night itself. It repelled rather than comforted her, and after a few minutes she placed it on the floor beside her. If the bear came again she would fire over its head first, to frighten it. She had read that it was dangerous to wound the animal; she would shoot to kill only if the bear charged.

It was true there had been trouble with bears and wolves ever since the end of the last century. Once the New Russia was laid on her back (as her father put it), the multinationals had rushed in to cut trees, drill, and mine intensively for as much of the year as climate permitted. The foraging, mating, and birthing patterns of large carnivores had been disrupted, their territories sectioned or reduced by new haul routes and large encampments.

Even the few game parks established by the harried government had been badly designed, according to her father. They were isolated, too small, with insufficient water and vegetation. The animals used them, she had heard her father say, as a retreat – a hideout. She had taught him the English word. For many species – not only bear, but ravens, mink, foxes, rats – had developed a taste for human refuse, and the largest had learned how to eviscerate locked vehicles or lunchboxes, or penetrate storehouses and silos in remote districts.

The question of the marauding bears was a sensitive one, of course, in Russia. A national symbol was becoming an embarrassment – or worse. A decade ago a starving brown bear had killed and partially eaten the eight year-old daughter of a prominent government official, right in the suburbs of a provincial capital. A massive hunt ensued, a slaughter of lone males and relocation of many sows with cubs, although an odd coalition of nationalists and naturalists objected vigorously.

Why shouldn't they wipe out a few of us, her father had demanded. *Oko za oko, zub za zub*. The most basic of natural laws. The bears were victims of a new *chistka*, a systematic containment followed by rapid extermination. Here Kenny would laugh in the careless, superior way that infuriated Doctor Kuznetsov. Anthropocentrism, the younger man would observe in a tone of mock regret, the chronic disorder of the field biologist. A tooth for a tooth means nothing to birds. A sensible policy would be to admit that Game Parks were as obsolete now as the so-called 'Wilderness Areas' of the last century. Big zoos were the only alternative, Kenny insisted; and eventually every large or exotic species would have to adapt to the conditions of captivity.

Satchi had usually sympathized with her father in these disputes, had thought of herself as on the side of the bears. But she felt very differently now, waiting and staring into darkness with a loaded gun beside her. She recalled that this station was, in fact, not far from the tip of one of the game parks. The huge bear could have watched, invisible in the snowy landscape, for the approach of her vehicle, stalked her to the station, waited for night to make his foray into the building.

A thought and a sensation struck her at once, making her bend as if from an abdominal cramp or nausea. In this season she was probably the largest single concentration of fresh meat in a very large area, perhaps hundreds of square kilometers. Her education, the fascinating play of idea and image in her beloved texts, her youth, beauty, vivacity, promise – they counted for nothing. Her blood, her bones, were rich and delicious only in a new and horrible way.

A fetching morsel, she thought with a small, bitter grin into the dark. She remembered a cheap scarf she had bought in Moscow on a holiday with Kenny, how secretly pleasurable it had been watching him and the salesman devour her in the store mirror. Feeling ridiculous, she poked briefly at the pile of her hair under the ivory clip, smoothed her eyelids with her fingers. As if she should look good to the bear, before he ate her. She was being ridiculous so she wouldn't be terrified. Also to remain alert, so the tension did not wear her away to nothing and allow her to drift off . . .

The stove kept the room too warm, and its blue flames cast dim, flickering shadows which seemed to match the moaning and muttering of the wind. She passed into the dream without even knowing it. She dreamed she awoke, a little startled, and found herself outside on a sparkling morning, watching Kenny as he came over the new snow toward her. On his feet he wore old-fashioned webs – hoops of spruce branch crisscrossed by leather strips. Though the sun shone and she felt wonderful – ecstatic with relief and bursting with the adventure of the bear – Kenny appeared anxious, moving at a swinging trot that kicked up a spray of white crystals. He gestured at her and his lips worked but the voice was too faint for her to understand.

Behind her the station seemed smaller and older – was in fact made of discarded wooden panels patched with sections of tarpaulin. Smoke rolled up from the chimney, so the stove had changed too, become an old iron woodburner. Then she heard a throbbing in the air, looked up and saw a single, blurred dot of darkness against the blue of heaven. The dot grew rapidly, developed a shimmering aura and a tail – a helicopter!

She was instantly afraid. She knew it was a company aircraft, powerful and swift. Inside there were men – Kenny's bosses, the meat-faces, wearing snow goggles and carrying rifles. They had come for her. The buttholes with guns. She looked down the path leading to the station, and saw Kenny was even further away – though he was running now, staggering, blundering through drifts, his arms windmilling madly.

She turned toward the station, which had shrunk to a mere hovel, but she felt bulky and awkward, hardly able to move her legs. The whapping of the copter blades was deafening and created a whirling cloud of snow. She could not look up, was too terrified, and for some reason held her hand in front of her face. Through the swirling white specks she was startled to see a fur-covered sleeve, an unfamiliar hairy mitten instead of padded nylon. But it was too late. She heard shots, a steady thunder . . .

She was fumbling after the Makarov on her hands and knees, the room still dark, her heart pounding in her breast in the rhythm of the dream copter. But it was not only her heart. There was a crashing outside, a door was rattling in its frame – the bear! She had the gun now, pried off the safety and with both hands swung the barrel to point at the door. She exhaled as she had been taught, began to count silently – and then heard a voice.

In spite of herself she whimpered, tears welling suddenly from her eyes. The voice came again, muffled behind the double doors of the airlock. '*Otkroi!*'

She secured the safety again with a trembling finger and got up to lay the gun on an instrument table. She cried out and the battering outside stopped immediately, and for an instant she thought it might be the dream again. She hobbled to the inner door, her joints stiff from inactivity, and cried out again.

'Who is it? Yes?'

She heard two or three voices then, in a low, hurried conversation. She brushed the door with her fingertips. The voices ceased, as if they could hear her movement, and she was aware that the wind had diminished. She glanced at her watch. 8:05. It would be daybreak soon. The eastern sky should be gray already. These voices had to belong to—

'*Ya golodnyi!*'

They wanted food, of course! They had to be tribesmen, Koryak villagers travelling for God knew what reason, and they must have been caught by the storm. Out of petrol perhaps, or too drunk to navigate in a blizzard. She found the lock on the door and opened it, stepping into the small airlock chamber. She heard exclamations of gratitude and again the cry for food. Her mother's people had become shameless, cheerful idlers, but there was nothing to fear from them, except the bother of dealing with their beggary.

She peered through the glass slot of the outer door and could just make out, through a haze of frost, the figure of a man standing on the other side. The others had to be behind him, out of sight. The night was indeed giving way to gray dawn in the East, but she could see no silhouette of a vehicle in the snow. The figure before her was only a dark hulk. He was garbed in furs, one of the people from the furthest out, most primitive settlements. They would probably all be missing some teeth, she thought, and would certainly stink.

Hastily she wiped her eyes, conscious of her own gratitude and relief. She would have them in for tea, serve them two or three of the rubber meals. Dirty and rude they might be, but she was glad – very glad – to see them. Government regulations forbade handouts to the Koryak, but Satchi would take pleasure in ignoring such rules. Also it was her duty to warn them about the rogue bear.

A moment before she opened the outer door the figure turned and shuffled away. She thought she caught a glimpse of light gray or even white hair under the hood of the man's parka. She pushed on the door; it wedged against drifted snow, opened just enough to admit the frigid outside air, like a hand reaching in to slap her. She cursed under her breath and shouldered the door harder.

'Wait!' she called, and managed to get her head and upper body outside. 'Come in, you are welcome! *Eh yeti!*'

The man had already disappeared around the corner of the building into the parking area, without looking back. *Shit!* she thought in English. *Little kids. Like the Americans.* There was no answer, no sound but a little scuffling of wind. A bar of silver had appeared on the eastern horizon, beneath a layer of cloud.

'Please,' she shouted into the stillness, hugging herself and lifting first one foot, then the other. 'Come in!' The cold was at her, nipping at nose and ears and fingers. She took a careful slow breath, so as not to sear her lungs, preparing for a final shout. Then a slight sound made her whirl and there, behind her, were three of them.

The biggest, the leader she supposed, must have walked clear around the building. He did have graying hair, although his features were not deeply creased with age, and he was quite tall for a Koryak. He stared at her, without expression, while his companions were nodding and simpering. The other two were very old men; one had no teeth at all and the other only a half-dozen yellowed stumps. Satchi judged the toothless one, who bore a flat, oval drum on his back, to be senile.

She jerked the door again, got it half-open, and gestured at them to enter. The two old men grinned like idiots and hurried over the threshold. As they passed, Satchi noted an odd assortment of clothes: fur hats and fur-lined boots into which were tucked ragged, quilted trousers from Mongolia, an old nylon parka several sizes too large, a bright red shirt under a sealskin vest. Indeed they stank. She noticed great, dark stains, and with a shock of fear, recognized the oily sheen of old blood.

The big man moved more slowly, ponderous and almost stately. He was dressed entirely in furs, spotted here and there by wool or canvas patches, and carried nothing except a knife and small bundle thrust through his belt. He maintained a steady, unblinking stare at Satchi. It was a look she found difficult to meet, so she was glad to shut both doors and return to the interior gloom. One of the old ones was flipping a light switch over and over, exclaiming in pettish astonishment.

'No,' Satchi said. 'No electricity. A bear tore out the power line. A big bear.' She signed with her hands the size of its paw. 'Sit. I will make tea.'

She moved to the cook stove, fired a burner, and filled two pots of water. In a moment she detected over her shoulder a buttery glow. When she glanced at her guests she saw they had lit a small lamp taken from one of the shoulder bags. It was only a metal can with a hole punched in its cap, through which a cotton wick had been drawn, but it gave enough light for her to see the other things they were taking from their bags. Pipes and some wooden and soapstone bowls, a leather pouch, and a flat board, thick with grease and pocked with holes – a *giegie*, a fireboard, the guardian emblem of all Koryak households. It was carved in the crude image of a head and torso, and this one was so dark it had to be very old.

'Bear come for you,' the big man said. 'We come for you.' His voice was low and measured, and though his Russian was accented and ungrammatical, it was clear. 'You not married.'

Satchi flushed and made no answer. No alcohol, at least that she could smell. Perhaps they wanted money, and planned to stage a little ceremony and then argue they had earned something by charming away the bear. A pang of suspicion shot through her. Could the bear be trained, a part of this act?

No, that was absurd. No one had ever made pets of arctic bears, either the big browns or the whites. A coincidence only. Though of course this crew could have tracked the marauder, coming or going, and seen the opportunity for their medicine show.

'What your name?' The big man barely moved his lips to ask.

She told him, and he gave her theirs, a single word for each. He was Kainivilu; stump-tooth was Tatka; and the brainless one, Tolek.

'I must get power restored here,' Satchi said, after a silence, and was immediately conscious of irrelevance, of how flat and unnatural her voice sounded. What could these beggars do for that problem? Their own villages had electricity only a few hours a day. They were entirely dependent on the government substations, and knew less about machines than she did.

Kainivilu threw back his head and laughed, as if she had said something very witty, but made no other comment. He seemed to be staring at her hair, and when she stared back he made a motion suggesting she should unpin it, shake it loose.

Again she felt blood heat her face, and turned away to ignore the suggestion. The water was simmering, so she tossed several bags of tea into one of the pots and sank three foodpaks into the other, larger one. The old men watched these preparations with unabashed lip-smacking and tummy-rubbing, as if she were about to serve a pudding to grandchildren. The big man in furs, however, did not waver in his sober stare; she could feel it even with her back turned.

The room was full of gray light now, the sun up but filtered by an overcast. She was hungry herself, ravenous in fact, and very tired at the same time. She kept thinking of her pack, the two small oranges flown out of Africa to the company commissary. She felt a twinge of mingled guilt and frustration. She had no intention of sharing them, but could hardly eat in front of her guests. She supposed that is what they were, though certainly she had not planned the invitation.

The three were conversing in their own language. Since she had heard her mother's tongue in childhood, had visited villages, she understood phrases, enough to know they were talking about someone ill, haunted by a bad spirit, and then about the radio and the *pawka-pawka*, the Sno-Klaw. Doubtless they were planning to ask her to go for a doctor, or even to bring her medicine kit to the village. These people, she knew, would take anything they came across – aspirin, purgative, antibiotic, tranquilizer – for whatever ailed them – flu, diarrhea, boils, dementia.

When she set the tray of steaming cups before them, Kainivilu spoke to her in Koryak. 'You come with us,' he said. 'No good here. Your things don't work.' He laughed again, a sudden sound like the bark of a fox on a cold night.

Satchi hesitated, considered pretending not to understand. She could tell he would not believe her. Perhaps something in her movements, the set of her head, had betrayed comprehension. It was too late, then. They would try to treat her as one of their own, a Koryak woman, and hence a being with no purpose other than to serve them. She would not collaborate, of course. She would not even give them the satisfaction of knowing she was aware of such claims.

She returned to the stove with the tray, and began to fish out the three bloated, steaming plastic bags. 'I am closing up this station today,' she said in Russian. 'Returning to the base. The generator is out and the batteries too. This is government property, and you can't stay here. If you need a doctor, I will relay your request to Indigenous Affairs and they may authorize a flight.'

She slid a stack of three plastic plates beside the hot food, added silverware, and brought the full tray to set before them. She put it down hard, rattling the plates. 'My father is expecting me.'

The instant after the words came out she cursed herself silently, in a rage of shame. She sounded like a green, fearful girl, hiding behind the tradition of the patriarch.

'Your people are seal people,' the large man said in Koryak. 'Not reindeer.' He blew noisily in his cup, sending a flare of steam in her direction.

The two old men, grinning and chortling, were busy stripping off the plastic sheath around the food, but they looked up long enough to nod in agreement. 'Whale people,' Tatka said, and licked his lips with a tongue dark as liver.

'My people are Russian,' Satchi said, quiet and careful in her fury. 'I am a citizen employed by the government of New Russia. Doing my job here.'

Kainivilu only stared at her again, his face smooth as stone. The old ones ignored her utterly. They had taken out and opened old, brass-handled knives with which they diced and shoveled food, eyes closed in bliss.

'If you will excuse me,' she said in the same soft, throttled voice, and picking up her pack, she walked stiffly to the tiny cubicle of the w.c. She let herself in, shut the thin metal door, and sat clumsily on the toilet seat. She dug out the oranges and peeled the first with angry little stabs and wrenches of her thumbnails, fighting back sobs even as she crammed sections of the bright, acid fruit into her mouth, her stomach convulsing with anticipation.

She should have called her father, first thing, or at least the moment she knew there was a bear snuffling about. He would be worried by now, and if he did not hear from her by afternoon, would begin to badger regional headquarters to send a plane. They could broadcast to her on the Sno-Klaw's shortwave, but the vehicle's own transmitter was too weak to respond until she got over Stanovoi ridge.

Or perhaps Kenny had come back. If her father were not too proud to ask, Kenny could easily secure a company plane. The company would be swift and efficient. The helicopter she dreamed might actually appear in a couple of hours. She hiccuped a sob, jammed a knuckle in her mouth. Humiliation nearly overwhelmed her: to be *grateful* to the buttholes. Because of a bear. *Sonofabitches*, she thought in English, not distinguishing between the men and the animal. She could see them in her mind's eye: the raucous meat-faces in their flourescent rescue garb, slapping each other's hands, leering at her as they offered hot chocolate.

A damsel in distress. The role they preferred for her. Even Kenny. Wide-shouldered and hair tousled by the wind, he would leap from the copter when it was still off the ground, ready to rescue her, defend her honor. So he could have his knotty girl back again. So everything would be back in its place – the trees keeling over, thrashing snow from their branches, the dollars trickling in to keep her father's bureau alive, the big men swooping down to shoot wolves and drink and brag in the bars . . . and the natives – Koryak, Chukchee, Tungus – would go on being stinking beggars like those three in the other room . . .

Even as she recalled them with a start, she heard a hollow tapping through the door, and a chorus of voices. Hurriedly she finished skinning the second orange, quartered it and ate the sections one after the other, a dribble of juice escaping to drip from her chin. They would see the stain, pick up the odd smell of another continent, but she no longer cared. If they were through eating she would begin buttoning up the station. She would start the Sno-Klaw, warm it up, flip on the radio. They would have to go; she would give them a sliver of chocolate and throw them out.

CHAPTER THREE

When she flung open the door between the w.c. and the main room, Satchi was startled to find it almost dark again. They had hung their coats over the two windows and pulled in the wick of their oil lamp until the tongue of flame was no bigger than a housecat's. The result was a small, inconstant pool of dull gold surrounded by a throng of wavering shadows. Toothless Tolek was tapping on the oval drum, and he and Tatka were crooning a slow chant to its beat. Kainivilu was gone. Satchi, her mouth open to dictate departure, was left dumb with astonishment.

She had heard no footsteps, no opening or closing door. In a light, rigid structure of metal, she was certain she would have sensed something. They must have done this as a trick – a child's trick. Must have laughed or sneezed to cover the noise of the door. She could remember voices, she thought, while she ate her oranges and brooded; but perhaps she had been too preoccupied to register other sounds.

More time must have elapsed than she realized, too. She saw that the plates had been scraped clean and removed to the kitchen counter, the fireboard propped nearer the lamp, and new objects arranged beside it. A little stone bowl full of what looked like withered nuts. A necklace of shells and bearclaws. Then another and more violent shock – one that drove the breath out of her. There was her heirloom ivory hairclip, sitting atop a rectangular block, a box . . . no, a book. The new novel she had been reading, left on the table across the room. But the clip!

One hand crawled up her shoulder, tentative and light as a spider. She was dizzy, too unsteady to take another step. How could he have stolen it, right off her skull? No, impossible! She felt her own hair, long and heavy and free down her back. She remembered his gesture, impolite and imperious, a brushing of his mitten behind his ear that said *undo, let it loose*. Then she remembered turning from him, irritated and self-conscious, his eyes boring into her back.

She had been distracted, then. Forgot herself, as they had it in English. Her fingers must have taken out the clip by themselves, even as she burned in resentment, and set it by the sink. That was it, had to be it. Brought on by fatigue and stress. They had snatched up the clip and the book as soon as she went into the w.c.

For what purpose? Some rite of sympathetic magic, no doubt. Her spirit transposed into objects. Books would be appropriate in her case. But this one ... She smiled, struck by the irony of these primitives coveting, as some sacred icon, a cheap novel on time travel. She had stopped reading just as Craig – a handsome, bohemian young genius – had confided to his love his hope of escaping, in a space shuttle experiment with centrifugal force, the rigid space-time continuum, if only for a phantom nanosecond. Craig likened such escape to the visions and out-of-body experiences of meditators and shamans, and now this pretty fiction of the future rested on the floor with bits of bone and wood which doubtless represented just such ancient fantastic notions.

Without looking at her or altering his chant, Tatka motioned her to sit beside him on the floor. Then he dipped a hand into the stone bowl, took out several of the withered lumps, and slung them into his mouth. When Satchi did not move, Tatka exposed the discolored stumps of his teeth in a broad smile, or perhaps it was a snarl. Then he reached out suddenly and took up the hair clip. Satchi saw very clearly the crane, which seemed for a moment to be moving its wings, a trick of the licking cat's tongue of yellow flame, before the knobby dark hands enfolded it. Tatka turned slightly away, looking into her eyes over his shoulder. His hands were kneading in his lap, she saw his shoulders hunch with effort, heard the brittle snap of the ivory.

She cried out and lunged so abruptly she stumbled and went to her knees an arm's length from the grinning old fool, who now lifted his cupped hands swiftly, showed her the fragments, two or three large ones and half a dozen bits, then closed his fingers around them again in a double-fisted cage. She waddled nearer on her knees, raked at his forearms with her fingernails, and in an instant his hands fell apart and the clip tumbled out on the floor, whole and perfect, rocking gently on its curved back. She snatched it up, her lips compressed in a white line, and stared. The discolorations, the slight dent in the silver hinge of the clasp, the crane's worn wing – it was certainly her clip, and it was seamless and sound.

Tatka had her by the wrist, and tugged until she sat down, but still did not interrupt his chant. Nevertheless, she could hear the laughter behind their singing, a suppressed glee. She glared at them in turn, to no effect. The *tump, tump-a-tump* of the drum was, if anything, more energetic. She should have been furious, should have worked up a simple, sharp speech in Koryak, recalling her mother's commands to her as a child, but she could not get over her wonder at seeing the clip made whole. The fragments had been there, she had seen them, curved bits of ivory. They must be even now hidden in the folds of the old man's clothing.

She had to admit the substitution was very skilled. There was no fumbling, no elaborate gesture, nothing but the slight turning away and the clasping and unclasping of two hands. The trick was all the more impressive because, sitting so near, she saw plainly how frail they were, how pitifully garbed.

The odor she had predicted was certainly there too, and strong, but not so unpleasant as she had imagined: a complex layering of smoke, sweat, musk, pitch, and ferment. Probably they were hosts to whole colonies of lice as well, and their diets must have been poor indeed for them to savor government emergency fare. Yet here they were, singing and pounding a drum after a night of blizzard, apparently gaining strength and vigor by the moment.

All at once her resentment left her, pushed away by the weight of exhaustion. She realized the foolishness of her plan to depart at once, when she had been up already for more than twenty-four hours, in a state of alarm. It was day now, the bear was gone, she needed rest and time to collect herself. She sat motionless, her eyelids heavy, letting the high, crooning voices and the hollow pulse of the drum move through her. What was the point of getting angry at these ancient, skeletal children? They probably only wanted to repay her hospitality with a little ceremony, a few tricks pulled from the ruins of their culture.

Where was Kainivilu, anyway? She glanced drowsily at the door. He was the one who made her uneasy, with that flat stare and talk of her going with them. It was only Koryak custom, she guessed, to make extravagant propositions and offers of favor. Still, she was glad he was gone for the moment. Skulking about outside, she supposed, waiting for some signal – a quickening of the drumbeat perhaps – to launch an impersonation of wolf or raven.

She had heard the word for Big-raven in this chant. *Quikinnaqu.* The bird figured in the handful of stories Satchi's mother had taught her. Some of these were gross, involving much excrement and cannibalism, and the loud black bird was more often fool than hero, but she remembered him with affection. He was a god more amusing and intriguing, she had thought, than the white-bearded despot who lived in a whirlwind and made you bow your head to his priest's gibberish.

On mornings when they were shivering on their knees on the stone floor of the old Orthodox Church, gilded icons glimmering behind banks of candles, she would think of the story of *quikinnaqu* and the mouse children, which made her want to giggle. Her father would frown and shush at her, while her mother smiled a guarded, secret smile, as if she knew what her daughter was thinking.

They were different from other families, a difference Satchi sensed as soon as she knew anything at all. Yet they never talked about it, in any direct way. Her mother would joke now and then about dark skin, a sign that *quikinnaqu* had made them out of spit and ashes, but Satchi could not tell whether the joke signified pride or shame.

The memory of her mother brought a sudden and poignant emotion, a kind of deep, delicious sadness. They had not had enough time for stories, for exchanges of the special knowledge a mother gives to a daughter, for all kinds of confidences and consolations, even the minutest, everyday kind – her mother's swift, almost rough fingers plaiting Satchi's hair, the way she slit a fish with a comic apology, the dolls made of sticks and bits of cloth . . .

Satchi was not at first aware of the tears beneath her closed eyelids, of the hand on her wrist. Only when her mother spoke aloud, softly yet very clearly, did these other sensations register, and then the tears scalded and the grip around her wrist was like an iron band. With no preliminaries and no sense of transition, she was beyond terror, beyond sanity, unable to breathe or move, even to open her eyes.

'You have wings,' her mother said. 'You have a tail. You are a little black one who eats everything. Eat . . . eat . . .'

Her hand was pried open, stuffed with something, and brought to her face. She smelled earth, mould, flesh. A grave had opened. She wanted intensely to lift her eyelids, and could not. Somewhere within, in a narrow chamber of her brain, her own voice was shrieking, *Ventriloquism*! *Falsetto old man*! *A trick*!

'Come with us,' her mother whispered. 'Eat.'

Not her eyes but her mouth opened; and the hand guided her hand to shove into it three small, soft clods. She tasted leather and earth, dust and rain, a darkness that shone with decay. Mechanically she chewed, and in a few moments there was a splinter, and then another, and then another, of extreme bitterness, a bitterness so powerful it seemed alive, like a mouthful of writhing, foul worms. She gagged, had to spew or swallow, and so, as the hand lifted again, swallowed to make room for another charge of earth.

The drum sounded in her skull, and the chant lifted under her ribs, the voices seeming stronger now, and much younger. They were singing of Big-raven again, and Satchi heard it, flapping behind and above her, felt the wind from its wings, but still she did not open her eyes, but now for a different reason.

The voice deep inside had explained to her this trick, how one of the old men was creeping around the room, fanning a pair of bird's wings now near, now far from her. The same voice had told her what she already really knew, that the withered clots she chewed were fly-agaric mushrooms from the tundra. The old shamans supposedly received their visions from the poisonous fungus. But there were no modern reports of the practice; the anthropology of all that had been done generations ago.

Sermons in stone, the voice told her in English, *fear in a handful of dust*. She took a deep, if irregular, breath, and was at once relieved and exhilarated. The bitterness was so intense, so startling, that it fascinated her. And the imitation of a woman's voice – truly astounding. So perfect in timbre and inflection that she had hallucinated her mother, had even believed in the hallucination for a moment or two. Enough to suspend judgment and take this bold step, which would allow her unusual experiences, certainly. And in a way – wasn't the concept always a metaphor? – these ragged derelicts had resurrected her mother, or at least that side of her so different from the Russia created – a tiny island of church and school and home – in the vast taiga.

She lifted her eyelids a tiny bit, so as to surprise the sly old children at their antics, but found them both still seated beside her, Tolek tapping his drum and Tatka handling and arranging his little store of objects. Her hairclip was back on top of the book, so she must have let it fall again before she ate from the bowl, which was now nearly empty. They had also lit a wooden pipe, left smoking in a copper bowl, and there was a skull with sharp teeth in its jawbone positioned between her knees. It seemed to her the room was darker, though light still pricked cracks and holes in the coats over the windows. The flame of the oil lamp was guttering, and the moving shadows on the walls reminded her of a cave. Everything was ordinary again, the same as before, except . . .

Somewhere outside there was a thump, as of a heavy object dropped near the door, and then a deep, muffled groan. She smiled. It would be Kainivilu, cavorting as some sort of demon or bogey man. The old men saw her smile and grinned back at her. Without breaking the rhythmic chant, they mimed awe, a huge animal, surely a bear, and the hurling of a spear, firing of an invisible rifle. Tatka dragged from his pouch a thick bundle, which turned out to be, when he unrolled it beside her, the hide of a brown cub.

He gestured to her, patted the hide, closed his eyes, feigned sleep. His expression was again gleeful, confidential – one prankster to another. She was to lie down, pretend to go to sleep, so Kainivilu could make his dramatic visitation. She laid a hand on the thick hair, and the old men nodded approval. The hide was wooly, soft, and did not appear filmed with grime or grease like almost everything else these men produced. Anyway, this was clearly her part, to pretend to retire. The coats over the windows and the lantern were supposed to establish night. It was all a child's imaginative play, and had the same primitive charm.

She felt a twinge of nausea, tilting over to curl up on the bearskin, and closed her eyes against the wavering shadows. Let the play go on. She was Hamlet, and would start a ghost. The drum and chant moved in once more, and she let the words run by like a river, picking out those that eddied back twice or thrice or more. *Quikinnaqu* was disappearing now, into the tale of his own origins, the origins of all things. His black wings rose out of dark nothing, *naqu ye quikinnaqu* as the seal people – her mother's people – said it. All these primitive cultures had such a being – an invisible wind of creation, god's breath, a formless power emerging into light and time and . . .

Naqu. The coincidence struck her so hard she laughed out loud, and one of the old men laughed with her. She opened an eye, seeing him, toothless, leaning toward her to crow over his drum, apparently leaning into space, against gravity, since from her perspective the floor had become a vertical wall. In the novel she had started the night before, *Naku* was the name of the sultry Asian woman who – she could already foresee – would become Craig's mistress and then betray him. She was supposed to represent mystery and danger.

Another silly coincidence. She felt like giggling. She thought she was disoriented and giddy from exhaustion. How absurd and delightful and serendipitous that two syllables should converge in this way, after such an extraordinary night. She murmured them to herself and smiled. She sighed, relaxed and pleased for the first time in days. It reassured her immensely that words had still their wonderful, strange magic, their illogical, irrelevant beauty.

Na-qu, na-qu, na-qu . . . the syllables and beat of the drum seemed to match the stroke of wide wings so dark they shone, flashed like a mirror in the sun. They were bearing her high and away, into the great cave of the sky, and the feeling was so restful, despite this residual giddyness and slight nausea, that she kept her eyes closed and burrowed into the soft fluff of the hide. She no longer tried to understand the words but heard them like the songs of birds – pure yearning or celebration or lament – or the moaning of branches in a breeze.

When the muffled growl woke her again, she thought the hide moved beneath her, so she tried to sit up. A heavy swell of nausea came over her, and she had to wait, propped on one elbow. The peculiarity of darkness in the room was more pronounced. Tolek was nothing but a yellow, grinning skull over the drum, but his striking hands seemed to trace fire over the pale disk of stretched skin. Tatka was another skull, nearer, simpering at her, and in its eye sockets the same fire flickered. Everything else was vanishing into the darkness, actually moving away, it seemed to her. Even the pinpricks of brightness coming through the coats on the windows had receded. The fireboard seemed to rock and skitter, its wooden mouth drooling grease. They were sinking into the earth and catching fire at the same time.

The voice inside had been babbling, she realized, in more than one language, though the phrases lost meaning as soon as they took shape, or confused one another . . . monstrous puns . . . *hallucination . . . hallowed sin of nations . . . frisson . . . free zone . . . freezing.* It was desperate, panicked silliness, and in another moment all words were blown away like so many dry leaves.

Tatka had picked up the soapstone bowl, now empty, and gotten to his feet, still singing. To Satchi, looking up, he seemed huge, lurching into the darkness. The toothless skull beat fire from the drum, sang now for the second time in a woman's voice. There was a snarling outside the door, which began to shake in its frame. The yellow cat's tongue licked once and withdrew inside the oil can lantern, leaving a single, silken thread of black smoke.

Tatka stood with his back to her, a black shape from which she heard the rustle of clothing, a clink of the stone bowl, then a splashing. At the same moment the airlock door was thrown open, and another even huger shape blotted out the instantaneous rectangle of brightness. For a time she could see nothing but whorls and coruscations of a fiery dark. Then the splashing stopped and Tatka loomed near again, bearing the bowl, steaming now, to the drummer. Tolek took it with one hand, the other still thumping his drum. Agape with mad glee, he stretched his thin, wrinkled neck and clamped his bare gums on the stone shell, like a turtle. Satchi could hear him sucking and burbling in the hot urine, while his small, glittering eyes watched her over the rim of the bowl.

She could hear also the heavy tread of the other, feel the floor spring under her. The voice in her brain had become tiny, thin, distant – meaningless as a fly buzzing in an empty room. She was motionless, unable to think of anything at all; she was a corpse, upon which her face had been set like a wooden mask. Feet shuffled and clicked on the floor; she heard a deep, coughing grunt, and smelled an odor so rank and alive she had to clamp her jaws to keep her gorge from rising.

She resisted with all the inertia of a corpse, of a being bereft of consciousness, but the wooden mask of her face pivoted ever so slightly. Just enough so that she could see the hulk with hair flaring lighter at its shoulders, see one eye flat and small beneath a tufted ear, see, just before she stopped seeing anything more, the foot still with a fringe of snow caught between the long, curved black claws.

CHAPTER FOUR

Though she leaned ahead and planted her feet firmly, Satchi had the impression she was walking backward in time, the snow and wind hurrying her further and further into a darkness where nothing of her former life existed. Her mind went on trying and failing to explain what was happening to her, what would happen to her. Instead, odd images were rising up, as in a dream.

She recognized them. They came from a book she had pored over as a child. *The Vanished*. Photographs of robed figures on camels in a desert of white dunes that reminded her of snowfields. Of men with braided hair and curved swords, mounted on shaggy little ponies. Of tents like black wings perched on the slope of great mountains. They were all from a chapter entitled 'The Golden Band: The Mongols,' and they all looked a little like her mother's people.

Though it made no geographical sense, she felt she was walking toward these figures, which were on the other side of the darkness. They were alive there, the people and camels and horses; the sun shone and flies buzzed and things stank. But if she reached them, she would never be able to come back, to Russia in the twenty-first century . . .

Perhaps it was already too late. Her hallucinations, the delirium brought on by the mushrooms – they seemed to have happened days ago. She thought a bear had entered the station, she had seen its hair and claws not three feet from her, and the resulting bolt of terror had left her catatonic. She remembered being carried to the back of the Sno-Klaw, rigid as a corpse.

Then they were moving, bouncing and skidding. Someone – something – was driving recklessly. She thought, absurdly, it was the bear. When the fuel ran out they walked, hulking shapes beside and behind her in the blowing snow. At times they turned toward her the grinning faces of the old Koryaks; other times she glimpsed a black snout.

They had come to a tent of some kind, a frame of sticks covered with reindeer hides, and Satchi fell into the deepest, most death-like sleep of her life. Nor had she any idea how long this sleep lasted. Waking up had been like climbing up through a tunnel driven deep in a snowdrift; she emerged into consciousness with a feeling of fragility and lethargy, as if reviving from a prolonged, almost fatal fever, or – she understood the phrase for the first time – as if she had been born again.

Weak and wordless she had smeared into her mouth the paste they gave her – some tundra berry pounded together with dried dog salmon. Later, there were steamed willow and alder shoots and a haunch of reindeer that she gnawed long after she was full, for the comfort of it. The old woman and girl who gave her food only smiled and would not speak to her.

The woman had pointed over and over at Satchi's foam insulated plastic boots, and when Satchi slept again, must have pulled them off. She awoke under a bulky fur blanket, and beside her was a pair of sealskin boots. They had brought also, incongruously, her book bag; and while she ate for the second time she went through it. A heap of the medicine bottles and bandages from the first-aid kit, her whole supply of chocolate, the flashlight – its batteries dead now – and two books: the notebook log from the station, and her novel. She remembered seeing the men pass around the Makarov, but it had vanished before her hallucinations began. Probably into Kainivilu's bundle.

As soon as Satchi had licked the fish-grease from her fingers, the Koryak woman motioned her to go out. She pulled on the sealskin boots, zipped up her nylon parka, then took the bag and wrestled her way through the cramped entrance chamber. When she pushed aside the hide flap to the outside, the men were waiting for her, standing beside two reindeer hitched to a sleigh and four others with packs lashed to their backs. It was overcast, warmer and calmer than it had been – a dead white world that seemed to absorb both light and sound into itself, returning nothing. When Kainivilu spoke his voice seemed diminished, distant; she could barely understand him.

'We must go,' he said in his own tongue. 'Sick people. We bring help.'

Tatka had already taken her bag and was securing it to one of the reindeer packs. Satchi was trying to bring forth words, a peculiar experience of grasping after things that had always been familiar, close to her, dependable, but now seemed cold and slippery and elusive as minnows in a shimmering pool – suspended there, perfectly visible, but gone in a flash as soon as she reached for them. *Help. Return. Please. Airplane.*

They were already moving, and her own feet moved after them. She uttered a sound, a groan and sigh combined, and Tolek laughed. She saw his pink, toothless gape under the fur cowl of his parka when he turned to look at her.

'Woman-who-sleeps,' he said. 'You must come. Wapak wants you.'

'Wapak?' she whispered, and yet he heard her.

He made a gesture of stuffing into the pink, steaming hole of his mouth. 'You eat him. Wapak, he took you away!'

Ahead of them Kainivilu made a sound. Tolek turned from her, the snow blew between them, and she was trudging again in emptiness.

Wapak was the mushroom then, or its spirit. She knew the power of the poison now, could understand the grounds of their superstition, how they could believe a god inhabited a handful of dried, bitter nubs. She had really believed she heard her mother's voice, had seen a bear beside her. Her flesh still rang, vibrated imperceptibly, with the shock of those impressions.

But she had not been prepared for this peculiar, floating lassitude, for her inability to reason and decide. After a great effort, she had managed merely to orient herself in relation to the world she had left behind. The station had been at the very edge of the tree-belt, the last spruce and stone-pine forests before Stanovoi ridge. Here she saw only a few straggling alder along water-courses, indicating they had moved eastward. From a brief period when the sun was visible, a pearl behind the clouds, she guessed they were also drifting north, therefore toward Okhotsk – the most desolate and forbidding coast.

She remembered an off-hand remark of her father's, about native culture owing its survival to a barren, inhospitable territory – which was, unfortunately, scarcely able to support the natives themselves. There were few trees to interest the timber companies, no scenery for tourists, and the fabulous gold of the Kolyma country lay mostly to the south. In the brief summer the tundra was a mosaic of stagnant, impassable bogs, the soil beneath them still frozen. In winter the fierce storms lashed out of the Bering Sea across Kamchatka, and not even the most advanced craft of sea, land, or air would risk traveling through them.

She grew anxious, trying to imagine the rescue team. She could carry them as far as the station, where they would find the damaged wall, the severed power cable, the four used plates and cups. She could see them begin their search, a widening circle . . . But then the planes would grow tiny, swallowed up in the dead, gray sky. They would be looking for smoke flares, a red snow-marker. She understood – again with an effort – that she ought to have stayed at the station, or with the Sno-Klaw (which was by now, she supposed, buried in drifts), or even at the tent.

She did not know why she had not made those choices, or how to explain her sitting, stupidly, with these beggarmen, listening to their drum, eating the mushrooms. She had felt bound somehow. Invisible fetters. The golden band of the Mongols. In the old children's book it was only a trade route, the silk and ivory and tea moving one way and salt and gold and furs the other. A tenuous linking of the most ancient and the most primitive. The nomads of East and North. The herdsmen – horse, reindeer, yak – and the ice people, the seagoers. *The pan-Arctic cultures*, she remembered reading, *remained almost as they were in the old stone age – frozen in time*.

But she was not frozen in time, she was moving, as over white hummocks and swales of sand or ice, lurching backward, toward whatever it was that preceded time. The reindeer that shuffled and loomed beside her occasionally, their tread a soft hushing, were already gone into that place. Against the fringe of snow on their antlers and muzzles, the black eyes, the black, steaming nostrils were startling as holes bitten out of the universe.

So it seemed natural when their party came to a halt before another, larger hole, in a dish-shaped cavity at the crown of a great drift. Nor was she surprised when Kainivilu led her up the steps chiseled in the steep slope, and they found a dead dog, a wreath of dry grass knotted to its neck, hanging on a stake beside the opening. She found herself relieved, almost joyful, to see the fur-clad shapes below, huddled around the fire. They came down through the smoke on an upright split log, setting their feet in the holes cut through it at intervals to make a ladder.

There were three women, one very old, two children, and a man who looked like Kainivilu's younger brother. The children smiled and the littlest ran to Kainivilu, but the women only stared at Satchi, open-mouthed. The men spoke rapidly, and she understood only the Russian words for medicine and radio, and the name Tolek had spoken to her – Woman-who-sleeps.

'*Eh yeti*,' the brother said to her. She could not read his face, though it seemed empty of the fear and hostility she sensed among the women.

'*Yeti*.' After a moment she swallowed and said, haltingly, 'My mother was Yayocanaut.' Yayo, as they had all called her, or red-tail, because she told them the name meant Fox-woman. Satchi had not even known she remembered the nickname, until this very moment.

The reaction was unexpected. The old woman gave a little shriek and fell to her knees, and the two younger women began to jabber, pointing toward one of the four large posts that held up the roof. The light from the fire was weak and inconstant, but Satchi could see the room was surprisingly large, eight-sided, made of vertical posts of alder with moss stuffed in the cracks. The lower roof slanted to the square made by the four pillars, in whose center was the ladder to the entrance and smoke hole; and from these rafters and walls hung furs, snowshoes, rifles, lumpy sacks and fuel cans.

Kainivilu moved to the pillar and bent over what she had taken to be a chest covered with a wolfskin. He motioned to her then, and when she approached – the women shrinking out of her path – he drew back the skin and she saw that it was a kind of crib. Another child, perhaps five or six years old. 'My son,' he said. 'Very sick.'

The small face in its nest of hareskins was wet with perspiration, the lips almost black. Behind slitted lids, the eyes moved restlessly. The child's skin was like a dark shade over an oil lamp; there was a flame somewhere within, giving off a faint glow, consuming slowly. Instinctively Satchi lifted a hand, wanting to touch, but again she felt the hostility behind her, and hesitated.

She looked at Kainivilu, who was watching her with the same unwavering intensity. It was the nearest she had been to him – at least with her wits about her – and she saw the fine seams in his face, the yellowed eyeballs and coarse white hair in his ears. He was an old man, despite his size and carriage, almost as old as her father. If this was his son, one of the younger women must be his wife. She noticed also, for the first time, the necklace of bear claws at his throat. Very likely the source of her hallucination.

'My mother's cousin had a girl called Yayo,' he said. 'She run off with a soldier. Maybe Wapak make her speak to you.'

Satchi stared at him. The wind and darkness were at her again, so she could not think. But she heard the voice. *You have wings. You have a tail.*

'Her mother was a doctor, great doctor.' The yellow eyes would not release her. 'You are not Woman-who-sleeps. You have other ghost inside.'

'Bad ghost.' It was one of the women behind her, hissing like a cat.

Kainivilu said something sharp, his eyes darting from her finally. Then there were voices overhead, a warning, and a moment later Tolek and Tatka swarmed down the ladder, packs over their shoulders, with amazing agility. They dumped their burdens by the fire, then jerked back the hoods of their parkas, their ancient, yellow skulls gleaming, and called out boisterously. The children rushed forward, trying to climb up into the old men's arms. There was some giggling and roughhousing, and Satchi saw that the younger women were, at last, smiling too. But the old one remained on her knees, her hands clamped over her mouth, still staring at Satchi.

Finally Tatka pushed away the children, shaking the skirt of his parka as if to rid himself of ants. He untied one of the bundles and unwrapped, with great care, the *giegie*. As he did so the room became utterly still, and Satchi found herself holding her breath. The fireboard, black and glistening, was placed reverently at the hearth. Satchi saw the niche that had been worn in the floor, the stone with a tilted face used to prop up the board. Tatka took a twist of dried grass from a bunch hanging on the wall and draped it over the wooden head.

Tolek had unlashed the drum from another pack, and now held it momentarily in the smoke from the fire, then dipped it before the *giegie*. He sat quickly then, and began to tap the drum and chant. Tatka sat beside him and joined in, and a moment later Kainivilu and his brother followed suit.

It was some kind of greeting song for the fireboard. While the men sang, one of the young women hurried to a blackened iron pot near the hearth and scooped out a bowl of steaming mush. She picked up a wooden ladle, knelt beside the fireboard, and with great care served the little wooden figure. She tipped the ladle and dribbled food into the gash of its mouth, while the chant became softer, almost a lullaby.

Satchi felt a tightness in her throat, watching this tableau from the shadows. She was still standing by the sick child, and the group around the hearth seemed as separate as a painting on a wall – a rude Rembrandt with dark, swathed figures grouped around a central flame that touched homely features with supernatural glory. Their pathetic reverence toward a slab of greasy wood, she knew, no longer had anything to do with the Promethean magic of fire-starting. The holes in the base of the board were made half a century ago, and these people used matches, she was sure, just as the cans hanging on the wall proved a dependence on kerosene.

The Vanished. They had, she guessed, already disappeared as far as any formal records were concerned. Most of the tribes of the whole area – Chukchee, Yakut, Tungus – lived around government stations, in government housing. A very few families chose to live by themselves, following herds in summer, wintering in traditional houses like this one. They trapped a few fox and marten, hunted seals, embroidered parkas and boots to sell to the timber workers as souvenirs. She looked again at the sick boy, his eyes closed now and each breath long and shallow. They were vanishing before her very eyes.

The chanting was over, and Tolek had placed the drum ceremoniously on a peg in the wall to the left of the fire. The old men smiled again, rubbing their stomachs, while the women filled more bowls from the pot and handed them out. Kainivilu had recovered her bag from one of the packs and now brought it to her. He had spoken to the old woman, and she came fearfully behind him bearing a bowl.

'You must eat.' His voice was still guttural and peremptory, but for the first time she heard something of kindness and solicitude in it. He stepped back and with one hand urged the old woman nearer. 'My mother, Pipik.' He smiled. 'Mouse-woman.'

The old crone was indeed very small, humpbacked and twisted with arthritis. Her eyes, however, were bright, unblinking, fixed on Satchi's face in what seemed to be a fascinated terror. She said something too low and rapid for Satchi to catch, and held out the wobbling bowl.

'She asks why you have come back.'

Satchi looked at him, pleading.

'She sees your ghost. Her mother's sister's child. She was the great doctor.'

Satchi took the bowl, tentatively, and the old woman snatched back her hands. It was an impossible question, and without premeditation she gave the only answer she thought Pipik might believe. 'Wapak,' she said. 'He made me.'

Pipik looked at her son, then at the smoke hole. She seemed on the verge of panic, her eyes glittering as they rolled here and there in the room. Gently, Kainivilu pushed her back toward the others, then turned to Satchi again.

'You will help my son, after you eat,' he said stolidly, but his eyes seemed to be pleading. Nothing in his expression changed, but she sensed the pain in him.

'He is—' She stopped, unable to form the question.

'Yina. Only boy. A girl two years old first. Five days ago she die.'

He spoke matter-of-factly, already moving away from her to take his place before the fire. None of the other women, she noticed, had served themselves yet. Nor would they look at her. Her legs felt suddenly unsteady beneath her, so she sat down next to the little bed, the bowl between her knees and her book bag beside her. They used matches, loved plastic boots, but fed their wooden guardian, believed in reincarnation. Their children were dying, so they sought the tablets and syrups of the invader, and kidnapped her to administer them.

For she knew that they would expect a magic cure. There would be no way out for her, no excuse. She had been given a name and had accepted it. Here were her sacred implements – the bottles of antibiotic, coagulant, aspirin, disinfectant and sedative, the gauze and scissors and needles. Here was her book, which they doubtless thought was full of spells.

She was eating as she was thinking these things, eating voraciously. The steaming matter in the bowl tasted of blood and rancid fat, which had been mixed with flour. A cup of tea had appeared at her elbow, though she did not remember who brought it. She blew and drank, blew and drank. There would be no sleep for a long time. Water would have to be boiled, cups sterilized, special food prepared. Then she would have to watch, be ready, try to remember every scrap of information from her perfunctory reading of the first-aid manual.

Satchi kept her fingers moving, licked and sucked them after dipping up food, because they would tremble if she didn't. She was afraid of what would happen to the boy, afraid of his mother in the room watching her. If he died, would she leap and strike with a knife? Would they drive her away, into that snow and darkness where she would surely perish?

It was a pure coincidence that she had the blood of these people in her veins, spoke a few words of their tongue, was haunted by memories of her mother. Even more remarkable that a man desperate with grief himself, practiced in imitating a bear in various ceremonies, should arrive only hours after the attack of a real bear. She saw now how vulnerable she had been, how she had collaborated in some obscure way in this whole journey. And now she was – without any experience or preparation – to be some kind of shaman, a witch, one with power over other souls.

Her new work did not, however, go as she had imagined. During her examination, she gave what she thought was a creditable performance as a physician. The boy had a temperature of almost thirty-nine degrees, and he had fouled the moss they had bunched under him and secured with a triangle of deerhide. She guessed he was probably dehydrated from diarrhea, and ordered sugar water. With surprising alacrity, the women carried out her every instruction, sterilizing vessels and cloths and preparing a clean, flat stone for her instruments.

With cotton swabs she cleaned mucus from his nose and ears, but not a great quantity. Nor was he coughing up sputum, which might have indicated pneumonia. She hesitated to try any of the antibiotics without more clues, in case of an allergic reaction, so she gave him only aspirin and vitamin C. The boy was passive in her arms, occasionally following her with his eyes, but at other times seeming not to focus on or even register her presence. A brain fever, she had begun to suspect.

When he was clean and wrapped securely in the rabbit-skin blankets again, apparently drowsing and not in immediate discomfort, she sat on a sealskin beside his bed, hoping for some rest. But within moments the others had gathered around her, and Tolek had taken down the drum. Only Kainivilu was absent; he clambered up the ladder without a word or backward look. She caught her breath, just as the bulky body disappeared through the black hole above.

They were all staring at her, Tolek and Tatka simpering like idiots. She put her hand on her bag, as if the bandages and bottles inside could protect her. She had done everything she could, she would watch away the night if necessary – what more did they want?

'*Quikinnaqu e Ememqut e Annamayat!*' Tatka crowed at her, gesturing at his face, protruding his tongue.

Big Raven and his son, the famous Ememqut. Most of the stories the Koryak told were about this son, a clever, ribald hero with a huge family. Her mother had told Satchi some of these tales – silly exploits, often scatalogical, full of exclamations. Did they expect her to repeat them?

From the bed beside her came a low, urgent moan. She raised up, and found the boy looking at her through half-closed eyelids, his mouth twitching. She took his hand and felt it contract a little in her own. There were soft cries from the women and the other children, who so far had only giggled and peeked at her from behind their mothers.

Tolek reached out and pulled at her sleeve. In his hands was a strip of deerskin, densely embroidered, which he placed in her lap. He, too, gestured at his mouth. Tatka snatched up her bag, plunged a hand inside. Satchi felt a tremor of alarm, and released the sick boy's hand. They were following her every move, hunching toward her as if she were an animal they had cornered.

Tatka had produced the novel and shoved it at her. In a Russian barely comprehensible, he said 'tell story' and 'Gospel.' The others nodded aggressively. Satchi stared stupidly at the novel's cover, the flames reaching into shadow. A mad thrill, a desire to burst out laughing, flickered through her and was mercifully gone. They thought she had brought a Bible! This absurd story of the future.

She looked up and found them all expectant. Tolek had begun to rap the drum gently with one knuckle, grinning idiotically at her. It occured to her that this culture might find a curative power in stories. Hadn't her mother in fact told Satchi those tales of Ememqut when mumps and flu had kept her in bed? So they expected her to be the complete witch doctor, to comfort the afflicted by reading from her chosen book!

It was true that she remembered little of her mother's lore, except the pleasing melody of her voice, which changed from gruff to wheedling to sweet, depending on the characters. Whether she understood or not, there was comfort in the flow of words, as in the music of a fountain or chimes swung by the wind. She could not hope to have that fluency in their tongue, could not hesitate to translate into Russian. They would have to hear it in English, then. Though first she would relate the simple outline of the story . . .

She took a deep breath and opened the book, leafed through it to the point where she had been interrupted – a very long time ago, it seemed to her – by the failing generator. Then she looked up into the ring of intent, brown faces, and haltingly began her summary.

'Long time, very long time, a hunter –' she patted the bed beside her '– like this one – hunter fly very high, see everything. Want to make everything . . . stop. No go any more. Only him, the hunter, can go. Walk right up to anything . . .'

CHAPTER FIVE

The other men had gathered around the table, where Inspector Sokhalov sat cataloguing and bagging the evidence. The men stamped their boots now and then, or hunched shoulders inside the heavy parkas and flight suits. They were pretending to be cold, an excuse for their impatience. Actually, the snowdrifts under the eaves were extra insulation, and with so many bodies in it, the little building was barely at freezing, thirty degrees above the new winter outside.

'What was in it?' McFarlane asked idly, pointing at the rude stone bowl the inspector had just examined and was now wrapping. They had seen him sniff at it and smile.

'Peess,' Sokhalov said, without looking up. Very gingerly he tugged at a sheet of paper on which were assembled three fragments of yellowed ivory.

McFarlane looked around at the rest, mystified. He had, Kenny saw, understood *peace*. One of the men made a quick gesture, as with an invisible hose, between his legs. McFarlane grinned, until he saw Kenny watching, and then tried to convert the expression into a yawn. One of the other men laughed in disbelief.

They blamed him for the delay, Kenny knew. For poking everywhere, around and around and inside and outside. For picking up every stray hair and bit of lint. And of course for making them feel guilty. Guilty because they did not match his glum intensity, his anxiety and self-blame; guilty for merely wanting to accept the obvious and get back to camp, to hot showers and a drink and maybe a movie or game of pool. He caught them exchanging looks, the upside-down smiles or puffed-out cheeks that signalled bored suffrance, the attitude of parents dealing with a willful child.

And Sokhalov, of course, blamed them all: for being here, for being Americans, for hauling away his country, and most especially, in this particular case, for creating a tremendously embarrassing situation for his bureau. Technically, Satchi was not supposed to be doing her father's work in the taiga. Technically, the Koryak herders were supposed to be on a restricted range. Technically, Russia was a civilized country, and the Moscow crowd did not like to hear tales to the contrary.

'This,' Sokhalov said, and looked carefully at Kenny as he tapped the paper under the heap of ivory fragments. 'Your frand was favorite of this. Was fond.'

Kenny swallowed and forced himself to speak in an even tone. 'Very fond. She had very long hair.' He swallowed again. 'Kept it pinned with that. An heirloom.'

Sokhalov nodded, pursing his lips. 'Yes. But pratty common. My grandmother have one. But you see is broken.'

There was a brief silence. Kenny did not trust himself to reply. 'No shit, Sherlock,' one of the men said in an undertone.

'Except torch, nothing else broken in this room.' The inspector reached out with one finger to nudge one of the fragments. He smiled. 'Foods and teacups okay. Bear not come in here.'

Harris, who was also a forester and therefore management and co-leader of this expedition, uttered a pointed sigh of irritation. 'So what's he saying, the bear ripped up the generator shed and then these Eskimo dudes scared him off? And she left with them, without any struggle?' He addressed the question to Kenny, as if he were a slow interpreter. 'I mean, why would she?'

There it was, the real question. They had been skirting it, implying it, assuming it. Harris was looking at him defiantly. *You were doing her, you were supposed to be cool about it. You tell us, Hotrocks, what's going on here.* It was a question, Kenny realized with dread, he would face over and over, in various forms. It was in Satchi's father's eyes, red-rimmed and bleary from insomnia. Pendergast, the big boss, had asked in a grim fury, before authorizing the company copters. Sokhalov, too, was asking, in his smiling, carefully oblique manner.

Kenny ignored Harris. 'The generator,' he said to Sokhalov. 'It was dark. She could have stepped on it, or one of the . . . visitors.'

Sokhalov shook his head, meditative. 'Koryak boot very soft. Also, see, smooth broken.' He ran his finger along an edge of one fragment.

'Clean,' Kenny corrected. 'Clean break.'

'Yes.' Sokhalov smiled mournfully and then quickly folded the paper around the fragments, slid the package into a plastic sack, and placed it with the other sacks on the table. 'Deliberately on purpose.' He stood up and looked around at the other men, surprised and apologetic, as if he had forgotten they were waiting. 'Somebody . . .' He made a quick gesture of snapping a thing in two with clenched hands.

'Yeah, well,' McFarlane said in a derisive drawl, 'why'd they piss in a bowl?'

'Ceremony,' Sokhalov said. 'Special ceremony.'

The inspector gazed steadily at Kenny, during the mock groans from some of the men. Kenny read the look as cautionary, but there was no need. He knew a little about the practices of local medicine doctors, and could guess all too well the Russian's line of reasoning. Satchi had not resisted, had perhaps invited the illegal herders into the station, where they had conducted some sort of rite. Perhaps she had herself broken the hairclip, a symbolic revolt of some kind, before departing – willingly.

Kenny felt himself on the threshold of dread. His boss and the authorities in Moscow also had good reason to fear. Journalists had picked up the scent, and some very unflattering rumors were likely to circulate. A beautiful young girl had been eaten by a bear, because an outmoded generator failed. Or she had been abducted by outlaw herders, perhaps raped and left to freeze. Or – speaking of rape – the girl had been jilted by a rich young American working for a greedy lumbering corporation. Unbalanced by despair, the power out and no radio contact, she had simply driven into a storm to die.

Kenny wanted to believe this last fabrication was absurd, wanted to dismiss such preposterous innuendo completely. But a certain unease persisted. If anyone felt jilted, he did. Not in the conventional way, but in the sense that Satchi had turned away from him in the last few weeks, become distracted and melancholy, even withdrawn and combative. Yet as far as he knew, Kenny's only rival was the stack of books she buried herself in, the novels and collections of myths about the future.

He saw in her a perverse, elusive desire for solitude. After a weekend of inflammatory, exhaustive sex she would leave him with hardly a backward glance, eager to flee into the icy wasteland and her arcane texts. Doctor Kutznetsov had mentioned once to Kenny that her mother was also given to moods. The Koryak blood, he hinted. Λ happy people for the most part, but superstitious. Enamored of ghosts and magic, even after a century of exposure to civilization.

He remembered then some titles, idly noted, from shelves in the Kutznetsov apartment: *The Mongol Destiny*, *Shamans of the Ice*, *The Raven People*.

Sokhalov had now stowed everything and slung his pack over his shoulder. 'So,' he said gently, 'here we are finish. Now I write up report.'

'She wouldn't go off like this, on her own.' Kenny was aware of the pleading undertone in his voice, and hated himself for it. 'Never.' He swallowed. 'Normally.'

Sokhalov sighed and nodded vigorously. 'Here in Siberia,' he said, 'normal is extremes. But I am encouraging now, in this case. No blood. No breaking, except hairclip and torch. Not foul play, I think.' He smiled tentatively at Kenny. 'You are encouraging too.'

Harris opened the door, and instantly the cold was in the room – a current heavy as water moving over them. The light, too, was paler and heavier. Another hour and the sun, dull and small behind overcast, would withdraw beneath the horizon. 'We're going,' Harris said. 'Like the man said, we are finish.' He looked at Kenny, not a challenge this time but a comradely chiding. 'Let's give it up, man. For today. Talk to Pendy tomorrow and maybe –'

'They didn't take the trailer with extra gas. The Sno-Klaw in this terrain would only be good for seventy-eighty kilometers. They've got to –' He stopped short. *They*. For the first time he had accepted them as a group. Satchi and whoever they were. Three, Sokhalov judged, and Kenny assumed they were all men.

The others looked back at him, silent and restive. They had all assumed, from the first, what he was at last admitting. Either the girl was nuts enough to drive into a blizzard, in which case she was surely dead by now, or she had run off with the natives, and this was a search for someone who didn't want to be found.

'Hundred and forty klicks is a big circle, Ken.' It was Jenkins, one of the pilots. 'You've flown, you know. We could hardly get started.'

The others were already shuffling out the door, beginning to converse in low voices about other things, ordinary things. Someone laughed, a soft burr of relief and satisfaction. Harris and Sokhalov were flanking Kenny, talking about the next phase. This would be contacting the Indigenous Peoples Bureau, to get a couple of agents in the field, checking out the villages and winter camps. The air search could also begin tomorrow, weather permitting. Sokhalov hoped aloud that the company's helicopters would be available. The Russian army's machines were not dependable and very poorly insulated. In any case, the inspector said with a smile, they should know within a few days where the girl was. They should be encouraging.

He felt the careful manipulation behind their matter-of-fact manner, and when Harris gripped his elbow he almost wrenched away. They were trying to ease him out, lull him for transport, as if he were a dangerous mental patient. But he said nothing. He let himself go numb, and stumbled out the door through cold blasts of wind toward the helicopter, whose motor was beginning its long, ascending whine, cranking on the drooping rotor blades. He wanted to defy them – Harris, Pendergast, the Russian government – wanted to strike out on his own and do something worthy, grand, heroic – rescue his beautiful Satchi and restore their life and love . . .

But it was not that simple. The nobleness, the grandness, depended on how he might find her. Sokhalov was convinced, he saw, that Satchi was simply an over-educated young woman full of bookish nonsense, who had run away from a wearisome father and a failed affair with a foreign trifler. The others would have put it more crudely, but the result was the same. If they located her in some herdsman's tent or stinking fish-camp hovel, there would be no opportunities for heroism. He would look ridiculous, the laughing stock of the whole community.

Slumped in his narrow seat aboard the copter, he shook off Harris's preferred cup of coffee and sat with his head in his hands, glad for the chance to be isolated in a cave of shuddering, bellowing sound. He had never been so miserable and worried and confused. They were wrong about Satchi. They didn't know her. Her playfulness and softness and trust, her passion . . .

He drifted rapidly into the stream of memory, a sentimental, erotic grief. How riotously they had loved, in the beginning! They discovered and explored each other in a fever of curiosity. Like new continents, she said at the time. *We are jungles and mountains and canyons, but I am so afraid I will get lost in us! But I want to go everywhere!* He had sensed no shadow in that remark at the time. Nor had he admitted fully to himself how often her casual talk, her moods, even her dress puzzled him. He was sure now it was not the strangeness of the culture, her mixed blood, or this harsh, primitive land. It was the mystery of Satchi herself, which he had, clearly, only begun to apprehend.

He groaned as the copter lurched on its landing gear and tilted into the air. He had begun as her guide, introducing her to reckless delight, but perhaps he had gotten lost himself. He only knew it had changed between them, imperceptibly but inexorably. He had begun to look no further ahead than their next night together. He stopped thinking about what would happen when they had finished the cut. When he did imagine home, Satchi was no longer there beside him in the vision. For her part, she dropped a remark or two about studying abroad. She had not said America or the United States. Just 'abroad.'

His schoolmarm in a black garter, his wicked little bookworm, was all at once casual and cool. She talked of conferences and publications, like an ambitious young scholar. She, too, had stepped back, and he could not be sure now who had been the first to move. Study in England or Canada was of course a believable, a reasonable alternative dream. He could accept such a choice. But surely the same person who nursed such a dream could not slink off with a band of illiterate, lice-infested herdsmen or hunters. Without so much as a word, a sign, a hint? Surely, surely not.

The copter had its altitude now and thrashed along, regular as a washing machine, over the vast sweep of the taiga. Below them outlying crews would have parked the laser-fellers and cats and loaders, hooked up the engine block warmers, and boarded the big weasel crummies for the ride back to the bunks. Through the small porthole of the copter one might see points of light along haulroads bounding the great blocks of white space, the new cuts that checkerboarded the forest. The lights would converge at the base camp, a luminous cluster visible to pilots for hundreds of kilometers.

Satchi had been upset by the checkerboard and the equipment yards, when he had first taken her up in a little company five-seater cruise plane. On the ground the extent of the cut was not so apparent; the forest seemed to predominate still. She had not realized, she cried, how fast it was vanishing.

He argued that her perception was old-fashioned and flawed. It *was* all forest – including the huge squares of what might look like blank snow. They were already planted with seedlings, were in fact a future forest in its recovery and regeneration stage, and eventually an *improved* forest, after selective thinning and pest control. But Satchi only flushed and glared at him.

'You call these improvements?' she demanded hotly. 'You come with your mechanical Gorgons and Golem and—'

'Wait a second,' he had said, laughing and tangling his hand in her luxurious black hair, while the pilot banked the plane into a lazy circle, 'I don't know a Gorgon from a blue goose, but if it wasn't for this flying machine you would never have *seen* all this at once. I mean, what's holding us up? Show her, Charlie.' The plane banked more steeply, while he kept his hand in Satchi's hair until she squealed and they were thrown together and he was kissing her and they flew around and around, suspended a mile in the air, while Charlie grinned and sang 'My Girl.'

He had to stop remembering, stop thinking. The base doctor had given him a prescription sedative, and he intended to go directly to his quarters, take a tablet, and plunge into oblivion. He would need all his strength to resist what they wanted him to believe about her. To resist humiliation. Maybe better that . . .

He was stricken by guilt then, at what he was on the verge of thinking. He couldn't have meant it. Good God, of course he hadn't, he was exhausted and demoralized and in shock. He didn't want that, not freezing to death alone in that emptiness, not having to identify her. Great God, no! The likelihood was she had been taken, perhaps because she was ill, or even against her will. She had a gun, but the raiders could have ingratiated themselves and then surprised her. That was what he had to believe in. The possibility for hope, for heroism, for ending everything nobly, if not exactly happily.

They would not reach the base camp before darkness, and Kenny was glad for that. This day had contained too much light, too much glare and exposure, beginning with the floodlights on the airstrip before dawn. Then, at the abandoned station, the men had stroked the floors and walls and shelves with electric torches, looking for clues. He had found the broken hair clip himself, and would have wept but for the faces and probing beams all around him.

But the clip had not shaken him so much as another find. A little heap of orange peels, darkened and crumpled by the frost, in the wastebasket of the bathroom. He had given her the fruit the day before leaving on a timber cruise, and she had been touched and delighted in the old way, like a child who has witnessed a magic trick. She must have saved the small, sweet oranges to take on her trip to the most desolate station. What struck him, however, was not the poignant irony of this gesture, but something unsettling, almost obscene in that heap of discarded peelings and bits of pulp and seed. He had been startled by the thought, before he could stop himself, that it looked like the refuse of some foraging animal.

CHAPTER SIX

Kenny reached his destination, the sleeping tablet and soft bed in a dark room with a pillow over his head. He was out for twelve hours straight, though it seemed to him he had only rested a moment or two before there were voices at his door, a midday sun pouring through the window. The voice at the door was a security man, come to hustle him to the executive office as soon as he could shave and throw on clothes.

Pendergast met him at the door with a cup of strong coffee and a smile. The shades were drawn and the office lights burning over a heap of papers. A phone was blinking but Pendergast ignored it and ushered him to the soft chair beside the desk.

The boss was a compact man in his early fifties, with an unruly shock of gray hair and the kind of weathered and lined features popular in advertisements for expensive whisky. He wore clean and sharply pressed workingmen's clothes, a homage to his origins. Dick Pendergast had paid his way through school with a chainsaw, and worked most of the jobs in the woods before he became a manager. Even now there was nothing to mark his position except an air of quiet mastery, and the bracing aroma of an expensive aftershave cologne.

The solicitude of the coffee and soft chair did not comfort Kenny. It made him think of the rituals reserved for a condemned man. In their brief session day before yesterday, when he had authorized the helicopter, Pendy was furious. He had been forced to fly in from the main office in Yakutsk, where he was busy moving logs and chips to the Japanese before the weather on Kamchat worsened. He had no desire, he told Kenny brutally, to use company men and equipment to chase after some environmental officer's little piece.

Missing persons were a government responsibility, but since Dixie Pacific was involved, indirectly – Pendergast stressed the word through his teeth – they would of course cooperate. Up to a point. This point, Kenny assumed, would also mark the end of his career with Dixie; and he sipped the coffee mostly to brace himself for getting fired. But Pendy was smiling, stirring in his sweetener, and asked off-handedly if Kenny thought Sokhalov had done a decent investigation.

'I . . . well, yes sir. I think so. As far as gathering evidence.' He waited warily for some clue to the significance of this new mood.

'Find much?' Pendergast lifted a spoonful of coffee, tilted it, and let it trickle back into the cup. 'No blood or hair or sign of struggle, I already heard from Harris, but anything promising at all?'

Promising. Kenny tried to think, to imagine what would hearten his boss. 'There may have been a ritual of some kind,' he said finally, 'a native ritual.'

Pendergast came alert, and his pale blue eyes were luminous and steady as gas flames. 'These are the Koriks – Koraks – you are talking about? What kind of ritual?'

Kenny looked down, to keep his mouth under control. He had thought for a split second of saying *a peace ritual*. He felt foolish, giddy, dangerously unbalanced by fatigue and uncertainty. 'Probably a religious thing,' he got out. 'Sokhalov thinks Satchi went with the Koraks.' He took an easier breath and looked up again into the pale, burning eyes. At least he had been awake enough not to correct Pendy's pronunciation.

'Religious.' Pendergast appeared to think hard for a few moments. 'They don't go in for sacrifice, mutilation, that type of thing, do they?'

Kenny looked solemn and careful. 'Not that I know of.'

'Went with,' Pendergast continued, again as if musing to himself, but watching Kenny closely. 'Not taken by. That's Sokhalov's theory?'

Kenny nodded. Pendergast waited, so he said it. 'Not mine. She wouldn't have done that. Not Satchi.'

Pendergast smiled at him, a sympathetic, indulgent smile, but the eyes of blue flame burned without a flicker or shadow. 'Satchi,' he said. 'Yes, Satchi. I'd heard the name. Beautiful young woman, I understand, and well-educated. This must be tough for you, Kenny.'

Kenny was too surprised to hide his expression. This morning she was a little piece, a half-breed slut, and now she was a beautiful, intelligent young woman. Something had happened and no one was telling him what it was.

'I know I was hard, when I first heard what happened. I had a lot of things on my mind and this situation was damned inconvenient, I can tell you. I lost my temper, and I say frankly I regret it. I realize now it's partly my fault, too. I helped set the company's policy on relations with the locals, and I could have said something months ago.' Pendergast made a gesture of dividing something neatly with the flat of his hand. 'Put it behind us. By the way, were you guys engaged, in any formal way?'

Kenny was dumbfounded, and just managed to shake his head.

Pendergast's smile broadened in satisfaction. 'That's all to the good. Terrible enough as it is, of course, but if you were planning a wedding . . .' He expelled a gusty breath of relief. For a time he tapped his desk rhythmically with one fingernail. The sound was like the ticking of a clock, and apparently reminded Pendergast to look at his watch, which he did now, with an exclamation.

'Good God, it's one-thirty and you've not had breakfast, let alone lunch. And no sleep the night before.' Pendergast clasped his hands and set his elbows flat on the desk top, squaring his thick shoulders and gazing forthrightly at Kenny. 'Let's get to it, and then send you to work. The thing is, Ken, we've got a ticklish development on our hands. There's a little pool of foreign journalists already camped up here in Magadan. Christ knows how they got wind of our little story, they were supposed to be doing wildlife and the economy and so forth, but they seem to be after us like a poolful of piranhas. I got a call this morning from our Atlanta office. NBC had heard of it from a stringer in Moscow.'

Pendergast frowned and Kenny saw the clasped hands tighten. 'These bloodsuckers would no doubt love to use this very unfortunate personal problem of your friend's – of Satchi's – to attack the international timber industry, stir up the environmental storm troopers and some of those save-the-aborigine outfits, the way they've already done in the Amazon. That would be bad enough.

We're concerned that some other types may start sniffing around. From the *entertainment industry*.'

He set up the phrase with a caustic pause, and Kenny understood finally that he was not going to lose his job after all. Pendy was afraid, too. They wouldn't cut him loose because it would attract even more attention, and because of what he might say, in revenge, about the company's policies. 'Studio people,' he said, and following blind instinct, gave the words a knowledgeable lilt.

'Yeah, I guess.' Pendergast examined him for a moment, then returned to his smile. 'You know how they talk. Everything's a great story, a colossal hit, public will love it and so forth. Mostly bullshit, but they can make it sound tempting. Offer what seems like a lot for rights to a story, which they will proceed to turn into *absolute* bullshit.

Again Pendergast paused. Kenny noticed for the first time the blue file folder on one end of the desk. Blue was for personnel records. He could not read the tab, but he was certain the file was his. He saw that Pendergast wanted a response, a card face up.

'Of course.' Kenny shrugged, as if at the weather. 'Hollywood.'

'Exactly. No telling what kind of garbage they have in mind. They're like vultures. They hear about the bear and a beautiful part-Eskimo girl in exotic Siberia and a bad old logging company, so they smell some kind of calamity or horror which they think they can make money off of.'

'Right,' Kenny said, and took a sip of his coffee. He ventured to look speculatively at the blue file.

'You've been with us five years now, Ken. An excellent record, and I know you're very committed to your work. To helping us make this a clean, responsible job. The environmental office is in some ways like the conscience of a project.'

'Thank you,' Kenny said. 'I'm really glad to hear that.'

'I tell you frankly we don't want to lose you, and particularly in circumstances like these. The whole incident is a little out of hand, and folks – in Moscow, in the Dixie headquarters back home, and the storm troopers – are looking for somebody to blame. Even before we *know* what has really happened.

'But a company like ours is always a target. And so is an individual like yourself, somebody caught in the middle, tired and under emotional strain – somebody who is already one of the victims in the thing. So I think we've got to stick together, work together. We want to protect your feelings and your privacy, Ken, and we want the company to get a fair hearing.'

Kenny was experiencing an extraordinary buoyancy. His fatigue was gone, replaced by a quiet, but intense glee. He thought he knew what Pendy was going to propose, and so put down the cup to look his boss directly in the eye. 'What I want,' he said, 'is to find Satchi. I think, sir, that—'

'Exactly. Exactly, Ken. I think that is the nub, right there. We want you to give that absolute priority.' Pendergast got to his feet and came from behind his desk. Kenny rose also, effortlessly. 'She comes first. The company will give you a copter and two crewmen, with other aircraft for support. We already have the government's promise to allow us to work with them and coordinate the air search. You can call me Dick.'

Pendergast put out his hand, his lips crimped in a tough but affectionate smile. 'I would guess you will want to get started just as soon as you can. Knowing how you must feel.'

Kenny waited the barest fraction of a second, then clasped the older man's hand in an active, strong grip. Pendy would honor this compact, he knew; a decision to link their fates had been taken. His job was to stay in the field away from the press, to find the facts and give the company the first opportunity to arrange them. He might even locate Satchi in some heroic way, complete the story in a manner beneficial to them all. In that case, no doubt, he could not only keep his job, with a hefty promotion, he might also listen to propositions from Hollywood. He and Satchi, their story. It might be a fantastic dream come true. They might even become stars. He moved to the door, Pendy's arm around his shoulders.

'Get some rest, and then find her, son. Bring her back to us.' Pendergast spoke softly, almost in Kenny's ear. 'We'll take care of everything.'

CHAPTER SEVEN

Coming up from the black oblivion of sleep, she thought at first the dogs had gotten in. There were growls and grunts, and in the dim light she saw fur rumps jerking. For a moment she thought they were worrying a live thing. She sat up, breathing in sharply to cry out, and saw then that it was the women, all of them on their knees. Old Pipik was trying to get between the younger ones, who were fighting over something.

The children, who had been romping gleefully at the edge of this struggle, fell silent instantly when they saw Satchi was awake. Pipik drew back, hissed a word, and all of them were looking at her, black eyes like a ring of sharp stones. Satchi saw then that each of the young women clutched one of her plastic boots. She threw back the fawnskin blankets and rolled onto her hands and knees. She was all at once angry and afraid, and for a moment stared back at them, but then she remembered Yina, and crawled quickly to the cradle.

Under the rabbitfur coverlet he was on his stomach, head turned to one side. A stain and odor indicated he had vomited the sugar-water. She fumbled at his throat, just above the collarbone. Her trembling fingers could detect nothing. An avalanche of dread struck her in the back, wrung a cry from her, and she lunged over the edge of the cradle to press her ear to his mouth.

He moved, made a tiny, gagging sound.

'*Yina, Yina, baby . . .*' She blinked back tears, as her hands went all over him, turned him on his side. He felt hot again, his skin dry as paper. His eyes were open and seemed to register her, though she could not be certain. How long had she slept? She was reading to him, she remembered, from the ridiculous book, as she had for three nights running. Had apparently fallen asleep between sentences, so they covered her and left her where she was.

But here was light now through the smoke hole. Evening or morning? The men gone, it was probably morning. Even so, at least fourteen hours had passed. She checked under Yina, but the moss pad was clean, and now she noticed that the flask of sugar-water beside the cradle was also nearly empty. They had done as she asked them, or rather as Kainivilu had ordered. Yina whimpered again, and one of the young women got up and sidled to a position across the cradle from Satchi.

This one was Paqa, Kainivilu's wife. Satchi had seen on the second day that the younger brother was married to the other woman – or girl, rather – and the relief she felt at this discovery made her angry with herself. The domestic arrangements here were none of her concern; she was no anthropologist. No doctor either, for that matter.

Paqa looked wary and sullen, and instinctively Satchi sat back on her heels, away from the child between them. The woman put her hand on her son's cheek and began to croon a song. Her voice contained a deep, soft, weariness. Satchi knew a surge of yearning, a desire to touch the other woman, reassure her.

What was it? The same woman only moments ago had disgusted her, scuffling on the rug over a stolen boot, apparently without a thought for her dying son. Yet her song had entered Satchi like an arrow, and in a moment evoked fragments of a scene long ago. A white coverlet, trimmed with startling red roses. A cloud of steam, an odor of camphor. Voices in another room. Something pressed into her hand . . .

She shook off the memory and turned away from the cradle to rummage for her little bag. Yina should have an aspirin immediately, for the fever, and more sugar-water. She had to concentrate. It had become difficult for her to push away these odd and unsettling images and thoughts that were confusing her. She did not belong here, she had to get that across to them – and to herself. Her decision – but it wasn't a decision! It was a tremendously stupid muddle, brought on by eating the mushrooms, which apparently had some long-term after-effects.

Anyway, now that she was here, however pitiful her preparation, she found herself the responsible nurse.

She located the aspirin, and when she looked up Pipik was

already there, extending the cup of water, her eyes still averted. Satchi took the cup and pointed to the nearly empty sugar-water bottle, which the old woman dutifully snatched away. At the cradle, Yina's mother had gotten a hand under his back and raised him. This small gesture of assistance produced another odd thrill in Satchi, a pleasure that continued as she deftly slipped the tablet onto the boy's tongue and tilted the cup to his lips.

Their cooperation continued through the feeding of the sugar-water and a little of the dark paste of berries and fish oil, yet Paqa never once looked at her or acknowledged her. It was, Satchi thought, like having a shadow that moved whenever she did. She also noticed that when Paqa went back to the other women there was no further sign of contention among them. The boots had been tossed aside and forgotten. She knew it was unfair, but she could not help thinking they were indeed like children, thoughtless and inconstant.

She watched them pull some kind of twisted fibre from sacks and begin fashioning what she guessed would be baskets, whipping together coils with the help of steel awls. The two oldest girls helped by unreeling the fibre, flexing and smoothing it for the weavers. The women kept up an incessant whispering and often laughed – a barely audible sound like rapid, hoarse breathing – but each time the laugh was supressed immediately, often with a swift, sly glance in Satchi's direction. She was surprised to see how rapidly the baskets took shape, amid this constant prattle.

Meanwhile the men were off hunting. Or so she had assumed. Though perhaps she was quite wrong. Outside was a hut of tight-woven willow branches perched on stilts, and the hut was full of dried, frozen salmon carcasses. And last night they had fresh reindeer meat, surely from the herd she had seen on her brief trips outside yesterday, between snow-squalls. The animals were in a crude corral, brush woven along and through a scatter of naked alders, while the dogs huddled in the lee of three sleds drawn up by the dwelling. One detail of this scene had struck her: two of the sleds were handmade, of hides lashed on a wood frame and runners, but the other was of steel and plastic, fairly new, and still bore a load lashed under a tight canvas cover.

Pipik had finished a basket, and without ceremony tossed it aside.

On impulse Satchi got up and moved around the fire to squat near the group of women. They froze – as she knew they would – but she reached out boldly and picked up the new basket.

'*Ai yeti*,' she said in a friendly way. 'Good. Good work. Whose?'

Their eyes were again black stones. No one moved. Satchi mastered her frustration, maintained her smile. 'This one, good. Who for?'

They went on gaping at her. It was maddening, but she held the basket aloft, pointed to it, the smile carved on her face. It might be baby Koryak, broken Koryak, but they understood. She would stay there until they answered.

Then Pipik spoke, so softly and rapidly Satchi barely caught the words.

'For Magadan.'

The old woman made a slight gesture, and following with her eyes Satchi saw leaning against the wall a sack that once held flour, and peeking out of it were a half-dozen more of the baskets, tightly nested.

A rush of anger then, mostly for her own stupidity, but she managed to nod politely, drop the basket, and retreat. They sold them. Of course they did. Hanging on these walls were battered, blackened aluminum pots and old plastic bottles strung together. And she had seen such baskets before, in Magadan and Yakutsk in the tourist shops and street-side stalls. Sold them. Took them to market and sold them. These people carried on regular trade, no doubt visited their domesticated relatives in government housing, had probably seen television. She remembered the way the old men had flipped the light switches. And of course one of them, surely Kainivilu, had known how to drive the *pawka-pawka*.

Rage buoyed her across the room to the ladder. Yina was asleep, his breathing shallow but regular, and she would go out. They had better not try to stop her. She jerked on her parka and the fur-lined boots they had given her, which, she had admitted to herself secretly, were comfortable and well-made, besides being valuable for their rarity. Earlier, she had wondered if it was possible they meant to do her a favor, supply some kind of payment for the service they were extorting.

The children watched, but the women hardly glanced up from their work, and said nothing, so neither would she. Thought she was helpless, a captive, a slave. Jamming her feet into the holes cut through the log, she began to climb and was again conscious of how narrow and precarious this perfectly vertical ladder could be. The holes were worn smooth, and barely wide enough for her feet. She had remarked with some envy how swiftly and effortlessly the whole family swarmed up this pole, even with a rope or bucket in hand, and she tried now to emulate their confidence. Just before she reached the smoke hole, four meters from the floor, she looked back in spite of herself.

The faces of the children were still upturned, brown moons in a deep well, but what she saw most clearly was the *giegie*. The fireboard was tilted beside the two great parallel stones of the hearth, so the blackened features also seemed to gape up at her, to shift and grin in the fluttering yellow light of the oil lamp. She paused, felt at once tremendously full and heavy, almost lethargic. She heard her own blood thumping within her, and then felt the foot she was balanced on begin to slip.

She lunged for the pole rim of the smokehole, caught it with both hands, and for one moment of terror hung with both feet flailing, before she got a toehold in the last hole and propelled herself up and sprawling over the rim. She lay for a moment, taking ragged, deep breaths, and heard the burst of laughter from below. Not a hoarse, muffled hiss this time, but a sustained, raucous clangor.

She got to her feet and thrashed out of the funnel structure of poles that kept snow from sliding in. She had to stifle her sobs of indignation, for the air was keen as a knife and in a moment the tears starting down her cheeks turned to crust. No wonder their God is the raven, she thought, the women are spiteful, black-eyed bitches and the men are thieves and liars. They could have gone in to the medical post, the Bureau of Indigenous Peoples, they could have taken the Sno-Klaw at least into radio range, here it was – she saw by the dim globe of sun through overcast – midafternoon of the fourth day . . . She thought in a jumbled rush, slogging away from the underground house and following unconsciously a narrow trail in the snow.

She had had enough. She was a Russian citizen of the Oblast of

Magadan, Autonomous Okrug of . . . A momentary uncertainty deflected her anger. Could they have come far enough East to be now in Kamchatka? Surely not. Suppose there had been more gasoline than she calculated, and they had come a hundred kilometers or better, then two days further on foot . . . No, impossible. And what did it matter? The point was they were taking advantage of her. They might even be counting on the search party, as an excuse to get the sick child helicoptered out and also collect a reward for finding her. *Finding* her!

She intended to find Kainivilu, and confront him. She had been a fool, a thorough idiot, she did not deceive herself about that. Imagining that she was recovering her racial identity, or her childhood, or spiritual contact with her mother, by hanging around with these beggars! She could never excuse such stupidity. Even though, each night, Tolek had gotten down his drum and they had chanted and told stories and urged her to talk and smiled encouragement at her halting attempts. It was all a sham; these people were unscrupulous, and no doubt held her in secret contempt. They were using her, keeping her against her will.

Her mind shied, balked, even as she marched on through the snow. The scholar in her remonstrated that this was not exactly true. She had not resisted, except for her barely articulate pleas to be taken back. And she had not really known – still did not know – the quickest *way* back. Nor could she condemn them for eating mushrooms, without being a hypocrite. She had some experience of her own. Kenny had brought hashish from Tajikistan and cocaine from Vladivostok. The memory of how they had used it yielded a blend of shame and heat, which she shook off irritably.

None of that had anything to do with this mess. She had gotten into this because . . . because of a bear and because of Yina, primarily. When old Pipik had been so excited, claiming her as some sort of tribal kin, and Kainivilu had begged her to minister to his son, she had acquiesced. How could she possibly do otherwise? The child was probably dying, and she had been shaken, deeply moved by his frailty and huge, feverish eyes.

And while she had watched over the boy for hours, for days now, wearing herself down, those women were fighting over a pair of boots! And the men off God knew where. She was again outraged and disgusted. Tramping savagely along the faint trail, hunched into her parka, she did not see the four men and the dog until she was a dozen steps away. They were crouched over the dog, flat on its side but moving its paws as if treading the air. Steam rose from a wound behind the front leg, and a wide splotch of bright red had sunk into the snow. Tatka held a long spear, and leather thongs dangled from the hands of Kainivilu and his brother. Behind them Tolek stood guard over a reindeer fawn, its back legs trussed tight. All of them had turned to her, startled, for they had been engrossed in their work.

Satchi was too shocked to speak. The stain was so bright, she could not for a long moment look away. The reindeer would be next, she thought. She backed up in quick, small steps, turned, and moved away over the unbroken snowfield in a sort of lunging half-trot. Inexplicably, under her shock and revulsion, she felt ashamed. Her anger, her desire to have it out with Kainivilu, had sunk away abruptly, shifty as a fish. This was probably a sacrifice meant for Yina, to ward off the malicious spirits – *kalau* her mother called them. And probably she had ruined it, an intruder and unbeliever blundering into a solemn ceremony.

The blood on the snow connected all at once with her earlier memory of the rose-embroidered coverlet, the camphor smell, her mother's tales of the *kalau*. Satchi had been very sick and her parents were very worried. She was four, or perhaps only three, so they were not yet in their nice new brick house. They must have been living in the concrete dormitories. Her father had stayed home from work, his face pinched and pale, and then someone came and they were all arguing in the kitchen. Satchi remembered being restless, afraid, and then the visitor came in to look at her . . .

She heard a sound behind her. When she turned, Kainivilu was there, a single dark shape in the white blank of the land. He came, unhurried, to within two strides of her and stopped. For long seconds he stared at her with a familiar, unblinking penetration.

'Come back.' He spoke in Koryak, and when she did not answer immediately, repeated himself in Russian.

'No,' she said. 'You must take me to the nearest post or lumber camp. In Momski or Kolymskoye, whichever is nearest. Yina needs medication, and a doctor. I can do no more.'

He shook his head, continued to stare at her. His flat, brown face seemed to register and track her like a magnet.

'Listen. Listen to me. Your son is very sick, and he needs a *doctor*. You *must* get someone here from a medical post. They will bring a helicopter or a big *pawka-pawka*. And I must go in and report. I am a government employee.'

She stared sternly back at him, but there was no reaction. 'You *must* understand.' In spite of herself, her voice warped louder and higher. '*I wish to go home.*'

'No,' he said. 'You are doctor.' There was a hint of unease in his voice. 'You are *nymyl'u*. From old time. Whale people.'

'I am Russian! My mother was only part, part *nymylin*, so I am—' Satchi felt hot blood in her face, and threw up her arms in exasperation. These people were hopeless. '—Russian. Do you understand?'

'Also we are Russian.' He looked away from her, then back. 'I have card.'

'Well then.' She took a determined breath. 'You are obliged to . . .'

At exactly the same instant his mouth bent up and she understood that he was making a joke. And he saw that she understood, and uttered a big, sudden laugh, his eyes wrinkling into slits. 'You have card?'

Now she looked away, her own mouth deformed slightly with the effort of keeping straight. All Russians had a card, had a whole wallet full of cards, for identification and admission and discounts and refunds. They were mostly worthless, but dutifully waved and recognized in various daily routines. Indigenous Peoples issued them too, so this illiterate dog-slaughterer, who thought she was a reincarnated ghost, had a niche in the grand disorder of Siberian officialdom, and he seemed to appreciate that absurdity quite as much as she did.

'I mean that people will search for me – are searching for me – but you cannot wait for that. We must go! We should have taken my *pawka-pawka* the other way, at the beginning . . . Where did you learn to drive it?'

Kainivilu's mirth was gone without a trace. 'Big mine,' he said and reached out to touch her sleeve. 'Come back now. Eat.'

She jerked away from him, fierce again. '*No*! You cannot keep me here, some kind of hostage!' She wheeled away from him and resumed her trudge over the snow. She expected him to come after her, and felt a quick pang of triumph when he did.

'No,' he said behind her. 'Come back. My son.'

She ignored him, tried to take longer strides. For perhaps five minutes they went on like this, Kainivilu a few paces away, before he said again, 'Come back.'

She waited another two or three minutes before she said, as if to the air, 'Leave me alone.'

'Cannot go this way. Bad way.'

Her rage had returned, solid and filling her heart completely, a kind of grim exaltation. A driver in the mines, traded his wife's baskets, had an almost new sled, claimed to believe in ghosts . . . *Promyshlenniki* – a Siberian type. What was the English? Scoundrel? Riff-raff? Hustler! That was it. Taking advantage of her after the bear had cut off the radio and frightened her into a bad decision. If he whined at her once more she would turn and slap him.

But for twenty minutes he said nothing, followed her like a dog, and then when he finally spoke again, his voice was distant and she realized he had stopped. 'Come back.'

She tramped on, happy for the first time in days.

'Storms coming. No tracks. You die.'

She took six more steps, then stopped and whirled around. He was further away than she expected, a little ball of fur with a shadow for a face.

'I AM TAKING A WALK!' she shouted. And then, in wild glee, she added, in English, 'BUTTHOLE!'

Within a half-hour Satchi had calmed down, though she was still exhilarated by her first real exercise in the better part of a week, and by the awesome emptiness of the terrain. They were well past the ragged edge of the taiga here, on high tundra breaking gradually – to the East – into a more rugged range, but everything was shades of white, edged here and there with blue or gray shadows, rising and rolling like a frozen sea. She had no intention of trying to cross this expanse, of course. But she would show Kainivilu that he could not control her movement. She hoped he would begin to think now of the consequences of holding her, of a major search party coming to her rescue.

There would surely be such an expedition, after four days without a report from her. The storm had not been that severe, and a supply vehicle at least would be dispatched, would find the station deserted and the Sno-Klaw gone. Her father had a friend or two in the Oblast administration – but she was not counting so much on the government. Without dollars under the table no Magadan office would do more than a routine check, for at least a week. But Kenny would . . .

The thought was so uncomfortable it could not take shape in words at first. And this obstacle coincided with her arriving at the edge of a sharper notch in the terrain, a fork of some watercourse running from the high eastern ridges. The wind had scoured snow from the eroded banks, and last summer's melt left layers of seamed yellow silt and a scatter of cannonball boulders far down the slope. The air was clear, and felt even colder. From here she could also see further, to another vast expanse behind the first, another sweep of rises and dips and broken edges that seemed finally to become the sky, a gray nothing, neither substance nor shadow.

The confidence she had known a moment before was sucked away, like a bank undercut and collapsing into a racing stream. She had assumed she knew, roughly, at least where she *could* be, but in this immensity there was no such knowledge. A circumference of a few hundred kilometers, she had calculated, but from what center? From this single point, this ridge, she could see an endless emptiness. What if she had been wrong and they had gone west? To the Yakut province, huge and with an unfamiliar bureaucracy even more corrupt than that of Magadan? What if there was delay in securing clearance from Moscow? She was not, technically, authorized to do station work. Man, they said in English. Man the station.

Her mouth became a taut line. They would all be men. Those who were looking for her. Or not looking for her. Her father and Kenny and even, an hour ago, Kainivilu. The thought she had avoided hit her now, as a single brutal phrase. Kenny had taught it to her, one of a number of terms of bedroom slang they had exchanged. *Piece of ass*. She had laughed at the time, at its novel crudity. American boys bought it, he had said. And that was what she had not been able to say to herself. She was counting on Kenny, the American with dollars, with a company behind him, to get the search party going. Kenny would buy her back. His naughty girl. His piece.

For a savage moment she felt an urge to go on, into the emptiness, to keep walking as far as her strength would carry her. They would never find her. That was ridiculous, of course, yet the bright flame of the urge startled her. In the next moment she realized the shadow of the crest she was on had filled the crevasse at her feet, and within the hour it would be dark. The wind at her back had increased a little too, and when she turned around it struck her immediately, numbing her nose and chin. She had, she realized, counted all along on retracing her own tracks to find Kainivilu's camp. The snow from the last storm was coarse and partially compacted, but a very strong wind could eventually blur and erase the trail.

She reached inside her hood and clumsily drew the nylon and wool flap over her nose and mouth, then plunged back the way she had come. Eyes slitted against the driving, cold air, she could not find the trail as easily as she expected, wherever the terrain was uneven and already in shadow. Several times she had to stop and crouch down to be sure. Within a half hour she was hurrying, concentrating utterly on the gouges and slashes in the gray surface just before her. So far, she had not encountered two sets of tracks, which would mark the point at which Kainivilu abandoned her.

At a certain point she felt, under her ribs, the tiny seed of a very great fear. Whenever the trail seemed distinct for a few steps, she was heartened and tried to attain a lumbering trot, but always the way became treacherous again and she had to lurch to a halt, or even go back a little. Finally she fell, and when she got back on her feet, batting the snow from her coat, the sun was nearly down and the fear had struck roots and begun to sprout.

She stood in the gray light, working to control her breathing, telling herself she was being a fool again. She could not have come more than four or five kilometers from the camp. She was a matter of minutes from the fire, from some food. She would soon see the sacrificed dogs hanging on stakes, stiff as iron, then the reindeer, the sleds. She should move deliberately, carefully. Making no mistakes.

There. Better. But even as she lifted a boot to set forth again, she heard a faint, but familiar sound.

It was an engine. A Sno-Klaw, a Wolverine, an Ice King – or perhaps a bigger vehicle, a military crawler-carrier. The sound seemed to be coming from the direction of the camp. She began to run, fell again, was up and still running. She was crying, calling out without any sense of what the words meant, and then abruptly she stopped to listen. Yes, the sound was a little nearer, distorting occasionally as if the vehicle was passing between or over hills!

She had to be calm, it was over now, they had come for her. She had to stop crying, for the tears froze and caked on her eyelashes so she could not see. It was over. This adventure, this mad twist of fate – even a good scare here at the end – it was over. Yina would get a doctor, and she would go home! She was glad for them all, she held nothing against Kainivilu and the old men, she would laugh about it, they would laugh about it – it was over!

She glanced down, located the trail and saw that it was finally two sets of overlapping tracks. She could follow it with little trouble, stride normally, collect herself. They would possibly have brought things – emergency rations and coffee, even brandy! They might even have called already for a helicopter. By the time she got to camp – but the engine sound was louder still now, coming from a point rather further to the West.

She saw it then. It was a crawler-carrier, a modified GAZ-75, moving fast on a path roughly parallel with her own. In a few moments it would pass her, going the way she had come. Searching for her! She broke away from the trail, running again. The crawler looked to be perhaps three hundred meters away. Surely they would see her any moment. She came to the top of a slight rise and stopped, waved her arms like a great bird, her heart full and hammering in her breast.

The carrier pounded on, disappeared behind a knoll, emerged once more in a spray of snow. The vehicle was painted a light gray and bore no numbers; the glass was tinted so she could not see how many were inside. 'HERE!' she screamed. 'Over HERE!' She beat her arms in the air so violently one of her mittens came off, sailed over her shoulder. Where were they going! The engine was snarling, wound up to the maximum. The carrier was passing her, now at its closest point, a hundred and fifty meters away! They had to see her!

At that instant the carrier decelerated and executed a sudden quarter-turn. All the air went out of Satchi's lungs, and her knees almost gave way. They saw her! She said the first line of a prayer to the Virgin, one she had not uttered since her childhood. She kept waving one arm in a slow, grand sweep, while she stuffed her bare hand under her parka. A great wave of relief and gratitude broke over her . . . she foresaw the embraces, the tears and jokes, the brandy . . . but even in this tumult of anticipation she sensed, far beneath, a reef of exhaustion and some hidden, obdurate doubt.

The carrier had stopped, the engine idling. They were no doubt preparing her place, maybe blankets and a pillow. She wondered, in quick succession, what they had done with their spare fuel trailer, what she would say, whether the radio would reach her father. Then she thought of her mitten and turned slightly to look for it in the snow, and ever afterward she would remember the next events in a kind of surreal slow motion.

The engine raced again, explosively, and when she turned to look the carrier was reversing itself in a great spew of snow, swinging its snout back through the quarter turn and then further into another quarter turn, pointing directly away from her; she heard the gears shift, and then the cleats dug in so that the body of the carrier seemed to squat and then leap in another spew of snow; and before she could move, before she could speak, the carrier was diminishing, was gone between two low hummocks, had disappeared except for its sound, which was fading too, so fast that she could already hear the wind again, which seemed louder now, as if roaring through the leathery leaves, the gnarled branches of that fear now full-grown and flourishing in her heart.

CHAPTER EIGHT

octor Kutznetsov had always hated the Ali Baba Pizza Emporium, even when it was only a rumor in the early planning of the downtown hotel complex. Inside, the reality was far worse than he had guessed. The arched ceiling was an electric blue, held up by pink columns, and a neon sign, dots and curls of arabic letters, burned purple over the bar. The waitresses wore transparent veils, harem pants of black rayon, and so much eye shadow they looked like raccoons. From speakers in the ceiling, a woman wailed over the whine and throb of zithers and flutes and drums.

Though he caught sight of Malenky gesturing grandly at him across the room, he pretended he hadn't, and proceeded methodically to remove his hat and gloves. The maitre d' glided up immediately, uttering officious little coos about the need for reservations, even in bad weather. Kutznetsov clenched his teeth in a smile. Lunch in a place he reviled with a man he detested. Served by impertinent fools. And probably he would have to pick up the check.

It had to be done. Anything that would help bring Satchi home, he would do. 'My party is already here,' he said. 'Doctor Kutznetsov.'

He took a grim satisfaction in watching the maitre d' absorb this information and begin fashioning a new expression of tentative servility. The head eunuch (as the Doctor immediately cast him) had assumed this old man in a worn coat and muddy boots had slunk in seeking refuge from the wind and ice.

'Ah, yes!' Now the eunuch had spotted Malenky, waving from a prime table. 'You are with Georgi, of *course*! Here, allow me . . .'

Kutznetsov forced himself to be still as other hands removed his coat. Then one of the raccoon houris scurried over to bear it away, and he set out behind the maitre d' to cross the huge dining room.

It was a passage he dreaded. The Ali Baba was designed to allow everyone to see everyone else. Around a low fountain in the center of the main room, a wide space remained clear. Belly dancers and acrobats performed here on weekends, he understood. Ranged along every wall were raised alcoves, Islamic in style but crusted with Roman vegetation, where the wealthy and powerful could survey the ordinary patrons at table below them, and these accountants and smugglers and engineers and assassins could in turn gaze up and even wave now and then at their employers and benefactors.

Kutznetsov walked stiffly, eyes fixed on the emerging bald spot at the back of the eunuch's head. In his first glance around the room he had seen two others he knew besides Malenky. A man from Fisheries, who was rumored to have pioneered the use of cannery ships to smuggle automobiles, and a beautiful young woman he had seen occasionally in the main Bureau offices.

There were Japanese and Americans, of course, sponsors of various lumber, seafood, and money enterprises in Magadan. They sat with their dollar whores or the Bureau chiefs and politicians they were bribing. They were the reason for the Ali Baba. The *boom*. Everyone used the English word, which Kenny had told him originally meant the sound of an explosion, a bomb.

He had hoped to go unrecognized, despite the stories in the paper and on television, but he was conscious of whispers in the room. They could all see his age and poverty and sadness, his pathetic black suit, and would note his wind-bitten cheeks, the mud on his trouser cuffs. Poor old duck, they would think, couldn't afford a taxi – and such a gorgeous young daughter, what a shame, what a waste.

Malenky must, of course, have rented Magadan's only Mercedes limousine. Appropriate enough, since that vehicle also was fat and pretentious and expensive. Even as he made this comparison, the Doctor recognized its jealous tinge, and hoped, in spite of himself, that Malenky would insist on having the Mercedes take him back to the office after lunch.

They arrived at the table. Malenky got to his feet and threw wide his arms, his eyes rolled up like Christ's in one of the bloodier old icons.

'Alexyvitch!'

It was a bray loud enough to cause a lull in the whole room and draw every eye to this pageant of adversity and compassion. Kutznetsov groaned aloud, wincing, as the large, obese man embraced him, but realized in a flash of maddening irony that his reaction would be taken as grief.

'Ah, Alexy, Alexy! What can I say? What can we do? Our beautiful Satchi! You must be – of course you must be! I know, I knew as soon as you called. But now – sit down, man, get your breath back, order a drink. You walked? Of course!'

Malenky brayed again, this time with an affectionate slap to the Doctor's arm, and shook his head at someone at the next alcove. 'Like father, like son. You remember, Alexyvitch, how your father always went second class on the trains? And cold as a nun's quim, those old coaches! How are you? How *are* you, my friend?'

Doctor Kutznetsov had put both hands under the table, so Malenky could not grasp them. He could not, however, prevent a muscle in his cheek from jerking, and he spoke mainly in order to disguise this sign of his loathing.

'I am well. I have been busy, helping with the inquiry.'

Malenky smiled wryly. 'Helping with the inquiry. Of course. You must tell me the news. But what first? Vodka? A wine?' He snapped his fingers and one of the houris hooked into their alcove. 'You know we are all concerned. The whole city . . . the whole Oblast, everybody feels terrible. Nothing? Come, Alexy, at least a red wine. Yes, good, bring the Beaujolais, the whole bottle!

'So, my God! Last night's news, they gave it the lead, a good five minutes! That young fellow, from Dixie, was saying he flies around the clock. And journalists here from all over! Stockholm, London, New York . . . some of them in here right now . . . at that table over there by the bar. Because of the bear, you know, but also Satchi herself – her picture throughout the world, maybe, eh? She was so beautiful, so promising – everyone is saying it, comparing her to a movie star. Of course your young fellow was all broken up. Satchi's fellow. Kinny, is it? Ah, you know, Alexyvitch, seeing him there, I couldn't help thinking . . .' Malenky leaned nearer, his lips curved in a smile intended as commiseration, but tightening under the pressure of real mirth.

Doctor Kutznetsov did not move. He had told himself, on the long, cold walk here, that he would be prepared, that he would concentrate on the main business he needed to conduct. At the same time he knew he had limits: it would be all he could do to swallow his revulsion and make a civil proposition. After that everything would depend on Malenky. If he leered triumphantly and brought up his worthless son's rejected courtship, or made any rude inquiry or improper suggestion regarding Satchi . . .

He had not, he saw now, sufficiently analyzed this possibility. He had thought he would simply terminate the conversation and leave, plan to offer his proposal in a different context. What occurred to him now, however, was a very vivid, and utterly compelling image of himself heaving one of the huge, hot, sauce-smeared pies into Malenky's fat face.

'. . . of course whenever my Domi is home he always asks about her – and you too, Alexyvitch, for you might have been, you know, that is, *we* might have been—'

Kutznetsov felt his muscles beginning to tense, but before he could speak or move the waitress swished into their alcove with the opened bottle of wine, another vodka for Malenky, and a tray of appetizers. She smiled with conspiratorial adoration. As if he were a celebrity of some kind, despite his age and his shoes.

Malenky went on talking, as she poured out a swallow of the wine. Kutznetsov tasted it and nodded irritably, momentarily distracted. Then, as the glass was filled, he simply stared, concentrated all his hatred on Malenky's thick nose. A hint of rawness at the rim of the nostrils, where a few stubs of coarse hair emerged. Twin dents of yellowed skin where his reading glasses pinched the bridge. A mottled flake of darkness on one side, a sun spot. Eventual cancer, perhaps.

'. . . the choices one makes in life, and then of course luck! Domi has been lucky, the import business is fantastic, and moving now into computer things – but how could Satchi know – anyone know – I hardly knew myself – when he was such a—'

'I am not here to talk about the past, Georgi,' Kutznetsov

interrupted. 'I have other things on my mind. And you are directly concerned.'

'Ah, Alexyvitch! Of course you—'

'The investigation. We must concentate on that. I am not part of this . . . *salon*.' The Doctor waved a hand once, as one clears a shelf, at the whole room, and gave his final word both perfect French pronunciation and all the acid it could bear. 'I want to find my daughter, and I will give everything I have to expedite the work of accomplishing this task. So I cannot waste time in small talk, and I will not.'

'Alexy! Alexy! Of course you are serious. My God, what you have been through! And of course I want to offer my help, everything in my power . . .' Malenky now appeared mournful, slightly offended. He sipped his vodka and sighed at Kutznetsov. 'It is true, Alexy, you do not belong here, and neither do I, in the real and final sense. A nice club, is where we should be. A quiet place with good food and a bar and billiards and cards and sometimes a program, a speaker or a musical thing – a place for gentlemen and scholars like yourself to discuss life, important matters, philosphy and so forth. But we must face what Siberia is today, we must deal with her as she is, and Alexy – I must say this – you have turned your back on compromise, on making these adjustments to how things are done. You—'

'I know what I am and what I have done,' Kutznetsov said between his teeth. 'And I know I need your help – the help of your department. That is what I am here to discuss.'

'*My* department. Oh, good friend! I am a functionary – that's the word, right? I merely make things function. I don't decide what should be done, the actual policies. I am one cog in a great machine – no, actually, I am just a bit of grease – yes, a tiny grease-blob in the mighty Bureau of Resource Management!'

Malenky laughed expansively at his own irony. Someone at a nearby table laughed in response, then waved. Doctor Kutznetsov laughed too, but in quite another key.

'You are recognized by everyone in here. They depend on you to – as you put it – make things function. To arrange the details. Which is all that matters. Policy?' The Doctor laughed again, a swift burst. 'Siberia has only one policy. Very simple. To sell itself and ship itself away. Nothing is important but who gets the dollars, and how soon. And that is arranged through the Bureau, by certain people. Mostly it is timber and oil and gold, but one tiny part of the Siberian economy, still worth a little in our region, is salmon and reindeer and furs, which involves the Tungus and Yakuts and Koryaks and Chukchi, and so the Office of Indigenous Affairs is also under you, and that is why I am here.' He let the other lift his hands in protest, shrug off this allegation of power and influence. In Malenky these motions took on the manner of one reveling in a clean, hot, deserved shower.

'Mikhail Sokhalov is the Inspector in charge, and he will tell you his resources are exhausted,' said Kutznetsov. 'He has had to rely on the Dixie people, and what the television says is a lie, for they have withdrawn all but one helicopter. The military pilots claim they have looked everywhere, noted all the visible encampments, and they are not obligated further. A civil agency must contact those encampments.'

'But the Dixie people, your young man—'

'He is not my young man.'

'But . . . ah well . . . forgive me. It is not my business. But this Kinny was very upset, he was very emphatic the search would go on, he is dedicated. Surely the Dixies will help! Why would they withdraw their helicopters?'

The effrontery of this pretended naïveté left Kutznetsov speechless for a moment. He almost laughed again, before going on in the cold, spare manner he reserved for particularly meaningless staff meetings. 'Because they do not want to appear responsible. Kenny was an employee, which is embarrassing. They gave him the helicopter to keep him out of the way, pretending it is a grand favor to a bereaved fiancé. On the other hand they want Satchi found as soon as possible. It would surprise me if they have not contacted you already.'

Malenky lifted a finger from the side of his glass, puffed out his cheeks and released an explosive sigh.

'Of course they did. They would offer help, but not in a public way. I presume substantial help.' Kutznetsov paused pointedly.

Malenky's sigh was now one of light, false, existential sadness. 'Alexy, Alexy . . . how can I explain this? Of *course* they are anxious to help. They understand what it is like for you, that you are in a difficult position, because of course your daughter was not actually, officially, qualified to service that station . . .' Malenky grimaced and hunched, as if witnessing a collision. 'But just as you say, it is very delicate for them also. You have much in common, actually.' He looked at Kutznetsov with sly sagacity. 'Which is ironic, eh? Your office monitoring habitats and wild animals – like that bear – and filing reports on the lumbering business and so forth . . . but anyway, yes, you are right, they have spoken to me. But you would not guess why, I think. They spoke about you.'

Doctor Kutznetsov blinked.

Malenky's bulk rocked a little with pleasure. 'Yes, Alexy, about you. Now let me speculate on something. You invite me to lunch – for the first time, as far as I remember. You wish to discuss 'the investigation', a possible role for me. We both know – and you much better than I – that our government has no funds, never has funds for special investigations, never has funds for anything, except what comes in under the door. And we both know what is the most honorable way to do this. Therefore – I am a detective, now, eh? – you have gone over your affairs and what you can sell or borrow, and you are prepared to guarantee a sum. And this sum would be allotted to Indigenous Affairs, as a reward in the American manner, offered for information leading to recovery, though my agents would spend it in field trips into the herders' camps. Yes? Yes, of course. What is that sum, Alexy?'

Malenky was beaming at him, with just a hint of impatience. Like a father, if a father could be twenty years younger than his son. Kutznetsov flushed and looked down. He could not find his balance, his tongue. The waitress was approaching again, bearing their soup. Malenky lifted a palm and she veered away. 'Three thousand.' He swallowed. 'Dollars.'

Malenky's mouth began to stretch, wider and wider, and he lurched forward a little with the effort of sucking in a deep breath, then fighting to keep it. His laugh, when it came, had the gasp of real hilarity barely under control. His eyes glistened with tears. 'Oh! Oh yes!' he got out. 'Dollars . . . to be sure!'

Kutznetsov had gone rigid, and his blush faded. A colder shame moved into his heart.

'Forgive me! It struck me . . . a little coincidence . . . I will explain in a moment. Yes, a reward then. And yes, my dear, ready for the soup! Come along!'

Malenky opened his napkin with a flourish, his eyes skipping on and off the Doctor's drawn, empty face. 'The thing is, Alexy, that is exactly what the Dixie people wanted me to discuss with you, actually. They are very rich, compared to us, my friend! We are nothing beside them. But Americans operate under peculiar rules. Medieval, byzantine . . .' He looked up mischievously at the waitress, now setting down their bowls of hot, green soup and a platter of black rye bread. 'Not you, my dear. You are exquisite, a Siberian orchid. But leave us alone now. For main course I'll take the Spanish, olives but no peppers. Alexy?'

Kutznetsov looked dumbly at the card on the table. He knew nothing of pizza, except that it was awkward and ridiculous. Spanish, Thai, Indian, American Special . . . His thoughts were a chaos. Kenny's bosses had already discussed the reward – no doubt the exact amount – with this fat crook, had foreseen his cooperation, so the whole idea he had nursed for days, thought over and rejected and readopted, was perhaps already in motion . . .

'Special,' he blurted.

'Good! Cannot go wrong with a Special. Now, Alexy, to business, as we savor the soup this beautiful creature has brought us, yes, thank you dear, bye-bye now.' As the waitress rustled away, Malenky tore a piece of the bread in half, sank it into the steaming bowl. 'The Dixie men could offer a big reward, very big. Five thousand, ten thousand, twenty even – this is nothing to them, Alexy. A set of tracks for one of their bulldozers. But in America everything is recorded, every dollar has a name on it, even in huge companies. Amazing, eh? In the great nation of Freedom, money is not free! It cannot move about easily, as it does here.'

Malenky ate the sodden chunk of bread in one bite and followed it with two swift spoonfuls of the soup. Then he wiped his mouth with the napkin and smiled ruefully. 'Dixie cannot simply give Indigenous Affairs ten thousand, unfortunately. As you point out, it would seem they felt responsible. But in your name, as the father, there is no problem. A sum of ten thousand, say, or even fifteen . . .

something appropriate . . . they would be very happy to contribute that. Then I could manage to put three or four men over the area for a week, with a supply truck, fuel trailer, and perhaps a couple of snomos. Men who speak enough of the language to find out something. We would of course offer a few dollars, perhaps three hundred, to any herder who can lead us to Satchi. Whatever we turn up, you would know as soon as I get the report. A generous proposal, yes? What do you think?'

'In my name.'

'Yes, of course. As the father.'

'They want to give you money in my name. Just enough so people will believe it is my money.'

'Well, Alexy, you see the problem. You said yourself—'

'No.' Kutznetsov had already stopped eating the soup and now placed his spoon carefully on his plate. 'No. Never. I offer my own money, in my own name. That is what we are discussing, and all we are discussing.'

'Ah! God, be reasonable, man! We were thinking this through so well. Dixie *would* do this – and much more – if it were not for the bastard reporters and—'

'How much,' Kutznetsov interrupted, 'are they giving you to persuade me?'

For a moment Malenky looked as if he would pretend he did not hear. He had been dabbling another bit of bread, had lifted it dripping, ready to take in, but now he paused. His eyes seemed to change color slightly, to a paler gray. When he finally ate the bread it was a swift, efficient motion, a gesture of elimination. He chewed, swallowed, then settled back in his chair. His pale eyes had not moved from Kutznetsov's face.

'You don't seem to understand, Doctor. Or perhaps you refuse to understand. So I will have to be frank with you. Your three thousand – even the whole sum – is of no interest to me, whatsoever. It's beans. It's shit. I could spend as much in three nights on that young woman over there.

'You are very out of touch, Alexy. Or else your temper has the best of you. Either way, you are quite wrong to think I am here to pick up a little percentage.' Malenky paused, belched in contempt. 'You come to me – slog through the mud like a martyr

– and say you want help, for a very honorable cause, to find your daughter. I sympathize, I hope the best, but I must say – and I regret having to bring this up, but everyone knows it anyway – a lot of people do not believe in this business of the bear. They think reindeer herders came to that station and Satchi ran away with them. She knew some of their language, from her mother, so there are people who think this is a hoax, that she was unhappy with her Kinny, or with you, and just wants to create a big stir or make herself famous. *That* is why neither your Bureau nor mine nor the Army is particularly anxious to launch an all-out search. Therefore you need help – you say.

'Then Dixie comes to me, because they want the same thing, they want Satchi found, of course for different reasons, but who cares? It is logical for you to join forces. And now they ask *you* for a very small thing. You see? They give you back your life savings, and only ask that you allow them to post the reward, in your name, for triple that amount! And you tell me no, never. You cannot touch the money from these foreigners who, you say, are eating up our country. No, not even if your daughter's life is at stake! And then you insult me. A double insult, by the way. You price me so low. If I have lunch at the Ali Baba with someone in this Oblast, I can assure you, Alexy, it is not over some shitty three thousand dollars.'

Malenky laughed in a new way, a low grunt of ridicule. Doctor Kutznetsov sat very pale and still. The rage he had nursed was being buried under an avalanche of despair, which also scattered his thoughts like rabbits before loose boulders. He realized he had known some of this all along, had simply, stupidly, refused to accept it. Three thousand was nothing to Malenky, nothing to the man from Fisheries or these Japanese and Americans. He could not bribe them. He was a poor buffoon, an impotent, threadbare enthusiast for antiquated ideals.

Nor could he ignore anymore the hints all around him. The television had dwelt on the tentative conclusion of Sokhalov's field report – that Satchi had apparently gone without a struggle. A runaway. He understood, in a flash, the appeal. Run away from all this – Malenky, Magadan, money, the Ali Baba, the boom – *BOOM!* it all to high heaven! – Dixie would have everything anyway, in the end ... His hands, without his knowledge, had been refolding his napkin, and Malenky saw this and shrugged impatiently.

'Don't be stubborn, Alexy. You are a scientist. Stay and eat your Special and listen to the facts. We do not have a lot of time. At least I don't.' As if to demonstrate the point, someone at another table beckoned vigorously and called out his name, but Malenky only glanced that way and with one hand gestured postponement. 'Remember none of this costs you a dollar, eh? Mainly Dixie is worried about reporters, the piranhas and little shit-smellers already here. They could attract some big sharks. Now all you have to promise, Alexyvitch, as a man of principle—'

'I regret the insult,' Kutznetsov said. He had finished folding his napkin and placed it beside his uneaten soup, the half-full glass of wine. 'I am, as you say, out of touch. To me three thousand was a respectable sum.' The words he knew he would have to say came slowly, carefully, like heavy cargo on a frail bridge. 'In any case, it is all I have, and I would appreciate your arranging to use it in the fashion you have described.' He pushed back his chair and got to his feet.

Malenky looked up and laughed in mild disgust, his eyes pale and steady again. 'Suit yourself. You're a fool.' He glanced away to the other table, summoned with two fingers. 'I'll tell them—'

'What Dixie does is their business, but they must do it in their own name,' Kutznetsov said evenly. 'Good day.'

Malenky hesitated, his mouth pursed, and the gray eyes speared into the Doctor. 'What if we match you, dollar for dollar? I will keep the funds separate – but spend them on the same field work, to find your Satchi? Eh? And you, you do one thing Alexy, you *acknowledge* the gesture. Could you do that? The man of high principle express his gratitude?' He grinned in derision.

Two young men from the other table were bearing down on them, already smiling and chattering, and behind them came the houri with their pizzas. 'I will consider it, and speak to you in a day or two,' Kutznetsov said. 'And I will cover the check on my way out.'

Malenky grunted once more in amazed disgust, before turning to beam at the newcomers and throw wide his arms. Doctor

Kutznetsov walked back across the main dining room, keeping as straight a line as he could. He collected his coat and waited, staring at the wall, while the cashier hastily figured the bill. Then he paid a week's salary and walked out, the eunuch gazing after him with an amused, incredulous pity.

Traffic was heavy on Spiridonova Boulevard, at least for midday after a storm. A couple of ships had come in and he saw a cabful of drunken foreign sailors go by, Dutch or German he judged. Their cargoes were already arriving in the stores, so there was the usual run of shoppers. The wives of wealthy blackmarket dealers and gangsters, or of upper-level employees of Dixie Pacific, the successful young whores and sometimes their bulls, and packs of adolescents with thundering and shrieking music boxes, gold rings through ears, noses, eyebrows, and God knew where else.

Doctor Kutznetsov passed these by in stony silence. He nodded once to an old woman and a boy, apparently on their way to the waterfront. They were dressed in shabby woolens, and the boy swung a white block of frozen milk on a string. Quite out of place in the New Siberia, Kutznetsov thought, as he was. Though no doubt this pair, especially the grandmother, would have fainted with delight at the prospect of dining at the Ali Baba.

It was clear to him at last that he would be doing things he hated every day now. Malenky was right, he was a fool. Until yesterday he had not allowed himself to consider certain possibilities. He had been certain Satchi was too intelligent, too able and knowledgeable to have made the blunders people were attributing to her. He had gone with her in the beginning, had seen how quickly she caught on, how accurately she followed procedure. But that was not the issue, of course. Someone came into the station. Someone took her. She –

Here Doctor Kutznetsov's mind always stopped, as if a wire had been cut. If he knew his daughter, she would not simply go along with a band of herders. But what if he did not know her? There were no signs of violence, except for the broken hairclip, though the gun was gone and the noise canister had been set off. Malenky had forced him to remember Satchi's eccentric behaviour as the summer ended: the signs of trouble with Kenny, her flashes of savage humor, her retreat into books, her fetish for English, the absurd contradiction between her dream of studying at Cambridge and her love of the lonely, ice-bound stations.

He thought again of the bear. Only once in forty years had Doctor Kutznetsov seen a documented report of a bear attacking a research station. If it happened, then Satchi must have been distraught and vulnerable, just when the herdsmen intruded. If it happened! He had pretended outrage at Malenky's hint of a hoax, but now he found himself hoping – in an odd, dismal way – that such jeering cynics were right, that Satchi had indeed simply run off. Rejected him, and her whole education, for some ridiculous notion of recovering her – what did they call it now? – ethnic identity. He preferred that alternative to the others, dark and huge and unbearable, that lurked beyond the range of his speculation.

This wretchedness would go on until he knew, finally, what had happened. Until someone scoured that tremendous, wrinkled plate of ice from the Okhotsk Sea to the Kolyma River. And someone would have to pay for the search. Malenky was right again there. It came down to money, as always, and Dixie Pacific had the money. He would have to swallow his pride and pretend to thank Richard Pendergast, perhaps be photographed with him.

Doctor Kutznetsov cringed inwardly. He wanted to spit, clear his mouth, but he had left the covered walkways of Spiridonova and was slammed by the cold, stiffening wind coming up the long avenue that led to the Resource Management building and his laboratory. Smiling beside Pendergast, he would throw away two years of labor documenting the shrinking away of riverine and arboreal habitat, the vanishing of red fox, marten, otter, and squirrel. *So*? Satchi would have said, *Who cares enough to do anything*?

Thinking of his research, he found his revulsion giving way to puzzlement. There were bothersome aspects, he realized, to this offer from Dixie, and Malenky's part in it. Kutznetsov had been reviewing satellite photos from the military, secured finally after two years of badgering. He could see that almost all the significant larch and stone pine from the eastern slope of Stanovoi had been taken, and from there to the north and east was tundra, with only poplar and aspen along the river courses. This was no surprise, but it was odd that Dixie had given no sign of diminishing their presence. Their crews continued to occupy the camps, ships unloaded the usual supplies, the company had even begun remodeling its office in downtown Magadan.

It was even odder, then, for the company to approach Malenky with this scheme. He could grant three thousand dollars was a laughable sum, but it was difficult to believe Dixie cared about its image if they were on the verge of pulling out of the whole region. And in any case surely they could arrange a payoff to Indigenous Peoples some other way. Why would his name seem important, vital even, to them? Poor old Kutzchik, compiling reports nobody listened to, with the help of his unbalanced daughter, who – if he believed them – would turn up any hour now, a spoiled runaway brat? *Wood from the same tree*, he had imagined them whispering in the Ali Baba.

They were hiding something, playing some other game, he would wager that. He decided all at once to agree to the joint reward. For Satchi's sake, yes, but also for the purpose of observing Pendergast and his minions more closely. Apparently they had concluded there was something left in this corner of Siberia worth hauling away. If so, even if he could not stop them, he would compile the record, he would bequeath to the future an inventory, at least, of their pillage.

He leaned into the wind now, felt a surge of dreadful exhilaration. Perhaps Malenky was right once more. Perhaps he enjoyed punishment, tilting his old bones over the frozen slush on the sidewalk, inviting an unholy union with his enemy. A masochist, then. But that – he smiled a savage and humorless smile – would be a redundancy, a Siberian masochist.

CHAPTER NINE

The men took two reindeer to pack the fish, if there were any, and traveled swiftly in the early morning hours, when they would not need snowshoes. The little river was always the last to freeze over, because there were two springs on its upper course that came warm from the earth, and sometimes a few late spawners could be picked up easily downstream from that point. They were ragged and dying, their red bellies startling against the white banks, but they were good enough for the dogs, and sometimes, as was the case now, the last chance to build up supplies in a lean season.

Choti and Kainivilu had gaff hooks, and dragged the carcasses to the bank where Tatka and Tolek had built a fire under a frame of willow sticks. The old ones gutted the fish, split them, and propped them on the frame to dry the first layer of meat. It was late for such work, Tolek had grumbled. He was right. It was too cold and the fish were scant and poor. They had spent too many days of the late summer ferrying supplies to the Brick-Heads' camp. Sled after sled of the strange food in plastic and metal and glass. Now they had money, but barely enough food for themselves. They could afford ammunition and a new sled, but there was little time to hunt and they had already butchered too many of their herd to feed this camp. It was as Tolek said: they were living more and more like the Russians, needing things that had to be brought from somewhere else, wasting or forgetting what was right underfoot.

'But they brought medicine,' Choti reminded Tolek, looking up from where he was prodding under an ice shelf, trying to hook a salmon that had gotten off his gaff upstream and lodged there. 'Yina sleeps now when Navilineut pokes him.'

The old men laughed, and Kainivilu smiled at this pun. He had brought three small fish from a bend downstream and shook them off on the bloodied snow at Tolek's feet. 'She is only Woman-Half-Asleep now,' he said.

'Good for Yina, I think,' Tatka said. 'The medicine and the reading and talking.'

They were quiet for a minute or two, while Choti pulled out the narrow, shuddering body of tarnished silver and dull flame, and Tatka and Tolek began swiftly cleaning the new catches. They were thinking of the sick boy, but unwilling to speak of hope yet. He was so thin, the fever burning so high. They had seen before, at the medical posts, how sometimes the needles and injections preceded death.

'They are afraid of her,' Choti went on. 'You say they want us to keep her away from them.'

'From everybody. The government. The Big Eater. Her father.' Kainivilu bent down and seized one of the cleaned fish by the tail, hoisted it for a closer examination.

'Tshaa! What can she do to them? She saw them drive away, but she doesn't know anything.'

'Foolish woman,' Tolek said, hissing his laughter. 'Nice-looking though. I take her. I'm not afraid. Make this old man smell like that fish you hold up.'

'You think a little minnow like you got would last two breaths with a big girl like that?' Tatka croaked and hopped from one foot to the other, waving his red knife. 'Hey! She is maybe Kilu, with that pretty black hair, eh, Kainivilu?'

Kainivilu tossed the fish at him and said, 'Big Raven has to feed her first, and better than this,' and they all laughed. It was a signal they understood. The fish was too old and no good; the sunlight was thinning, the shadows lengthening. It was not a time to think of pretty black hair. They had time only to warm themselves by burning the last of their scavenged wood. Then they would load the two dozen barely dried fish and depart; but for these few minutes they would talk frankly, freely, about the things most on their minds, and find a way to laugh at them. That was how an *eyem* spoke with those who believed in him.

'She brings *kalau* for the Brick-Heads,' Choti said. 'But what about here? Maybe we should be afraid too.'

'Always plenty of reasons to be afraid,' Tatka said. 'She is *nymylin*, like us.'

'Part. But Russian in her wants to go home. And people will come looking for her.' Choti stared at Kainivilu keenly. Shorter and wider than his brother, he had a way of tilting forward slightly, as if about to climb upward. 'They know that, the Brick-Heads. And they have seen her now. She said she tried to stop them, so they know she has seen them too. She can guess they are nearby. She will notice that they took away the load on that sled.'

Kainivilu did not look at any of them, but at the little river. He was waiting, they divined, for them to say everything.

'Tshaa!' Tolek flipped a batch of guts aside with his blade, his gums bared in the hissing laugh. 'The young bears are sniffing.'

Kainivilu grinned at the river.

'Be quiet, uncle. So they will pay us to pen her up, eh? So you think they will be afraid of us, too, now? But it is maybe dangerous to make the Big Eater afraid. It is hard to understand – all this to hide some blocks of frozen mud.'

'Not hard,' Tatka said. His wrinkled features contracted into a frown as he spread out a fileted carcass on the rack. 'They have cut all the trees. Now they look for something else. Money, all money. That is easy to understand.'

'There has always been gold in this mud. Who cares? Too far from the ships. Their machine – why should they care who knows about it?' Choti gestured with one mitten.

'Nice big bricks,' Tolek observed.

'Brick-Heads,' Tatka said. 'Mud brains.' The others laughed. It was their usual summary explanation. Men who made everything into blocks – their houses and food and roads and machines. Men who counted and ordered everything like bricks. Who looked like bricks, all of them the same.

'Tshaa. I wish we could just leave them. Let them feed themselves.' Choti glanced at the rack full of fish, at the reindeer staked by leg-lines behind them. 'They are bad men and they are afraid. That is dangerous.'

No one spoke, and in a moment Choti sighed in impatience. They all knew and had been over many times their reasons for staying. At first it was because the Big Eater, Malenky, had sent his men to tell them they could do this and their registration and allotments would be reinstated, without penalty, and besides they would be paid well. All they had to do was supply the camp with fresh meat and an occasional load of supplies from the post at Dukat. It was never explained why those in the camp could not take their own GAZ and travel to the supply depots Malenky's bureau had set up for the *nymyl'u*.

They assumed the camp was some kind of important secret. Helicopters – one of them very big, from the Army – went in occasionally, but did not stay. They had in fact heard a smaller one pass to the south early that morning. Kainivilu believed they were chosen to supply the camp because they were always moving, were never long at any one government post or settlement. No one knew their business, or cared to notice them. They were outcasts even among their own people, everywhere except in the Taigonos.

That was the other reason they had stayed with this peculiar business. Without updated registration and unwilling to live in the government's housing, they were eligible for no payments or services. The market for reindeer was entirely controlled by the post agents, so they could normally sell meat only through their middle brother and a cousin still in the Taigonos, which was far away and a weak market besides. Everything was funneled, coming and going, through Magadan, through Malenky and the other Big Eaters. To survive, they found themselves perched in this place, the furthest edge of that funnel, a barren, cold place with poor fishing and too much wind.

'So tell us what is in your heart,' Choti finally said, and Kainivilu laughed.

He had a great number of laughs, some loud and some soft. This one was like a seal's bark and startled them, but in a moment they laughed with him. He did not have to explain what he meant, for it was clear. They were not afraid, and they were not dangerous, which was not a bad position to be in. 'We are protecting the Big Eater from this mean woman,' he said, and they all laughed again. 'We are the only ones who can handle her.'

Tolek was grinning again. 'Only because she thinks you are a bear.'

Kainivilu lifted his head, his eyes squinting, and let his shoulders droop. He began a shuffling, swaying walk. They laughed in earnest now, remembering how The-Woman-Who-Sleeps had fainted when she saw Kainivilu in his bear-mask, how he had been perhaps at his best, the most convincing ever.

'Eh! He comes back!' Tolek had rolled on his back beside the fire, his eyes wide. He was joking, but they remembered how a few days ago, in the woman's station where they had tracked the bear, he too had believed, like the woman, that his nephew had changed himself into a great brown bear. The others knew this could happen, when one ate the black, bitter nubs, and it was as true a happening as any other. They were even envious of Tolek, because he could see such things as easily as a little child.

'What do I smell,' Kainivilu growled, sniffing and wrinkling his nose. 'I smell bricks.'

Tatka had also collapsed beside the fire, gagging with laughter. Choti looked away, behaving like one in a fit of sneezing. Kainivilu approached them in his swaying shuffle, sniffed at the tops of their heads.

'Any bricks here? Any good bricks? Br-r-a-a-gh! Bad! Only stinking *nymyl'u*. Smell like old women's pee, and no meat, all bones.'

Tolek sprang up and seized one of the drying salmon by the tail. 'Eh, bear! You like fish? Like big girls? Come on!'

Kainivilu pretended to be interested in the fish, shook his head and imitated the loose, swinging gait of a running bear as Tolek hobbled around the fire. They kept it up until Tolek threw the fish at his pursuer. Kainivilu sniffed the carcass, snorted in disdain, and pretended to urinate on it.

They had laughed until they were breathless, and now all at once were quiet, though Tolek continued to grin in silent glee. Tatka had recovered the salmon and began lifting others from the rack over the fire, laying them on a section of light canvas that Choti had removed from one of the packs. Kainivilu took the neck halters from the second pack and handed one to Tolek. They moved easily, lightly, and together in their work, happy to be heading home. The mood had changed. A child was very sick and the winter was beginning and they had no good prospects, but Kainivilu had made them forget it all and laugh. That was why he was *eyem*.

'So?' Choti said finally, watching as Tolek tied up the bundles of salmon and Kainivilu was strapping the packs on the reindeer.

'Ah my brother, you are a true hunter. You never lose the trail.' Kainivilu smiled and slipped a loop of thong over a wooden toggle pin on the harness. 'It is like that bear. The Big Eater is dangerous, but he is only interested in one smell. If we do not get between him and his berries – money, you know – he will not bother us. But we can be bears, too.'

Choti had hoisted the pack stuffed with salmon, but paused before he swung it up on the reindeer. 'What is this?'

'You do not bother a bear, or he will bother you. The Bricks know we have this woman, part Russian. Her father is an *eyem*. She knows about them, too, as you said. They cannot take her, or they might have to kill her. And we would know, so they would have to kill us too. Too dangerous. So they will tell us to keep her away from everybody. Then they will not bother us – as long as they are still playing with their bricks.'

Choti spoke soothingly to the reindeer, then heaved the pack of salmon onto the harness. When he had two loops secured, he said, 'And we will do this?'

Kainivilu laughed shortly. 'For now. Then we will see. Maybe tomorrow or the next day we have to take them meat. We will see how they are.'

They left the little river just before sundown, their shadows immensely long and jagged. Tolek sang to the reindeer, slapping his leg rhythmically with his thong whip, and they began to make good time as the cold of night moved over them and the snowcrust rang like metal. There was a nearly full moon and they knew this trail very well. Also the air was unusually calm, so the severe cold would not bother them much. They could keep moving and even talk now and then.

They spoke no more of the Brick-Heads or Big Eaters, or even about the woman. This was perhaps because Tatka had called her Kilu, the Big Raven's wife. A very beautiful and strong young woman might be teased with this name, but it had startled them to hear it applied to a newcomer. Especially this odd one. Pipik was sure she was a distant relative from an intermarriage with the Whale People of the Taigonos. The old woman even believed she had seen her before, as a small child. This could be true. Pipik remembered things from long ago, and forgot what happened yesterday.

They spoke mostly about the delivery they would have to make soon. The Brick-Heads wanted more fresh meat. They ate an astonishing amount, and wasted a great deal. They never used forelegs or heads or tongues or intestines. The main crew of six and the transients – three or four at the moment – could devour two animals every moon. Choti was unhappy already at the number of good breeders they had sacrificed, and they had nothing left now but their own pack animals, calves and the brood does. That was why they had come so far for these poor fish. They could no longer afford to eat their own tender calves.

It was Choti's opinion that they should take Tipa and Enalit, the oldest draft animals, but Kainivilu argued that the smallest of the does would be a better choice. Tolek paid no attention, but Tatka listened as he trudged along beside them. The loaded reindeer were stumbling a little over the rough crust, and there were long pauses in the discussion when they navigated a steeper slope. After one such pause, just as they reached a ridge top and lined out along it at an easy, swinging pace, Tatka finally spoke. 'We are rich men starving to death,' he said, and laughed out over the moonlit land. 'We are eating our own arms and legs.'

No one answered. Of course it was true the herd was diminished either way. But a herd could be restored over time, if the weather was not too perverse and they worked hard. They all understood Tatka meant something more. They were all at once aware that they had been talking about themselves, and not just the reindeer. They – all the *nymyl'u* – were disappearing from this region. They had withdrawn to the settlements. Or the children died of sickness and the old ones of grief. Kainivilu's band and one or two others were all that remained of the true *nymyl'u*.

'In time—' Choti began, but Tatka laughed again, louder. It was a wild, gay laughter.

'Staying or going. That is all we talk about.'

'All going. Sooner or later.' Tolek laughed too, a long cackle interrupted only by gasps for breath.

'*They* are feeding on us,' Choti insisted, 'eating our herd. We should say to them we can do no—'

Kainivilu had stopped the lead reindeer, causing some momentary confusion. 'Those foxes are eating something,' he said with bemused curiosity. He was looking down the ridge and slightly behind them. The others turned and stared.

The western sky was still pale, and snow crystals sparkled in the moonlight, but the land was wrinkled and slashed by shadows. It was several seconds before Tatka said 'Yes.'

'Kits. Three, I think.' Choti glanced at Kainivilu. 'It is not far.'

Kainivilu grunted and set out down the slope again, angling back the way they had come, toward the flecks of shadow clustered at the edge of a lesser ridge whose top was almost flat. After a moment the small shadows moved too, and vanished behind the ridge.

It was a bear, and the ravens had been at it earlier, stringing entrails about in a series of fugitive raids. The foxes had only begun to work on the carcass, nibbling at the inner cavity. It was a very large emaciated male, dead for a day or less, Tatka estimated. The hunters had taken only the head, hide and front paws. There were boot tracks around the carcass, but none leading away, so they knew the hunters had come from the sky. Perhaps the helicopter they had heard that morning.

They stood around the headless, naked corpse, mute with the shame and waste of it. The torso without its skin looked like a big old man with slumped shoulders and a distended belly. There was nothing wrong with the meat, but they would not touch it. And there were songs for the killing of a great bear, but they would not sing them here. The men who leaned out of the sky and shot caribou and wolf and bear did not know these songs. In the mines Kainivilu had seen what these men did. They laughed and shouted and made jokes with a wolf they had killed, sitting it up and putting a hat on it so they could take pictures, and then they drank and shot their rifles into the air.

It had become a rare night. The wind had almost stilled, and the silence was immense. The glittering snow all around and the plumes of frost made by their breathing were the only apparent movement. Even the reindeer stood quietly, staring. They were all as if under a spell, or like men who were lost and did not know where to turn, and so remained motionless in despair or wonder.

They did not speak what they thought, which was that the bear deserved respect and had been wronged, and that this was a bad omen. Finally Tolek uttered a faint, querulous, whispering moan and then Kainivilu said, 'We must go home. He does not care if we go home.'

They moved then, the packs creaking and feet and hooves rustling, and formed their line to climb back up the low ridge. They did not look back, and did not speak again until they were within sight of their camp.

CHAPTER TEN

'Couldn't afford her,' Peter observed. 'On your tight-ass Lutheran budget.'

They were in the Apache Lounge at the Ermak Hotel, a dank cellblock where the second wave of journalists into Magadan had settled. A young woman in very tight jeans and spike-heeled boots was coiled on a stool at the far end of the bar, smoking and practicing certain provocative expressions borrowed from magazine covers.

'Fok you.' Lafe watched and when the woman looked his way he nodded and grinned, beckoned with a large, hirsute hand. She tossed her head and smiled cruelly, lifting and tilting her glass.

'*Prastity!*' Lafe pointed imperiously at the bartender, then at the woman. 'Come here, sweetheart.'

'Fucking hell.' Peter drank from the bottle of Sapporo before him. His laugh was a kind of deep, hoarse cough. 'Down to ethnic pride, is it? Men with square-headed dicks?'

'Interview,' Lafe said. The bartender finished recharging the woman's drink, and she began her complicated, hydraulic stroll across the room. 'Whores know more than ministers.'

Peter's laugh boomed again. He was over six feet and weighed almost seventeen stone. Barely thirty, he was balding and ruddy, with a dense black mustache. Together with Lafe, who was nearly as tall, they might make up half – by weight – of the corps of six journalists housed at the Ermak. Even so, at the moment there were more reporters than there were people to report on. Everyone had already interviewed the one available ministry official at least once. Also the police, the army, and the Dixie people. So Lafe might be right; it was perhaps time to go back to the old standbys – taxi drivers, street vendors, bartenders and whores. They were there for a late afternoon talk with Carraway, but that was tentative.

'Ah, sit down. *Zdrasstye*. You have a byootiful bottom.' Lafe had gotten up to pull back a chair at their table.

Peter winked at the young woman, who slid into the chair with a sultry smile and an audible creak of new denim.

'Halloo booys,' she said. 'I am Natasha. Ver' gut. Best aixpansif gurl. Woon hawndred dollars, aiverytank yoo wunt. *Shtaw vy loobeetye*? OK?'

'OK, da, sweetheart. Very pretty, Natasha. Like a movie star.' Lafe beamed at her and folded her small hand out of sight in his own. 'You talk to us?'

'You ought to be ashamed, you filthy Swede. Leading this poor child on. Ask her what she thinks of the bear-girl.'

'You are an esshole. Give the poor child five bucks.' Lafe spoke softly, soothingly. 'No big hurry, OK? *Ja govoroo poroosky*. I speak some, OK?'

Natasha was not exactly an amateur, Peter observed. There was a crease on each side of her young mouth, a little scar on her upper lip, and he saw the way she glanced at his shabby knapsack, at the row of pens in Lafe's breastpocket.

'OK,' she said. She withdrew her hand, in the same motion stroking Lafe teasingly on the chin, and then sipped her drink. 'I tok English. Pratty soon I am go Moscow. Gut gurl. Best gurl. I hef blud tist, gavarmint tist. OK, no problim, I do aiverytank. Tree togedder is OK, planty fun.' She looked from Lafe to Peter and back. 'Two hawndret feefty dollars.'

Lafe smiled regretfully and nodded at Peter. 'No, too bad. My friend is unable. Lost in war. The Foklands.' He pointed primly with one finger at Peter's crotch. '*Nitzshye vo, nyet*, nothing. Shoot off. All gone. Can only talk.'

'You cunt.' Peter cuffed his friend lightly and grinned at Natasha in a monstrous parody of modesty. 'He is Meester Foolofsheet.'

Natasha reviewed them quickly, glanced again at Lafe's pocket of pens.

'Yoo booys meedya?'

'Uh-oh. Exposed.' Peter sighed and slumped, one eyebrow hoisted in fatalistic irony.

'No, not media.' Lafe paused at his task of removing a pack of Marlboro from his shirt pocket. 'I am a writer. Author. Most important intellectyal journal in Sweden. Just talk to you, Natasha, your story. Come on esshole, the poor lady needs five bucks.'

Hooting, Peter went for his wallet. 'An *awthuh* is'e? For a *joornal* now? Friggin' ecoterrorist rag, ponces for whales . . .'

Natasha had taken a cigarette but didn't wait for Lafe, producing her own lighter and then, with a clank and scrape, a tear of yellow flame. The men watched her eyes close, her cheeks hollow, the red mouth part to gush smoke. With wondering eyes, Lafe had extended his big hand again, palm up. She shrugged and placed the lighter there, then dragged again on the cigarette, watching Peter remove the five and slide it next to her glass.

'Yes! Zippo! A real one. Wonderful, wonderful! *Harashaw*!' Lafe shook out and lit a cigarette of his own, passed the lighter to Peter and then pushed the pack of Marlboro across the table until it covered the five dollar bill. 'A present?'

'Booyfran,' Natasha said with another shrug. 'Amricn. So whot we tok abut? Kutznetsova, yas? Yoo tank beers eet hir?' When Lafe hunched his shoulders and lifted his hands, she laughed. 'No, no beers. She tek off.'

'Why? Why did she tek off?'

Natasha smiled, playful and mysterious. 'Maybe booyfran.'

'Homestake,' Peter said. 'Who the fuck is that?' He had been examining the engraving on the gold case of the lighter. 'Must have been an old bloke, her Yank. This is a fucking antique.'

'Unhappy love, eh? Did you know her, Natasha? Satchi Kutznetsova?'

Natasha wrinkled her nose ambiguously.

'Her papa has offered a reward, you know? And Dixie too? Ten thousand dollars?'

Natasha laughed for the first time. A crow's call, short and harsh.

'What?' Lafe planted an elbow on the table to prop his cheek on the curled hand holding his cigarette, making his smile comically one-sided.

Natasha signaled for the return of her Zippo with an inch-long scarlet fingernail. Peter palmed the lighter a moment longer. 'What did he do, your Amricn booyfran? Black market?'

'No. Gif bek. Is kipsek.' She waited until Peter dropped the lighter in her hand. There was a touch of color in her cheeks. 'He wark Dixie. Drife bekho.'

'Again, love?'

'Bekho. Booduzer. Beg, *beg* bekho. Woz beg men.'

'Ah. Backhoe,' Peter explained to Lafe. 'A big tractor for—'

'I know what it is. But why are you laughing, Natasha? Ten thousand too small, you think?'

'Satchi Kutznetsova is chip gurl. *Kurva*. Fok lut of booyfrans. She is netif gurl. Nat woon hawndret pirsint Rooshan.'

'But very byootiful, no?'

A slight, mock spit between the front teeth. 'Too fet. And blek. Laik durt.' Natasha gave a coy shudder and extinguished half of her Marlboro.

'Good English, from the university,' Lafe goaded.

'She wunt Hallywood. Fur mawney. Hur Papa hes nodding. *Nyet*. All Dixie mawney.'

'Think she's right there, mate. Papa Kutz is an old crank, hasn't a pot to piss in. And that's an interesting theory, that our dusky beauty staged the whole cock-up to make herself a celebrity.'

'Not a good chance. She was a university student, a good one. Wanted to go to your country, study litteratyoor. I admit you have good schools, for a second-rate power . . .'

'Not good enough to teach square-dicks a proper accent, it appears. But that means fuckall, except to prove that people will do anything, even read T.S. Eliot, to get out of this icehole. Though I grant our good friend here is just imagining what she'd do in the same spot. Trace of jealousy, I'd say.'

'Perceptive of you. But Natasha, you still have not told why you laugh at this ten thousand.'

'Whot?'

Natasha was lighting another cigarette, and as the smoke bloomed she glanced through it around the room. More patrons had drifted in. A dark stocky woman and a narrow youth with bleached hair were serving drinks and clearing tables. A group of merchant seamen, Dutch or German, was getting loud.

Peter noticed that both the pack of cigarettes and the five dollar bill had vanished from the tabletop. 'Let me try,' he said. He turned to Natasha, and his dense black mustache lifted like wings above the white crags of his smile. 'You are good girl, best girl, yes indeed, and also a smart girl. This boyfriend, Satchi's boyfriend? Carraway? You know him? Did you ever fuck him?'

'Booyfran of Satchi? No.' Natasha wrinkled her nose again. 'I navair fok him. My fran, oder gurl, she fok him.'

'Ah. Not a surprise, really. But is this a true story, love? Your friend is sure of it?'

'Of curs. See hem on teevee. Booyfran of Satchi. My fren say hey I fok dis men.'

'Was this recent?'

Nastasha looked doubtful. 'Raysin? No raysin. Just fok, setesfy coostmer, mek lidel bit mawney.'

Peter laughed, saluted her. 'I mean, did your friend – the other girl – fuck him yesterday, day before, a few days? Or long time ago, before this Satchi goes off with the natives or whatever?'

'Long tem. Two munts.'

A motive,' Lafe said softly. 'Woman spurned.'

'Premature,' Peter said. 'Don't know she knew. So—'

'Nas tokin' to yoo booys. I hef to go . . .'

Natasha had swiftly crushed her cigarette, but a large, firm hand on each shoulder kept her from rising more than a foot from her chair.

'Oh, sweetheart!'

'No no, love, this is fascinatin'.' Peter grimaced urgently around her at his partner. 'Your turn to help the poor lady, square dick. Make it ten this time. Just a couple more questions, love, promise.'

'Yoo booys nas booys, but dunt wunt to fok.' Natasha, impatient and cross, was eyeing the table full of sailors.

Can't blame her, Peter thought, maybe five hundred bucks over there. 'You're right. That's true. But you are our smart girl, Natasha.' Lafe had dealt out two five dollar bills at her elbow, and Peter picked them up, folded them quickly and stuffed them into her purse. 'Five minutes. Two dollars a minute. And they will wait.' He jerked his head at the sailors. 'They know who is best girl.'

'Queeky, OK. Bot fest, I hef to go. Isk me.' Natasha's blue eyes were hard and level now.

'Better be foking good qveschuns,' Lafe muttered.

Peter ignored him. 'Everybody looking for Satchi,' he said, and made an elaborate show of scratching his temple. 'Boyfriend and Army and Dixie. Everybody says she is with the natives, the reindeer herders. But nobody finds anything. Ten thousand dollars and nobody – not even the Army – finds *anything*. Why? Why do you think, Natasha?'

Natasha gave again her crow's laugh, and then pulled her mouth down in wry dismissal. 'Dunt wunt to fine har.'

Peter and Lafe looked at each other. 'Don't *want* to find her?' Peter appeared incredulous, and waited.

'Dunt wunt to. Army *wunt* to fine you, dey fine you.'

'But *why*?'

Natasha shrugged. 'Dunt know. Shame. Sheet hoppening in gavarmint.' One of the drunk sailors had crooned in her direction, and she shot him the ruthless, inviting smile. 'OK. I hef to go.'

'Wait, my dear – just one more – who would know why? Know about this shit in government? Who's the sheet-hoppening man?'

She was on her feet, looking down at them as if they were tiresome schoolboys too dull to follow a lesson. 'Magadan? Yoo dunt know? Yoo spik to Malenky. Sheet in gavarmint, tok to Papa Malenky. OK?' She turned and left.

They watched her undulate to the whoops and whistles of the sailors, who had prepared a chair for her arrival.

'Not a backward glance. We, who cared about her higher nature.'

'She makes more money than us today,' Lafe grunted reproachfully.

Peter regarded his companion in wondering pity. 'She *works* for a living, cunty. Christ, I feel sorry for her. Feel sorry for most of these poor beggars. A thousand fucking degrees below zero outside and nothing to do in here but screw each other, in all the known senses of the phrase. And you admit yourself she's given us a possible motive. Maybe our Satchi is just another jilted half-breed, or a shameless opportunist. In which case we might both take the next plane out and save our editors money. But the other notion – that the authorities don't *want* to find her – that could be worth a good deal more than bloody ten pounds.'

'I do not see. Why would they not?'

Peter was rolling the empty Sapporo bottle between his big hands, thinking. 'Possible they did find her, or what the bear left of her, and they don't want to admit they fucked up. Or she knew something. Found out something.'

Lafe was shaking his head, squinting in doubt. 'They fok up all the time. They would blame her, or old Kutznetsov, for sending her. And what is to find out, in a weather station?'

Peter hummed noncommittally, gazed out over the room. The bartender and a bouncer were conferring quietly, probably about the sailors. They wore black and white striped turtlenecks and dark berets, and the bartender sported an earring. Above the bar, behind layers of cigarette smoke and a final film of greasy glass, hung a row of enlarged photographs of Montparnasse, the Arc de Triomphe, and Brigitte Bardot. From the black mouths of ancient speakers came the noise of a heavy metal band, apparently playing underwater. So much for atmosphere, Peter thought. Everything else was concrete or plastic in horrible shades of blue and green, the decor of a bad American motel.

''Tis a mystery,' he said finally. 'Maybe we should ask this Malenky. But you talked to him already, right? He's the man for the natives?'

Lafe's squint had turned into an outright frown. 'He was a fokking eel. Can I help you, do you need anything, my dear friend, Sveden is our neighbor – all shit. He said nothing, for thirty minutes. Only hinting that our girl is a bad one, a heart-breaker, always fokking around. He didn't look like a big fish, but who knows?' He shrugged. 'We are here . . . what? Five days?'

'Centuries, by my clock. Anyway, I think our Natasha has given us a clue. Think of her and the Kutznetsova girl. You're almost thirty, and your great hope is to be a Moscow whore or get a board and books scholarship in England. You're stuck in a place where for three hundred years the Tsars and Commissars sent their enemies, because it was a frozen hell on earth. The coldest place on the fucking planet, and huge. Biggest country in the world, Siberia – if it was a country – did you know that? But unlivable. Nobody lives here voluntarily.' He cocked an eyebrow at Lafe.

'For money. Yes, we know. And so?'

'Large sums of money, mate. Very large. That's what brings people to frozen hell. That's what will explain this little mystery eventually. If the government – the Army – doesn't want to find the Kutznetsova girl, it's because she would cost them money, or they get something out of her absence.'

'I have gone over all that. Does not add up, as you say.'

Peter bared his teeth in a growl, his habitual expression of frustration. No scenario they could dream up supplied a motive for hiding a bureaucrat's daughter, or her corpse. Lafe's journal was especially interested in finding some scandal involving collusion between the government and the giant American lumber company, whose royalty payments funded the research and monitoring program the Kutznetsovs worked on. But both these players would be anxious, one would think, to bring Satchi out of the bush dead or alive, just to get the media circus over with. Which was what Lafe and he wanted. A circus, all right, and a juicy one, but quicker.

The magazine he was stringing for was mainstream with a flavor of young money and fashion. So his own angle was the beautiful natural princess, saved from a wild bear by the nomad herders. He had the opening graphs basically written. They were stuffed in his knapsack after two mornings' work.

The beauty of an Oriental courtesan, the passion and brilliance of a young poet, and blood-kinship with a primal, nomadic race – Satchi Kutznetsova is as fascinating and contradictory as her savage, desolate, Siberian homeland.

Satchi learned intimately the tundras and mountains of her Koryak ancestors. When her Russian father, a government environmental scientist, became too ill to gather vital data from far-flung climate stations, she took over the work (against regulations) in order to save his research and monitoring program. That program was funded by the giant American lumber company Dixie Pacific, and – according to company spokesmen – was run efficiently and safely.

So Satchi drove a powerful half-track snowmobile, carried a gun and short-wave radio, and followed an established route on a known schedule. By Siberian standards, her work would not be rated difficult or hazardous. Routinely she spent her evenings at the lonely stations reading in her specialty – utopian science-fiction novels in English.

Ten days ago, with the year's first ferocious snowstorm roaring in from Kamchatka, the twenty-eight year old scholar became the protagonist in her own astonishing drama. Satchi Kutznetsova vanished without a trace from the most isolated station on her itinerary. Investigators found two sets of tracks leading to the weather shack: those of a great bear, and others belonging probably to Koryak herders.

Peter could fill in the rest of the version he was leaning toward. Ravishing but troubled girl-woman throws over her own utopian future (promise of a Cambridge degree, chance to meet some rich young sport with exotic taste, eventual role as an Anglo-Slav expert) in order to go native with descendants of her primitive ancestors. But he had no facts to go on. Nobody did. The story could go anywhere. Girl Eaten By Bear; Girl Bags Trophy Bear; Girl Raped and Murdered; Hoax Makes A Star ... It was maddening. They were reduced to sniffing out the merest scraps. The bear business was of course only a suggestive metaphor, but it supplied atmosphere. The previous romance with the young Dixie employee would also make a good setup, whatever the outcome. You couldn't go wrong blaming shit on American corporations – you would usually be right – and if Carraway had been whoring around behind her back, it would be absolutely perfect.

'Money explains nothing,' Lafe said finally. 'And you are wrong, that no people lives here for any other reason. These reindeer tribes, the Koryaks, they are yost like Laps. They prefer it here.'

'Ballocks. Give the Laps laptops and stand back, they'll be on Mediterranean cruises next thing you know. Say, do you suppose they took our girl as a hostage, to get something out of the government?'

'That police inspector. Sokhalov. He thinks – he is sure – she runs off with them. For herself.'

They looked at each other, and Peter heaved a sigh for them both. They came back to the same impasse, tantalizing and frustrating, every time. They had hooked up on the plane from Moscow, gotten drunk together on their second night in Magadan, and very soon sorted out their common interest. Lafe had already seen the piece in the *Times* on the bear-bride myth, and just like Peter, had gotten keen on the possibilities. Beautiful young woman, hybrid of two cultures, world's last wilderness inhabited by a vanishing race . . .

The whole situation absolutely reeked with movie potential, even before the subplot of a turbulent romance with a young American engineer. Even before they found out Satchi was on her way to becoming the first female Siberian aborigine to get a foreign doctorate – and in English Literature to boot, Peter had gotten through on their third day to a friend who had worked on a couple of Africa epics done out of a London studio, and the man had been very encouraging. With an important qualification. One had to have a shock-o ending, a corpse or two or a serious scandal, a fantastic trek against odds, at the very least.

But the material hadn't taken its shape yet. They didn't know the outcome. They were stalled, stymied, stiffed. Normally he would never write two graphs of a story before he knew where it was going, but Peter understood that to movie people getting the jump was everything, the pitch had to be ready for instant delivery, backing had to be available to secure rights. They had to be first with solid magazine pieces, had to have good contacts with the key parties – Satchi preferably, of course, but if she was already bear stool then her father and Carraway. Which was why they were willing to wait in this hole to chat him up, away from the other vultures. Peter glanced at his watch. Carraway was forty-five minutes overdue.

'I don't believe our boy is coming,' Lafe said. 'Goddamit.'

Three Russians had come into the Apache, changing its atmosphere. They wore expensive jackets and boots, but these were not clean, and they needed a shave. Local dockside mafiosi, Peter guessed. They were very drunk, especially a short, broad man with a face like an imperfectly scoured potato. With a stuporous arrogance they shifted bloodshot eyes around the room, table to table. For a long five seconds they looked at Lafe and Peter, then moved on to the group of sailors around Natasha.

'Probably not. Maybe we should have asked him to meet us at the Ali Baba. Bit pagan, this place.' Peter noted that the bouncer had moved to a point near the archway leading to the hotel lobby, and the bartender looked fatalistic, even glum. 'I had a dim hope of charming him into taking us out in his helicopter for a look.

Maybe share the secrets of his tiny teflon heart. The bereaved philanderer. What a twunt.'

The sailors were aware of the newcomers now, and some began to return the heavy stare. A bottle cap spun and clattered to the floor only inches from the nearest Russian's boots. Natasha, Peter saw, had lost her provocative pout.

'A what?' Lafe was watching the bartender studiously wash a glass. 'Maybe we should go.'

'Philanderer. Fellow always wanting a bit on the side. Human male—'

'No, the other one. Twunt? What is – Yesus Christ.'

The short Russian had taken a compact black semiautomatic pistol from inside his coat. He was smiling, and a slender track of drool shone at one corner of his mouth. He bellowed something, pointed the pistol at the bartender and waggled it. The bouncer eased along the wall as the bartender nodded vigorously, one hand already foraging swiftly through a row of bottles while the other stacked three glasses, rap rap rap, on a plastic tray.

One of the sailors said something, a curse by its intonation, while others skidded their chairs back from the table. '*Tzat knyesh!*' The man swung the gun to cover this distraction. '*Chortyim.*' He was smiling with a furrowed brow, his eyes narrowed, as if he could not quite find the right expression. He let his aim drift, talking softly to himself, and the sailors kept still, watching. Except for the music and the sound of vodka pouring into glass, the whole room was quiet. One of the other Russians belched and said something to the gunman. After a long blear-eyed moment, he laughed, like a motor turning over, and pointed the pistol at Natasha, digging it slantwise into the air in a beckoning gesture.

'*Milaya, prijhady ka' mnye.*'

Natasha stood, her smile wide and tight, and glided the half-dozen steps to the Russians' table. She left behind her purse and a still-smouldering cigarette. Without looking aside or moving his lips, Peter risked a whisper. 'What's he saying?'

The gunman shifted in his chair, spreading his thick legs to provide Natasha with a knee to sit on. When she did he beamed at the sailors, his eyes almost squeezed shut, and lifted the hand with the pistol to drape over her shoulder, so the barrel hung between her breasts. For the slightest fraction of a second Natasha's eyes skipped to Peter and Lafe. 'What do you think,' Lafe whispered back.

The waiter with the bleached hair came with the tray and slid it on the table, then withdrew like smoke chased by the wind. The Russians picked up their glasses and drank, as men scratch themselves or dust off their trousers. The gunman addressed the sailors again, this time in a series of phrases interrupted by guttural wheezes of laughter. As he talked he raised the pistol just enough to tease a few strands of hair from behind Natasha's ear.

Peter could hear the sailors breathing, the creak of a chair under stress. He saw the bouncer smile furtively at the gunman's epithets, just before he slid out of sight through the archway leading to the lobby. The gunman jiggled Natasha on his knee and she uttered a soft, coy sound. He grunted into her ear and the pistol barrel came up along her cheek. She bit her lip, demuring, and he grunted more insistently. He tapped the barrel smartly against her jawbone and held the muzzle an inch away until she kissed it. The potato face wrinkled into a full grin, directed at the sailors. The other two men laughed when he tapped and she kissed the barrel again, and then again.

The man resumed his commentary, even as he pushed down on Natasha's shoulder and straightened his leg so that she sprawled to her knees in front of him. He positioned her head to face his crotch and serve simultaneously as a rest for the gunbutt while he kept the weapon pointed loosely at his audience. His two companions were greatly entertained now, bellowing laughter and making kissing noises of their own at the sailors.

Peter had been dimly aware of subdued voices and footfalls coming from the lobby of the hotel. Swiveling only his eyes, he could just see the connecting archway. 'Yesus, Yesus,' he heard Lafe whisper. Then, in the same moment, he heard the sound of a zipper opening and saw Kenny Carraway appear in the archway. Carraway saw them immediately and set his course for their table, at a long easy stride. He carried his parka over one arm, his gloves and hat stuffed in its side pocket.

'Hey, guys!' he called, showing one palm up, a kind of placating greeting. 'Sorry, held up all morning, but I've got—'

His casual look around the room had come back and lodged,

finally, on the tableau of a woman on her knees with a black gun sprouting out of her hair. 'What . . .' He had stopped so abruptly that Peter saw the heels of his boots rock up off the floor. Carraway was tall and was also the only person in the room actually standing – the bartender was slouching almost prone at the bar and the waiters had vanished into the backroom. Even Natasha was looking over her shoulder, and the gunman himself stared up at this lofty apparition.

'What the hell is going on here?' Carraway addressed Peter and Lafe in a tone of wondering outrage.

Peter had been looking at the Russian's open fly, and glanced up as if startled out of a daydream. 'Market forces,' he said, 'trade wars.' He coughed out another laugh.

In a brilliant stroke, Lafe got to his feet and tugged Peter up after him. The Swede was speaking rapidly in his Russian pidgin, apparently addressing the room at large. Peter understood only 'Amricn' and 'Dixie,' as they moved to Carraway's side. Now there were three standing, in command of the stage, and Peter grasped that they were playing the roles of important foreigners with a pressing engagement elsewhere. The potato-faced Russian was dimly intrigued. Without zipping himself up, he stuffed the gun back into his coat and lurched away from his chair.

He stopped only inches from Carraway, talking loudly with sloshing vowels, spittle-drenched consonants. He kept the frowning, squint-eyed smile, but his manner seemed conciliatory, expansive. 'Dixie,' he said. 'Gewd. Dixie gewd for Rooshya.' He slapped Carraway on the chest. 'Amricn, da? Amricn, Rooshya. Gewd! *Vyeepyem wheesky*!'

Behind him the sailors were sidling to the archway, Natasha with them. The last two were emboldened to mutter on their way out, and one of the gangsters spit perfunctorily after them, but their focus had shifted and in another moment the room seemed almost ordinary again. The three of them were also moving toward the archway, Carraway and Lafe saying what they could in Russian, Peter grinning and showing with his two fists how close the Russians and Americans were, while potato face tried to lumber after. But they were too brisk, and he too encumbered by vodka. They heard him fall over a chair and curse. Then they were in the lobby, putting on their coats, then through the glass door into the airlock, and finally outside.

'Follow me, I've got a company heap,' Carraway said, and strode toward a utility wagon with oversized snow tires, parked in the hotel's small side lot. He looked back at them once, puffing out his cheeks to signal humorous amazement. 'Guess you guys got to sample the local culture alright!'

'Indeed,' Peter replied. 'Dramatic folk, the Russians. And your own timing was perfect.'

'Missed the climax.' Carraway laughed modestly at his own wit and unlocked the vehicle. When they were inside, the engine running, he turned to them, still smiling. 'I knew it was late and we were tentative, but I came because I actually have some news.' He spoke in a confidential tone, with an undercurrent of excitement. 'We may be closing in on this thing. We have a lead in a new location. I heard just this morning, and I thought, hey, the two European guys, maybe they could do a fair and honest job on this one. Maybe they'd go along.'

Peter and Lafe glanced very swiftly at each other. 'Go along,' Peter repeated carefully.

'I mean, not sensationalize the whole thing. Just look at what there is, be fair, report what we've got and not a lot of pardon me, bullshit.' Carraway cocked his head at them, narrowed his eyes to convey shrewd assessment.

'Of course,' Peter said, 'we think of ourselves as responsible journalists. We try to be fair.' A rueful smile. 'Lafe and I were just saying we feel uncomfortable writing about a region we haven't yet actually *seen* . . .'

'Well, now there is something to see.' Carraway struck the steering wheel lightly with both hands. 'Real evidence. We've found Satchi's Sno-Klaw.'

'Ah,' Lafe breathed. 'And . . .'

'No sign of anything wrong. Nothing broken, apparently just out of gas. And much further away than we thought it would be. I'm sure now someone was with her. And it sure as hell wasn't a bear.' He looked at them for a moment without smiling.

'That's encouraging,' Peter said. 'But you must be anxious to—'

'Find her. You bet I am. We're fueled and stocked and ready.' Carraway revved the engine and put one hand on the gearshift lever. He looked sidewise at them, wearing now the thin smile of a fighter pilot. 'So you guys want to tag along?'

This time Peter and Lafe did not risk looking at each other. 'Well, I'm sure . . . that is, of *course*.' Peter's smile was dazzling. 'Would be splendid.'

'A very great favor, Mister Carraway—' Lafe began, but the American was shaking his head benignly.

'Kenny.'

'Yes. Okay, Kenny. Very grateful. Thank you. A very great opportunity. I wonder – do you mind if I ask – why you chose us? I have to be honest, you know, and my journal has some objections to cutting so much of the taiga . . .'

'Sure. Hey, look guys, that's cool. I know – Dixie knows – a lot of people are going to see us as the bad guys in this thing. Believe me, we're used to it. We know we've got only one option. From the top down, Pendergast and stateside management, I can tell you the policy is now to lay everything out. Let people know exactly what we are doing, how hard we are trying to find Satchi. That's why I'm in charge of coordinating the search. Because Satchi and I – well, of course you know the story.' Kenny looked out the window at the gray slab of hotel, the gray street and gray sky, then back at them. 'As far as you guys . . . this is something I thought up myself, because you know how it is, the prophet has no honor at home. In the States they're going after the environmental angle, the woman angle, the big bad corporation. Enough of that hype and somebody will start sniffing TV special or even a movie. I figured you guys at least are working for straight magazines with class, and we like the idea of being international, respecting that dimension.'

Kenny slipped the wagon into gear finally, but kept his foot lightly on the brake so the frame only rocked once and remained poised, shuddering faintly. 'So I figured you guys would stick to the facts. The straight story, for its own sake?'

Peter and Lafe were leaning toward him, eyes shining. 'Absolutely,' Peter said. 'We want the whole thing, Kenny, absolutely. Straight up.'

'Oh yes. The facts. We need the facts.'

'Okay, then. Let's go get 'em.' Kenny held up his gloved hand and released the brake so they rolled out of the parking lot. It was a moment before Peter caught on, remembered the American custom, and slapped his own gloved palm against Kenny's, and then Lafe did the same, and they all laughed as they surged down the street.

CHAPTER ELEVEN

In the corridor Craig broke into a long, reaching stride. He had to get the accelerator warmed up. Had to coordinate the axial chronometers. Had to pray Walsh and the Commander would stay interested in their work, would not get suspicious when the others drifted along after him.

They were lucky. The great electromagnetic beam had reached maximum focus and force just as Naku and Steve joined him, breathless and alert. It was tracking perfectly, thirteen thousand megatons of centrifugal force orbiting soundlessly around a single porcelain chamber. The Time Cannon. It would shoot them in a few moments. Shoot them one infinitely tiny slice ahead of themselves.

They hoisted up into the chamber and belted down. Craig gestured gingerly with the remote. 'Ready?' he whispered. They breathed their response together. 'Ready.'

He pressed a key, then another, then another. The chamber began to rotate, and the deep hum, below the threshold of hearing, invaded their bones. The increased gravity came suddenly, like an anvil through the heart, and a sudden, terrible sheet of lightning wiped the brain blank.

They were through. They were fired into a new time, a new future at a precise vertical angle from a single flowering nanosecond of the old – ninety degrees plus just the width of one electron, so that they could, finally, come back. This time the vertigo and nausea passed more quickly, and no one retched. Climbing from the chamber, trailing the dusty glow of shattering atoms of atmosphere, they were giggling in a euphoria of triumph and relief.

'Wheeeee!'

The exclamation was only a bright fog from Naku's mouth. Putting on the helmets and packs they looked at one another in wild delight. The thrill went on and on. The thrill of moving in absolute dead *silence, and – in relation to everything around them – at almost the speed of light.*

Back at control center Steve leaned down and delivered a casual, foul lecture into the Commander's ear. The Commander and Walsh continued to stare down at the papers before them. Walsh was apparently saying something, his lips contorting slightly, his eyes widened. It would take until next year, on their new time axis, for the first syllable to emerge, and of course they could not hear it –

The children erupted in a chant that drowned her out, and Satchi had to stop reading. *Teike'mtilla! Teike'mtilla!* they chorused, giggling wildly and pulling at her shirt. She looked back over the text and saw that this time they had seized on 'take until'. From the cradle Yina was watching them, and though his breathing was still a bubbling rasp, the antibiotic injection had reduced the fever and given him rest. His look now followed the children's movements closely, and his lips twitched now and then in a smile.

Satchi smiled too, in spite of all that had happened. This game had become the children's favorite, in the time after the first meal when the men went to tend the herd and the women were busy at their blankets and baskets. She could not begrudge the children her attention; in fact their round, brown faces full of innocent joy were her only relief. And Yina seemed to respond to this game, this guessing at random echoes of meaning in a strange tongue and then fitting them into a story. For her part, she could ignore at least for a while the monstrous irritations of this place. Not only the rank odor of stewing fish-carcasses, the women's hissing and giggling, the drum and the droning of chants, but – far more infuriating – Kainivilu's maddening deception.

She looked serious, as if thinking hard. 'Numtila,' she said and pointed to Yina and Itu. Navakut, the eight year-old, squealed approval and gestured between her legs to show something swinging. The others doubled up, hysterical, when Satchi pretended shyness. She looked puzzled, rolled her eyes. '*Teike*?'

They all pointed overhead, made a circle with both hands. Satchi pretended amazement. She mimed sleep, waking up, then imitated their circle and, with twiddling fingers, a man walking through that circle. A Sun-Man? Navakut pointed immediately to the fire, stuck out her tongue and began to pull off her skin shirt. A man warm as the sun. Itu had his arms spread as wide as possible, seemed to be staring up at a mountain. A man big and warm as the sun? Then they were jumping up and down in delight and impatience, pointing at her, the book.

Now it was her turn. Acting out the story, she tried to recall Koryak words from her childhood. Navakut helped with long asides to Yina and Itu – jabbering so much that Satchi was sure the girl invented a good many additions. She had been surprised at how elementary the novel was, under its clap-trap of technology and pseudo-philosophy. Strip away the references to Relativity and diverging time-vectors and hyperspace fractals and the story was for children. Three people get into a magic box. When they come out everything around them is frozen. Their friends left behind cannot move, cannot see or hear them. They can walk around and do tricks on these friends who cannot move.

The children saw the fun of it, and took turns being in or out of the box. To make the Sun-Man fit in, they had him heat the box so those inside were safe from the freeze that struck the unlucky outsiders. Very quickly it was apparent that the challenge was in remaining still. The children vied for this role, and Satchi was amazed at how motionless they became. Not a quiver or blink, even when another child took a bit of yarn and tickled an eyelash or nostril. At each thawing, of course, they exploded into laughter and rolled and batted at each other like kittens.

She had taken up a position by Yina, and saw that not only were his eyes following the play, but he also moved his lips, whispering along with the others: *teike'mtilla*, *teike'mtilla* . . . She placed a hand on the edge of the crib, and his look moved to take her in. Then he reached and placed his own hand on top of hers, light as a spider at first and then stronger, like a bird claw, and to her amazement he pulled himself up a little, his head and shoulders lifting from the moss pad. His mouth was bent in a smile, and he tried to whisper something before he fell back.

She was over him immediately, stroking his brow and crooning his name, tears in her eyes. He lifted his hand again, brushed her chin, and she was shaken by a maelstrom of emotions. He was conscious, he was communicating with her, trying to tell her about the game, the story, the Sun-Man . . . his skin was not so translucent and heated, he might live, would live, *had* to live . . .

She was aware that the other women and children had gathered around the crib, crying out in excitement and pleasure. Paqa was beaming at her son, and at Satchi too. Pipik stared in deep reverence at the book Satchi still held. Just as if the Time Cannon had worked and blown them into a new universe of hope. It was, of course, the antibiotics. Satchi knew this and yet she was herself beaming, holding back sobs, believing the story-games had helped, had roused and cheered the boy a bit, at least.

She stepped back from the crib and let the family close its circle, then tucked away the book and went for her coat. She wanted to be away, to cry by herself, partly out of happiness, yes, but also because of the loneliness and frustration and fury that were still jammed together deep within her. Whenever she thought of the cargo carrier swooping in, the technician or doctor casually handing out medicine and syringe, then driving off, driving right past her . . . How could they not have seen her? And who were they, who could they be? Surely they had a radio, surely the search was under way . . .

She gritted her teeth and swarmed up the log ladder, no slipping this time. It was very cold but the wind had ceased. The sky was intensely, deeply blue everywhere above the brilliant incandescent sun. The men had come in late last night, bringing a few salmon, and she saw they had this morning also brought in four reindeer, penned them into the rude corral, and then gone out again. They were mature reindeer, what looked to be the best of the herd. Why so many? She looked here and there over the whole bright, barren scene. The stark skeletons of a few trees, dogs tied to some of them, the pole ramp around the entrance to the house, the high heap of the fish-shed, the tracks of the vehicle printed sharply in the snow – and following these tracks she saw something else. One of the three sleds, the new one with steel runners and a plastic shell, had been unloaded. The tarp cover was folded and lashed to the handles.

She stamped her foot and marched over to examine the sled more closely. The GAZ-75 had drawn up and a cargo had been transferred into it – perhaps while someone was tending to Yina. Then they had roared off, struck out over the tundra to the West, and run into her, so they turned aside and drove away at full speed! That's how it had looked to her. Why would they be going West? Toward Kedon? Toward the Kolyma country – land of three million ghosts? That was impossible, for they towed no fuel trailer.

Kolyma. Just the word made people shudder, and brought back ugly memories even for her generation. As a college student in post-Soviet Russia she had finally encountered, in the foreign press, some of the dry, irrefutable, ghastly facts about her native Siberia. The forced confessions and secret trials, the torture and execution of 'politicals' who were otherwise systematically starved and worked to death in arctic gold camps. Most of it had happened before she was born, but Magadan was the port of entry for the three million convicts whose bones now moldered in the permafrost, and she had glimpsed in her parents the legacy of that horror.

Her father said little about those years, and she remembered only one personal anecdote. He had taken her to see the Tummany camp, now a museum, where fifty years ago he had been sent to work on a 'health problem.' The problem turned out to be lice – lice so numerous he could see them crawling on the skeletal prisoners, could hear them dropping onto the floor. 'I was young and idealistic, a good communist,' he told Satchi with a mirthless smile. 'So I pinched my nose and threw myself into helping my country recover from the war.'

They had reached a dim, bare room in what was once the infirmary. 'Here I tried to believe,' her father had said, gazing down at the filthy concrete floor. 'I wanted to believe these shrunken, stinking bone-heaps were enemies of the people, undergoing rehabilitation, and I was there to make their reform easier. And the very first prisoner I touched – while I was taking a blood sample, while I was talking to him – coughed a little and died. Died right in my hands. Of exhaustion and exposure and – I came to see eventually – of despair. I cried out to the guard, saying something idiotic, "This man is dead! He is suffering from scurvy . . . poor diet . . . he needs attention!" And the guard smiled and winked at me. "So," he said, "his lice are out of luck, eh?"'

Her father had laughed then in a way that shocked her, and

walked quickly out of the room. Her parents and their generation had learned so well to hide, to ignore, to forget. 'Survival,' her father would bark with a frown, whenever she asked for reasons. Then he would turn back to his book or his papers. Turning away – that was what made these monstrous atrocities possible. She would not, she thought, be capable of such evasion.

Anyway, nowadays Russians were secretive and hypocritical and deceptive out of greed, rather than fear. It was the age of petty atrocities. Vicious little gangsters who killed for money. And more and more profiteers and smugglers and drug dealers and thieves. Though some were not so little, she reflected. Her father called the Japanese and American companies the biggest thieves of all. Yet what did he do about it? He did what any ordinary Russian would do. He shrugged. *Survival*.

Some such monkey business, as Kenny called it, must have brought the GAZ to this remote place. It galled her that she could not guess what that business might be, had not even the comfort of indulging in high, moral outrage. She was not a martyr like those once doomed to the Kolyma camps, not exactly a captive at all – though she certainly felt like one. She was in a place that no one escaped from – a huge prison of white earth and empty sky and sun that blazed as cold as death – unless they had a vehicle or plane or at least a radio. Then, in just a few hours . . .

It was maddening. She scuffed her boot toe again into the frozen rut. The bastards had *been* here! Russians, on some kind of business. Official, surely, for there was nothing to smuggle or steal here. No one had any money, or anything to sell except these miserable reindeer, a few furs sometimes, and the women's baskets and blankets. Nor would anyone send an agent to this godforsaken place to buy such things. She uttered an explosive sigh of exasperation, looked down once more at the tracks, and saw a bit of color, exposed by her boot.

She bent down and pried from the compacted ice a scrap of cardboard with a strip of green packing tape across one corner. She peeled away the tape and underneath were two printed words and part of a third, all in English. *oil*, *salt*, *spi*

Food. Yes, of course. Some common food, with such ingredients. Yet food of a special kind and provenance. There were stores in

Magadan where imported delicacies were sold, and Kenny had laughed to see them in the shopwindows. Everybody ate these things at home, he said, even the people who lived in the street. Chips, nuts, twists, spreads – the company imported these by the carload because workers were used to them, and now they appeared regularly in the dollar stores. At such prices, Kenny said, he ought to have brought over a trunk full of peanut butter.

There was no sign of such food in Kainivilu's household. No one would haul a hundred kilos of candy and chips out here to trade. With no fuel trailer for a return trip. She searched for more scraps in the snow, but found nothing. She looked up, stared about her at the brilliant, stark world she was in. The reindeer, nostrils folded tight and eyes like gouts of a deep gold amber, watched her in turn. The sleds, an old collapsed lean-to kennel, the wisp of smoke from the roof entrance – all of it insignificant on this tremendous sweep of heaving, frozen earth. Yet they were not here alone. There was another camp somewhere nearby. There had to be. A place with medicine and food stored, with at least one support vehicle.

Why? Why was there such a place? And why would the people there come here? What had they unloaded from the sled? She should have looked more closely at it, pulled up a corner of the tarp to see what was there. She had been so busy with Yina, so exhausted by the effort of getting here and bearing the strain of living in a chamber in the ground with nine strangers, so worried at how her father and Kenny would be taking—

She stopped herself with another sharp sigh. It wasn't exactly true anyway. It was booshit, as she first misheard it in American slang. And so fashioned a pun – or was it a coinage? Booshit was something false that scared you or could be used to scare someone else. Anyway she had not thought of them so very often, and when she did it was sometimes with a peculiar thrill of satisfaction. Their little worlds must have broken open. Their helpmate and ornament was gone. Their knotty girl had untied herself and slipped away. Like the Russian countess in *Orlando*, one of her favorite English novels.

During these musings she had been walking along the track made by the GAZ. Their encampment had disappeared behind a low ridge. When she reached the top of the next rise and could see it again, it would be no more than a smudge on the horizon behind her. The tundra was very like a sea, an immense yawning distance in every direction. How many days would it take to reach the hidden camp? Not a serious question, of course. She would not forget soon the panic of her last sojourn, which was no more, really, than her realization of what it meant to be on foot in this place. One needed a dog-sled, or at least reindeer to pack supplies. No chance of that. Impossible to steal food or catch the animals unobtrusively, let alone harness and drive them – even if she knew how. She would have to wait until the mysterious visitors came back, whoever they were.

She walked on, just fast enough to keep warm, and gradually her thoughts steadied and organized themselves. Yina seemed to be growing stronger, and there was no denying that help was somewhere nearby. The adventure was over. She would confront Kainivilu and demand that he guide her out of here, or put her in touch with those who could. A matter of two or three days at most. She would take no excuses, no more of his evasions and tricks.

When she reached the top of the second rise, she stopped. The tracks of the GAZ still aimed ruler-straight at the western horizon, but just before that edge they jogged to the north. The place where she had intercepted them. Now, from this vantage point, she could see what she thought was the ghost outline in the snow of a second set of tracks, not quite paralleling the first, but diverging north.

She breathed in slow measure, her eyes roving and probing, and in a moment she located what might be a third set, or more likely several sets, braided over the second in long bellying arcs. Earlier in the fall, as the ground alternately froze and thawed, the drivers had swung out from the old ruts where they were too deep and treacherous.

One of her father's obsessions was the damage done by wheeled and tracked vehicles, especially the cargo sledges, whose cleats destroyed the tundra's fragile cover of grasses and lichens and led to irreparable erosion. Flying with Kenny in the Dixie survey plane in summer, she had seen the stars of twin yellow lines radiating out from base camps, looping and converging and branching. But to be visible as a depression beneath a meter of snow, the erosion had to be significant, more than that of a single season.

Vehicles had been around here for some time, then. At least since last spring. And they had made several trips to Kainivilu's camp. A routine. She breathed in and out slowly, carefully. Monkey business. In rapid succession she underwent a wave of apprehension, another of curiosity. Kainivulu had to be supplying them with something besides food. It would be absurd to send a herdsman with a reindeer or dog sled to haul one-fourth of what the GAZ could transport in one-tenth the time. She would watch, she would be there the next time they came, and she would find out.

She turned, looked back to Kainivilu's camp, which was indeed now only a cluster of dots on the horizon. It occured to her then that the reindeer brought in this morning were possibly to draw the three sleds, that the men were going to freight in more supplies. That would mean they were not more than a few days' travel from some small community, a trading center. They could be harnessing the reindeer even now. It was likely – highly likely, now that she considered the incidents of the past two days.

She was already marching purposefully downslope, but at this thought she broke into a shambling trot, kicking chunks of frozen crust high and to either side. She would insist on going. She would strap herself to the sled, if need be. He wouldn't trick her again, do his preposterous impersonations. She wasn't afraid! He couldn't booshit her this time!

She stumbled once and got up without even being aware of it, only noticing the sting of the rough snow-crystals on her cheek. Starting up the final rise she had to go slower. She drove her boots grimly, steadily into the snowy slope, and held her mittens over her mouth to keep the cold air from cutting so deeply into her lungs. She was almost at the top when a dark shape started up, a silhouette against the sky.

For an infinitesimal instant she was on the brink of terror, and later understood that she was remembering the moment when the bear reared up outside the window at the station. But it was only Tatka made larger and faceless by the light behind him and the angle of her view. She had cried out, she realized, and so spoke to reassure him – and herself.

'*Ai yeti!*' She moved to the side, squinting to shut out the sun. 'What is it? You surprised me.'

He uttered something about *kalau*, his voice high and sing-song, and turned immediately to hurry ahead of her.

'What *kalau*?' She trudged after, and did not catch what he said next. He was in a big hurry, and she had noticed his face was distorted into a wincing grimace. Maybe the other men were indeed getting ready to leave, and Tatka was angry at not being included.

'*Quikinakku yeni melgene!*' Tatka again sang the words, but not as if answering her.

A fire-place for Big Raven? What did that mean? *Kalau* were bad luck, but her mother's people believed they were everywhere, in animals and even stones and trees, put there to bedevil humankind. Also to make us strong, her mother had always said. She remembered suddenly, and with a clarity that startled and disturbed her, that her mother had pressed one of the little wooden guardians into her hand when she had been so sick, long ago, and the stranger had come to their house. A guardian against the *kalau*. And the stranger . . .

Tatka was actually outpacing her. His thin, bent form could scuttle as swift as a crab, and she could no longer make out much of what he was moaning. Something about fire and her clothes. Had they burnt up her things? Exasperating! She began her lumbering trot again, crashing through the snow, down the slope of the last ridge. The camp was now in plain view. She could see a figure had emerged from the roof entrance and was hauling up something from the interior by means of a rope. It was Euna, the brother's wife, and beside her a heap of baskets was already stacked on the snow. The gate to the pole corral was also open, and the reindeer were moving. A moment later she saw Kainivilu and his brother among them, harness draped over their arms.

So they were about to set off! She was excited, full of determination and relief. Kainivilu must have realized his little game was finished, must have sent Tatka after her because he had decided to take her in to the authorities. A reward, probably. Of course! The visitors had told him what she was worth – and the consequences of trying to hold her hostage. She exerted herself to keep from running, managed to slow down to a brisk walk. She would not betray her feelings. She would be civil. She would thank them all. She would hug the children. Actually she would miss the children, their games and laughter. After all she and this family were, at least biologically, of common ancestry.

Kainivilu saw her and said something to his brother, at the same time gesturing at Tatka to receive the leather lead-ropes to two reindeer. He came toward her then, still bearing the harnesses, the hood of his parka thrown back despite the cold and dazzling light. He took only a few steps and then stopped, as if weary. He did not seem to be looking at her, but at something on the horizon behind her, and his expression had an odd, fixed quality.

She crafted an attentive, cool smile. Let him make his excuses and speak his piece. She would be straight, as they said in English. Absolutely straight. It was very simple: he could get her out of here and all would be forgiven. By being reasonable he would gain all he wanted. She would see that he got the reward, that a doctor was dispatched. She strode up to him, still smiling, and stopped. Still he did not look at her, and she waited, noting now that his cheeks were losing color, becoming wax-like. He should put up his hood or he would have frostbite.

'My son dies,' he said in Russian.

Satchi saw the words as a small plume of ice-fog coming from his mouth, and when that vanished the world was completely still in the merciless light around them.

'No,' she said, the smile gone numb on her face. 'No, he is . . .' She stared for a moment at Euna, now slinging aside the basket she had hauled up, and uttering at the same time a single, barely audible whimper.

Satchi heard her own breath drawn in, abrupt as the sound of fabric tearing, and then she was trying to run toward the entrance, but Kainivilu had moved in front of her, held her away by gripping her shoulders. She was not conscious of what she was saying, only that the light was splintering through her tears and she could not see any more, could feel nothing but Kainivilu's hands keeping her away, a force that she ran against and which moved only to steady her, keep her from falling, but otherwise did not yield.

Then all at once her strength left her and she stood like a post propped on his hands, the breath heaving in and out of her. 'Yina?' she whispered hoarsely. 'Yina?'

'He dies. Cannot go in now. Paqa says maybe you are *kala*, sent by whale-people, your mother.'

She looked up, blinked, saw into his eyes for what seemed the first time. They were mottled brown, tobacco and amber, with no visible pupils. Under lashes crusted with frozen tears, their emptiness appalled her. 'No,' she said. 'No. I . . . I tried so . . . I did . . .' She sobbed, long and hard, and clutched at him. 'The medicine! He must be, he *must* be better . . .'

'Shhh.' He shook his head and glanced toward the house. 'Dead. But spirit inside, *yayani*, is still here. Pipik says your mother was not *kala*. Yayo was good mother. You wait now. No crying yet.'

He took his hands from her shoulder and they stood apart. 'No crying yet.' He waited, immobile and heavy, the empty eyes now looking into and through her.

She tried to speak twice, three times. '*Etin*,' Tatka called out behind them and shook the lead ropes in his hand, but Kainivilu did not look away from her. She stepped toward him without thinking and reached out to grasp the fur trim of his hood and pull it up around his head. Then she turned and walked away.

CHAPTER TWELVE

They were already dressing Yina when Satchi clambered down to the hearth. Pipik greeted her with a quavering *ai yeti* and Paqa at least looked up, before they both went back to the work of folding the dead boy into what appeared to be new trousers. The children did not come to Satchi as usual. Navakut was sewing tiny colored beads on a belt, and Itu played with one of the little wooden *kalaks*. They gave her wan smiles and went on with what they were doing.

Her heart was heavy and cold as iron, her stomach in a knot. She knew her guilt was irrational and extravagant, but she cowered under it all the same, and sank down silent on her bedding, unable to speak or lift a hand. She watched Paqa open out a beautiful little coat, more elaborately embroidered and fringed than any she had seen. Saw then that the trousers were also richly worked, and recognized the color and pattern. She had noticed Paqa sewing a bit of that trim one evening soon after her arrival, and again only three or four days ago. She stared at the trousers, the coat, and the belt Navakut was finishing, all made to match. They had been preparing this funeral suit for weeks, had accepted long before she came that Yina would likely die!

And yet they seemed unwilling to grieve, unwilling even to admit their child was gone. There was no wailing or sobbing, only now and then a turn of the head or hunching of shoulders. She watched as Paqa lifted her son's arm and worked it through a sleeve, then raised his torso from the bed to drape the coat across his back. She murmured what sounded like a soft urging, and when she bent the other arm into its sleeve the dangling fingers brushed her cheek in an awkward caress. Meanwhile Euna busied herself at the fish-pot, talking to herself in a tone of forced cheerfulness.

It went on that way the whole night. At the evening meal a bowl of fish chowder was prepared for Yina and placed beside him. They had thrown a blanket over him loosely; his face was hidden but one hand curled from beneath, as if beckoning. After the meal Pipik took down the drum, and with Paqa sang to the still form. It was a song Satchi had heard before, an ordinary lullaby, and the children joined in hesitantly, glancing sometimes with wide eyes at their hidden brother. Only now and then the singing wavered, or Paqa furtively wiped away tears with thumb and forefinger.

Satchi had eaten in dumb silence, and turned away from the song to hide her own tears. This stubborn, perverse denial of death left her desolate, more alone than she had ever felt, even during her mother's illness. That trial was shared with her father and their friends; they had done everything possible – two surgeries, the best doctors at the military hospital, fruit flown in from Azerbaijan – and yes, her father had even given in and allowed a shaman from the Taigonos region to come. An old woman, like Pipik, who had brought a drum and some bitter, bad-smelling tea. Satchi remembered her father's embarrassment, trying to explain to the nurses, and the drumming, how it was soothing in its monotony and her mother had gotten good rest that night.

They had done everything, and death had advanced in inexorable, orderly stages, which they foresaw and met together. Nothing prepared her for this appalling, arbitrary end, this ghastly trick. A few hours ago Yina had listened to her story, smiled at her, taken her hand, been stronger and happier than ever, she had stepped out to see the sky and rejoice – and in one breath the sun was blown out like a candle. He was dead, being stuffed into his funeral dress, and she felt utterly alone and irrelevant.

She found herself yearning for a storm, a fierce ice storm that would rage and roar to end this emptiness, the vibrating stillness of this household. Some mark of terrible grandeur, of monstrous force, that would unite them in suffering. But even as the women sang the lullaby, Tolek snored at the fireside until Tatka prodded him awake, and Kainivilu brought lamps to set near Yina's body.

The men had been gone all day, scavenging limbs and sections of logs, dragging them to the site of the funeral pyre. Yet they gave no sign of grief or fatigue. They gathered around and, as Satchi watched in disbelief, Kainivilu produced a pack of worn, dirty cards and they began to play there, directly on the blanket covering the dead boy. She watched Kainivilu's face in the lamplight. He did not flinch in picking up his cards, even smiled once at something Tatka said. He spoke in tones lower than usual but with no tremor or hoarseness. Only once, so briefly she almost missed it, he let one hand rest for a moment on the blanket, and she sensed the heaviness and darkness within him, a kind of tremendous gravitational force that made every movement deliberate and minimal.

She had understood intuitively that no one except the children would sleep this night. It was as if they were simply extending Yina's last day. After the first hours she had tried to read a few pages of her novel but could not bear it, had tried to doze but each time the weight in her heart would not let her. She ended by simply sitting, dull and withdrawn, on her bed place. What thoughts she had were scattered, petty, maddening in their circularity. She was aware again that she stank, that her nails were dirty and bitten. She wanted to but could not recollect the portion of the Death Mass that came after *Sluzjba*.

She wondered if Yina's birth was registered in the Oblast Civil Record, if she should not have given him the injection, if her father could have saved him . . .

Near dawn the card game ended and the women began to rummage through the baskets and boxes lining the room. Paqa came with a handful of moss she had dipped in the water pot, lifted the blanket from Yina's face and washed it quickly, keeping her eyes averted. Pipik had taken out a hat and mittens, and these she brought to her grandson. The mittens did not go on easily, and Satchi saw that the right and left were reversed. She had an impulse to point out this mistake, but when Pipik also turned the hat backward before pulling it over Yina's head, she understood the confusion was deliberate.

Euna was filling a basket with scraps of material left over from the new coat and trousers, trinkets and small carvings kept in Yina's bed, a tiny bow and arrows evidently once his. Satchi guessed these were gifts meant for the fire; she remembered the old shaman had told them to burn her mother's best clothes and jewelry, the *kalaks* she had kept in a drawer for years. So when Euna came with the pair of plastic thermal boots and held them out to Satchi, she shook her head no and pointed to the basket. Euna looked away uneasily. Too big, she whispered. *For you then, or . . .* Paqa looked up at Satchi instantly, with eyes brilliant and burning. For a moment no one moved, and then Euna said in the same soft hiss, *Yayocanaut*, and put the boots quickly at Satchi's feet.

For her mother? Satchi stared stupidly down, seeing the familiar creases, the scar of melt where once she had placed them too close to a heater, the metal buckles worn dull. Yet the empty boots seemed utterly strange, too. As if she were someone else – or rather as if she were dead herself and able to see back into her former existence. Dead. Perhaps she was dead. She picked up the boots and set them in her lap and began to rock gently back and forth.

The men had brought a pole and some lengths of hide rope, and were making Yina's blanket into a sling secured to the pole. Euna had taken a dried fish from the bundle hanging over the fire and with a knife she sliced off two small ventral fins. Paqa took one, Pipik the other, and they folded them carefully and securely into the palms of Yina's mittens. Then Pipik removed from her belt a small, forked stick which she placed on his chest, running it under the flap of his coat. At the same time she tried to croon another bit of the lullaby, but her voice broke and she darted back. The ancient face was a silent, crumpled mask of pain.

Satchi saw the novel beside her, its cover of flame and steel, took it up and held it with the boots as she went on rocking. Paqa was fussing with the blanket, her hands quick, frantic, like feeding birds. The men stood behind her, waiting quietly, and the two children were behind them, still and watchful as mice.

She was dead. She was going to the land of the dead. She would leave everything but these. Her book and her boots, her boots and her book. She rocked forward and back, forward and back. Her Time Cannons. Only she had no fish fins. She opened her mouth and uttered a sound like a laugh, but sudden and sharp as the bark of a fox, then rocked harder until the sound tore out of her again, but this time it was transformed into a long, gagging sob. As if this were a signal, Kainivilu and his brother stepped forward and rolled Yina into the blanket-sling, and then Kainivilu swarmed up the ladder while the others lifted the pole to thrust it through the entrance hole.

Pipik made her way to the base of the ladder then and began to sing again in her high, cracked voice. As the pole was drawn up, the body tugged along in the sling, she mounted with it, pretending to carry it on her shoulder. All semblance of normalcy collapsed as the corpse reached the light of day. The other women were wailing now, their mouths bending and writhing, the tears running free down their cheeks, dripping from their chins. One by one they climbed out, Euna and Paqa laden with the baskets they had filled, Satchi and the children next, and Tatka last, after he had swept the floor carefully with a bundle of dried reeds.

Outside the world was gray and immense, with a tinge of dull red on the undersides of long windrows of cloud. A few light snowflakes drifted down, but the weather was mild and still. Tolek held two young reindeer hitched to a sleigh, and Yina was quickly loaded on and tied down. They had less than half a kilometer to walk, and the men dragging their firewood had already made a rude trail, easy passage for the sleigh and the smaller sled by which the women hauled their baskets.

They set out now, Pipik still crying a song as she hobbled beside the sleigh, which jerked and slewed because the reindeer wanted to trot. To control them Tolek held the neck straps and muttered commands, while the other men ranged ahead and on each side, carrying or dragging more deadwood. Paqa and Euna and the children kept up a chorus of wails and sobs, but Satchi's racking cries ceased abruptly, sucked out of her by the silence and sweep of the white tundra.

When she looked away at the horizon their small company seemed to shrink, a column of insects, the cries of the women disappearing instantly into the dead air, as the sound of their footfalls vanished in the snow. But when she turned again the sleigh and its cargo seemed unnaturally near, immediate and brilliant as a hallucination. The plunging reindeer, the blanketed form strapped down and unmoving as a log, the figures trudging alongside to guide its dipping and yawing – they had the monstrous scale and luminosity, the microscopic detail, of nightmare. And she was in that dream, seeing the fog of her breath, the dull mahogany shine of the reindeer antlers, hearing the icy tinkle of the bells sewn on Paqa's coat.

She felt a stirring of the same fear that had gripped her before, on the afternoon she ventured out and encountered the GAZ carrier. Here there was no reason for alarm – it was sunrise and the wind was light; they could even go with coats open and hoods rolled back. Swaying from side to side in his march, a large alder branch balanced on his shoulders, Kainivilu was sweating. She could see steam rising from the damp gray hair at his neck. Everything was entirely itself and nothing more. The tundra and sky, the sleigh, the reindeer, the people in their furs – these were a dense, stark, and final reality – the only reality – and she found herself on the verge of terror.

They reached the funeral site, a little swale between two low hills, where the men had crosshatched brush and heavy branches in a rough rectangle perhaps three meters on a side. The new wood was added to this pile, and the sleigh was drawn up beside it. The women began to unload their baskets and carefully set out Yina's effects. Tolek unhitched the reindeer, and Choti prodded them to one side with a spear he had taken from the sleigh. Then Pipik and Paqa began to unstrap Yina's body, moving with great deliberation even as they wept and cried out. Kainivilu had removed a short-handled spade tied to the back of the sleigh and began to dig beneath the snow, into the frozen earth.

Satchi heard a squeal and grunt, then a thrashing, and turned to find that Choti had speared one of the reindeer, and the animal was struggling to rise from its knees, while Tatka tried to cut its throat. A moment after she looked he succeeded and the blood geysered out over the blade. The reindeer lunged up and floundered two steps before going over on its side, where it seared a patch of startling red into the snow. The second reindeer, which Tolek held tight by its neck strap, stamped and trembled uneasily.

When Kainivilu had finished scooping out a hole, Euna dropped in, one by one, the scraps of hide and embroidery left over from Yina's suit, a carved bone spoon, the miniature bow and arrows, and various child's toys of wood, bone, beads and leather. Paqa spread Yina's blanket over the stacked wood, and then helped Pipik carry the body and lay it upon the blanket. The faces of both women glistened with tears, and they murmured and moaned as they worked.

The second reindeer had gone down. Satchi heard the ripping and chopping of butchery, and soon after smelled the reek of hot blood and bowels. The children had turned around to watch in solemn fascination, but she could not. She was watching the others lay more things beside the body: a bundle of matches, a knife, an embroidered shoulder bag, a small harpoon, a photograph, a plastic cup with a cartoon animal on its side. It was the rabbit named Bugs, she thought.

From Euna's second basket came things apparently not Yina's. A needle-case, a comb, a pair of bracelets. A pipe, a handkerchief, a small bowl hammered out of blackened copper. Half-kilo sacks of sugar, tea, and tobacco, some beads. Before Euna finished setting out these items, Paqa and Pipik and even Navakut began wrapping them in squares of bright cloth. Pipik delivered a kind of short prayer or chant over each, and it struck Satchi that these were meant for others – surely the members of the family who had died earlier. She remembered the daughter Kainivilu said he had lost. For her, no doubt, the needle case and comb.

That must have been what Euna meant by handing back the boots. For her dead mother, Yayo the Fox-Woman. She moved forward, swinging the boots in her hand, to stand beside Euna. She remembered her mother sitting up in the white bed, her face drawn and intent, listening to the old woman chant and beat the drum. Her mother had clutched something in her lap, bits of paper or cloth Satchi seemed to remember. This was before the priest came, and Satchi attached no importance to these scraps. Yayo must have seen ceremonies like this in her childhood, must have still believed in them, or at least yearned to believe. But she had been surrounded by doctors and nurses and even a family that understood nothing of such things.

The other women were staring at her, stifling their weeping. She did not flinch from that stare, but gave it back, as she set the pair of boots down beside Yina. She said her mother's Koryak name, and on impulse added a few words of the old lullaby about the mouse-children. Euna looked at her with a small, uncertain smile. Satchi stepped back, and her feet were light under her, almost as if she were rising slightly, lifted by an invisible wind. She looked out again at the horizon, the frozen gray sea sweeping away to infinity, and saw a tremor there. A flicker of movement that was gone, then flashed again. A black flake dancing.

'*Kutka!*'

Kainivilu had followed the direction of her gaze. He did not gesture, but kept watching the moving point as others looked up and also cried out. '*Tenantomwan! Quikti!*'

With astonishing speed the flickering grew nearer, became recognizable as the stroking of black wings. Pipik had fallen to her knees in the snow, sobbing and gazing up at Satchi, her face a wrinkled mask of wonder. Gently Kainivilu drew her to her feet again, and spoke to the others. At the same time the raven flapped higher and banked in a long hook, as if to view them carefully, and then set a course to the east, into the sun that had risen behind the massed clouds and edged them in dull silver. With the same swiftness the bird shrank to a pulsing fleck of darkness, a skirring mote, and was gone.

When the group turned back to look at her again, Satchi sensed immediately a difference in their attitude. Even Paqa regarded her with a new attentiveness, perhaps an apprehension. She stepped back from the pyre and Pipik hurried forward with a patch of red calico, which she wrapped around the boots, murmuring a broken, uneven chant. *Yayocanaut*, Satchi heard again. Then Kainivilu moved to the wood stack, and for a single moment his eyes met Satchi's. She could not read his expression, yet a pang of obscure, powerful emotion went through her.

The fear she had known a few moments before was still there, shimmering like a sea under her, but so was the lightness at her center. That feeling had become a kind of unsteady motion that contained an element of excitement or mystery, as if she had balanced like the raven in the wind just long enough to be noticed by these creatures hulking on the earth.

Kainivilu went down on one knee, opened his coat, and took a plastic litre bottle from his belt. At the same time Satchi felt a tugging at her sleeve. She was short of breath, disoriented, and realized she had begun to lose awareness of her surroundings, of this ceremony. The women had already tied their empty baskets to the little sled and seemed to be waiting for her; the children stared at her with huge, brilliant, black eyes. Euna was saying something but she could not grasp it.

Kainivilu had unstoppered the bottle and was pouring dollops of kerosene on the wood at the base of the pile. Without looking up he spoke to her in Russian. 'Our women go now.'

'I am not your woman. I want to be here.'

She had released the words as easily as breathing, without thought. When their import came home to her, she felt her face heating up. Why had she said that? She did not want . . . what did she want? Surely not to see . . .

He hesitated and looked at her again, and again she could not decipher his face. He shook out the rest of the kerosene and tossed the bottle into the stack of wood. When he raised up and came toward her, his appearance had changed. He seemed not so large, so solid in his ragged sealskins. The bones in his face were more prominent, his eyes deepset and dark like pools in a cave. She took a step backward and he stopped.

'Not *voyemtivolu* today. OK. You see from a little away. Some steps away.' He gestured toward one of the knolls, and then spoke to the women. Satchi heard *qoyani*, the word for reindeer.

Tolek and Choti had in fact finished their butchery and were loading the sleigh with the quartered carcasses. They would, Satchi guessed, drag the sleigh themselves after the burning, and meanwhile the women were to prepare for a feast at home. Slowly the women turned from her and began to trudge away. Pipik looked at Satchi over her shoulder, gape-mouthed with grief and awe, and the children also glanced furtively back.

She was hot with shame now, and tried to speak but could not. What did you say to a father who had lost his second child to sickness? Who was about to burn his only son? For him and for Paqa it had to be terrible, pain of a magnitude she could scarcely imagine. And she had defied them! Had insisted on . . . on what? Her right to grieve? Her separateness? The depth of her guilt? The realization of her selfishness stunned all the words out of her.

'Excuse please,' he said. There was nothing in his voice. It was as remote and opaque as the call of a bird. 'Two days, we go back. You go to your father. You tell him excuse me please. Excuse bad man. Now, few steps away please.'

He turned and shuffled back to the heaped pyre, where the other men now waited in a half-circle. He had bent over the wood and struck the match before Satchi began a lurching run. She got part way up the little hill and stopped, the sobs heaving in and out of her. For a few seconds the flame was quick and high, bright yellow flags with a long fringe of black, silky smoke, and then the smaller, steadier red fire began to spear around and through the bottom logs. She could hear it, an avid, brisk sound.

A piece of the calico wrapping caught and went up in an orange flash. A patch of fire began to grow on the fawnskin blanket. The red tongues licked higher, luminous and nearly invisible at the tip, making the air warp and shimmer with intense heat. Satchi could see the snow banks nearby glaze, melting and refreezing when the wind shifted a little. The flames worked their way higher, the red spear points rising around Yina, shriveling and curling the hide blanket, and the wrapped gifts were periodically flaring, bursting, sometimes with a loud report or sizzle.

The men stepped further away, but remained turned to the fire, their backs toward her. They made no sound, and only Tatka carried something in his hands – the spear they had used to kill the reindeer. Within a few moments the blaze had completely ringed the body and began to concentrate itself into a single column. The sound became a throaty, steady cataract. The blanket began to drop away in flaming pieces, while smaller flakes and embers went whirling aloft with the smoke.

Satchi could see Yina now, curled on his side, arms crossed over his chest. The fine coat and trousers were blackened and shriveled in their turn; the whole body seemed to be moving, as in a restless sleep. One hand slowly clenched in its smouldering mitten; a shift in the column of fire made the whole form appear to shudder; the feet bent together, as one, pointing the toes like a dancer's. The flames were sheeting aloft now, alternately hiding and revealing. Then a loud hiss, and the torso jerked and seemed to sink in slightly.

All at once Tatka ran toward the fire, his hood pulled up and wrenched to one side in order to protect his face. He held the spear in both hands, and with it he poked into the fire, into the body of the child. Satchi did not understand his cry, but as Tatka retreated he beat his arms and made a darting movement of his head, very much like a bird. Then he walked completely around the fire, reversed himself, and walked the full circle back again.

Satchi watched Kainivilu, but he stood still as a stone, and none of the others approached him. Tolek had found some twigs or shreds of bark in the snow, and these he was scattering around the pyre. Choti busied himself over the meat on the sleigh and the harness rigging. The flames roared up in a long, sinuous column, but Satchi guessed the ceremony was now ending, and she dreaded being there when the men turned finally homeward. The raging ardor of the fire was at once horrible and irresistible, she would have to *tear herself away* – the English phrase had a new and unsettling force – and she felt as she wheeled around, almost falling, exactly as if her flesh were sundering, sloughed or seared from her bones by the image now behind her.

She ran as best she could uphill, through the snow, and did not look back. She ran down again, at an angle, to pick up the trail, and kept running almost the whole way to camp. Her heart was bursting with a strange grief, a violent grief she did not understand until she saw the fish-shed and fallen-in dog shelter, the two other sleighs, the house entrance with a broad ribbon of smoke rising from it. Two days. She would leave this place in two days. What she had begged and demanded and cried for, what she had known would finally happen.

She came to a stop, her lungs sucking and whistling like bellows, sweat and tears steaming from her face. Some of the dogs had trotted out when she approached and were barking at her, curious or alarmed at her running. She spoke to them, and when they quieted she could hear voices and the clank of a kettle rising from the smoke hole. She could hear Itu asking a question, about Sun-Man, and Navakut answering, too softly for her to grasp the meaning. But she could guess. If only the Time Cannon could have shot them away a day ago. Instead, in two days, she would be torn apart.

CHAPTER THIRTEEN

Dick Pendergast usually took the company jet to Seattle and flew first class from there, so he could catch enough sleep to minimize the physical toll of passing through five time zones. After three years in Siberia, he also got used to sunlight at two in the morning or twilight at the same hour in the afternoon. What tried his nerves was the rumble and flash of the cities in his native land.

The problem was adjustment. In Irkutsk and in the field camps of the Stanovoy he was the equivalent of a medieval Shogun. His immediate environment – the office, the log landing, the Magadan wharf headquarters – was always tuned to his rhythms, ran or halted at his command. Just beyond, however, there was always the ultimate desolation of Siberia, vast tracts of abandoned clearcuts that frayed away into an endless, barren wrinkling and humping of the earth.

He had learned to define his operation and himself against this final, overwhelming reality. It conferred an odd sort of freedom. The gales bearing in from Kamchatka, the sudden floods and freezes, were far more powerful than the schemes devised by men in the soaring, climate-controlled office suites along Nihonbashi or Fifth Avenue. He had grasped at last the perverse, fatal attraction of the place: the absence of even the slightest shred of concern for humanity and all its achievements left one free to make his own rules.

And then he came back here, and ran up against something like this mix-up over a rental limousine at the JFK terminal. He felt himself a bull in a china shop. He had glared and spat a very ugly word at the poor dithering counter attendant, who was desperately offering her blazing hygienic smile and taut, upthrust American bosom as amends for the limousine she wouldn't be able to deliver for another twenty minutes. He had to adjust all over again to his own country's notions of damage control. Bright smile, free coffee, a comfy waiting room. He had almost come to prefer the brain-dead indifference or leering insolence of Russian clerks, because it gave one grounds for healthy tantrums, great salvos of profanity.

He hauled his own bag to the waiting room, huffed down on a couch and shook out the business page of the *Times*. He had barely scanned the Dow when he heard his name and looked up to see Jim Hart grinning at him not two strides away, a bald old hawk in a smoke gray overcoat, hat and gloves in hand, behind him a porter with a luggage cart.

'The barbarians are here. Get out the raw meat and whiskey.'

Pendergast delayed a beat, cocking his head, before tossing the newspaper aside. Then he was on his feet and the two of them shook hands and gripped each other by the shoulder. 'You old outlaw, Hart. This must be a bigger raid than I thought.'

'I'm just the chauffeur, Dick. Heard you were trying to hitch a ride.' Hart allowed himself one of the thin, opaque smiles he was famous for. 'You can tell that fetching little trick over there to cancel your cheap stretch, because your man's here with the car.'

'You're full of shit, Hart. But I'll take you up on it. Are we in the same hotel, or is your intelligence that good?' The porter had already stepped up to load Pendergast's bag on the cart, and they were moving back to the rental desk, purposeful but not hurried.

'Waldorf Towers. Screw Trump. We've got four suites and a couple of conference rooms.'

'Really. What the hell are we doing? Selling the company?' Pendergast leaned on the counter, spoke to the attendant with a swift automatic smile. 'Won't be needing the limo, Sunshine. Cancel and shred it.'

'How did you guess.' Hart indicated with a flap of his gloves the direction and Pendergast had turned when the attendant called out, quavering and slightly breathless.

'Mister Pendergast! Our policy . . . I mean for a cancelation we have to . . .'

Pendergast turned back, smiling. 'Sweetheart, you make your arrangements,' he said softly. He slid a hand in his trouser pocket, took out a small roll of bills, snapped off a twenty. 'You've got my card number. Do the paper and let it go. And buy yourself something nice. You deserve it.' He dropped the bill on the counter and winked.

The woman hesitated, her smile worked and she moistened her lips, but before she could speak the men turned and strode away.

'Self image.' Pendergast grinned at Hart. 'It's everything, I hear.' Now, all at once, he felt at home in his own country. 'And speaking of which, what's the old Stack got up his sleeve this time?'

They met as a group four hours later, in mid-afternoon. Pendergast had showered, shaved, napped, and dressed, then gone for a short conference with Harry Stack, the CEO. After that he quickly reviewed his notes for the brief presentation he would be called upon to give, before making his way to the larger of the conference rooms.

Two things surprised him: the small number of players and their apparent magnitude. Stack was there, of course, along with the stateside manager Phillips and Mendez, the chief of South American operations. Also Stu Lehmann, Dixie's top counsel, and a youngster he didn't know but recognized as a legal hound of some sort.

The real shock was Willy C. Dobbs, the notorious market raider. Pendergast recognized immediately the lank frame, oversized ears and trademark bolo tie he had seen in newsclips or on magazine covers. Chatting behind Dobbs was a group of three. The Japanese with the fixed, sad smile and hornrimmed spectacles was George Watanabe, who bought about half the logs Pendergast shipped. The two others he didn't know: a heavy-set man in a flower-embroidered vest, eyes rapid and shrewd, and a fortyish woman in purple silk, a Bahamas tan and diamond earrings.

They were biggies, though. Their power was evident in every gesture and easy laugh, in the way they were fielding people with deft handshakes, light smiles, a just-warm word. Pendergast moved that way, introduced himself to Dobbs first as the Siberian project boss. He pressed flesh a little more firmly than the norm. That was appropriate, he figured, coming from the most far-flung and barbarous of Dixie's outposts.

Dobbs gave him a once-over with narrowed eyes the color of burning alcohol. 'So you're the logger,' he said. 'When you fellas gonna wind up that cut?'

Pendergast laughed, easily enough. The billionaire was famous for his bluntness. He understood that Dobbs had been briefed and knew already that the fading Siberian operation figured in this meeting. 'Not yet,' he said. 'Winter's actually our busiest season.'

'Heard that. Freezes hard as the Ten Commandments. But I also heard you've about done the course out there. Plus problems with the local enviromaniacs. Say, what about that girl who ran off with a bear, or whatever it was? Want to hear about that.'

'Not much to it, but I'll tell what I know.' Pendergast smiled and moved on. He had managed, he hoped, to dissemble his surprise. Global village, they used to call it. Well, the tundra was no village, but everybody seemed to know the news all the same. He slid off at a tangent and worked his way back to Hart, wanting to compare notes. The two of them were the lowliest members present: understory management, with an insignificant block of shares, worth maybe six million between them, picked up as bonuses over the years. Everyone else was probably a percentage owner.

He caught Hart at a side table offering coffee in urns and punch from a glass bowl. No hotel employees to serve, which confirmed his theory that this gathering was essentially clandestine, with the tightest security possible. As he picked up a napkin and a cup he said quickly, 'What the hell are *we* doing here, Hart?'

'Was about to ask you the same.' Hart took the ladle and filled Pendergast's cup with punch. His smile was so swift and neutral it might have been a fleeting gastric discomfort. 'Like I said on our way in, we're the Siberian connection. So I suppose our little dirt-slicer is involved.'

'I didn't think it was that big a deal. An experiment, you told me.'

Hart tilted his head ever so slightly and Pendergast drifted with him away from the table toward the big windows with a view of the city. On the way they smiled and nodded at others who were into their own whispered speculations.

'That's how I set it up. And the results I've seen look very good. But this isn't an operating system. Take years – two, three at least – to find out whether the sonofabitch will make anybody rich. Anyway I can't say anything more about it, Dick, or Stack will personally amputate my balls. I'm supposed to follow you with a four-minute talk on how improvements in the little elephant and thinner kerfs and all that bullshit will keep us competitive. But I can tell you that's *complete* bullshit.'

Pendergast gazed down the canyon of Fifth Avenue, the glittering ant-trails of cars. He was thinking hard and fast. His own instructions from Stack, received during his seven-minute audience two hours earlier, were to stress the long-term viability of taiga operations, the white pine replantings in Krasnoyarsk, and to downplay the fact that they were running out of pulp, let alone sawtimber, in the whole Eastern zone. But Stack had also made emphatically clear that he was to leave out all mention of the diversification of Dixie's resource base in Siberia, specifically the pending open franchises, good for timber, mineral, gas, or fertilizer extraction. And absolutely no reference to the experimental research project.

'Who's the flower boy, and the dish?'

'Henry Kravis, Jr. The money.' Hart lifted his cup of punch in fleeting salute. 'We're in the big time.'

They heard a briefcase unsnap behind them, a rustle of papers. Not much time. Henry Jr., the chief dealmaker for Kohlberg, Kravis, Roberts. No bigger player in the game. Pendergast was wondering now if Hart knew more than he was saying. If the right question would prompt his friend into dropping a clue.

'So we're borrowing or selling?'

'You tell me.' Hart set his empty cup on the windowsill and looked at Pendergast directly. 'And figure this for me. His lady friend owns Kismet. So Dixie's moving into jewelry and cosmetics and diet plans? Jesus Christ.'

Chairs were being moved now, more briefcases were opening, and laughter and parting sallies marked the end of conversations. He and Hart turned smoothly and separated, heading for their places at the great oval oak table. Stack was arranging two charts on easels behind his chair, while the young lawyer seated immediately to his left had raised the lid on a laptop.

Opening flourishes were always important, not usually for their content but for their style, their body language in the broad sense. Pendergast normally looked for traces of warmth or chill in certain words, a tell-tale flicker of tension or excitement behind the reading of a graph. But Stack, for a change, set forth the main course of red meat at the outset.

He greeted everyone, picked up a pointer, and the room quieted. Then he said, rather softly, '"Dixie Pacific is a big, strong international lumber company that hasn't learned to blaze trail."' The CEO did not smile and did not frown, but the room was instantly alert. 'That's a quote from the *Journal*. The Oracle from the Rear.' A low murmur of laughter. 'Now I'll give you the short form: We're not making money fast enough to take advantage of some opportunities to modernize and diversify – opportunities that could mean a very substantial profit. Put even shorter, we're in danger of missing a pretty good-sized boat.

'So we have a choice: we can solicit straightforward limited loan guarantees and ride the situation as is, hoping we can get the problems solved in time, or we can be bold. We can invite friendly support, anything from a takeover to a limited partnership. Fortunately, we *do* have a few friends.'

Stack smiled swiftly at Dobbs, the woman in the purple dress, and Kravis. Stack was a piece of work, Pendergast thought. A full-service predator, steely but flexible, with a concentration that was at once incandescent and perfectly steady.

'Those of you who know me pretty well, can guess where I come down . . . when there is an opportunity to be bold.' Stack smiled for the first time at a second wave of chuckles. 'So we're here today to discuss that option; but first I want to give you a quick profile of what your company is doing right now, including briefings from the field and a look at some new possibilities. Now . . .'

Stack turned to the chart, and Pendergast darted back to his former train of thought with renewed intensity. So it was true; they were for sale, all or part. Dobbs already owned a piece of them, acquired in the buyout wars of the last decade. 'Your' company, Stack had said, so no doubt Kravis had picked up shopper's shares too. Sniffing around, possibly as a prelude to squaring off. Audacious, indeed, to invite two big sharks to the same pond. And any sale would surely lead to a merger and a new package, or, alternatively, a breakup; and if Pendergast knew anything for sure, he knew that the Siberian operation couldn't survive on its own.

However he bent or shaded his reports, he could not hide the fact that they were running out of decent trees. After almost two decades of heavy cut, twelve billion board feet or better a year, they had gone through the nuggets. Their camps on the edge of the tundra were essentially salvage operations, the office in Magadan hardly justifiable, except for . . .

That had to be part of this complex. The little dirt-slicer or hole-heater at the research camp, with its potential for mining. He glanced covertly at Hart, who sat with head bowed slightly, as if in meditation. A pencil in one hand made a slow doodle on the pad before him. A circuit or structural diagram, no doubt. Hart knew. He had to. He'd been the designer for the whole thing.

Hart was a little company unto himself, an oddball renegade tech adviser who had worked on contract to Dixie for years, and saved the company millions. His adaptation of the laser-faller, the 'little elephant', was the first small enough and maneuverable enough to function in the rugged terrain of the northern taiga; and his simple, brilliant expedient of constructing snowberms and a compact solar refrigeration system to keep them frozen had allowed skid roads to remain open almost two months longer into the melt season.

Pendergast had known him for ten years. They had been sympathetic opposites: Hart the bald, laconic, slightly disreputable engineering genius, and Pendergast the tough, shrewd, gregarious manager in hardhat and boots. Together they had flown in to check out the site of the research facility a year ago; and Hart had been back twice for lightning visits. Only now did he realize that he had no clear idea of what this monstrous cookie-cutter was for, why it had to be so secret. Early on Hart had said something about drilling and quarrying, and Pendergast had gotten the impression it was a sort of experimental laser jackhammer, a construction tool.

He hadn't been smart, hadn't paid attention, that was clear now. His last trip, just last week, he'd simply flown over the site and seen the strange rectangular blocks the device had heaped up. He remembered the trip mostly because on the way home he had shot a nice bear right out in the open, so the pilot could drop in and secure the hide. He should have been thinking about those franchises, and what Malenky's Indigenous Affairs and the Army were up to – their bribe to old Kutznetsov, their pretense of a serious search, at least until the little whore could be picked up and things would die down. All this to protect Dixie's image, he had been led to believe, but the affair clearly went beyond that. Well beyond a patent improvement on a hot shovel.

Stack had introduced Phillips and Mendez for their four minutes apiece, and Pendergast listened with half an ear while he kept circling the mystery of the tundra project. The Western hemisphere report was obviously pitched to argue for diversification within the natural resource field. But the company had no interest in Venezuelan oil, and jungle biomass wasn't going anywhere. So what then? Copper? Titanium?

It was the usual humdrum stuff, the material of in-house reviews, self-critiques, biannual brainstorming. Why would Dobbs and Kravis waste their time on such small-gauge matters? Now Mendez was finishing up his spiel on the system of solar-powered small mills strung along Amazon tributaries, the big power barges pincering up and stowing bundles of precut furniture on deck without any need for stevedores or flagmen. The future lay with this kind of chic pennysaving? Christ, this was embarrassing, and it would be Pendergast's turn next.

In his last few sentences, Mendez noted that when logging slowed in the rainy season the barges were adapted to freight ore from the Orinoco mine pits. The sideline was lucrative enough that he had recommended that Dixie look into acquiring a production interest as well. Pendergast happened to be covertly watching the Kismet woman, his notes already in hand, at just that moment; she had moved her arm slightly to glance at her watch, which gave off a tiny flash of gold.

Heat, cold, and gold. Diversification, mineral property, production interest. He was momentarily disoriented, almost dizzy, and had to exert every ounce of himself to focus on his presentation, upcoming in a matter of seconds. It had all fallen into place, with one tiny flash, he knew it without having to think out every detail. How had he been so dense? He saw why the company hadn't pulled out of Magadan. Saw why Hart was so oblique. Why the little runaway whore was potentially dangerous. Why he must, somehow, whatever it took, get hold of himself and give no sign, absolutely not the faintest breath of a suggestion, that he understood what was at stake here.

Stack was turning toward him with easy, offhand grace. Pendergast had no idea what his boss had said as introduction, but he stood up and made a small joke, something about coming to New York in a heat wave – it was a nippy late fall day, just above freezing – which got a good laugh, and then he glided into the remarks he had rehearsed a time or two in his room. Everything he said was now irrelevant, an empty but necessary show, requiring sincerity for its effect. But he managed it. He was straight and tough about the shortage of prime timber, sketched the measures they were taking to offset it, waxed briefly eloquent on the ultimate wisdom of maintaining a presence in Siberia – the richest, most underdeveloped real estate on the planet – despite the difficulties of climate and culture.

This was his segue into a closing anecdote, about the little tundra flower who allegedly ran off with a bear. He set it up by observing that environmental extremism had met its match in Siberia, where the muggers and molesters weighed half a ton. 'We're thinking,' he added, 'of turning security over to those big fellas. Don't expect any problems with tree-spikers.'

After the laughter he looked at Dobbs with a rueful smile. 'Actually, as I think even our sensational journalists have admitted, the abduction probably involved some local native herders. Just before I left, the snowcat this young woman had been driving turned up not far from a main road. The supposition is she's a runaway, pure and simple. Took up with one of the herders, and since they mostly live in town now she is no doubt enjoying her own drama on TV while she microwaves some popcorn.'

Pendergast shrugged and rolled his eyes. 'Dixie was involved only because the woman had an unfortunate liaison with one of our young field officers, and by coincidence her father was part of the local regulatory bureaucracy. Of course the media wishes for something sexier or bloodier, but there's just nothing there, folks. Nothing. She'll be found soon, and we'll go on as we always have, moving the logs.' He sat down, and one lightning glance at Stack told him his approach had been right.

He was breathing harder than he meant to, and sweating a little now. He wouldn't listen to Hart, couldn't bear any more of these routines, all camouflage and bait. It shouldn't have hit him so hard. Every logging show came to a natural end, and he'd known the Siberian operation wouldn't pay for itself much longer. When he had allowed himself to speculate, he imagined himself back in Atlanta for a year or two, or maybe Seattle again. But always as a honcho, with major responsibility for a big cut, in a company that was, and always had been, one of the premier timber movers in the world.

Of course Dixie was not going to stop cutting, or milling, or fabricating wood products. He wasn't going to lose his job . . . probably . . . and there would no doubt be other challenging assignments. But he wouldn't be at the center of things anymore. The heart and soul of the company had been captured by something more durable and rarified and valuable than timber, and even more treacherous.

Were he a gambler, Pendergast would have bet his entire nest egg of stock bonuses that within a matter of weeks Stack would announce an impending acquisition, or possibly even a merger. Dixie would diversify into mining, would select a medium-sized producer, Amco or United Mineral or Homestake, as target or partner. And then, Malenky having already arranged the new leases and contracts, the rumors would start. Hart's wizardry would be ballyhooed, the new wintertime technology. All would see that the logging operation was only a screen, behind which lay a glorious new opportunity – the vast Kolyma gold reserves, accessible the year around, the permafrost permeable at last.

It was, he saw, a trap for sharks. His own operation was merely a ruse, an elaborate delaying tactic to forward yet another ruse, which depended on exquisite timing, a convergence of rumors. He was, in all this, a kind of decoy. Dobbs and Kravis were meant to see a company trying bravely to regain its footing, stumbling toward reorganization and the barest hint of a new and promising direction. The sharks would be ready and primed, when things began to unfold, to bid ferociously for control. Dixie's stock would go through the roof. He would end up utterly useless, Pendergast thought, and – if he sold at the right moment – extravagantly rich.

CHAPTER FOURTEEN

The second day after the funeral, Satchi heard a helicopter. She clambered up the ladder pole, shoved aside the cover over the entrance, and raised her head above the log barrier just in time to catch a glimpse of the huge, fat, gray-green insect, flying very low, as it slipped over the horizon to the west. The direction, she was now sure, of the nearby camp.

She stepped over the barrier poles and stood for a moment in the midmorning sun, breathing deeply. The others had no doubt noticed that she did not scramble out in a great rush. Nor did she feel frustrated and angry at a missed opportunity. With a quiet amazement, she felt relief, a perverse gratitude that she had been overlooked or ignored. The truth appeared to be that she was no longer sure of her yearning, once so hot and spiteful, to escape from this place.

She could see in retrospect that this reversal had begun the moment Kainivilu stepped forward to give his apology and promise to make amends. She had backed away dumbly, unable to think of any future. She had stared into the fire, seen a child, whose wet bedding she had changed the day before, shrivel and fall to ashes. And then, still dumb, she had eaten and slept the profound, dreamless sleep of exhaustion – and when she rose finally in the afternoon, blinking and yawning, and took the bowl Tolek had shoved into her hands, she had known in an instant that everything was changed. He was the same ancient driveler she had recoiled from before, his yellow and purple gums bared to her in a mindless grin, the reek of fish offal and urine about him; but she saw an alertness now in the quick shift of the rheumy old eyes, felt a force both protective and pleading in his handling of the bowl of broth. He watched her drink; nodding, nodding, nodding, as if at a wondrous event.

When the children came to her finally, they were solemn and shy for a few minutes, and then grasped her hands and smiled fiercely, wanting her to read a little and then play the television game before the light was gone and the evening meal ready. They had all heard Kainivilu say he would take her away in two days, and in their faces she read affection and sadness and a brave effort. She felt her heart convulse painfully when Navakut said in her best Russian, 'You come back and be the guest for us.'

And then Itu had said, with his lower lip trembling, that he wanted her to be his papa's, like his mother, and Satchi stumbled over her words, mortified, in hurrying to tell him, miming with fingers and eyes, she would begin their play as soon as she had combed her hair. She was fervently glad that Kainivilu and Choti were gone to the herd, and she listened intently for any unnatural silence behind her, where Paqa and Euna were pounding willow twigs on the fire stones, and the two old men wheezed and snuffled over their tobacco and occasional talk, but she sensed no tension.

Part of the change was perhaps the weather. Late October, and the Kamchatka winds were unpredictable. Patches scoured by the blizzard were now bare, with an edge of melt in the afternoon. Some re-exposed lichens were rich green and rose. The reindeer cropped them greedily, and the men went with coats loosened, their necks and sometimes a shoulder bare.

The night before Yina died Satchi had heard the men talking about *inat*, a root or tuber of some kind, which she had tasted in the pudding they sometimes made. She gathered that they might go on a last short journey to gather this root, and there was some joking at Pipik's expense. The old woman looked sly and proud, and when Satchi asked the children they demonstrated how their mothers robbed the plant, and also cedarnuts and other seeds, from the burrows of mice. She had felt a twinge of excitement at the prospect of getting away on such an expedition, out of her underground cell and walking free and at ease on the tundra.

Of course she could not go now. She was going home. Back to it all. There would be a stir of some kind, she was aware. No doubt the search for her was still going on, an investigation or two also. She hoped her father had not gotten into serious trouble. Or fought with Kenny. Or, on the other hand, collaborated too closely with him.

Her mind shifted away from such reflections with a furtive alacrity. Thinking of Kenny was vaguely uncomfortable. That situation, at least, was clearer. She had been a bit of a fool. Because he was handsome and dashing. Because he flew her off in a company plane and gave her champagne and cocaine. Because they had enthusiastic and creative sex, and talked about it in English. She shook herself, her mouth tightening. Kenny would find her a knotty girl indeed, when she returned.

She had walked now past the reindeer holding pen, following the track of Kainivilu and Choti. She guessed they were bringing in more animals to butcher. It was obvious to her now that they must be supplying meat, as well as goods from some trading post, to the hidden camp. She could see how much they ate, and one animal would have fed them all for at least two weeks, even without the salmon and puddings of berry or *inat*. If they killed today they would have to make their delivery soon, in case the weather held warm for another day or two.

It occurred to her all at once that it was terribly wrong for her to burden Kainivilu so soon after the tragedy of Yina's death. Wrong and unreasonable. There was nothing but her own pride to keep her from telling him that it was not important, just at this time, for her to return. Especially if he had work to do, other responsibilities. She felt immediately better, clearer-headed, and strode at a faster pace along the track. She would be quiet, but pleasant and respectful. She would help by staying out of the way, by waiting for the family to recover some measure of stability and peace.

Before ten minutes had gone by, she topped a slight rise and saw the two brothers ahead of her, bringing along four reindeer. They saw her too, and Kainivilu signed her, rather imperiously, to turn off the trail and give them a wide margin to pass. She was taken aback and felt a familiar pang of irritation, but did as he directed. When the reindeer had eyed her and sidled by, he handed his neck-bridles to Choti and came to her, his face flat and without expression.

'We kill these and go,' he said. 'You go. Eat first, take your bag. Take everything.'

A sudden hollow appeared under her ribs, where her confidence had been. She tried but could not get out the words she had prepared, the kind, calm words of support.

He waited another moment, then swung his head toward their camp. 'We go now.'

He had already turned when she spoke.

'No . . . please. You don't need to do this for me.'

He stopped.

'I am sorry I have been such trouble. Right now you must do only what you need to do.'

He turned back to look at her fully, his eyes steady beneath the thick gray line of eyebrows. She wanted to look down, but she did not. She wanted him to see that she meant to help.

'Who is this? Where is *Navilineut*?'

It was a moment before she remembered the name. *Woman-who-sleeps*. What the old men first called her. She managed a tight smile and shook her head.

'So. Yayo's daughter does not want to go, *ey yeti*!' He laughed, a single grunt, and beckoned to her as he turned back to Choti and took up the halter-lines to two of the reindeer. 'Too bad. We must go this time. Enough snow, and warm now.'

They set off and she walked beside him. The hollow place in her deepened and widened with every step. 'You are taking meat to the camp over west of here, where the helicopter went. I could go too, and we could ask them to bring me back, or call on the radio.'

She spoke this with a forced matter-of-factness, without looking at him. He did not answer.

'You would not have to trouble yourself any more.'

She waited, listening to their footsteps breaking and grinding the snow, still brittle from the night. She glanced at him quickly, saw his intent profile, his exposed throat and the string of bear claws around it. When he did speak it was in Koryak, to Choti, a command of some kind to keep the reindeer from crowding together.

The old anger invaded her heart.

'Why? Why can't we go there? *Tchort*! I know it is near. There is a doctor, a vehicle, now a helicopter. They must be government—'

'You do not trouble yourself about this any more.'

She breathed hard once, choking on the phrase she had used herself, which he had deliberately thrown back at her. The effort she made to hold her tongue brought tears to her eyes. She had to remind herself he had just lost a son. He was a simple reindeer herdsman, with his own odd cultural notions, he was – No! That was false, ridiculous. He knew Russian better than he pretended, he had driven the Sno-Klaw, had dealt with the people in this camp, and his womenfolk traded trinkets for goods from Magadan. He was no primitive. There were no primitives left in Siberia. Only a handful of derelicts too ignorant or stubborn to accept the support available to them. There was no need for any of them to live here.

'Why won't you say the truth?' she burst out.

Nothing. Only the rustle and crack of boots and hooves on ice. Her question might have been the scream of a gull. She plodded on, woodenly, and when her mind went utterly blank he finally spoke.

'They would not take you back.'

This time she was silent. Four, five, six, then eight strides.

'Not government.'

She waited. Four, five, six more.

'Amricn.'

She almost halted, then stepped like a startled deer until she was ahead of him. '*American*? How can that be?' She tried to read his expression, but he had none. He was watching the trail and the reindeer.

'Two Amricn. Four Russian.'

'But why? What are they doing here? They must be army.'

He glanced at her, quick as a spear-thrust, and walked on. She read in that glance both reluctance and an obstinate, unequivocal refusal to say more. She knew, with a certainty she could not explain, that he must have given some kind of promise to keep silent about this camp. A promise he now found hard to keep.

Russians. *Arkharovtsy*, no doubt. Hunters, packers, traders without scruple. But *Americans*! What could they be doing here, with a helicopter? In Magadan she knew of no enterprise in this class, besides Dixie of course, and a small trading firm – owned actually by Moscow Jews who had gone over to the U.S. after the collapse of the Union. There were a few consultants to the government, scientists and engineers who came for a few months and did whatever they did (very little, according to her father), and occasionally a small military detachment or some professors on a field grant.

Will Baker

But a helicopter and a big GAZ meant either the Army or a very rich and influential company. Her thoughts were hurrying pell-mell now, in several directions. Kainivilu could be mistaken. The foreigners might be European, German or English probably. But that explained nothing. What did they want? Why would the camp be kept secret?

They were too far east and north of the taiga to be linked to the lumber industry. Furs had not been a serious factor in the economy for fifty years. Minerals were at best a remote possibility. Just to the west lay the Kolyma goldfields, which had yielded a fantastic fortune to the Union, and still contained immense reserves, more than could be effectively mined in the short summers when the permafrost softened. Even a major new discovery would be of no great immediate value. The same was true of iron and coal and oil and gas, huge deposits of which occurred in the western steppes, much closer to market.

Nearer Magadan or Yakutsk or Vladi she would have guessed drugs, but there was no reason to route them here, and every reason not to. Hashish and heroin and cocaine moved easily by ship, like everything else. Away from these cities, the truckdrivers and miners drank their bitter *chifir* to stay awake and vodka to knock themselves senseless. So here were six men, two of them foreigners and possibly American, hiding in a frozen waste and living on fresh meat and peanut butter dragged to them by itinerant herders. It was baffling, irritating, and exciting.

They were in sight of their camp now, where the children were playing outside, dragging each other on an old hide, and Tatka and Tolek were at work attaching dog harnesses to one of the old wooden sleds. They had already rigged the other two cargo sleds for reindeer. They were almost ready, everything done with an unfamiliar, almost miraculous speed.

Satchi knew at last, and definitively, that she did not want to leave. Yet there was nothing more to do or say. Kainivilu understood how she felt. She heard it in his single bark of bitter laughter, saw it in his one swift look. Yayo's daughter, the fox-child, could not make up her mind. When she wanted to go she had to stay, and now she wanted to stay she would have to go. Taking her bottles of medicine, her new fur boots and her book. No one had mentioned the Makarov, and she supposed they would count the revolver a tacit gift.

'Your gun. Take with you.'

She was startled. He had spoken in the same flat, low voice, exactly as if he were responding to a question she had just put. The hollow space reappeared under her ribs, but it had not the same quality as before. A vague anxiety, as if she had failed to grasp something, or prepare for something.

'I don't want it. It is yours, please take it.'

He ignored her. Or rather he turned stone deaf an instant before she spoke. He and Choti were crowding the reindeer toward the corral, its entrance winged out to receive them. Satchi stopped and let them all go by. Tatka had hurried up with the spear and thongs and stood ready to swing shut the gate. They were cooing, cajoling the nervous animals, who in a few minutes would be kicking out their lives in the bloody snow.

She stood there, silent and miserable, and watched it all.

When the carcasses had been skinned the men began to butcher, wrapping the cuts of meat in oilskin and stacking them on the sleds. They ignored her until Kainivilu simply pointed to a basket beside which they had tossed hearts, sections of intestine, and livers. As they whetted their knives and rolled up hides, Tatka laughing soundlessly at something, she understood they meant her to load and carry the basket to the house. They simply assumed she would serve them, while they finished up and then squatted in the bloody snow, faces to the sun, smoking and waiting for their food.

Her face hot and her lips a thin, straight line, she bent to retrieve the chunks of slimy, purple liver, the rubbery guts and tough red hearts. She worked bare-handed, head down, telling herself that she had after all talked herself into this role. She was helping a family in a time of great tragedy. Only they seemed already to have abandoned their grief; they moved and spoke in their familiar and ordinary ways. Behind her the men were discussing the route they would take, estimating the time for the trip. Her gesture was not acknowledged, not even subtly. She rubbed the blood from her hands with wet snow, picked up the basket, and walked away without looking at them. They fell silent and she knew they were watching her. Tatka said something about *quikinnaku* and wheezed. Choti and Kainivilu grunted. The raven god. She took it as a reference to the bird they had seen at the funeral burning, just as she had committed her old boots to the flames. She had thought she was being honored at the time, but apparently not. Certainly she did not feel herself soaring free, as she swung the basket awkwardly from both hands and lurched toward the house.

Even the children, playing by the fish-shed, ignored her; but the three women were around the hearth when she descended and could not avoid her. Euna received the basket with a weak smile, and Pipik began to chatter nervously. Paqa was fanning the fire, her face red and sweating, but she glanced at Satchi. Swiftly they began to separate the meat into piles and chop the livers and hearts into chunks, while Satchi went to her corner and gathered up her small stock of possessions. After placing her bag by the ladder, there was nothing for her to do but wait.

She glanced furtively once more at the spot where Yina's bed had been. Empty now, everything gone. The sight of the bare earth and unadorned support post gave her a physical shock. She edged a little nearer, remembering the moment when Yina had put his fingers around her wrist, pulled himself erect and smiled. At the top of the upright log which had once anchored his bed something dangling caught her eye. She took another step nearer and saw that it was one of the *kalaks*, this one with a leather covering and a more elaborately carved face.

Seeing it she remembered a word, *enayiskamaklo*. Almost simultaneously, with another shock that went entirely through her, like that from a bare, high-voltage wire, she saw again the scene from her childhood, a woman bent over her white bed. The woman's face was in shadow except for one cheekbone and eye, which caught a soft light from what must have been a candle or lantern. She held out her hand to Satchi, in the palm a tiny carved figure, and her voice was subdued and hoarse. Satchi did not understand what the woman said or perhaps sang. She had been six years old, and very ill, so that most of what happened to her seemed part of a dream.

She was trembling from the wave of emotion that had slammed through her. Her hand had curled up and she actually felt again the small form, a forked willow stick with a leather corset, notched into a face at the thick end. But the shock came not from the carved charm, but from this sudden memory of the exact line of the woman's cheekbone, the timbre of her voice.

She had been troubled since her arrival by this memory, had assumed that it was simply that Yina's illness reminded her of her own. Yet these recollections had centered more and more on the dim, shadowy visitor holding out an object, and gradually the scene had gained definition and detail, like a developing photograph. She had thought – on no reasonable grounds, she understood in a flash – that a relative or neighbor must have come by late at night with a small gift. But now there was something familiar, immediate, dreadful about the memory. The contour of the face, the posture . . .

She reached up on impulse and grasped the charm. Again the sudden, intense feeling, as if the thing were charged.

'*Enayiskamaklo!*'

The cry and the lightning-stroke of her understanding came together. She was already turning swift as a bird in flight to stare at Pipik, who had seen her reach for the figure and had cried out. An old, bent, withered woman whose eyes had turned to fiery jewels, whose mouth was wide in terror or ecstasy. A woman who had again leaned suddenly out of the shadows after twenty years.

There was a second cry, then a short, searing burst of words. It was Paqa, who had seen Satchi and what was in her hand. Paqa's face was grotesquely contracted and she had dropped the small knife in her hand. She hopped abruptly to the side, almost knocking Euna off her feet. Her hands jerked to her face, clawed down once, leaving thin streaks both red and white, and her body began to shudder, a vibration so rapid and violent Satchi could hear the slapping of flesh.

More words came, as shrieks and grunts delivered with sudden, rictus-like frowns and smiles. Euna and Pipik had moved to either side of Paqa, and were trying to capture her arms gently, but she avoided them or knocked their hands away. Now she leaped over the fire, tipping the great pot of fish-broth off its rest so a considerable amount sloshed out on the floor in a cloud of steam. She was shouting, looking around the room wildly.

Satchi found herself pressed against the wall at the furthest possible remove from the others. She was still trembling, and the fragmentary thoughts that came to her seemed huge, unwieldy, impenetrable. She might be related, somehow, to these people, as they had first claimed. They thought she was a saviour, a witch-doctor sent by their Big Raven, and her refusal to stay meant something dire or sinister to them. Had caused a death, and now madness.

'*Pakuku!*'

Satchi flinched as if struck with a rod. She recognized the word, learned from her mother in the bath tub, the word for the slit in a woman. She was weak with panic, unable to speak, and began to edge along the wall. She felt like a creature trapped in a cave, dumb with terror at the spectacle before her, another animal gone mad and tearing at itself.

Paqa was sitting on the floor now, her head jerking spasmodically every few seconds to a new quarter of the compass. She stared now at one person or thing, now at another, and Satchi had never seen such a look of incandescent madness. Euna was beside her talking in a soothing way, trying to interest her in wiping clean some wooden trays, as if Paqa were a distracted child. And that is how she behaved, repeating exactly Euna's words and gestures, then jerking away to stare at something else.

Satchi had now come all the way around to the other side of the hearth, and found herself working, silent and furtive, beside Pipik, bent over the heaps of meat. They were again slicing strips of the heartmeat and chunks of liver, their hands swift and instinctive as small creatures. The shock Satchi had undergone rendered her body strangely fluid and alert, though her mind felt suspended, orbiting still around that tremendous flash of recognition – a sudden certainty that the woman beside her bed more than twenty years ago, glimpsed in a feverish dream, was no other than Pipik, who had recognized Satchi too, from the beginning.

The old woman had also understood Satchi's stunned reaction. She beamed at her with a kind of adoring complicity, and as she worked whispered a stream of exclamations and hums and broken phrases. *Yayocanaut . . . you grow up! You are well! Hi! My songs for you . . . Ah! Whale people! Namalu! You are also Taigonotolu!*

Then her mouth would twist awry and she would squint out tears. *Ai! We lose our Yina, we are almost gone! You stay! Stay! Paqa is sick . . . menerik! Menerik!*

Satchi kept slicing furiously, with the flat of her blade herding the chunks of meat to one side, while Pipik threaded them on long wooden splinters which she laid over the fire. *Menerik*. The arctic sickness. A herder's disorder, though it struck mostly women, and her father claimed it was simple hysteria. Or a psychosis triggered by isolation, by the dreadful searing endless emptiness of the tundra. And to lose a child to this blank horror without horizon . . .

She dared not look at Paqa, though she felt the other woman's eyes on her at intervals, felt a presence like a wave of heat on her skin. She heard the ugly word muttered again. No woman had ever called her that before, reduced her to a slit, a hole. It was malevolence of a proportion new to her, but she understood now, knowing that all around them was nothing, nothing but the expanse of snow and sky. No policemen, no nurses with medication, no counselors or priests. She had appeared as the sole representative of all that, the other world, and had brought nothing but more pain. Had read a stupid story, and the child died anyway, died almost in her arms . . .

And now she understood why they burned their dead. For those left alive it was a way to seclude the spirit finally, cage it with articulate and antic brightness, drive it into the wind, into the sky, and far away. She did not understand this in her usual way, but as a sensation, almost hallucinatory, rather like the lightness, the lift she had felt seeing the raven approach the funeral fire. Only this sensation took the form of a secret, mad desire, the wish to burn herself. To know the whip and surge and bellow of flame all through her body.

Yet she would do nothing. She would simply take the skewers of hot meat, haul them up the ladder and over the snow to the men. She would not look at them, or linger. She was paying back Pipik, and the whale people. She would walk there and back, burning, and no one would know.

CHAPTER FIFTEEN

The vehicle had been hauled to Susuman on a truck after the army cargo copter delivered it to the main Kolyma road. It sat now by itself in the equipment yard of the Oblast Transport Authority, with a hand-lettered warning sign on the window. Both doors were open, and Sokhalov had removed everything inside, even the coarse floormats, and spread all of it on a plastic sheet weighted down at the corners with old parts from other wrecked or partially dismembered vehicles in the yard.

'She didn't smoke, absolutely.' Kenny was hunched over one of four small plastic jars, sniffing. 'Didn't even like the smell of it.'

Peter uttered a sound unintelligible but sympathetic. He was making a pretense of examining a box of fuses, waiting for some sign that this phase of the investigation was drawing to a close. The case of the Half-Breed Who Ran Away With A Bear was, so far, colossally boring. Everything seemed to point to the same conclusion. Carraway's little muffin had absconded with a pack of natives, apparently willingly. There was no blood, no scratches or dents on the inside.

'She couldn't have been lost,' Kenny said plaintively. 'She must have been taking them somewhere. But this far . . .'

He trailed off. *As far as possible from some whoremongering nitwit*, Peter thought, but said, 'Quite right. Though perhaps they had some sort of emergency. Somebody ill, perhaps.'

'I think of that,' Lafe commented from the other side of the sheet of plastic. 'But there was no hospital hereabout.' He put down the old, worn glove he had been examining, though they had determined already that it was surely Satchi's, probably lost behind the seat months ago.

'Vary inturasting. A medical problim, yas?' Sokhalov had

emerged from the Sno-Klaw, smiling inquisitively. 'You thank she wos playing doctir?'

'It could happen, I suppose. But I agree with Lafe. Wouldn't she try to take them to the nearest medical post?' Kenny got to his feet.

Peter and Lafe also stood, sensing that the Police Inspector had put something together.

Sokhalov was holding up his bare hand, forefinger and thumb pinched tight. His narrow face was pink with exertion, his gray eyes alive with interest. 'Oh Mester Kanny,' he said, 'your yong lady Kutznetsova has so much byootiful blek hair. A big gurl, no?'

When he stood directly in front of them and swung his hand slowly back and forth, they could see the three or four long dark strands waving in the light breeze. The Police Inspector watched their faces. 'No?' he demanded with a soft chuckle.

On the surface he seemed to Peter an exact copy of the slightly seedy, middleaged men who were nominally managing most of the bureaus he had dealt with in this country. Hearty, corrupt, and utterly without spine or hope. But in the five hours they had been together, he had noticed that Sokhalov's deferential, garrulous chatter had a certain drift. Despite – or maybe because of – his fractured English, he managed to elicit a surprising amount of information from all three of them, while concerning his own work on this case he had offered only the vaguest generalities.

'Meny hairs,' Sokhalov went on. 'I was sorprise at so meny at first place, bot you know, that thing, that clip, was broke. Hairs all loose. Bot fonny thing, I find all bot one in cargo place.' He produced another of the plastic cups from his coat pocket and handed it to Kenny, gesturing for him to remove the top. 'Tobacco come from seat.'

'One of these workers,' Lafe said, and tilted his head toward the concrete blockhouse at the far end of the yard. Its steel doors were open, and they could see the blue-white flash of a welder in the gloomy interior. 'Or the loggers crew who find this first.'

'Ah yas! Vary gud! I thank this same thing, because these warkers set any place, go any places, hends all over avarything.' Carefully Sokhalov coiled the strands of hair into the cup, looking up brightly at Kenny as he did so. 'Bot this tobacco is vary chip, blek tobacco.

Vary bed. Even warkers get gud cigarette now. This tobacco wos for herd pipple.' He recovered the cup, snapped on its lid, and dropped it beside the other four on the tarp. 'So!' He beamed at them as he moved around the sheet, gathering up its corners. 'Fenish here. Time for lonch?'

'Wait, so what are you saying?' Kenny was all at once anxious. 'About . . . about the cargo space?'

'Oh, I dunt know whot to thank.' The Inspector turned one corner of his mouth downward and allowed his shoulders to sag. 'Maybe she is slipping, maybe not filling gud. Dunt know.'

'You mean you think she was back there the whole time?' Kenny began to pace around Sokhalov, watching him knot a cord about the gathered corners of the plastic sheet. 'Yes, tied up maybe. Goddamn it, we've got to locate whoever it was that did this. Have you heard anything from Indigenous Affairs? About itinerant herders in the area?'

'Would one of these herders, these Koryaks, have the knowledge to drive?' Lafe was pondering the Sno-Klaw, and spoke as if talking to himself.

'Ah, yas! Excellint. You should be detectif, Mester Nelsen. Yas, some herder pipple know how to drive. Wark in mine or roads. Bot these pipple lives in Magadan or the Taigonos, not here. Here is rendeers. This is gud.' Sokhalov swung the bundle he had made judiciously, as if judging the weight of the evidence, and beamed at the others.

'Good, how is it good.' Kenny's anxiety was turning into irritability. 'Are we supposed to trace them through their reindeer?'

'Yas. Vary gud!' Sokhalov set down the bundle again. 'You should be detectif too, Mester Kanny. I hef three gud men now.'

'Shit!' Kenny turned away, looked at the ground, then said over his shoulder to Peter, 'You know what the hell he's talking about?'

'Not exactly.' Peter grinned warily at the Inspector. 'You mean *almost* all the Koryak who know how to drive are living in town. Maybe there's only a couple left out in the bush, which would make it easier to find them.'

Sokhalov nodded vigorously, hummed his assent and encouragement to go on.

'Do you have anybody special in mind? A suspect?' Peter asked, and had the satisfaction of catching Sokhalov with his mouth ajar for an instant.

'No, no, I only talk to pipple in Nayashan, vary far from us, on radiofun. An agent who wark with Koryaks all his lifetime. He tell me about some men, men I hef heard about before.'

They were all looking fixedly at the Inspector now. Peter and Lafe were alert and poised, sensing for the first time an acceleration in the development of their story.

'Who? Who is the man?' Kenny was pale, his mouth set.

'No, no special men. But the agent say some men, just few men, stop wark in mines and go back to old time way. Ketch fish in sommer, go wid rendeers for winter. Nevar listen to gavarmint. Bot why coming so far away, by themseffs? Whar is rendeers?' Sokhalov shook his head. 'Now I dunt know what to thank again. It sems impossbul.'

'*What* is impossible?'

Sokhalov gazed at Kenny mournfully. 'Ah. I am sarry. Forgif me. Bot . . .' He picked up the bundled plastic sheet and turned toward the Sno-Klaw, motioning for them to follow. No one said a word until they surrounded the vehicle again.

Both doors were still wide open and Sokhalov leaned inside, resting one fist on the seat. He looked for a long moment at the cargo space behind the seatback, then at the floorboards. He shook his head again and withdrew it to stand erect.

'I dunt thank it is possbul. Too far.'

Before Kenny could explode, Peter said quickly, 'You don't think they hauled her the whole way? Or that they all came?'

'Well, vary vary small place. Four teacops at station, so we thank four pipple. Kutznetsova gurl pratty big. Vary small in cargo place. One men set on other men, if they wos small men, for few kilometers, maybe sixty, sivinty kilometers. Bot three hunred? Oh! Avarybody be sick.'

'And the petrol. Wasn't there some question about the petrol?'

'Yas. Also. We must beleve she mek mistek at first place, an' den find mar petrol, maybe fifty liters, and take along, bot no . . . no thing for carry . . . what is it?'

'Trailer,' Peter guessed, feeling the excitement now.

'Yas, traler, gud. Bot traler left at station. So two, three big kens? On tup four pipple? Or fand other traler some place, but whar? No traler here. Maybe drop off, bot . . .' Sokhalov did his mouth bend and shoulder sag. 'I thank impossbul.'

Looking at the narrow cargo slot behind the seat, trying to imagine three men on that seat made for two, Peter understood that of course it was impossible. Even without three cans of petrol. The available space would be jammed, the air fetid, no room to change position. Even sixty kilometers would be hard to believe, unless there were frequent stops – and a blizzard had been underway at the time. And the three herders would certainly not split up, in such weather.

He laughed, and so did Lafe, in self-disgust. 'Right. Impossbul is the word. We've still got a mystery.'

Kenny had taken on a flush, was making an obvious effort at self-mastery. 'All right. So you're saying it's hard to imagine four of them in here for two days, so they may have dropped . . . that is, left . . . somebody somewhere? That she . . .'

The Inspector looked away, sighed. It was an uneasy moment. 'I hef to sey yas. Possbul. *Bot* I dunt thank so. No blud, no mark of trubles. If they are thiffs, no need to tek her at all. Bot I hef strong filling she wos here.'

Peter glanced speculatively at Kenny. He could see the man was suffering and confused. He was an asshole and a fool, no question, but with a measure of basic generosity. He sincerely wanted to do his job, find his lost fiancée, or piece – the label depended on interpreting Carraway's various sighs and grimaces – and find her alive, even rescue her, in the best of all scenarios. But Sokhalov was giving him no vantage point to work from. In fact, the Inspector seemed to be undermining every hypothesis, indiscriminately.

'Well tell me – please, tell me – what you *do* think.' Kenny was taller and heavier than Sokhalov, but leaning down, pink-cheeked with humility and frustration and private agony, his manner was that of an altar boy before a Bishop with power to exorcise.

Sokhalov lifted his hands to resist such a role, and bared his teeth in the grin of one who hears a piercing sound. 'Ah! I weesh, how I weesh I know what to thank. I hef to mek guesses. Bot I know what I wunt to know, at first place.' He nodded, looked at each of them in turn, once more solemn with a deep crosscurrent of slyness. 'I wunt to see the place whar they fand this.' He stepped to the Sno-Klaw and struck its top solidly with his doubled fist. 'Wunt to talk to the loggers crew who fand it. I hef defficulty to beleve *anybudy* drive here.'

The three of them looked at each other, at the Sno-Klaw. Finally Kenny spoke, his voice a little strangled. 'Fly to Druza? That's in Khabarovsk. We – I don't know – I didn't clear that with our people for today. Our pilot is expecting to run us back to Magadan, so we can make our report, organize to relocate the search up there. I'd have to call. I mean, we can be sure they found it, and we know the Army has already run several flights in that area, nothing so far. Is it really important?'

Sokhalov puffed out his cheeks, blew out a slow jet of breath. 'Is mystary, as your fren say. No rison for drive almust three hunred kilometers. Four pipple and petrol is impossbul. Also, wedder change any time now, snow and cold. Better go see, I thank.' He smiled, innocent and cheerful again. 'Okay?'

'I'd say make the call,' Peter said. 'I'm humble. And I'm ashamed that I couldn't see it. The damn thing is just too small.'

'I also,' Lafe said.

For another moment Kenny remained as the bewildered altar boy; then his jaw lifted and set, he remembered his other archetype – the lone horseman squinting at the desert horizon, alert to any ambush or showdown.

'Okay,' he said. 'Let's move 'em out.'

It was late the next morning before they stood, finally, in the clearing where the Sno-Klaw had been recovered. There was difficulty getting the call through to Dixie headquarters in Yakutsk, more trouble locating extra fuel in Susuman, and they had ended up spending the night in a truckdriver's rest stop, a concrete dormitory with bare mattresses on iron cots. Peter still itched, and he was grateful for the cold, sharp, pine-scented air of the taiga, which cleared his head of the dormitory's odor, a compound of sweat, diesel, tobacco, and cheap cologne.

They had seen nothing extraordinary. The snow had melted a

little during the brief warming of the last week, but the tracks were plentiful and told an obvious story. A bulldozer had dragged the Sno-Klaw away to a larger clearing where the helicopter picked it up. The loggers' lighter carrier came in from the uphill side, and they found a number of footprints left by the crew.

They had already spoken to the foreman and one of the crew members, an interview arranged during Kenny's call from Susuman. They found out only that a cruiser plane photographing a nearby stand of trees had first spotted the abandoned vehicle, and assuming that it was company equipment somehow overlooked, had called for a ground crew to investigate. They noticed nothing, the foreman claimed. The blizzard and then the wind and melt had erased any clear tracks, and they had themselves walked all around it in wonderment, before someone remembered the search going on over in Magadan.

'Vary opin here,' Sokhalov murmured. He was not even looking at the palimpsest of cleat and runner and boot tracks, but straight up at the sky, which was a deep, intense blue.

'They ran out of gas. And then just walked off. Just like that. And where?' Kenny turned and stamped where he stood, like an impatient horse in its stall, for Sokhalov had asked them to move about as little as possible. No one answered.

Peter was thinking longingly of the heater in the GAZ they had borrowed from Dixie, parked now a hundred yards behind them in a stand of stone pine. His boots weren't meant for this climate, and no one at the lumber camp in Druza had a pair large enough for him. It was nice to see trees again, their sharp, dark shapes against the brilliant snow, nice to see the open sky and inhale the startling freshness of this air, but his toes were going numb. His mind, too, from thinking around and around the impossbul. *Where* was not a meaningful question, until he could see the *how* of it, and Sokhalov, he had finally understood, was bending them all to that way of thinking.

He uttered a short, derisive laugh and said without any fore-thought, 'Maybe it *flew* here.'

Sokhalov turned to him, gray eyes wide with apparent glee, the brows above them arched high. Peter understood in a flash he had made a double joke. To Sokhalov, the joke was it *was* no joke.

'Ah! Mebe so! Lat us follow bekwards, and see!'

They looked at one another furtively, bewildered by the direction of their own thoughts.

'What? Oh, come on . . .' Kenny tried to laugh, but the effort died in his throat. 'Really,' he said, but with no force.

'Follow little weys. Why nut?' The Inspector was beaming again, the genial idiot. 'Go fest. See whar he come from.'

'Very reasonable,' Lafe said, 'to me. We would at the least determine direction.'

Peter could detect, under the Swede's calm, the thread of a new and fierce excitement. 'Another day of this thaw,' he added, 'and we might not be able to. Even with more vehicles.'

So they did. They climbed into the GAZ and set off, backtracking the Sno-Klaw. Kenny drove and the others scanned the ground, leaning out the windows.

It was cold, windy, and frustrating work. The Sno-Klaw was a light vehicle with broad cleats, and had crossed the terrain when it was partly frozen under a layer of new drifts. But this far from the coast the snowfall was lighter and more scattered. The track was intermittent: clear when the Klaw had broken through to the ground, no more than a dubious trough in the snow crust elsewhere. In big clearings the snow had blown and melted away entirely, and the exposed permafrost bore no certain impression, so they had to scout ahead to pick up the track.

For three hours they worked east and north. It was clear the Klaw had kept to the cover of trees whenever possible, and had been driven sometimes recklessly. The larger GAZ had to detour around two thick stands of larch, while in crossing the wide swaths of clearcuts, they sometimes had to follow the trail on foot over ground now boggy, while the GAZ picked its way gingerly off to the side. Peter had cracked his chin when they jolted over a gully, and his insufficient boots were like blocks of ice on his feet, despite the heater.

So far they had confirmed only one thing. The GAZ was made to carry up to seven, but they found that three large men and one medium-sized, with their overnight bags and briefcases, crammed the vehicle to the hilt, and frayed tempers accordingly. The Klaw could never have hauled Satchi Kutznetsova and three grown men for three hundred kilometers.

Nothing else of any interest whatsoever. The taiga was beginning to thin and scatter, turning into tundra, and though they could go faster here, the horizon also receded suddenly, yawning away into a bleak, gray-white haze. Along with this depressing vista, Peter was beginning to reconsider his view of Sokhalov. Perhaps this was all a wild goose chase, a way for the Inspector to get out of Magadan, pretend to do his job, and torture some foreigners for sport.

For his part, the Inspector chattered on as usual, ignoring the disgruntled looks of his three companions and the broad hints Kenny threw out, that they were wasting time on this expedition. He pointed out the hoof marks of a band of reindeer that had crossed their trail, theorizing that the travelers in the Sno-Klaw had spent nights with relatives or at temporary camps already set up en route. He drew their attention to a few squirrels, a gyrfalcon, and two red-crowned cranes, great gangling, creaking things that started up from one of the boggy places.

'Doctir Kutznetsov, he tell you vary much about these animuls of Siberia,' Sokhalov said. 'His dotter too. Vary inturasting.'

'I know Alexy's ideas,' Kenny said rather shortly. 'He's a good field biologist. Just doesn't understand what we're trying to do here.'

In the back seat Lafe and Peter traded a glance. They had given faint hums and nods of accord to Kenny's unsolicited explanation of a new ecosystem developing in the clearcuts. Yes, good for the mice no doubt, which was good for the hawks and foxes. Lafe had opened his mouth to ask where the hawks would nest, but Peter saw and quickly asked how big the mice were and what they ate.

'And I'm beginning to wonder,' Kenny went on, 'what *we* are doing out here' – he glanced at his watch – 'at one o'clock in the afternoon. It'll take us two hours or more to get back, going all out, from right here.'

'Ah, I know.' Sokhalov sighed, lifted his elbows and tightened his biceps. 'I am frostrated too. Detectif wark is too frostrating.'

'I mean, we *see* they came from the east, probably just below the Kolyma.'

'Yas. Bot so far. Vary strange.'

Sokhalov yawned and crossed his arms again, gazing out the half-open window. It was colder in the open tundra, because of the wind, and the Sno-Klaw's track was more fragmented. They were simply driving in the same general direction, picking up every fifty meters or so an indentation of the cleats or a vague double furrow in a snowy patch.

'We've got to get back.' Kenny spoke authoritatively. 'Just about enough fuel left, without dipping into the emergency reserve.' He glanced aside at the inspector. 'We don't want to travel in the dark.'

Sokhalov sighed and made a soft, rapid kissing sound. 'Yas,' he said. 'Is true.' Then he leaned forward, peering intently at the horizon ahead. 'Okay! Whot sey we go to this place, high place?' He gestured vigorously, a few points to the left.

'Look, Inspector . . .'

'Last place! Okay? Small mountin, bot no top. Mebe one, two kilometers? Gud place to see from.'

Kenny's jaw tightened. 'Whatever we see, that's it. We've got to get back. One quick look, and we are gone, fella.'

'Thenk you,' the Inspector said solemnly. 'My hups are not all gone yet.'

They drove in silence, Kenny gunning the GAZ between rough spots. There was no mountain really, only a more definite rise, like a great frozen ocean swell with a flattened top. The Sno-Klaw track angled up the rise in almost a straight line. They lost it twice, recovered with no special effort, followed it then over the crest and onto the plateau on top. The blizzard had left long windrows of light drift behind a few hillocks, had filled the occasional depression, but the plateau was largely bare to its rim, where the snow had piled deeply on the downslope.

'Well,' Kenny said brusquely, 'this is it.'

'Nice view,' Lafe said with undisguised irony.

My God, Peter thought, this must be the end of the world, and if so why all the fuss. *Barren, endless, desolate* . . . all the words he could think of failed to convey the feeling he experienced. The idea that people could live here was preposterous. He was certain, suddenly, that Satchi Kutznetsova was a frozen corpse, or possibly less. Scattered bones, picked over by ravens after the bear was through. He wanted only to leave this place. Now. 'Okay,' he said. 'Back we go.'

Kenny had already begun to brake and turn, but Sokhalov reached out and grasped the steering wheel. 'Ah, excuse,' he said. 'Bot whar is track? Whar go?'

Kenny glared at him. 'Beg your pardon? I'm driving. The goddamned track is right . . .' He swerved to one side, rolled down his own window. The wind came from that side, a blast strong enough to whip the laces on the hood of Kenny's parka and make him squint. 'It's right here, we just saw it.'

'Dunt see now.'

'All right, we'll pick it up then. And that's it, Inspector. I want you to see that track, for your own satisfaction, and then *we're getting the hell out of here.*'

'Thenk you.'

Sokhalov sat meekly while Kenny, in a silent fury, ran on across the plateau for fifty meters, then a hundred. Peter kept his eyes perfunctorily out the window, but saw no tell-tale marks. Then they were at the opposite lip of the plateau. Kenny cursed and turned to drive along that edge, instructing them to watch for any track in the band of snow drifted there. After another two hundred meters he uttered an oath even Peter, with his long experience with English profanity, had to admire, and wrenched the GAZ around to strike across the plateau on a second lap.

'Ples,' Sokhalov said. 'May I mek suggestun?'

Kenny braked to a stop, set his forearms on the steering wheel, and spoke to the Russian with soft, murderous politeness. 'Yes inspector. What *is* your suggestion, inspector?'

'Mebe go bek same wey, follow own track? Not distroy our evidence.'

'Yes. We wouldn't want to destroy *evidence*, would we? Not if it takes all fucking night. You—'

'Easy mates,' Peter said chattily. 'It's a point. Why not just wing back to where we dropped it? Pick up again and go a few yards, all right?'

'Oh fine.' Kenny jammed the GAZ into gear again. 'Oh fine.'

He drove wide open, slithering dangerously a time or two, back over his own track until they were at the point where they first entered the little plateau. Just beyond the unmistakeable double dent made by the Klaw when it crossed the lip, they found one fairly clear cleat track. Then nothing. They crawled along slowly and looked hard. They doubled back once, twice. Then Sokhalov cleared his throat and made a slight, comical gesture of walking two fingers along his thigh.

Kenny stopped the GAZ, threw open his door, and jumped out. The others followed silently. Peter dared not look at Lafe, or the insane hilarity building inside him would erupt. The American was a bright pink, with a jaw musculature now beautifully defined, and lunged along bent from the waist, scanning the ground at his feet. If he found a track, Peter imagined, he would rub Sokhalov's nose in it.

'Here!' Lafe called them. He had drifted to the left, onto a large patch of bare ground, its surface a pebbly scree. They had glanced at it before and gone around because it was not likely to bear an impression.

'Thank Christ,' Kenny said and broke into a jog.

They all hurried to Lafe's side, veering a bit because he warned them with a gesture away from a space in front of him. There, clearly visible in the earth, were two lateral gouges, perhaps six inches deep and six feet apart. The men stared, uncertain, for several seconds.

'Well, it's a track of some sort.' There was challenge in Kenny's tone, as well as impatience. 'It had to be them.'

'Not like anything we've seen, though,' Peter said. 'What the hell did they do here?'

'I see nothing on other side of this place,' Lafe offered, gesturing somewhat grandly at the perimeter of the bare patch.

Sokhalov had edged carefully nearer to the gouges, almost tiptoeing. He looked back and forth along the ground, as if trying to guess at the size of something invisible. Then he moved further away, opposite the rest of the group, and went down on hands and knees. They watched him, as men might watch a bird hunting for insects or nuts.

'Dedication,' Peter said, and emitted one tiny, stifled bubble of laughter. Then he remembered his feet, still freezing.

'Ah. Yas.'

They heard the Inspector's whisper. He had picked something up from the ground. A worm or curl of moss, something black and dangling. He got to his feet and came to them, mincing carefully as before. He reached Peter first and, chuckling, thrust the dark little strip directly under his nose.

Peter reared back a little, eyes crossing slightly. Gasoline. He recognized the half-circle of rubber, a piece of a gasket of some sort. Sokhalov passed eagerly to the others, Kenny last, holding up the fragment of gasket for each to smell.

'Yeah, all right,' Kenny said. 'So they had extra gas. I see that's the sealer gasket for a GI gas can, so . . . where's the can, but . . . I mean . . .' He sounded shaken.

Sokhalov continued to beam a delight beyond bounds. 'No,' he said. 'Track start here. Fill op petrol first, check avarything, tek off!' He held up his arms, as if about to dance.

Peter gazed at him. The bastard was something, really something. 'So,' he said, 'how did it get here?'

The Inspector waggled his eyebrows, mouth a wide O of glee, and extending one finger on each raised hand he began to rotate his wrists, faster and faster, and make a rhythmic shooshing sound, the sound of great metal blades whopping around and around and around.

CHAPTER SIXTEEN

They stopped the convoy of sleighs on a bench between two low ridges, where a stand of dwarf cedar provided cover. For two or perhaps three kilometers they had broken new trail, forking away from the main route, climbing out of a valley and then along and over the first of the ridges. Satchi threw back the lap robe and climbed out of the dog sled, listening intently to Kainivilu and the other men, Choti and Tatka. They had gathered beside one of the reindeer sleighs loaded with meat to discuss or argue about something.

They had been on the trail for nearly three hours, longer than usual, she guessed. She tried to help by leaving the sled and trotting along beside Kainivilu as he drove, but their pace hardly varied. Even the reindeer stumbled and labored. The mild spell, with its alternate melt and freeze, had made the snowfields lumpy and coarse, with here and there patches of bare earth.

Now snow was falling again, and the wind had stiffened and chilled. Satchi heard *mainicaican*, a word she had heard them use during the last blizzard, so she knew they were apprehensive about the weather. But they were also worried about something at the camp, which by their gestures she inferred was directly over the ridge, perhaps not far. Twice they looked at her, speculative and furtive, and their talk tailed off. The second time she stared back at them briefly, and then turned away in silence.

She kept a few paces apart, as a good Koryak woman would. In what she thought of as her last hours with these people, she had meant to keep her vow and cause them no more inconvenience. But nothing she did seemed to matter, in the face of such overwhelming tragedy. It was clear, leaving the camp, that Kainivilu had ordered the other women to pack up for a permanent move of some kind. This cargo of fresh meat would no doubt be their last delivery, which meant the arrangement with the hidden station was being abandoned. Satchi had witnessed them basting the *giegie* with fish paste, singing into its wooden head a long song – a farewell song surely. She also knew that she was herself more than a little responsible for the ceremony.

She told herself this tiny clan was a doomed anachronism, and with or without her they could not hope to endure much longer on the desolate tundra where their ancestors had lived. Kainivilu was *eyem*, a strong man, she had heard the women say. So he must have been, to have left the mines with their heated dormitories and dining halls and medical clinic, in order to risk living here on reindeer and salmon and the few baskets his womenfolk could sell. But it was a kind of madness. A fierce, unreasonable pride or some mindless superstition; in any case something unbending and final, that had cost the lives of his children.

He ought to have been crushed, and yet he was not. He seemed calmer, more at ease than the other two, who were remonstrating with him vigorously. A time or two he even smiled. From what she could gather – mainly from Tatka, who said over and over, *You go! You go!* – they wanted Kainivilu to take her away, setting out immediately for one of the settlements nearer the coast, she supposed, while Tatka and Choti made the delivery and then returned to camp to get the women and children and Tolek.

She was sure now that the camp over the ridge was a criminal operation of some kind, involving probably armaments or drugs. It seemed preposterous, so far from the normal routes of commerce, but it had to be something of that nature. They had apparently relied on Kainivilu and his reindeer for transport and food, but were perhaps now fearful that he would betray them. Or that Satchi herself would reveal their secret, if she reached a station or settlement with a radio.

Yes, that was it. Surely they knew her identity by now. Surely the men in the GAZ had seen her that day, had noted her unusual parka, and of course also saw that she was aware of them. They would have their own radio, would be alerted that a search was under way. So they would be anxious to keep her from being found. Perhaps they had pressured Kainivilu to hold her captive, which would explain his evasiveness and silence. Perhaps more. Perhaps . . .

She knew a chill of fear beside her curiosity. If this camp was in fact a hideout for gangsters, they would be capable of more. Perhaps they had even offered Kainivilu a prize if he got rid of this unwelcome intruder. Or switched to threats if he failed to react. These speculations made her dizzy. They were either ridiculous or terrifying. Why *had* this *eyem*, this strong man, brought her to his camp, kept her there for weeks, knowing his employers wished for secrecy?

She sneaked another look at the men, who had apparently reached a decision. Kainivilu had gone to the dog sled and was rummaging through a basket. He found something and called to Tatka, who was turning around one of the meat-laden reindeer sleighs. The old man grumbled, but handed his rein to Choti and shuffled to Kainivilu, who passed him a small packet which Satchi recognized with a shock. It was the Makarov. Kainivilu had wrapped it in a soft bag of fawn skin and tried to give it to her before they left the camp. She had refused, offering it as a gift. The gun was the only thing of value she had, once her boots were burned.

They were coming toward her, two dark humps in the pale afternoon light, their faces hidden in the shadow of their fur hoods. For the merest fraction of a second she wondered if they were going to kill her. It was the obvious solution to the trouble she had brought them. But she did not move or flinch; she did not even regard them. She felt quite calm, and listened when Kainivilu spoke.

'You stay,' he said. 'Tatka too. We take them the meat and come back, and then you will go home.'

She could see his eyes now, black and steady, unblinking. 'What if they do not let you come back?' She smiled as she had seen him smile, with a bland, mad cheer. 'They are bad men.'

Kainivilu laughed. 'No. Not so bad, I think. Only talk, maybe one hour. If we do not come, then go back with Tatka to the others. Wait there.'

He reached out then and took her arm. She could feel his grip even through the glove and thick down of her parka. 'You are not Woman-who-sleeps any more,' he said. 'They will not kill you. Not so bad. But they do not want you to leave.'

She stared at him, head high. 'But you. You do.'

He said nothing. For just a moment the grip on her arm increased, and then he took his hand away slowly.

'What is this gun for?'

'For a signal. If snow comes very hard and we cannot find you.'

He had looked away and she knew he was lying. They were in some serious danger, she was now sure. Kainivilu and Choti had brought one rifle between them, leaving the other with Tolek at the home camp. There would be at least six men in the camp over the ridge. They would have automatic rifles and pistols, as well as the GAZ.

'You must go home.'

She waited. She had not taken her eyes from his.

'Kainivilu has no home. He would say *ey yeti*, stay here, but he is not any place now. So I take you home, to your father. That is all.'

He said something quickly to Tatka, who pulled at her sleeve, cajoling with his gap-toothed leer. She did not move. She had caught a vibration under Kainivilu's terse statements, had heard for the first time a pulse of feeling, faint yet so deep and powerful that it shocked her through and through, as if the earth had moved. The upheaval in her heart was sudden, and beyond her understanding.

'*Hik anana!*' It was an old expression her mother had used, to register alarm at a pot boiling over or amazement at the first snow on the ground; but Satchi wailed it with a new, sharper agony. She reached out and took Kainivilu's arm in her own grip. It was hard and resistant, but she wrenched back and forth until he gave, staggered slightly. 'No! *Keinimtilla*, you say! Bear-people! Well, this is a trap! A trap!'

He pulled away suddenly, she did not know how. Tatka was between them, holding on to her sleeve again. They were both talking to her, but she understood only a little; Kainivilu, moving away, was telling her to sit under the sealhides on the sled for it would be cold; Tatka said something about the dogs. She was crying again, hating herself for it but unable to stop. She watched Kainivilu and Choti take up quirts and line out the cargo sleighs in tandem. With quick strokes and a guttural command or two they hurried the reindeer teams into a gradual climb up the flank of the ridge. The snow was still light, so she could see them clearly. They did not look back.

Tatka tried once more to urge her toward the sled, but she turned away from him deliberately and would not answer. He mumbled for a while about food and sleep, the coming cold, and then uttered a croak of disgust and shuffled away. In a moment she heard him going through the baskets lashed to the sled; then the dogs whined, and began to snap and gnaw at the half-frozen chunks of salmon the old man was tossing to them, one by one.

Her tears were only a skim of ice on her eyelashes when she turned back. Kainivilu and Choti and the sleighs were just crossing the crest of the bare ridge, gray but definite shadows in the thin veil of falling snow. Tatka had turned his back to her, fumbling after the split carcasses in the basket he dragged between his legs. She watched the sleighs drop out of sight behind the ridge, and when they did so she moved, not toward the sled but angling in the direction of the nearest of the cedars, not more than fifteen meters away.

Tatka tossed another salmon, but it broke apart and fell short. The dogs were in harness, and when two of them lunged at once for the pieces, they jerked another dog off its feet and in an instant the whole team was snarling and floundering. Tatka screamed hoarsely at them, took from his belt a leather-wrapped club and swung it vigorously into the melée. Satchi moved faster, her feet lifting smartly, cleanly, quietly. She was into the trees then, but did not turn her head when Tatka passed from her field of view.

She wove from one squat, shaggy tree to the next, a path designed to deepen and broaden the screen between herself and the uproar behind. She was not thinking, only gliding through the trees, stitching a swift pattern which took its form from a vision she had, remarkably clear, of the two men driving their sleighs. She saw them from above, slanting down on the other side of the ridge toward the long, empty valley where the main trail ran. That trail would hug the base of the ridge, and the camp would be located there.

The yapping of the dogs was fainter now, and she began to step more directly uphill. At the point where the bench connected the two ridges the cedars had overgrown both and ran in a thin scatter along their crests. She would go to the last tree at the very top, she would verify the camp, she would watch the sleighs and their drivers approach. She felt light, not at all tired, a feather unreachable by the cold. Quikinnaku's daughter, the Raven's child. There would be daylight for perhaps another two hours, and she would watch over Kainivilu.

It was a long time before she heard Tatka's shout, and it was audible only because she had stopped a moment to rub away the snow crust formed around the furred edge of her hood. He might follow her trail a little way, but he could not risk leaving the dogs for more than a few minutes. She would very soon be at the top and probably he could not see her even then. She felt a brief, guilty regret, for the old man was surely upset, but she knew he would do nothing foolish. He would simply wait, talking or singing to himself.

There was a lull in the snowfall, though more clouds were hurrying in from the northeastern horizon. Her strange mood, light and thoughtless, was also passing, and what came to her now was, like those clouds, dark and swift and without definition. There was fear in this new feeling, but also an excitement. When she came over the top of the ridge and made her way through the last of the cedars, stunted and bent by the snowdrift around and over them, she saw the distant dots below her, the sleighs and men, and in that instant understood.

She was afraid of what she was becoming, of this uncontrollable emotion emerging inside her. In its simplest, inarticulate form that passion had impelled her up this slope, as if her watchfulness, her presence, could protect Kainivilu. That was absurd, idiotic even. She could already see, a little further off, the camp, and the sleighs would be there in a few minutes. She could make out four inflatable tents and some vehicles, the GAZ surely but also something much bigger, perhaps a DT-35, and another machine with an odd beak, probably mounted on runners. There was nothing she could do here but watch.

It seemed to her now that this feeling had been with her all along. From the moment she threw open the door to the station and let him in, delirious with relief that he was not the bear – or at least the same bear, for she remembered how dirty and animal-like all three of them looked to her then. Ever since, as she had struggled to help, with her pitiful aspirin and plastic boots and a book, she had been intrigued and exasperated by Kainivilu's stoicism, his silence, his smiles as unpredictable as sun or storm.

She had fought with herself every waking hour over the last three days, trying to stand apart from Yina's death, from her lightning intuition about Pipik, from the haunting awareness of her mother's presence, which had been with her since she ate the mushrooms; she was still trying, in short, to recover the self she had been before that bear reared up out of the night. She thought she was succeeding; she managed to smile and laugh through her tears when she embraced Itu and Navakut for the last time and gave them the battered, stained, cheap book in a language they would never know. She bore up even under Pipik's wails, and finally placated the old woman with the last of the aspirin. But she knew now the heart of her turmoil lay deeper than rage and frustration, or fear or grief or compassion.

She noticed for the first time, just below the camp, an aberration in the valley's floor. A series of linear shadows, which resolved themselves finally into what appeared to be three rectangular piles of something, like huge bricks. She was too far away to make out what they might be, but their size was startling. The whole station was much larger than she had expected. Two of the tents looked big enough to house several men. A stack of fuel drums rose almost as high as the tents. Next to that was a shed open on one side, perhaps a repair shop.

The sleighs were almost there now. Two dots moved out from one of the tents. Electric lights glimmered, so there had to be a generator. Satchi rocked forward onto her toes, breathing lightly. She could hear nothing but the wind. In snowy weather the tundra deadened all sound except for this whispering and whistling and howling directly in one's ear. She wanted to hear the voices; she would be able to tell from their accents and pauses what they were thinking; she could caution her friends . . . She strained to decipher, through the muttering, hissing white air, what the dark dots were saying. She thought she heard a distant, mad laughter.

Another figure emerged from a tent. They all gathered about the sleighs, which then moved slowly to a spot directly in front of one of the large tents. She guessed this was the kitchen and dining area, for the dots began to stream in and out like ants, unloading the cargo, In a few minutes the job was done. Two people entered a smaller tent, and one figure remained outside with the teams and sleds. That should be Choti, but the stance was wrong.

So far she had seen nothing amiss. The laughter on the wind was no doubt her imagination. For several minutes she waited, shifting her position only a little, to avoid cramping. A dot came out of the repair shed and crawled to the large tent where the others had gone. Nothing more for another minute or two, and then the snow began to whirl down again. Almost immediately the camp faded until she could see nothing but the outline of the big tents. She blinked and looked away to clear her vision, and when she looked back everything was gone into the rapid, silent cascade of white.

This white was already darkened, however, by the shadow of night. She was suddenly aware of the cold, an aching numbness in her cheeks and fingers. She stood up, undecided, and began to chafe her mittens together. At that moment she heard the faint sound of a motor behind her. It seemed to come from the tree-covered side of the ridge, where she had climbed to reach this spot. Fear struck her like a gale. She began to run toward the sound, laboring a few steps until she had crossed over the crest again, then plunging down through the cedars in great, shambling leaps. On this side the sound was louder, and she could tell it came from the lower end of the bench, where she had left Tatka.

She was flying, crashing, flying again over the coarse snow, kicking it up in sheets like broken glass. It seemed to her that the engine noise grew fainter, was barely audible over the yelping of dogs. Hope surged through her. Perhaps she could reach Tatka in time! She fell and rolled, got up and kept running. Finally the trees thinned so she could run more directly, and she saw the sled as she had left it, the dogs jumping and being jerked back by their traces. And then, suddenly, there was another man with Tatka, looking at her, and it was too late to think of hiding.

She staggered to a walk, seeing at last the big Yamaha cabbed snomo pulled up just on the other side of their sled. It had been painted in winter camouflage colors, white with a few patches of gray and yellow. There was an emblem on the door, which gave her heart a sudden, dizzying bounce. The sea kayak with crossed harpoons above and reindeer horns below – the Office of Indigenous Affairs, an agency of the Bureau of Resource Development, which also oversaw her father's research. What did it mean? The snomo must have come from the camp over the ridge, for it was not an overland vehicle . . .

'Come here,' the man called. He wore a new army parka over old, greasy woolen trousers stuffed into his reindeer-hide boots. His gloves were of nylon, new and expensive. He was part something, Yakut she thought, because of his wisp of beard. 'Who are you? You know Russian?'

He was peering at her intently, beginning to grin. Instinctively she had hunched herself deeper into her parka. She was again conscious of her coat. Though filthy, it was still of nylon and down, with fur trim only on the hood and cuffs. She could see recognition dawning in the man's face, along with suppressed glee. She stopped, perhaps a dozen paces from him.

'Aiya! Who can this be? The little Magadan sweetheart? Da?' He came toward her, reaching, and she stepped back.

'Oh, it is! It's our lost girl!' He stopped, spread his arms wide to show the size of his excitement. 'Kutznetsova, eh? Ha! Everybody looking for you! Your father, your American boy, the whole Bureau, hey.' The man giggled to himself and took another step. 'Big star now, little girl. Big star, eh? Come on, now, I'm here for you . . . God help us, what luck!'

'Stay where you are!' she called out sharply.

She was watching Tatka, who had quieted the dogs but not himself. He edged back and forth like a crab, as if probing a rock face for some crevice in which to hide. His face was fixed in an expression of desperate anguish.

'We are already on our way home. You can contact your superiors and inform them if you like.' Satchi stared at the man, unsmiling. 'Or you can accompany us. These people need assistance. You are from OIA, yes?'

For a moment the man was too surprised to speak. No one moved and the snow whirled down around them, a light shawl already formed now on Satchi's shoulders. Then he laughed explosively, slapped his body with his gloves.

'*Tchort*! Ha! What are you saying? You can't go with this old walrus, you are crazy, you are coming with me. A place close by, ten minutes, very nice. Cognac, good food – plenty of everything. Then—'

He had stepped forward quickly to take her arm but she jerked it free and dodged away. He came after, still grinning, speaking louder in a tone of fierce delight.

'Whoo! What's this? Little *nymylin* fox with sharp teeth, eh? Snow crazy! Ai, little girl, it's time to come home now . . . good girl . . .' He was more agile than she expected, and retreating without looking she caught her heel on a clump of packed snow and fell on her back. He was on her immediately, pinning her hands at her sides, his face thrust near, a handspan away, so that she could smell his breath of tobacco and sour meat. 'You're worth plenty, sweet one, you know? On your way home, eh? That fucking lying Bear Ear. He wanted it but I'm going to get it, eh? Be a nice pussy. So I don't have to—'

He shifted his weight to straddle her, lifting his head and his leg, and she twisted under him and screamed something but never remembered what because of the tremendous smacking sound and the way he flopped away from her instantly. She pushed herself up on one elbow, dazed, and saw Tatka crouched just two or three steps away, the Makarov clutched in both hands and pointing at her.

'No,' she mouthed breathlessly, shaking her head. He stared at her and then shook his head too and began to moan. As in a perverse and mad dream, she was conscious of the snow whirling silently, swiftly down over them. She made a gesture then and Tatka lowered the gun. Looking the other way she saw the man from the Bureau, lying face down. His arms and one leg were tensing sporadically, as if he were waking up. But the back of his parka hood was badly torn, the exposed insulation spattered with wet, startling red, and the snow around the hood was rapidly staining a darker shade of the same color.

She rolled to one side, got to her knees, head down, and gagged for several moments, trying to control her breathing. She heard Tatka behind her, shuffling in the snow; a clink of metal, a rustle of clothing, then an odd sound, like a wet sack opened suddenly. She could not think, was conscious only of a hopeless, bone-deep yearning to go back before this last minute of her life, to change her mind, say different words, avoid this horror. But when she finally looked again, she saw Tatka bent over cleaning his knife in the snow, the man perfectly still now, the stain under him huge and brighter red. Tatka had cut his throat.

This time she threw up, quickly and violently, and when she was done she made her way back to the sled, which seemed a very long way. Tatka hung at her sleeve and she dragged him with her. He looked so worried and confused that she embraced him. He felt as dry and light as a child, and mumbled and crooned in her arms. They were both cold, and since the dogs had quieted, they huddled together in the sled under the sealskins.

She would not act, would not speak, would not think. She had been hurled, not out of, but into a terrifying present. She would be here, motionless, looking out from a small aperture in her blanket cover through the whirling snow, for light years. Until her life began again. Until Kainivilu came back.

CHAPTER SEVENTEEN

They came into the camp through the light snowfall, so no one saw them until they were very near the shed where the tools were kept and repairs done, where the generator was running. It was clear the Brick-Heads were preparing to make some expansion of the camp. A big GAZ and its trailer were drawn up by the shed, a cargo of steel beams and struts already partly unloaded beside a very large sled under construction. The yard was braided and crossed with ruts churned by the cleated machines, the tractors and the device that cut the frozen earth. Just beyond this area short metal posts had been driven to string an electric cable in a circle fifty meters across. Lanterns in red glass hung from the cable. They were not switched on now, but Kainivilu guessed they would mark a place for the helicopter to land in darkness or bad weather.

A man inside the repair shed saw them and shouted, so by the time they had driven the nervous reindeer to the commissary tent Sergei and the other Cossack with the flat face had come to meet them. Before the tent flap dropped they saw other men, more than usual, some eating and others smoking and talking in chairs around the heater.

'Hey, Bear Ear, what you doing here?'

Sergei called himself The Hun. He was thick, the color of tallow, with a straggly beard and sleepy eyes. He ran the kitchen and storehouse, and drove the GAZ on occasional trips to the post at Dukat. He wore his usual garb, old military winter gear and a red scarf and a pistol.

Kainivilu and Choti pulled up the reindeer and kept them snug with neck halters. 'Meat,' Kainivilu said. 'Good meat.'

'You come pretty late. Slip in here so quiet!' Sergei was smiling, his eyes moving over the reindeer, the sacks of meat lashed on the sled, the two herders. 'But you were going to come next week. Next week, you understand? Still got meat. Plenty meat.'

'Storm,' Kainivilu said. 'Cold.'

'Pah! Shit, a little one. You *nymyl'us* can fart a bigger storm than this one.' Sergei looked at Flat-Face, who grunted a laugh. The man had come out of the repair shed to join the others, and he laughed too.

Kainivilu smiled mechanically. He did all the talking on their trips to this camp. He pretended to know very little Russian, which had allowed him to learn a number of things from the conversations around him. Sergei spoke a few words of the *nymyl'u* tongue to supplement the pidgin he had learned from the Tungus and Yakut, and he savored his role as translator and expert in the ways of the simple aborigines. Kainivilu knew this type. Most of his bosses in the mines had been the same. Still, the Hun was no fool, and a few times he tried a trick to see if Kainivilu was indeed as ignorant of Russian as he seemed.

'Anyway, what now? What you doing, old Bear Ear? You want unload? Want money?' Sergei cuffed Kainivilu on the shoulder with another bark of laughter. Kainivilu kept his smile, but his eyes were empty. Choti stood by the reindeer, motionless.

'The boss – *eyem* – want to talk. Doktor Nikki, Okay? Want to know about that little *pizda* you keep for us. How is she, eh? Tight? Slick like a little calf? Pretty good for an old *hooy* like you, eh!'

The Russians laughed, stepping back from the sled. Kainivilu nodded, smiled wider, a parody of Tolek. He would be expected to know these words. With his raised forearm he made the universal gesture for an erection.

'Hey *yeti*! Can still lay some pipe, eh?' Sergei and Flat-Face and the other man grinned at Kainivilu. 'I bet the old *muzjik* could. Anyway, take him and the young bull there and unload the stuff. Hang it with the rest.' Sergei gestured for them to go with Flat-Face. 'Come back, get tea, we talk. Okay? Talk Doktor Nikki. Hey, how your boy? Your little guy? Medicine good?'

'Good,' Kainivilu said. He was already moving away, turning the reindeer after Choti toward the rear of the big kitchen tent.

Choti spoke softly, as if giving commands to the animals. 'What now? What do they want to talk for? They don't need us, or any meat.'

As if commenting on a broken harness or the weather, Kainivilu said, 'They only care about the little black bird. We have to tell them everything is all right. We don't care, we will say, but she is a bother, so we would like some more dollars.' He put a slight emphasis on this last word.

'Eh? They understand that much, these *muzjiki* with dirty behinds.' Flat Face leered at them. He and the repairman were a pace or two behind and to one side, ostensibly directing the herders, though they knew the way well enough.

Dollirs. An American word, universally used. He and Choti would go along, pretend that they cared only about the money. While the Brick-Heads pretended that they only wanted to be left alone, with a little fresh meat now and then. But it was clear that things were changing rapidly. It would not be possible to hide so much activity for very long. The bricks – each as long as a man on two sides and half as deep – were stacked into two huger versions of themselves, now nearing the size of warehouses. The great steel sled under construction, Kainivilu guessed, would soon begin hauling them away down the frozen river. And when that happened, there would be no possibility of secrecy. And so, he assumed, no need to worry about Satchi Kutznetsova. Then what would the Big Eater have them do? Take her back? Abandon her?

Unloading the quartered carcasses into the pantry, he and Choti exchanged a few words more of such speculation, but mostly he listened to Flat Face and the other man, whom he had not seen before. The grease on the man's clothes marked him as a mechanic, and his Russian was profane, salted with Moscow idioms. He was complaining about having to learn the English alphabet in order to follow instructions on the computer for the Little Elephant, and about how that American bastard made ridiculous requirements for its servicing. The thing was wonderful when it worked but it kept breaking down. And then you couldn't go anywhere, and the movies they sent in here were all shit. Sometimes not even subtitles. He felt like quitting, some days. That would be the last job you ever quit, Flat Face said. Or the last but one, if you count feeding the foxes for a couple of days.

The mechanic said nothing for a moment, watching Choti heave a hindquarter onto a hook. Then he laughed, but without enthusiasm. Ah, come on. They wouldn't. And now Flat Face laughed, low and quick. What did you think? What are they paying triple salary for? You don't fuck with this guy, man. Don't let anybody hear you talk about quitting. You stay until the job is done, and it's done when Malenky says it's done. The two Russians looked at each other and then the mechanic went on. All right, sorry. I just mean this place gets on the nerves. But what about these guys. Christ, they look like apes. What's the deal with them, they seem to come and go when they want.

They're too fucking dumb to leave this country. They've lived here ten thousand years and don't know anything else. No, I mean why keep them around, why encourage them, they'll stick around and beg to lick pot like dogs. If the idea is to keep the lid on – Careful, the old guy understands a few words, and he may be old, but I wouldn't call him any names. Anyway, they have their uses, I can tell you. Yeah, what does that mean? The mechanic was watching him closely, and Kainivilu appeared to notice this and beamed his empty, mechanical smile.

That's another thing not to talk about. Ah, the fucking mystery man today, aren't you. You think I'm a little green bull, just got here and don't know what's going on. Didn't say what you know or don't know. Just said keep it to yourself. So we don't talk about the little piece of chocolate cake worth what is it now, ten thousand? What are they giving these Yakut rag-asses, a couple hundred? They're not Yakut, they're—

Flat Face stopped because Sergei had poked his head through the open double door of the pantry, and the herders had hung up the last of the meat. 'All right, good, *eh yeti*! Come now, talk, come 'long. You lazy pricks can go back in the commissary and warm up. Better close up the shop before dark, though. Snowing a little harder.'

Kainivilu and Choti appeared confused briefly, but moved after Sergei when he gestured rudely. 'I didn't get most of that,' Choti muttered. 'The new one doesn't like it here and calls us dogs?'

'Never mind. Keep quiet. That's all they really want.'

'You, big bull, go in get warm, get some tea.' They were back at the front of the commissary tent and Sergei pulled at Choti's sleeve, indicating he should go inside where the men were gathered around the heater. 'Old Bear Ear and I go talk to the Doktor, eh?' He took the halters to both reindeer from the herders and called out to one of the men inside, who soon emerged, not looking pleased and still struggling into his coat.

Choti shuffled a half-step away, watching the man. 'What is this?' He glanced at Kainivilu. 'We should not be separated. The rifle is in the sled.'

'Do what they say. There are too many of them anyway. They have to let us go pretty soon, before dark.'

'It's all right. *Harashaw*! *Tikina tanyita*'. Good, no problem. This man take care of your stock and sleds. Rest up.' Sergei handed the halters to his subordinate, shoved Choti lightly toward the tent entrance, and took Kainivilu by the arm, leaning a little to steer him away toward the office and dormitory tents. Exactly, Kainivilu thought, as if they were reindeer too.

He went with the Hun, who kept a hand on his arm until they were at the door of the most elegant of the tents. It was in fact a door, made of some light, stiff material and set into an airlock. This was the tent for the little *eyem* here, Doktor Nikolai, and also the office with the radio and books and papers. He had been here once before, right after he had told them about bringing Satchi to his camp. Of course he did not call her that. A woman, he had said. A half-breed from a weather station. They took her because she was sick and had been attacked by a bear and had begged them. He had mimed all this, with very few words.

He was glad now that he had thought up this plan. Taking Satchi and then telling the Brick-Heads before they found out. He knew they would find out anyway, and he could tell by their reaction – and by what he overheard – that he had scared them. Others would come looking for the woman – she was important and was a rare woman, which he had seen himself – and might find the camp, see their pile of bricks. The Brick-Heads were very upset, but began to treat him with a new wariness, a kind of respect.

'*Zdrasstye*, Bear Ear. How are you?'

Doktor Nikolai was waiting for him, and the two other men in the room also. He knew they had been talking about him. He put on again the empty, unvarying smile. '*Harashaw, Doktir*.' It was too warm in the tent, as usual, and he loosened his parka, aware and pleased that he was releasing odor as well.

Doktor Nikolai seemed very young to Kainivilu, far too young to be an *eyem*. He was small and thin, and so was his smile. He had a narrow, sharp black beard and intense, unblinking eyes. One of the small computers that folded up was before him, surrounded by papers and some light canvas bags containing, Kainivilu knew, samples of dirt from the bricks.

He had not seen the other two men before. One was Russian, and even younger than the Doktor, a slender sort who looked as if he had never worked. The other was surely an American. His boots were white and new, made of plastic, and he grinned and nodded at Kainivilu and raised one hand, palm out. Kainivilu had seen this greeting in American movies that were shown to the mine crews. It was reserved for the dark ones with feathers bound to their heads, who looked like starving *nymyl'u*. All of these men were in shirt sleeves, and had been drinking coffee.

'And your little boy? Dina, is it? The medicine helped?'

Kainivilu kept smiling and nodded. Doktor Nikolai indicated with his hand a height, and patted an imaginary head. 'Good? All right?'

'Good.'

'Ah, I am glad for you. Now, Bear Ear, these are my friends, from Magadan and America. They are very interested in our work and the young lady, you know. The—' He looked at Sergei, who stepped forward with arms cocked, as if to lift something.

'*Navili. Tanitin, eh yeti.*' Sergei spoke loudly, eyes raised to the curved ceiling of the tent, as if he were preaching. He added the phrase for Russian bread and a slang Yakut word for wife.

Politely Kainivilu nodded again and made his smile more thoughtful. He was aware of Doktor Nicolai watching him closely. 'Good,' he said. '*Navilineut* good.'

'Their name for her,' the Doktor said to the Russian man, who in turn said something to the American. The young man was there, Kainivilu understood, to translate for the American.

'We are glad. She is comfortable? Not sick?'

The question sounded hopeful to Kainivilu. He wrinkled his

brow. '*Yeni*,' Sergei said and panted and wiped his brow to indicate fever.

Kainivilu appeared to consider deeply. They waited. The American cleared his throat.

'Is she sick or not? The *navili*? We are worried about her.' Doktor Nicolai spoke more quickly, his cheeks reddening slightly. 'Tell Mr. Robert we saw Kutznetsova last week and she was healthy. But don't mention she was on foot and a good two kilometers from these people's camp. Just say we continue to monitor the risk. And we have alternative means of guaranteeing security.'

The young Russian began talking immediately to the American. Kainivilu even thought he understood a word or two; the tongue now sounded familiar to him, because he had listened to Satchi reading to the children for many days.

Doktor Nikolai went on, speaking to him directly and watching him with an intense concentration, like a hunter. 'You are good man, *eyem*, very good. You say, you do, yes? You take care of this woman? Keep her? All the time?'

Kainivilu nodded slowly, but this time he did not smile. '*Da*,' he said. 'Bring meat. Keep *navili*.'

'But she is good now? Not sick?'

Again Kainivilu frowned in apparent deep thought. He waited until the Doktor became pale again and his breathing changed. 'Camp. Bear Ear camp no good.'

'What? You want to move?'

There was alarm in the Doktor's voice, but the American had been talking and the young interpreter broke in now. 'He wants to know if we are sure we know where Kutznetsova is right now. Who is watching her. He says they need just a few more days to get the machine working perfectly. Time is very, very important. Much money is involved. So nothing must happen to her, and nobody should find her. It would cause the wrong kind of attention. In a week or so things will change. She can be brought home.'

'I know that. Does he think I'm an imbecile?' The Doktor smiled at the American. 'Now let me find out what this problem is with the herders. Then you can tell him the usual, that Kutznetsova is watched at all times, and their camp is a hundred and twenty – no, make it fifty-kilometers from the nearest civilization. And the whole search has moved up to the Yakut frontier anyway. Now, Bear Ear, what's the matter? You must stay where you are. No going, no talking, remember? Tell him again, Sergei, that it would be very bad – very bad for them – if anybody sees this woman, or talks to her. Or if anything happens to her. Just for a short time more.'

Sergei began a long tirade, mostly gibberish taken from Yakut, with emphatic and unmistakable gestures for silence and immobility. Kainivilu allowed his smile to ebb away. '*Nyet*,' he said finally. 'No good.'

They stared at him. The Doktor was agitated. 'I knew this was a mistake. It's absurd. An affair like this in the hands of these people—'

But before he could go on Kainivilu began an elaborate pantomime of his own. It was a technique he had perfected in the mines, and he was good at it. He played the part of the captive woman: he minced about and shuddered at something given as food, sighed pointedly, made exaggeratedly glum and angry faces, pretended to throw something, all the time gabbling silent complaints. The American and Sergei laughed. When he was finished Kainivilu shook his head. 'No good,' he said. 'Talk talk all time. This woman too much work.'

The American said something and laughed again.

'He said she is driving the poor man crazy. Offer him more money.'

'Or tell him to kick her out. Let her walk to Magadan.' Sergei looked about, sagacious and merry.

Doktor Nicolai glowered at him for a long moment. 'Hold your tongue.' He closed his eyes, like the swooning, suffering Christ. 'Tell him he must continue to take care of the girl, or there will be serious consequences. Remind him he is no longer under the protection of Indigenous Law – we are his only protection. Technically, he is already a criminal. And yes, mention there is a reward. He must go on doing as he has, and in a week or ten days they can expect . . . what shall we say . . .' He gave a short, exasperated sigh. 'Three hundred dollars.'

'Three!' Sergei looked injured. 'One would—'

'Tell him.'

Sergei launched another pidgin discourse, this one with some imprecations and threats to break bones mixed in with cajolery. Although he was grinning, his eyes conveyed to Kainivilu the clarity of the message. The *nymyl'u* were to stay where they were, not try to run away. He, the Hun, had a GAZ and many automatic rifles, and regularly he sent men out to make sure no one came into this region, and nobody from here left. Right now there was a man out on patrol, who might even follow them to make sure they took the right path. On the other hand if they kept the woman properly they could count on a big bonus. A hundred at least – in dollars – for simply doing what they were supposed to do anyway.

Kainivilu appeared thoughtful at the beginning of this speech, but allowed the smile to creep back gradually, until he was beaming and nodding at the end. 'Yes. Good. Dollirs good.'

The American laughed and spoke again.

'He says he likes this man. He doesn't waste words and he's a good actor. He thinks the situation is probably secure, if his camp is as remote as you say . . .'

'Reassure him,' the Doktor said shortly. 'This is the end of the earth. In this season, without a good team of dogs and plenty of experience, nobody would last more than a day or two on the tundra. She can't go anywhere.'

When the translator began, Doktor Nikolai turned to Kainivilu. 'Very good,' he said. 'We understand each other. Dollars, yes. You take care of *navili*. Keep tight. No go anywhere. We are friends.' He looked searchingly into Kainivilu's smiling face. 'Yes?'

'Good.' Abruptly Kainivilu stuck out his hand, his arm extended straight from the shoulder. 'Okay.'

The Doktor shook his hand swiftly. 'Yes, okay.'

'Okay!' The American shook his hand too, still grinning widely, and said something more, making a double waving motion with his two hands. Doktor Nikolai looked inquiringly at the interpreter.

'He says the Bear Ear is lucky. This woman is a celebrity, very beautiful.'

Kainivilu had recognized this motion, too, from the old movies. It was the sign men made to signal that a soft, round young woman was around. But he only looked puzzled and uneasy, saying to Sergei in his own tongue, 'We must go. The reindeer do not like to wait.' He thought to himself that this was indeed how Brick-Heads were; he had seen it in these movies. They had only four corners: money, machines, liquor and women.

Sergei had hooted and slapped his leg, had translated the herder's wish to tend to his team. Doktor Nikolai was amused. 'As you see, no need to be concerned,' he said to the American. 'A *very* simple people.'

The Doktor bid him goodby then, the American gave him five dollars, and Sergei pulled him outside again. On their way back to the Commissary the Hun kept his arm around Kainivilu's shoulders. 'You see, *muzjik*? You do right, you get dollars? It's all right that you don't know anything. It makes you dependable. Makes you valuable. Christ, it's getting late, and you and your brother are going all the way home tonight? Back to a stinking hole in the ground. Tshaa! Not for me. Time for that's over. We're seeing to it. The ones who know what's going on, Malenky's men. That big bastard will turn Magadan into a little Moscow. The dollars are going to roll in – oh, man! Vodka in drums, plenty of juicy young stuff . . . Do you have any fucking idea what's going to happen? What we're sitting on here? No of course you don't. What the hell. If you did . . . that's the one thing I worry about. If you knew what that little piece was actually worth, how much they . . . Ah, but you care about your fucking *reindeer*, right? Reindeer!' He laughed and cuffed Kainivilu's shoulder.

'Yes,' Kainivilu said. 'Reindeer. *Chavchuvens*. All time. *Yaranga* people.' He smiled his smile.

'The tents, right? *Yaranga*. You must belong with the old Khan. The people who live in tents. But the Khan's been dead for a thousand years. Now me, in a couple weeks I'm going to be a new Khan, living in the best hotel in Yakutsk, with the most expensive whore in town. People of the hotels, eh? Ha ha! What are we to you, Bear Ear? You tell me. Me, what am I? Not *chavchuvens*, but Siberian. What? What like?' Sergei had stopped, taken with this problem. He peered intently into Kainivilu's empty, smiling face. 'Talk. Say what like?'

Kainivilu waited a long moment before raising one hand. 'Dollirs,' he said, and moved his mitten in a straight line to the right and then stopped short. 'Traktor. GAZ.' A line next vertically down a few inches to another stopping point. 'Vodka. Wheesky. Smoke.' Then another horizontal line to the left, parallel to the first. 'Woman.' He dropped the mitten again to his side. 'Is all. Siberian.' He laughed a single, soft note.

Sergei gazed at him in wonderment, before exploding into guffaws. 'Shit! You bastard! You got it, all right. That's what makes it go in this place, eh? You're going to see plenty of it, too – even old Bear Ear. Ha! Maybe you're not so slow after all. Hey, where's Markov?' They had come around now to the commissary tent and could see that Choti was outside now working to keep the tired and restless reindeer from jerking the sleds.

The tent flap was thrown back and a head emerged. 'This *'jik* got his tea and wouldn't say a damned word. Might as well talk to an iron post. Went right back out and took his gear away from me. Fuck him, he wants to freeze.'

'More likely you made him take over so you could sit on your lazy ass. Anyway, wait 'til you hear my new definition of a Siberian. Got it from old Bear Ear, can you imagine? Say, is Zamya back yet?'

'No sign.'

'Shit! What the hell is he doing out there? This crazy weather we're having. He ought to have been back an hour ago.' Sergei frowned, listening . . .

'There are more of them,' Choti said to the reindeer, with a little sucking sound meant to soothe. 'I count six here. That's nine with blowhard here and the new man with Flat Face.'

Kainivilu moved to take one of the halters, laid his mitten on the reindeer's neck and began his own muttering. 'A foreigner with the big boss. And one man is still out, in a vehicle.'

'The little drift-jumper. It's the Yakut breed. I saw he was missing.'

'Shit. Could he have broken down?' Sergei looked up briefly. 'This fucking snow. All we need now is a *buran*. The weather's fucked this year.'

'No,' Kainivilu said. 'No *buran*. Small.'

'Yes, yes, I know. I said that, you remember? But . . . did you see anything coming in? See snomo? Hear?' Sergei cupped a glove at his ear. 'See man? Look like you, dark?'

Kainivilu shook his head. 'No. No man. We go. Day going.' He pointed at the sky, at the stamping reindeer. 'Goodbye.'

Sergei looked uncertain, started to say something. A man shouted from inside the tent to stop the jabber and close the flap.

'Move,' Kainivilu said. 'The Yakut might have picked up our track.' He tugged on the halter and Choti swung the second team into line. He called over his shoulder. 'Goodbye. Thank you. Very sorry.'

'Maybe we should take the GAZ and go look for him,' Sergei said. 'I think—'

'Well, think in here,' the man at the tent flap said. 'The guys are pissed off at me for letting in the draft on their card game.'

'Siberian.' Kainivilu turned to grin at the Hun even as he eased the sled into motion. 'Four part. All same. Brick-Head.' He was sure Sergei would not know the word, and indeed the man bellowed out his laughter again and gave him an obscene gesture, then a grand wave, before turning to shoulder through the tent and relate his new anecdote.

They were picking up speed, jogging beside the sleds, until they passed the last tent and were traveling beside the equipment yard, the fuel drums and silent machines, then the great rectangular piles of blocks. There they sprang onto the sleds and urged the animals on with a snap of the driving rein. He could hear Choti moan in impatience above the shoosh of runners and the dull impact of hooves. They would take the trail back to their home camp for a kilometer or two, and then diverge to begin a wide, gradual turn that would take them over the ridge to the wooded place where they had left the others. If their luck was good they would not encounter the Yakut, this Zamya. The snow was in their favor, would hide them and dull their sounds.

'You are crazy!' Choti called back to him after while. 'Calling him that to his face.'

Kainivilu could tell by his brother's voice that he was pleased all the same. 'Maybe never see them again,' he called back. 'Better tell them what they are.'

He was thinking that the Hun would be in great trouble when their flight was discovered. There would be no reward money, and the Hun would lose his reputation as a man experienced in dealing with the natives. He himself cared nothing for the reward. He laughed, squinting into the snow swirling out of the darkening air. No bear would be so stupid as to trade a fine woman, fine as *Kilu* herself, for a pile of bricks.

CHAPTER EIGHTEEN

'Strong tea. Something to help me think.' Inspector Sokhalov spoke loudly as he worked his way out of the heavy, black overcoat he had worn to the press conference. He was by himself in Kutznetsov's small, cluttered salon, because the Doctor had already passed into the kitchen, and remained there rattling about in search of glasses and a tin of biscuits.

They had not left together, nor had they any opportunity to converse in the drafty, drab Yeltsin Chamber of the Oblast Judiciary, where the conference was held. Both understood that they would rendezvous as soon as possible, to assess together the meaning of the alarming events they had just witnessed. Sokhalov had called the Doctor's flat from his car, parked two blocks away, and less than five minutes later was at his friend's door.

'What is thinking, in an asylum for the hopelessly insane?' Kutznetsov called back. 'That is what Siberia has become.' He appeared in the doorway, a tray balanced precariously in one hand, a small samovar dangling from the other. 'These cakes are stale.'

Sokhalov waved in dismissal, almost irritably, before relieving Kutznetsov of the tray, which he set on a low, carved table between two padded chairs. 'I know how you must feel. These are indeed terrible complications. We are sure of nothing now, except deception. It is all, you know, the madness of money.'

'A safe assumption, if Malenky and Dixie are involved.' Kutznetsov indicated one of the chairs. 'But what is the money from?'

'That is the question.' The Inspector sat down and took a raspberry biscuit, which he began to nibble. He watched Kutznetsov place the samovar next to the tray and bend to fill their glasses. 'A considerable sum, if they are willing to tell such lies.'

He waited and there was no sound but the trickle of hot, dark tea into a glass. He watched Kutznetsov's precise movements, angular and intent as those of a feeding crane. An excellent man, Sokhalov thought. Steady and alert, even when every relief, every support is knocked away. Being a young doctor in the death camps fifty years ago would no doubt teach one to be awake and competent, under any circumstances.

Kutznetsov handed across a glass and a spoon, then served himself and sat down in the other chair. 'Lies tell their own truth,' he said. 'We know, at least, that they are not looking for Satchi anymore. Perhaps they never did. Yet they are anxious as ever to convince everyone that they have made great progress.' He shoveled two spoonfuls of sugar into his tea and stirred. 'The swine.' He spoke almost abstractedly.

'But hauling the vehicle so far away, and then these new crimes, serious crimes . . .' Sokhalov paused and looked down into his glass. 'It is convenient how this murder and the talk of drugs makes a little native herder into a monster. A monster now in another Oblast. Most convenient.'

The Doctor stopped stirring, but did not remove his spoon from the glass. 'I thought you yourself mentioned the man to them. You knew he was a fugitive of some kind, without a valid registration.'

'Eh! Yes, I did, of course. But many people know about old Bear's Ear. He was not a serious fugitive. Only an eccentric who has steered off the trail for a long time. And anyway, half the Taigonos men don't have up-to-date cards. The Chukchi are even worse. But this cocaine business – that is an invention, I would swear to it.'

'They said nothing to you about it, beforehand.'

'Nothing.'

They were silent, thinking about the morning's unpleasant surprises. Malenky had arrived with Vladimir Krutko, the head of Internal Security for all the Northeastern provinces, who had flown in from Yakutsk on a Dixie Pacific private jet. Pendergast had the delicacy to come in a separate limousine ten seconds later; but it was obvious the three had already met to prepare statements.

He and the Doctor had thought the press conference was called merely to maintain the illusion that a serious investigation was ongoing. They expected a briefing on developments since the discovery of the Sno-Klaw in another province, and a photo session with Pendergast and Doctor Kutznetsov clasping hands, to seal another contribution to the search effort – this time twenty thousand dollars. Kutznetsov had nearly revolted, and it took Sokhalov most of an afternoon to convince him that collaboration was the best way to glean information.

Until he saw Krutko, the Inspector had even imagined – very briefly and wildly – that his superiors had changed their minds and he might be called upon to sketch his theory about the translocation of Satchi's vehicle. But it had already been made clear to him that his suggestions were troublesome, and the instant he saw the Internal Security chief he understood his position was even more precarious than he had thought.

That impression was reinforced by Malenky's cool, evasive manner, and by the size and excited buzzing of the hive of reporters. Some hint must have been leaked, he thought, as Malenky completed his introduction. And then Krutko had stepped forward and delivered a stunning series of announcements, delivered them in the flat, measured tone that best suits a sentence of doom, or its execution.

The discovery of traces of cocaine in the storage compartment of Satchi's Sno-Klaw. The gangster-style execution of a field agent of the Office of Indigenous Affairs, the body dumped in a remote sector along the border with Yakut, less than a hundred kilometers from where the Sno-Klaw was recovered. A prime suspect – a reindeer herder named Bear's Ear, operating without license and now believed to be the leader of the small band that fled with the young woman, Satchi Kutznetsova.

Sokhalov had watched his friend covertly from across the room during the three or four minutes it took to relate these catastrophic developments. The Doctor had been perfectly still, his narrow face not appreciably paler, but appearing shrunken slightly over his skull; he did not look down or away, but his eyes were seeing nothing but what was deep within himself.

Sokhalov had absorbed such details automatically, the habit of a detective; his own mind was staggering under the impact of what he was hearing. Everything they had conceived or speculated or imagined about Satchi's fate was annihilated or wrenched into another nightmare dimension. All the contingencies and possibilities they had elaborated were abruptly suspended.

'I do not know if we should worry more or less,' Sokhalov finally began, realizing that it was his place to do so. 'At least as far as your daughter is concerned. If she was harmed, if they . . . found her . . . you know . . . then they would report it and the whole affair would be over, for them. If they moved the vehicle – and of this I am quite sure – then that is probably all they found.'

Kutznetsov was watching each word as it came from the Inspector's mouth. At this pause he said, 'The agent?'

'I don't know. It is peculiar, one of Malenky's men in so desolate a corner of this region. He will say, of course, they were part of the search Dixie has financed. Perhaps they transported his body also? But two things are now clear. The government does not want – very much does not want – any search in the Kolyma country. And they want people to believe this whole business has to do with drugs. I suppose because then people would dismiss it and forget it.'

'Yes.' Kutznetsov put down his glass, got up abruptly, and walked to the small, leaded window that gave onto the street. He stood with his back to Sokhalov, looking out. After a while he said, 'They would have my Satchi an addict. Because now we are bored by petty death. Petty horror.'

Sokhalov could say nothing, for his throat had constricted painfully. A moment later Kutznetsov turned and came back to his chair and sat again. 'I am sorry,' he said. 'Forgive me. I am bitter, too used to bitterness, and there is not time for it. We have to find a new path. You say that your Bureau will not listen to you, about the helicopter for example.'

Sokhalov smiled mournfully. 'My chief points out that we took no photos, and now there has been a snowstorm. The gaskets from fuel cans he says are a coincidence – so much traffic on the tundra these days.' He laughed once, sharply. 'And I was reprimanded for going out of the Oblast, with foreign journalists, to retrieve evidence. It is quite possible, Alexy, that I will be removed from this investigation.'

'That would be very bad for us.'

'Yes it would.'

There was an uncomfortable pause, which they occupied by refilling their glasses. Sokhalov felt for the first time a chill at the center of his being.

'We must think fast, then. Put this strong tea to work.' Kutznetsov sent him a swift, thin smile. 'Now, I have some thoughts to tell you. I have obtained the satellite photographs I told you about before. After howling and begging for months.'

'Ah.' Sokhalov looked up with interest, saw something in his friend's face. 'Did you find anything?'

'These only include timber reserves, of course, but this category is stretched a great deal by Dixie, it appears. Especially in the Kolyma district, which as you know, I have been familiar with for many years. There are very few trees there, and none of any value.'

'Of course. But everyone stakes out as much as possible, worthless or not.'

'Granted. But they do not *work* there. And yet in one sector, south and a little west of the Sugoy river, there is what appears to be a small camp. I believe one of those blow-up tents, and the tracks from a carrier around it, but none reaching any great distance.'

'Sugoy. Of course, but . . . how far from the station where the bear attacked? K-17, was it not?' Sokhalov had leaned forward, cradling his glass in his hands. He was smiling his familiar smile, elfin and perverse.

'Less than a hundred-twenty kilometers.'

'Ah! So?'

'So of course I called. Air Defense first, since they supplied the photos. No, they said, nothing of theirs. Identified as a non-military, non-strategic structure. Dixie next. No, they claimed to know nothing of it. Energy and Resources, the same. I called Documents and Geophysical Survey, and they also had no idea. Documents suggested that since the satellite composites were assembled almost six months ago, the structure could be gone now, a temporary operation of some kind.'

Kutznetsov paused and the Inspector frowned, pursing his lips. 'Possible. Defense would lie, of course. Or some little research project, a mobile post for a climate study, perhaps?'

'I am especially curious because a month or two before this time

– not long after Satchi brought him home – I heard Kenny talking about an engineer who had come from America to do some kind of special research. It was this man who invented the laser-cutter Dixie uses to harvest the taiga. Kenny remarked that no one knew what the research was for, and that is how I learned the English word *hush-hush*. Which means there is secrecy of some kind.'

'Indeed,' Sokhalov interjected drily.

'And then a Colonel Speransky called me back, from Defense. An oversight, he said. The camp was actually a little temporary emplacement, something to do with mobile soil-testing units, in the service of bunker-building. It had been noted in the daily logs but was too short-lived to warrant identification on the main chart. In any case, there was no reason for concern. He expressed his sympathy for my situation, his belief that my daughter would be found soon, now that we knew she had fled to Yakut province.'

'Fled.' The Inspector wagged his head slowly. 'This is the new expression, we see. But *soil-testing*?' He rolled his eyes in amazement.

'I did not pursue the issue with the Colonel, who was at once fervently reassuring and exceedingly vague. I went back to the photos and examined them with a glass, and indeed not far from the tent there are two small spots, oddly rectangular, which may be excavations.'

'Excavations?' Sokhalov smiled broadly. 'Ah, my friend, one does not—'

'Excavate a soil sample with a backhoe. Exactly. A hand shovel is usually enough, a two-man drill at the most. Nor does one set off five hundred kilometers into a watershed and then make tests in only one site. So next I called Kenny – a difficult thing in itself, as we are not on good terms – and asked to review Dixie's aerial survey maps for active holdings in the whole Oblast. They take their own, you know, because they cannot estimate the yield of a tract from satellite information. I am empowered to verify such documents, of course, but usually make my reviews in the spring. I pretended that I was old and confused and under a great deal of stress, and wanted to complete this job—'

'Pretended?' The Inspector squinted genially.

'Yes, all right.' Kutznetsov smiled broadly for the first time.

'Let us say I exploited my role as the bereaved septuagenarian just enough to serve my purpose. I was given unlimited access to the company's record room and yesterday I searched thoroughly, quite thoroughly.' He was beaming now in a way Sokhalov had not imagined possible, almost like a boy.

'And?'

'And fortunately – I may say – I did not find the original, because it was not there. Every inch of Dixie's lease was in the file, but there was a peculiarity in the strip along the Sugoy. That one section, where the camp exists on the satellite version, is represented by a copy of a much older photo, taken at a slightly lower altitude, though similar enough that one may easily overlook the mismatch in the composite. But it is certainly a substitution, because I checked the dates on the negatives, kept in drawers below the file. This one – the only one, as far as I had time to check – was not only developed two years earlier, it was film of a different trademark.'

Sokhalov planted his glass on the table top with a smart rap and then was on his feet, crumbs cascading from the front of his old suit. 'Alexy, Alexy! You have made a fool of me! I am supposedly the investigator.' He threw out his arms, as if beginning to waltz. 'You old wolf! So simple a thing. Look at Dixie's maps. Ha!' He clapped his hands and peered at the Doctor. 'It is Dixie. We have known that in our hearts. But you have identified their track. And you know what it is, too, don't you? What they want, where the money will come from?'

'I have an idea,' Kutznetsov said, attempting a dry calm, but his smile would not be banished.

'You are going to say gold. I have thought it myself a dozen times, and dismissed it, because Dixie has never concerned itself with mineral resources, and so many have tried and failed – the South Africans, the Australians, the Canadians – but . . . that has to be it, doesn't it? Soil samples! Ho!'

'I have wondered for a year what is keeping them here. I know what they have cut, and what it is worth.' Kutznetsov had recovered his cool, rational tone. 'Everyone knows – has known for a century – that the whole Kolyma region is rich in gold-bearing sands. The richest deposit on earth.'

'Yes. Everyone knows, as you say. But everyone knows as well that it can be mined for only three months a year, and then with great difficulty.'

'Because the tundra is a frozen rock the other nine months. The blessing and curse of half of Russia, the permafrost. Perfect for traveling over, but impossible to dig into. But what if . . .' Kutznetsov had taken on the manner of a tutor coaching a bright student.

'The engineer from America, the *hush-hush* engineer.' Sokhalov was pacing in the room now. 'But how would – ah! Malenky, to be sure. An experiment of some kind, a new technique, test-mining on a small scale. It could all be done with a few men, two or three vehicles, one or two pieces of heavy equipment from Dixie. Indigenous Affairs – a perfect liaison. But surely the army – this Colonel for example – would be aware, would demand some payoff? And why *hush-hush*? Why are they afraid someone may find out about this camp, what it does?'

'We are speculating now,' Kutznetsov warned. 'I have wondered about this and do not see an answer. Kenny is not bright enough to help us find out. And of course it is of no importance, except in making clear why this search has been a sham, an evasion.'

Sokhalov stopped before the window, turned to regard the Doctor intently. 'I told you about the two reporters who went along to track the Sno-Klaw. Well, they have a mind for this sort of thing. They are hoping for a scandal involving Dixie, and they want very much to find Satchi. Not for the best reasons, I fear, but they mean no harm. We might ask them about Dixie, about what it has done elsewhere, if it has ever been involved in some kind of mining.'

'Reporters.' Kutznetsov shook his head. 'I would share nothing with them.'

'We do not have to share anything, and you know, Alexy, we have no other allies. The foreign press has some influence in this mountainous ordure we call a government. What if . . . it must have occurred to you . . . Satchi could be at this camp?'

The Inspector immediately regretted his question. He could see in Kutznetsov's face that his friend had not merely thought, but had agonized over this possibility.

'I must say—'

Outside a car door slammed, and then another. Sokhalov half turned to look out the window again, and then began to walk swiftly across the room, digging under his coat with both hands.

'What is it?' Kutznetsov stood up, staring at the Inspector with widening eyes.

Sokhalov had by this time stripped away the harness and holster containing an automatic pistol. He folded the loose straps around the leather case and shoved it into Kutznetsov's hands. 'Hide this, quickly. Some place, any place!' He began to remove his coat.

'What in Christ's name?' the Doctor whispered. He stalked toward the kitchen again, a sleepwalker. 'What is—'

'So they cannot shoot me for resisting arrest.' Sokhalov sat down again, carefully, on one of the padded chairs. 'Be so kind as to answer the door for me, Alexy. They do not want you. Don't worry. Call Teresa for me.'

'I will put it in the oven,' Kutznetsov mumbled, and stopped in the open doorway to the kitchen. 'Who is it? Whom did you see?'

'Bushuev. Narcotics police. A Captain and a bad man. Say nothing, except I came for tea. Hurry.'

Kutznetsov disappeared. A moment after that Sokhalov heard the oven door clank open. Then the doorbell rang.

CHAPTER NINETEEN

Two hours after Inspector Sokhalov was bundled into a police car and driven away from Kutznetsov's shabby little house, three other men sat in a new four-wheel drive crew cab Ford pickup, its fenders and side windows splattered with mud, at the far end of a half-mile long loading dock.

Ten minutes ago the driver had parked and left the vehicle, engine and heater running, and walked a hundred yards or so through a light, spinning snowfall to disappear into a small concrete-block weighing station. Two thickset men remained in the back seat, which was fitted with a cover of soft reindeer hide, and a younger man sat in the front, but turned to face the others, his legs drawn up awkwardly. The windows were fogged with moisture, but the men had no interest anyway in what was beside them, a looming ship and a row of flatcars strewn with loose bark and chunks of compacted snow.

'Tell him I misunderstood. I wasn't prepared for his friend Krutko, and the whole thing has been a strain. But we don't want anything to happen to the girl. We'd like to see caution.' Pendergast did not look directly at Amon, the interpreter, or at Malenky. 'And tell him we think it is very dangerous to confuse this matter with narcotics. Whether or not the investigation moves to another district.'

Amon nodded solemnly and after one deep breath in and out launched into translation. Twice Malenky interrupted with what sounded like objections or expressions of incredulity, before delivering his response in a rapid, continuous torrent. The Russian made faces of wry pain, smiled bravely, creased his brow with profound concern. Several times he reached out to tap his gloved fingers on Pendergast's forearm or knee, making the American flinch.

'He is sarry for misunderstanding. He as well wants gurl to get hum, safe and sound, at right time. Narcotics is vury good opshin, however, vury good. Because they make pipple and reparters understand why gurl goes away somewhere else. But we still have big problim, which is these bad herdmen, nomad herdmen, who take gurl, shoot man, run away. Now whot?'

'You ask him,' Pendergast said between clenched teeth, 'now whot. And what about that detective, Sokhalov. He was there today. He's almost talked our boy into believing that a helicopter hauled the goddamned vehicle to Yakut.'

Malenky heard the name and began again without waiting for a translation.

'No rison to worry. Inspector Sokhalov is being questioned. He is not availoobul now, he is now suspect.'

'Suspected? Of what?' Suddenly alert, Pendergast turned to Malenky.

'This is narcotics matter also.'

'Oh, well. That's just fucking *wonderful*.'

The young man paused. 'I say this?'

'Ah, shit, shit. Never mind.'

Pendergast stared straight ahead now, as if he could see through the windshield and past where the tracks ran down the wharf and vanished into the whirling snow, to the low, bare ridges surrounding the harbor and then beyond to the empty white wasteland that went on and on and on until it folded eventually under the frozen arctic sea. As if he could see into the heart of this mad absurdity. See how it was possible for one little Russian bloodsucker to completely fuck up a half-dozen major international corporations.

Anyway it was never a plan, that was the goddamned problem. Merely an emergency response when their native packers showed up with the girl, for God knew what superstitious motives of their own. Malenky paid them simply to keep her out of the way, until the operation was ready to take public. But something had gone wrong. Maybe the herders were trying a ransom scheme, or – the nightmare scenario – the girl had persuaded them she could get them a higher reward at the nearest trading center. At any rate the station crew had let the whole lot slip away, and now the cannon was loose.

Even before that, when a couple of his Cossacks had recovered the abandoned snowcat, Malenky hatched the cockamamie plan of borrowing an Army copter to haul it out of the area, presumably to divert the media vultures onto a false trail. The effect was exactly the reverse. Sokhalov had seen through the trick immediately, and talked Carraway into flying him in for a closer look – with two journalists along for the ride.

Pendergast was dumfounded, in the position of having to generate a lockjaw smile to cover his rage and fear when Carraway rushed into his office with what he called 'evidence of conspiracy.' It had taken all his skill and every ounce of his self-control to get the young ass cooled down, to gently suggest that Sokhalov was interested in advancing his own career and journalists would always go for the most sensational version of any set of facts.

Then the shooting of the agent boosted the whole affair to a far more dangerous order of magnitude. The herders had done it, he gathered, but to compound that difficulty by belatedly planting cocaine in the girl's vehicle and publicly implying a connection between these developments, at the same time involving the most ruthless and corrupt arm of the police apparatus – the colossal stupidity of such a scheme left him stunned and very near panic. And he couldn't rage at Malenky, whose winking and smiling and pouting drove him crazy, couldn't acknowledge that he knew anything about who had arranged this package or why. Just as Malenky would never admit that his recent investments in property and the construction business were to be explained by advance knowledge of an impending boom.

No doubt much of this mess could be blamed on their dance of deniability and mutual mistrust, trying to communicate through hints and hidden signs and reverse spins, which had then to be filtered through an interpreter and across cultural chasms. But now they were down to the last days, the biggest deal of his entire corporate life riding on sheer timing, and Pendergast had to concentrate on getting across the most basic conditions. Words of simple pressure.

'He does understand, I hope, that we have to have more time. If we get the resource leases tomorrow, then we need another week. Five days the absolute minimum.' Pendergast tried to keep his voice neutral, but the emotion in him squeezed out the last two words with emphasis.

There was another long interchange, Malenky throwing up his hands, frowning, hooting once with laughter. Amon looked solemn, delivering his summary.

'He understands so well you have concern over this. He wunts to help. He knows it is impartant. He warks hard on these leases. All rady now, all done, waiting just for ministry signatyor. One, two days.'

'Fine. Give him my compliments. But we need the time for our work on the project. *Time*. We have to achieve a certain volume, then finish our financial arrangements. A week. Ten days would be better.' Pendergast held up both hands, fingers spread, before Malenky. The gesture was one of arrested aggression. 'Otherwise, we can lose everything. Bye-bye Dixie. He can kiss off his plans for a Super Mall and new housing.'

This time Malenky listened intently, and after a pause he spoke evenly and directly, and made no faces.

'Vury impartant to finish expermint, yes, he is agreeing one hundred percint. But we dunt have control on this reindeer man and Kutznetsova gurl. Dunt even know where they are. And our pipple maybe find them, but they have guns and are shooting. This could be big problim. No secrit if somebody getting shot every day. Also, this Koryak, he knows about expermint. He brangs meat to this camp many times. Used to wark in mines also. *Zolotishk'* – gold miner.'

'I know that. I believe it was his idea, wasn't it, to employ this guy? Another terrific Malenky idea. No, strike that. Fuck it. Not the time for pointing any fingers. Anyway, if they're going to be found in the next few days, *he* has to find them. We just supplied another twenty thousand for more field agents. Get that across, Amon, for Christ's sake. He has to find them. And tell him again this whole narcotics business is *very* . . . unfortunate. Very risky. Everybody knows what the narc police are capable of. It might . . . it could . . . is there a Russian word for backfire?'

'Bed fire? Bad fire?'

'Never mind. Just tell him I don't like it. Tell him—'

But Malenky interrupted again, this time speaking rapidly and quietly and briefly. Amon swallowed, then translated. 'He is sarry but he must tell you bad news. Vury sarry but Narcotics Police say they have record. Many foreign pipple here brang drogs to Russian pipple. Foreign warkers.'

'Yes, yes, we know. Dixie tests all equipment operators and pilots. What the hell does—'

'He means pipple like Kinny, this young boyfran of Satchi Kutznetsova.'

For long seconds Pendergast did not move. Then he said, 'What is he saying? He's telling me . . . he wants us to pay off the narcs because one Dixie employee supplied this little tramp with her coke? Does he . . . Jesus H. Christ!' Pendergast had taken on color in his cheeks, and was suddenly short of breath. 'Blow the whole thing, the whole goddamned thing, for a chickenshit little—'

'*Ai! Nyet! Nitchyvo!*' Malenky was laughing, with gusto. He laid his gloved hand again on Pendergast's sleeve, and Pendergast jerked away before he could master himself. The Russian did not appear to notice, but began to talk through his laughter, his tone cheerful and placating.

Pendergast took a long, deep breath, closed his eyes, and blew it out again, *Whoosh*. He had not hit another man for years, but his instinct for self-preservation was wearing dangerously thin. He held himself still, concentrated on waiting without thinking anymore. Through the window he saw a black, heavy car appear amid the veils of falling snow. It had come around the corner of a warehouse and now moved along the tracks toward them.

'Is misunderstanding, nothing at all! Nothing that you are thanking. This is vury small, two-three gram, not impartant to police, no rison to worry, but this is maybe big problim if reparters know this. Mister Kinny is not ordinary warker. He is high warker in your company, boyfran of Kutznetsova gurl, he takes helicopter to look for her, yes?'

Pendergast was watching the black car, which had swerved slightly to align itself on a course directly toward the Ford. He allowed himself a single thought, which took the form of a number, the maximum sum he would agree to. He would listen to the proposition, and then he would cite the number and call an end to this meeting. 'Yes?' He tasted corrosion in the syllable as he uttered it.

Malenky chatted further, still chuckling now and then.

'Mister Malenky warks vury close with autharities in this investigation. He knows they do not wish to make a problim for Dixie. But, on other hend, they must question. This is vury good opshun.'

Malenky was nodding and simpering again, delighted with himself, and Pendergast felt once more the urge, now slightly nauseous, to hit him.

'You see? Whoever finds gurl, Narcotics must question first. Take time, vury careful. You speak with Kinny. Tell him it was bed mistake, giving drogs to Russian gurl. So they both in prison, unless gurl agreeing to not say anything about station or expermint. I thank gurl agreeing, to protact her father, and Kinny agreeing, to protact self. No truble, everybody okay.'

The black car had stopped only twenty yards away, and a man got out. He was a big man in an overcoat and fur hat, a scarf drawn up over his face. It occurred to Pendergast that the vehicle had apparently passed through the dock's security gate without a sticker.

Malenky murmured something aside, pressed the button to retract his window, and leaned out to call to the man, who got back in the car without any sign of acknowledgment. The window hissed back up and Malenky sighed and smiled at Pendergast inquiringly. 'Okay?'

He was aware that his hands were clenched into fists, but he did not relax them yet. 'What else?'

Malenky answered swiftly, tugging a glove and wiggling his fingers.

'He says that is all. Simple, good plen. Get one week, two week, for sure. You finish business, then not impartant any more. Maybe make contribution to fund for police later, when boom going.'

Pendergast regarded the Russian, decided in a flash that his nerves could stand no negotiation. He wanted it over with. If they guaranteed him a week, he didn't care how they did it. 'Two hundred thousand,' he said. 'And that's *all*. He can take it or leave it.'

Amon was startled; he flushed and hesitated, but Malenky knew his numbers in English anyway. '*Dvah*,' he said, laughed and shook his head. He looked at Pendergast with a certain admiring curiosity as he spoke.

'He says this is Dixie business, Amricn business. Always buttom line. He is hoping police vury cooparativ. Maybe discussions later, he will help, if you wunt.'

Pendergast allowed himself a wintry smile. It appeared they would be close enough. The two men held each other's gaze a moment longer and then Malenky nodded decisively and laughed aloud again, with real glee.

Pendergast lifted a hand to stop him. 'There's another thing. What about the herder, this Bear Ear? He knows.'

Amon reduced the question to one phrase, and Malenky replied shortly, still beaming at Pendergast.

'He says no problim. He is fugitif committing murdar. Murdar for drogs. So Narcotics police will finish.'

Finally, Pendergast thought, a moment of rare clarity. He was surprised that he felt relief, and no particular compunction, at this bland death-sentence. He had enough to worry about, and the brutality of Russian law enforcement wasn't his responsibility. In some ways . . . the thought evaporated, leaving him uneasy, and with the same odd, metallic taste in his mouth. Too many things were becoming not his responsibility, out of his control.

'But we must bring the young woman home safely,' he said, enunciating firmly.

As Amon rendered this, Malenky nodded vigorously and gave Pendergast a look of benign, amused pity.

'He says of curse, of curse this is goal. This is Russian buttom line. Doctor Kutznetsova is old and dear special fran of his. So okay? He find her, or anybody find her, Narcotics will question for one week minimam. You speak to young man Kinny. Okay?'

Malenky tugged his other glove, and after stretching his fingers, lifted the hand in a quick wave. The smile he directed at Pendergast was a polite, bland query.

'Okay,' Pendergast said. The black car was moving, swinging out to pull in beside them.

'Thingyew vury mooch. Goot lock.' Malenky grimaced comically at his venture into English, reached out rapidly to shake hands first with Amon and next with Pendergast, then slid out the Ford's door even as it was being opened by the big man, who had left open the door of the black car only one step away, so that Malenky disappeared into it like a large, furry rodent passing from burrow to burrow.

Pendergast did not watch the black car draw away. He could see his own driver now, standing just outside the doorway of the weighing station, waiting for a signal to return. Amon was also waiting, he could sense, behind a discreet, attentive demeanor. Pendergast was aware all at once of his obvious place in this little drama. He was the audience, and he had had nothing to do with the conduct or timing of the performance. Now it was simply time for him to leave the empty theatre.

'Call him,' he said, and the words were thin and hard as two coins.

'Oh yes sar,' Amon said over the hiss of the window gliding down, and thrust his arm outside in vigorous semaphor.

Pendergast watched the driver begin to jog through the light snowfall. He saw he had underestimated again the monstrous gamble of life in this place. Who would have thought this wretched bunghole of the world, known mainly as the frozen grave of millions of convicts, would become an overnight sensation, subject of a lurid international soap opera? Because of one dumb little half-breed tart and a fucking bear? And exactly, *exactly* at the moment when a multibillion-dollar deal was teetering in the balance, when timing and confidentiality were everything, and a breath of the wrong publicity would monkeywrench the entire, complicated package . . .

The driver was close enough now that Pendergast could see his ruddy, smiling face, its expression of sly deference. The effrontery of these people, the range of their demented imaginations, was possibly the only defence against the malignancy of chance, the perverse unpredictability of this land. Malenky's crude, outrageous scheming was perhaps perfectly appropriate, their best hope, and his own shrewdness utterly irrelevant.

He could see how it might work. Drugs and murder would end the romance of Beauty and the Bear, the media would lose interest in crime so ordinary, and the narc police would hold up the investigation for as long as needed. The herder would be history, and Carraway and the girl would have no choice but silence. At the cost of another half-million or so, the boom could begin.

Pendergast smiled grimly to himself, as the driver opened the door and swung up into the cab. Right or wrong Malenky would call the shots in the short run, but there was a little surprise awaiting them – Malenky and all the greedy, crooked minor assholes who depended on him. The boom might come, but it would be very, very short indeed. For Pendergast alone it would be very, very big, and would last the rest of his life.

'Yas sir?' The driver had put the pickup in gear and was holding it back with the brake, watching him in the rear view mirror.

'You know where to go,' Pendergast said. 'Drive.' Then he laughed. It was a rather long laugh, and full of fierce glee.

Amon and the driver exchanged a lightning glance. Then the brake was released and they surged away.

CHAPTER TWENTY

T hey stopped in a narrow basin, a channel for runoff, where the snow was piling somewhat deeper. Kainivilu said nothing, but moved forward and began unharnessing the lead dog. Leaving the shoulder loops attached on the main trace, he slipped a short length of plaited hide strap around the dog's neck. Then he motioned Satchi to come up beside him.

'Hold them,' he told her and indicated with his head the rest of the team.

She was puzzled, since they had already stopped once this morning for a handful of cold meal, but she was grateful for any chance to rest. She said nothing. In the last two nights she had gone beyond speaking, beyond the boundary of words, in any language. She hooked her hand through the harness of the second animal, to keep him from trying to follow, and peered inquiringly at Kainivilu.

'Our dogs cannot go,' he said over his shoulder.

Satchi could not fathom this statement, or his intent, preoccupied manner. She was very tired, and the warmth of last night was still in her blood, so she was content not to move or think. The snow came down intermittently, almost as fine as sand, a shifting haze of light. She found herself hoping it would clear a little more, at least for a while, so she could see the horizon of the country they were crossing.

Of course they did not want it bright and clear. That first evening, stumbling desperately, tentatively, into the darkness, they had heard the thunder of the helicopter, had once seen its flashing lights moving swift and low very near them. They were grateful then that a storm was moving in. The next day—

She took in her breath sharply, for she saw Kainivilu's knife, streaked red, just as the dog jerked and lunged, nose down, into the snow. She had thought he was bending over the animal to check a harness sore or bruise. He had taken it a dozen paces and cut its throat and was on his way back to her, while the dog bucked and thrashed where it lay. She released the second dog and recoiled without thinking to the next in line. She must have uttered some sound, for he paused over her.

'Snow will stop soon,' he said. 'No more food for them. We have to go on foot now, and they would follow us, too many to hide.'

She stared back at him, and he knew before she did that her vision was going, because he sank to one knee in front of her, took her head between his mittened hands. '*Kilu*,' he said, 'Black bird wife, be still. Eh!' He leaned forward, knocked his own head lightly against hers. 'Don't go away now.'

His face appeared to be in a tunnel of darkness, far away from her, but she could hear him as if the words were spoken inside her own skull.

'Good dogs, my dogs, I have to give up. Dogs and sled very easy to see.'

She whispered, 'Tatka, he . . .'

'Ai! I know. Not the same. Do not look. This is like *apapel*, for the mountain, even if we cannot make the stakes. But keep away *kalau*. Many *kalau* here now, all around *nymyl'u*.'

She heard the strain in his voice, almost at breaking point, and it frightened her. His face drew nearer, the tunnel widening, and she could see into his eyes, like glittering black water.

Yes, the *kalau*, the bad spirits, were everywhere. The machines, the helicopters and bulldozers and cutters. The dogs could betray them, and so would become a sacrifice, even if they could not be hung on stakes in the proper way. The people, the *nymyl'u*, had nothing else to protect themselves. She swallowed and nodded, managed a twitch of a smile, and tugged on the main harness-trace to signal she was ready.

He pulled the second dog away to a new place, several yards from the leader, who lay almost still now. Satchi murmured to the dogs beside her, for some had begun to whine and scratch at the snow. She felt the warm back under her hand, saw the yellow eyes and dense, erect hair in the ear canals. She concentrated on these sensations, on soothing the animal, to keep away the vivid image of Tatka bent with his red blade over the dying man. It was clear to her, not as a thought but as a powerful magnetic force at her center, that sanity and survival depended on living entirely in the present, without memory or hope – living in her fingers, eyes, ears, breath.

Kainivilu came again, and this time she had already dropped the first loop on the third dog before shifting over to the next one of the team.

'*Eh yeti?*' He looked at her closely.

She nodded and gave him a quick, wide smile. He laughed, a sudden wheeze, and bent to finish the unharnessing. When he moved away again she watched his back, how he checked the dog carefully, firmly with the strap. The concentration that kept her floating here, from instant to instant, relaxed a little. She was aware of the warmth inside her, and drifted stealthily into the one memory she could entertain, because it had endured into the present, because it was in fact the source of that magnetic force suspending all the remaining past and possible future.

It had snowed fairly steadily the first day, and in the afternoon of the second, the stiff, gusty wind had become a gale, driving them to huddle behind a bank and dig in, for they could see no more than a few feet ahead. They unhitched the dog team, fed them, and tied them to a few clumps of willow that ran beneath the bank, then rigged a rude lean-to from the sled, using the doubled cargo tarp. With wooden pegs Kainivilu secured two fur blankets to close off the ends, and a third served as sleeping mat underneath.

Satchi had never been so cold. She had stopped shaking and could barely stand, but if she fell she thought she might shatter. Watching Kainivilu make this den she was aware of how narrow and precarious was the margin for survival. Without these hides and their small stock of food for themselves and the dogs, they could die within a day or two. But if the weather cleared the men from the mine would likely find them just as quickly. Kainivilu had therefore been vague about how long it would take to reach some haven. If the snow and wind were bad – but not too bad – they might reach one of the small government-run Koryak communities in four or five days.

They had spoken only a little at the outset, and during their hasty meals. She had learned that the men at the hidden station were miners of some kind, and the Russians, at least, were very dangerous. Kainivilu confirmed what she already had guessed, that he had reluctantly agreed to keep her from returning to Magadan, because they knew she had seen the GAZ and might know about the camp.

He thought she would be safer with the *nymyl'u*, he said. And then added that she also belonged there, and he knew this because Pipik had recognized her as Yayocanaut's daughter. She had come to help his son, because Pipik had healed her as a child, by driving away the *kalau* around her sickbed. Now he realized he had been wrong, he should have taken her back right away to her father . . .

'No,' she had interrupted him, and then said simply, 'I am glad I am here.' A great wave of astonishment and relief had flooded over her then. A moment later she half-sobbed, half-giggled at the absurdity of her words, and Kainivilu laughed too in his sudden, soft way. Just as he had a moment ago. She understood then, in an instant, how he could play cards on his son's corpse and laugh in the midst of slaughtering creatures dear to him. It was that, or never laugh again.

They had only four dogs to go now. The dead lay in a crescent, each carcass ten meters or so from the next. Kainivilu had kicked heaps of snow over them to hide the dark stains. She watched and did not watch, and moved again into the memory.

When the lean-to was finished, Kainivilu had held up the corner of the blanket at one end and motioned her to enter. She had to get down on all fours and squirm inside, desperate and clumsy because the cold worried her limbs like a pack of wolves. The grey light barely leaked through the blanket seams. She could hear him rooting in the snow, and clumps of it rained down on the tarp forming the roof, only inches from her face. Insulation, she assumed, and perhaps camouflage in case the helicopter came.

There was barely room for her to turn over, and surely not enough for them both. The night before, without the wind, they had simply huddled against the sled, each wrapped in fawnskin blankets. She wondered if he was making a second shelter, but then the end blanket was flung up and his bulk moved in and over her. When the blanket dropped again he reached back and contrived somehow to secure it with a peg on the inside. Then they were together, in each other's arms, because there was no room for anything else. Her mouth was breathing into his neck, and his into her ear.

'*Kain' eu pipiku*,' he whispered, and she heard his smile in the words. Bears and mice.

The force moving from her heart, lifting her breastbone, was like that of gravity. She had known for days – how many she could not say – it was there, in the form of pity or curiosity or anger. But these were contained and transient feelings; her self remained inviolate. This power leaned against her bones, her whole being, and even as she felt something like panic and tensed to resist, she knew it would pull the two of them together and move them at will.

She tasted the salt on his skin over a hard collar bone, and he chewed a little, delicately, at her earlobe. She could hear his voice rumbling softly, a grunt or croon, perhaps a chant. A dart of the panic came back, a sense of danger and vulnerability, the fury of the gale over them, and she tensed again, drawing her arms in, and his teeth took firmer hold of the soft nub of ear flesh.

She could not jerk away, for she would tear that flesh, and she could not roll without pulling down their shelter. So she bit too, into the looser skin at his neck. He growled a little in surprise, and released her ear, but his weight came against her so that she could not move. '*Kilu*, you say happy to be here,' he whispered. 'But you show your teeth.'

She did not release him. Her mind was a headlong race of fragmented thoughts and scenes. The force in her was mounting, inexorable, like a falling tree. She wanted her mother, she saw Yina curling in the flames, Kainivilu's face hollow with suffering and yet smiling, the helicopter . . . men and dogs dying in the snow and they too would die together . . . unless they flew on black silken wings she would take him with her . . .

Without thinking she had been tightening her jaws on the fold of his skin, and now tasted blood. Simultaneously she sensed his stillness, a reversal of energy, a withdrawal from her, and her panic returned, so strong she uttered a hoarse moan. The next instant she was moving her lips over his shoulder and neck and cheek, murmuring urgently into his body.

Her hands were out of their mittens and inside his coat, forcing it open so she could reach his chest, and he grunted in surprise and pleasure. The warmth was intense and deep, woven with their hands and mouths under their parkas and shirts, until it was a glowing coccoon within which they could move more freely. The heat was glorious, and she savored also the intimacy of their smell: sweat and smoke and fish and wet hide. He was worrying again at her ear, and muttering between his teeth.

'Up,' he said, and she loosed the drawstring at the bottom of her parka and pulled out her shirttails so he could reach underneath them and hold her breasts; her own hands were free to unzip her trousers and pull down the waistband of her thermal underwear. The flap of his fawnskin trousers was dropped easily by untying a single thong.

Then he was in her, and they were a single compact field of warm, dense flesh, inside an insulating sheath of fur and wool and down, for she pulled the flaps of her coat over his hands cupping her breasts, and he spread his sealskin around his buttocks and hers. He moved slowly, though she discovered she was dripping wet and offered no friction. His breathing in her ear and against her neck was long and deep, and she measured her own to it. She arched her back slightly, to take the curve in the shaft of his penis, and he began to rock her a little with deeper thrusts, his face buried in the thick black curtain of her hair.

The last fragments of her consciousness, the horror she had seen, the danger and fear and misery all around – they were swept away finally in a sea of blind ecstasy, a greedy, dark rapture like nothing she had ever known. It was something between and in them both, fiercer and more powerful than the cold death lurking outside this tiny cave of skins. This force animated her body without her volition, hoisted it, made it writhe and quiver as the hot strokes came faster, until they were one convulsing organism, bucking, squirting, groaning its transfiguration; and then loosening in release, panting more slowly, floating in exhaustion. She was warm, sweating, complete. She breathed his name and he laughed again, a barely audible hiss. '*Kilu*,' he said. 'Black bird is good woman.'

* * *

When he took the last dog, she stood and went to the sled to begin unpacking. They would need all of their food, and as many blankets as they could manage. She would have to carry one of the big baskets on her back, hung from a strap around her forehead. She did not question Kainivilu's decision, though she thought they could not go very rapidly over this broken and fissured terrain. She knew the idea was to become smaller, less obvious, because if the helicopter from the station found them they would likely be shot. It would be many days before they reached a settlement, and even then they could not be sure what would happen to them . . .

She shook off the thought. They would crawl over the frozen land until they were exhausted, then sleep together in their small den under heaped snow. She felt strangely calm, even exhilarated, at the prospect. The warmth between them would withstand cold and exhaustion and danger; they would go on, traveling lighter and lighter. She felt once more the lift and freedom of that lone, distant black bird soaring away with the smoke from Yina's funeral fire.

She put frozen sections of raw loin in both baskets, and plastic pouches of the fish and berry mush, and gave Kainivilu their one tin of biscuits. She kept in her basket the little tea pot and packet of leaves. He came up beside her and began to rummage in the driver's end of the sled, but after one smile she left him alone. She could read his face now, saw that what she had taken as emptiness or shock was in fact a kind of intense focus on what was directly before him. He went through grief for his dogs as he had gone through the death of his son and the madness of his wife, as one traveled a precarious trail, concentrating to maintain a foothold.

When she had finished loading the baskets he brought her the few items he had chosen to add. The flashlight taken from the dead agent's snomo. A small hide pouch that held the divining stones. A coil of fish line and two hooks wrapped around an alder twig. A bundle of dry sticks and a candle wrapped in paper. The Makarov and the last half-dozen cartridges in a paper bag. She stowed these without a word, and then Kainivilu drew something else from a large, flattened sack.

'*Velvi-yegit*,' he said, and knelt at her feet.

They were a crude kind of snowshoe, a bent willow frame laced with thongs, with a strap of hide looped to hold a foot. He gestured at her feet and made the motion of flapping wings. He laughed at her puzzlement, and shoved her boots into the loops of a pair of frames. With two quick kicks he jammed the other pair on his own feet and began to stalk around, bent from the waist. Again he stretched his arms and shook them as a bird does, and she burst out laughing.

'Black bird,' he said, 'like you.'

She tried walking and immediately tripped and went down on hands and knees. He laughed too, an attempt at cawing, and strutted around her with head cocked. She got up and tried again, imitating the way he lifted his feet cleanly up from the ground.

'Crow's feet?' she said in Russian.

'Ai! *Velvi-yegit*. You will hop along now.'

She kept her balance and with care stalked to and fro. The frames did help in walking over the rough, pocked, and uneven surface of the snow, which was variously a fine dust or solid ice. Still she felt ungainly, and with the basket slung over her back she would have to proceed very slowly, at least in the beginning.

Watching her, Kainivilu had indeed grown more serious, and after a glance at the sun, now visible through the overcast as a dim silver coin, he pointed to the sled. 'Have to cover up,' he said. 'Then we go away. Fast.'

He carried away the last of the frozen salmon for the dogs, three shrunken silver-grey boards which he buried under the snow at a distance. This was so no animal would tear up and expose the sled to get at them, she knew without asking. The harness he gathered up and stuffed under the runners. Then he removed one of his crow's feet and showed her how to employ it as a scoop shovel, and together they began to heap loose snow over the sled.

They talked as they worked, in spare phrases and hums of affirmation or doubt. Satchi knew without asking, as a simple, natural extension of the warmth that had awakened in her, that he would tell her everything essential about himself and his life, and she would do the same. When they finished burying the sled they slung the baskets over their backs and set off, following the same eroded watercourse. She asked him then why he had come to her station in the beginning, and why he had decided to take her to his camp.

Yina was very sick, he said, but there was no doctor at the mine camp, and the miners would not let them bring in someone from the native clinics that were nearest. But he knew of the climate station far to the west, and set forth with two fast sleds hoping to find it occupied. They got well beyond a relative's camp – the place they had hiked back to after the Sno-Klaw ran out of gas – when the blizzard caught them and they had to kill their reindeer and huddle in the warm carcasses behind a windfall. The next day they picked up the track of the bear and followed it – an omen – directly to the station. They were at first only going to take the Sno-Klaw, but they did not want to leave her, especially after she had eaten *Wapak* and called up her mother's spirit.

'I? It wasn't me,' she interrupted him. 'Tatka, he talked . . . he changed his—'

Kainivilu laughed, another cawing. 'Yayo talked. Talked through your mouth. Heh! Wapak made *you* listen!'

Was it possible? She had spoken aloud in some kind of trance? But she had heard her mother, heard her clearly . . . *You have wings . . . You are the little black one . . .* They were skilled ventriloquists, the Shamans of the *nymyl'u* . . .

They walked on and she thought hard. She was aware of him smiling beside her. 'But my hairclip . . .' She gestured at her head. 'You wanted me to take it out, you remember? And then Tatka broke it, but then it was . . .'

This time the quiet wheeze of laughter. 'Trick,' he said.

She glanced at him, startled into a frown, and found him grinning like a four year-old. She bit back her own smile and shoved him suddenly, so that he staggered, and this made him laugh until he had to stop and bend to get his breath. Nor could she stop herself from giggling. A trick! It was perhaps all tricks. She, too – entertaining children with her preposterous book, and eating mushrooms to hallucinate her mother's voice.

And yet the voice had told her she was a black bird before they called her Kilu; and gibberish from a bad novel had brought the dying boy to sit up and smile at his mother, after everything else had failed. There could be power in trickery. A bear had tricked her out of herself and into this laughter, the blood warm in her face, no longer afraid.

They moved on, matching their swinging, high-stepping gait, and the mad, irrelevant poignancy of her happiness was nearly unbearable to Satchi. She saw that it was indeed a precarious path, that to look back or ahead would be agony. She looked down, and thought of another question, this time about the mine and the men who were there, the Americans and Russians. She had opened her mouth to speak when Kainivilu seized her forearm and stopped walking.

She almost fell, but righted herself and saw that he was listening intently. The snow had very nearly stopped, a diamond dust in the atmosphere, under a light overcast. The wind was only a sigh, over a vast stillness. And then she heard it. Only the faintest pulse in the air, but rhythmic and deep. A helicopter.

CHAPTER TWENTY-ONE

For most of the night Kenny had lain on the couch in his apartment, no light but the blue glow from the furnace. A few times he had gone to the window to look out, and around two o'clock he had seen stars. The day would be clear and cold. There would be no excuse not to fly. He couldn't decide whether that cheered or depressed him.

A little before four he put on the tea kettle and went into the bedroom to dress. The previous afternoon, after a canned dinner alone, he had cleaned his boots and laid out his thermals and cold weather gear. He put on the body suit, then a woolen shirt and nylon ski pants, laying aside for the moment his old Army double-lined parka and his boots, mittens, and face sock. In a waterproof bag he quickly packed his binoculars, notebook, tape recorder, and the case containing the maps he had taken from the company files.

He felt like a soldier preparing for a last, desperate assault, and when the kettle began to whistle he was startled and hurried to remove it from the flame, as if stealth were already necessary. In some ways, in this whole business, he would have preferred the physical challenge of battle. All he actually had to do was sit in the copter and wait to see if the camp and the strange rectangular pits really existed, and hope that Lafe could get pictures of them. But it would be an agonizing wait.

If they were wrong, his career was over. He could certainly kiss goodbye a one hundred and twenty thousand dollar severance bonus, and he might very well have serious trouble with the Oblast police. But if they got those pictures, he would have a weapon. He could turn the situation around. Pendergast would do the crawling, the next time they met. He would demand not only the bonus but a commitment of support from Dixie when they brought Satchi in, and a commitment to give Lafe and Peter first access to the story.

He draped a teabag in his big cup and got milk, butter, and honey from the narrow shelves of the pantry cooler, then shook the last of a box of sugar flakes into a bowl. Two bread slices were toasted on a metal grill dropped over a stove burner. He ate swiftly, mechanically, his eyes empty. He was remembering vivid scenes from the last three days.

He ought to have known something was awry when Pendy was less than pleased at the expedition to Yakut. Or again when Sokhalov vanished. All the same he would never in a million years have foreseen the load of shit coming his way. Pendergast had summoned him to the inner office, and Kenny walked in proud and tall, thinking he was going to confer with the old man on the whole situation, reconsider some options, maybe look into Sokhalov's hypothesis again.

And the bastard had a smile on his face. For a half-minute he hadn't realized what kind of smile it was. The snake-hunter's smile, the set-up smile, the killer smile. Sit down, Ken. We have some matters to go over. Matters that concern you. A very disturbing turn in this investigation. Narcotics are now involved. Allegations directed at Dixie employees.

He had been taken off guard by the drift of this talk, the menacing smile. He had just begun to wonder – with a breath of unease – if the narc police were trying to blackmail the company's management, when Pendy simply shot him between the eyes. *So, you were doing coke with your little piece, your Satchi?* There was complete silence while he stared, blinking, into a contemptuous leer. Of course he ought to have stood up, exclaimed in indignation, protested somehow. But he was paralyzed.

He sat mute while Pendergast told him with crisp, cold disgust that the narcs had affadavits from the small-time hood who had sold him his two or three grams, and also from one of the prostitutes he had gone with in a weak moment. Such petty shit might have escaped notice, Pendergast went on, but for your girlfriend's running off with this renegade native drug dealer, who is now wanted for murder. And the whole circus timed just as a pack of media jackals was gathering. Did he see – had he any *conception* – what all this could do to Dixie's reputation? What kind of damage his fucking around would cause, if it became known in this context?

Kenny had at least presence of mind enough to dodge. He did his best to hide his humiliation and fear, and said the obvious, that he'd had no intention of causing a scandal. A little summer recklessness, an experiment that went too far – but he never sold anything to anybody—

'You don't understand something.' Pendergast leaned across the desk, his knuckles pressed on its shiny surface. 'What you may have done, or whether you even did it, doesn't matter to them. You cooperate, or they can arrange for you to spend the rest of your life right here in a Magadan prison. You *do* understand what a Siberian prison is like?'

Kenny listened to himself breathing, closed his eyes and nodded. He was trying, through a fog of confusion and anger, to grasp his situation, do the sensible thing. Cooperation? What did that mean?

Pendergast went on, in a voice moderating now almost into pity. There was a massive manhunt on the Yakut border and the fugitives would be caught very soon – at any moment, in fact. The police were going to be interrogating Satchi, and in that process he could be useful, working to help her supply information, explaining to her what her circumstances were.

His face had flamed and he started to object, but again Pendergast cut him off. 'Don't misunderstand. The police do not – believe me – give a shit about your fun-and-games last summer. They want just two things: a true account of who shot that agent, and an enforceable guarantee that neither of you will ever say a word publicly about any of this business – no interviews, no books, no tapes, no pictures, no nothing. They're afraid of publicity and so is this company, which happens to be at a very sensitive stage in its development. We want some control over how this thing breaks. Because whatever the facts, the media will twist them to blame the government and Dixie Pacific, and make heroes out of some killer and his tramp.'

He said nothing to this challenge, staring now at the front of Pendergast's shirt. It was a light blue workingman's shirt, but new and clean, with the emblem of a grinning gorilla stitched on the pocket. It occurred to him that his boss's cologne smelled like linament and old flowers, something to do with horses and money. Simultaneously the thought came that he was being told a lie, a string of lies.

'I have Krutko's assurance that no charges will be filed, if the two of you cooperate. As far as Dixie is concerned . . .' Pendergast cocked his head and smiled at Kenny. 'We'd fire you instantly if we could, of course. I hope you understand. But that would arouse suspicion, given the role you've had in the investigation. I might say I have no hard feelings, personally, Ken. I've done what I could to make it easy for you.'

Pendergast opened a drawer and removed a thin sheaf of papers which he slid across the desk top. 'This is a copy of the severance package we propose. We'll supply you with letters of recommendation also. You look it over and get back to me in a day or two. Then I think it would be best if you relocated to our branch in Susuman, where they found the Sno-Klaw. You'll remain as our liaison and stay in touch with Krutko's people, but keep yourself low-profile – and you say nothing, not one syllable, to anybody else. With any luck, in less than two weeks the whole thing will be done with. Understand?'

He didn't nod this time. He took the papers, stood up carefully and said, 'I understand.' Pendergast smiled tightly once more, and with a flick of the eyes he was dismissed.

On the way out he felt his first pang of satisfaction. He had managed a lie himself. He understood nothing, in fact, except that he had no idea what lay behind this sudden, radical transformation in his career. He was only sure that it was not simply a matter of adverse publicity, or a couple of grams of cocaine, or even a murder. There had to be something else.

He went back to his office and read the papers through, every word. It had been more than he expected. The document was not dated, but 'regretfully' accepted a resignation and guaranteed to the employee (left blank) or his designated agent with power of attorney, payment of a lump sum equivalent to twice current annual salary, in exchange for an agreement to refrain from any comment, public or private, on the Dixie Pacific Corporation or its operations, its officers or employees or representatives, and to likewise refrain from any portrayal, in print, television, film, or audio tape, of any subject or person based on or related to Dixie Pacific Corporation or its operations . . .

Kenny calculated the payment would come to about one hundred twenty thousand dollars, since he was getting hazard pay as a field man. He xeroxed the agreement, locked the copy in a drawer of his desk, and slipped the original into the pocket of his coat, which he then put on. He had left the office and was two steps down the hall to the exit when he heard the phone burring behind his closed door.

It was Doctor Kutznetsov. The dry, stilted voice made Kenny sweat and cringe. He hadn't spoken to the Doctor for a week, when the old man called with a request for access to the most recent aerial cruise surveys. After the humiliation and anxiety of the session with Pendergast, Kenny could not imagine another confrontation, or even a conversation with the Doctor.

But Kutznetsov was making a short speech, clearly prepared in advance, not simply inviting him to visit, but insisting that he bring the documents and come as soon as possible. Kenny was in no mood for fumbling painfully through a review of some stupid harvest plan, done in cracked English and his own pathetic Russian. But Kutznetsov would accept no postponement. His daughter's life was at stake. Very serious emergency . . . utmost significance . . . irrefutable documentation . . .

The old man was senile, he had thought, and partly out of a twinge of sympathy and partly to head off the rest of the lecture, he agreed hastily to drop off the material directly, within the next half hour. He jotted down the sheets the Doctor wanted – the oldest and newest surveys, he noted. It wasn't until after he hung up that he remembered Pendergast's emphatic prohibition, but he found himself taking pleasure in the prospect of defiance.

By the time he had filled his briefcase with the maps and was in the car, he had sunk again into puzzlement and a fretful dread. Pendergast's brutality concealed a vein of anxiety, he was sure of it. It simply wasn't credible that the narc police were using a trivial three-gram coke deal to confront and leverage the biggest foreign contractor in the Oblast. They wanted him quiet and out of the way, like Sokhalov. They were afraid he would find out something. What, he had no idea. He caught himself watching the rearview mirror furtively.

When he came into the Doctor's salon, Kutznetsov rose and approached like a mummy that had undergone a magical galvanic resuscitation. A fierce intensity of purpose had replaced his habitual chilly reserve, and he dispensed with all conventions of civility. He took the briefcase from Kenny's hand and said, 'You and me waste no time disliking the other. Come here and care to listen.'

Dumbly he had followed the old man to the table and waited while the Doctor spread out and arranged the aerials beside some maps and notes of his own. Kutznetsov matched up three sets of a section along the Sugoy River basin, and then began his lecture, using a sharpened new pencil to indicate various landmarks. The sets were supposed to be views of the same area, a square kilometer. One was a single plate enlargement from a military satellite series taken almost a year ago, and the other two were Dixie's composite aerials, one from the first survey three years ago and the other from the most recent cruise update, just over six months ago.

Kutznetsov called attention to a small disturbance near a bend of the river, below two converging timbered ridges, visible in the satellite photo but missing from the identical spot in the two sets from cruise surveys. A small blip and two odd rectangular marks. The Doctor gave him a hand lens, and ordered him to examine the photos more closely.

The blip was round, a tent he guessed, probably an inflatable six-man job. The rectangles were peculiar, possibly a huge regular boulder or a squared berm, and a trench. Around both were a number of yellow stripes, the ubiquitous sign of vehicle tracks. Now, the Doctor rasped in his ear, please observe that in second Dixie set, the northeast quadrant, where this complex should be, there is nothing. Empty, and matches poorly with the surrounding quadrants in the composite. That is because it is only a duplicate print from old negative of three years ago – see, here are identical scratches, this shadow – which has been substituted. Otherwise, even if the tent were gone and these odd heaps erased, the vehicle tracks would show up, since they are a permanent defacement of the tundra.

Kenny ignored this dig and said, 'Just a bad exposure or

something. Doesn't mean . . .' He was stopped by the Doctor's severe mouth and glittering eyes. 'Okay. Okay, it's a funny thing to do. I couldn't guess why.'

It was a puzzle; he would admit that. There were occasional unusable shots, sun-glare through the lens or a bad batch of developer, but unless an area was slated for immediate harvest the missed quadrant would simply be left blank in the file and reshot later. There was no reason he could imagine for reprinting and then substituting an earlier take of the same quadrant. Especially in an area on the outermost fringe of their lease, where there was practically no timber anyway.

'These,' Kutznetsov croaked, 'what do you say they are?'

He was pointing his pencil at the dim rectangles. Kenny bent and peered again. He had a depressing sense of being trapped and badgered. 'I can't tell. It looks sort of like a huge brick . . . or a block of some kind . . . cut out of the ground.'

The Doctor croaked again, this time in a tone of savage triumph, and launched a series of questions, as if he were a prosecutor. Yes, the whole point of cruise maps was to be current and accurate. Yes, it was true any time in the last year a plane could easily have been detached to pick up the shot. No, he knew of no other such substitution. No, it was not a critical area. Then why, demanded Kutznetsov, would a company falsify a meaningless document?

He ground his teeth, on the point of exploding with frustration. The damn maps were of no importance. Any company officer, any engineer or secretary or woodsboss could pull any part of the file any time and doctor it. It was some kind of . . . of what? Of petty monkey business. Maybe . . .

The Doctor was going on, inexorable. It was perfectly clear that someone substituted the old print in order to prevent discovery of the camp, which might by now be much bigger. It had been great difficulty also to obtain the satellite photos, and his request for more recent data had been ignored. The Army claimed a small, temporary station had been there for soil samples, though he had searched thoroughly and no agricultural or resource bureau in the Oblast had record of such a thing. But did not Dixie itself have some kind of research project going? Had Kenny not remarked some *hush-hush* affair just before this most recent survey was done?

Kenny found himself staring at the photos, the disappearing tent and swirl of tracks. Had this dried-up old loon actually run across something significant? It seemed ridiculous that management would go to such lengths to hide the location of a research project. But it was true Hart and his team had made a second visit only a few weeks before the last survey was done.

There were visitors, a famous inventor, no? the doctor pressed. Kenny always had trouble arguing with Kutznetsov, whose inquisitorial persistence he took as the legacy of those who grew up in a Marxist state. They were consultants, he admitted grudgingly. Equipment research of some kind. But they had no apparent impact on anything. They breezed in, were assigned a support staff, checked out a vehicle or copter, and disappeared for days, or sometimes weeks.

Kutznetsov raised the coarse frost of his eyebrows. Weeks? What were they doing? What kind of equipment? Kenny shrugged impatiently, but even as he did so he felt the first, strong twinge of furtive excitement. Research on methods, techniques of road building, he had heard somewhere. Some machinery and electronics came in at the dock a couple of times.

Who were these support persons? Americans? Two Americans, but mostly Russian temporaries. Temporaries? From where? What was the relation with Pendergast?

It occurred to Kenny that he didn't really know. They had been recruited from Resource Development, he thought through one of the bureau chiefs, Malenky, who had a reputation as an arranger and dealmaker. A team of four or five who were supposed to know the territory. He'd seen them only once by accident, getting ready to board a copter.

Before he could bring up this detail Kutznetsov was lumbering on, and what he was saying dropped Kenny through another trapdoor into the free fall of near panic. He had contacted this Swedish journalist, the Doctor said, upon Sokhalov's advice and because he had respect for the magazine which employed the man, and because he needed some information not available through his usual sources. The Swede had, by extraordinary good fortune, obtained this information yesterday. Very important information.

Dixie Pacific Company was creating a stir back in America, it seemed. The Swede—

'Lafe, his name is Lafe,' Kenny interrupted, and cracked his knuckles in frenzied frustration. The last, the very last thing he needed was to be implicated in exposing some environmental scandal. They had not overcut by much, and surely—

Very well then, this Lafe had some time ago, through his computer, requested his office in Stockholm to search all new information available on Dixie; and yesterday the editor whose specialty was economics had answered with a message about a new rumour, just now appeared, of a major transaction. A 'big deal', wasn't that the phrase? The impending purchase by Dixie Pacific of a company called Homestake, a mining company.

Kutznetsov paused after this announcement, for dramatic effect. Kenny had only gaped at him at first. Before he arrived he had convinced himself the Doctor was in a sweat over some minor bootleg cutting. But the old man brought him back again and again to the photographs, the coincidence of Hart's mysterious research and a camp that management apparently wanted to hide from its own employees.

Other things fell into place. Everyone had wondered for months why the company kept open its northernmost camps, which operated at an obvious loss, and wondered also about the applications for new resource leases. Kutznetsov had then informed him, with a smug look, that these leases allowed Dixie to control or hold hostage *all* resource development, including the region's vast gold deposits.

What if, the Doctor hissed at him, these deposits – so rich, but so difficult to remove – could be taken in the nine months of winter? What if a machine – a new laser, one might guess – could cut blocks of ore from the permafrost, stack them as one did bricks, and – Why not? It was the oldest and best way – put them on a sled to be taken down the frozen rivers to convenient refining places? What if Dixie transformed itself into a gold behemoth, instead of a timber dragon? There would be a great *boom*! would there not?

Such a thing might explain, Kenny saw, Pendergast's hidden anxiety, the urgency and ruthlessness of his moves. The company had to secure its position – the leases, the technology, the financing – before competitors or greedy government officials got wind of the deal. And Satchi had disappeared from a station not so far from the Sugoy. Maybe . . .

But it was all speculation; they had no concrete evidence except a single duplicated photo. He blurted out his own questions. What about the murder of the agent from Indigenous Affairs? The charge of drug-smuggling? A coincidence and fabrication, Kutznetsov rejoined immediately. That is what is so dangerous. Perhaps Satchi and the herders accidentally found the camp, so this story was invented to make them out criminals. Inspector Sokhalov believes someone hauled the Sno-Klaw three hundred kilometers away, and put drugs in it, to divert our attentions. My daughter has nothing to do with murderers or drug people.

He had looked away, an odd pang through his heart, a mingling of satisfaction and shame. Kutznetsov did not know everything. His daughter had once been naked, bent over a mirror with a rolled-up green bill up her nose . . . He shook himself, suddenly dizzy in the maelstrom of his feelings. The concept of a hundred and twenty thousand dollars flashed through his mind, like a light speeding by a window.

'But we don't know anything,' he said more loudly than he meant to. 'It's all . . . I mean it's very interesting—'

'*Interesting*?' Doctor Kutznetsov took a step and glared at Kenny, their faces not more than a foot apart. '*Interesting*? You do not seem to understand. You must *do something*!'

He began to ask what, but he already knew. The question died in his throat, driven back by the cold fury emanating from the Doctor. In the end he had agreed to it all, had made the call to Lafe himself.

It was a simple plan. He would pick up Lafe in front of his hotel in the next ten minutes, and they would be at the company's airstrip well before people began arriving at the main offices. Casually he would explain to McCloskey the detour in the flight plan – reshooting a survey plat along the Sugoy, in the Northeast quadrant – and how a photographer friend was taking the job because Harris was too busy, but after the shoot they could set him down in Galimyy where he could catch a company truck or bus back to Magadan. Then they would proceed as scheduled to the basecamp at Susuman.

He had imagined it over and over, and now it was less than an hour away. The three of them would climb into the helicopter, and before the white ghost of the sun rose through the ice-mist over the ocean, they would lift away into the brilliant, gunmetal sky, and finally, absolutely, there would be no going back. He would have committed. He had been through the long night of the soul, a night of these restless doubts and surges of determination, a night when he had to define himself finally, the kind of man he was. And he had chosen, he was reasonably sure.

It was visibly lighter, the window a gray rectangle through which he could see another concrete building like the one he was in. Practically all the structures in Magadan reminded one of prisons. Siberia was itself a prison, on the most tremendous scale ever conceived, a prison founded on the dream of escape. The gray light made him remember suddenly coming home to bed with Satchi, after dancing and partying away the night at one of Magadan's pitiful discos or dinner clubs.

That was their dream of escape, last summer. They had thought it all colorful and daring, the shimmering mylar panels and strobe lights, the bad and deafening rock music, the dyed, tattooed, perforated young people. They came home to throw off their clothes, sit on his bed and sniff the streaks of icy powder, then fuck themselves into oblivion. They woke at midday, tired and pale, but feeling – they thought – wickedly happy and free. It was adventure and rebellion with a spice of the forbidden, but it was not freedom, he saw that now. It was over and gone and they were now bound tighter than ever to this grim world.

Escape was a matter of fighting, of having a weapon to protect yourself, he had come to see. That was why he had to take this chance. The pictures would be his insurance, his firepower. Pendergast didn't want this experiment, whatever it was, to be public yet. Pendergast was willing to ruin people – innocent people – to keep his secret. Pendergast needed a lesson, a hard lesson. The notion of a half-million flashed by that side window in his mind. He got up suddenly, like a released spring, and set his empty bowl and cup into the sink. A man had to seize his moment.

He hurried to his pile of gear. He donned the face sock and clamped his gloves under one arm, then hoisted his bag over his shoulder. He glanced once around the whole room before he unlocked the door, and his eyes lingered a moment on the old framed photo he had brought from his family home. The Colorado Rockies, the Uncompahgre in the foreground. What the world was supposed to look like; snow bright and clean on its granite roof, and skirted with deep, lush forest. Elk and cagle and trout and bear. It seemed very far away. An old, old photograph. He shut the door abruptly and hurried down the darkened stairway to the garage.

CHAPTER TWENTY-TWO

In the morning Kainivilu consulted the divining stone by suspending it from a stick and then lifting the stick to see whether and which way the stone swung. Satchi squatted beside him to block the wind, so the test would be true. She wondered at the smooth rock, no larger than a quail egg in its leather cradle trimmed with hair and beads, and wondered at herself. Her life was being determined by this dangling pebble, and yet she was not disturbed.

They were also cold, hungry, and exhausted. They had been hunted by the helicopter incessantly, at least twice coming within seconds of being discovered, even though they had abandoned the relatively easy but exposed routes nearer the frozen river. These circumstances did not concern her very much either. She was waiting only for the next moment, for the sway of the stone, or Kainivilu's sudden laugh; and this waiting, and looking out now and then over the gray, heaving world, was her refuge. She had understood at last that freedom was not a permanent state, but a moment-to-moment experience, like the flight of a bird.

The stone spun slowly and swung very slightly from side to side, as Kainivilu lifted the stick. 'They will come out of the sun,' he said. 'Maybe one day more, Kilu finds a road.' He caught the stone in his hand and untied it from the stick. He smiled once. 'Eat everything now.'

She looked at him, beginning to shake a little. The last stars glittered in the dawn sky. The light snow squalls had ended, and it would be a day of brilliant, bitter cold. 'We have one day more,' she said.

He had wrapped the thong around the stone and returned it to its skin sack. His eyes held hers only for an instant. 'Kilu has many days,' he said. 'Now eat fast.'

She moved quickly, crawling to the baskets and digging into them for the food bags. The baskets had served in the night to keep the hide blanket and its load of snow aloft, creating the tiny cave they slept in. If the cold was severe, they might have to find shelter for part of the day too, and then walk into the night hoping to encounter an outlying herder's camp. They had seen old sign of a couple of encampments before they left the river, and Kainivilu estimated they came from small settlements just north and west of Dukat and Galimyy, where there was a road.

She was making the same mistake, his look had told her. She was thinking again of the future. It was a curious pleasure to know now, without effort, what he was feeling and thinking. She thought that was because her body had learned his so quickly, with almost no interference from words, and because her mind had flown beyond fear and despair, had become only a pair of eyes gliding on broad wings.

She brought out a packet of dried fish, only backbones and a head left, the last crackers and the last half-cup of sweet berry paste. She set these on the ground between them and they huddled knee-to-knee and began to eat. Chewing the splinters of rough, salty meat picked from the bones, Satchi shivered and laughed softly. Kainivilu nodded and smiled, but then looked away to scan the horizon. He would know she was thinking of how he had frightened fear out of her, two days ago.

The helicopter had already flown over twice, and the third time came from behind a ridge, flying low, and caught them in the open. Kainivilu had heard it only just in time to pull her down, her head on her knees, arms folded to her chest. Otherwise, she realized afterward, she would have run. Kainivilu had opened and spread his parka, then curled his body over hers. The noise was deafening; her breath stopped and as far as she knew her heart did too. The thunder of the blades was all around and in her, and, twitching, she waited for rough hands, or bullets.

But the thunder receded, grew faint, until Kainivilu jerked her to her feet and they made their way to a shallow ravine with dead willows on one bank. Hastily he built a lean-to camouflaged by the skeletal branches and they waited out the afternoon, but they heard the helicopter no more. They had been lucky, Kainivilu explained. They had become a rock, or so the men directly above had perceived them. Making oneself small and never moving, that was the best sometimes.

It was obvious now that they were mice, and the wolves in the helicopter had picked up their scent. But mice with the brains of foxes. So they were eating fish. She laughed to herself again. Everything ate fish. But bears most of all, and that was how he had scared her again, scared the terror out of her. She had been exhausted, had dozed in the willow lean-to and then felt him beside her, wrapping his heavy body around her. He had made a sound deep in his throat, and she felt a stirring, a warming.

His growl deepened. Along with her heat came a vague alarm that escalated suddenly when hair brushed her cheek. She opened her eyes with a snap and twisted to look. The snout lay on her shoulder, tufted ears flattened, the small red eyes glaring into her own. The current slammed through her body and was gone, like an electrocution, over in a fraction of a second. For she saw it was a mask even before his muffled laugh. He reached up with one mitten and turned her head away.

'Trick,' he said. 'Bear with man mask.'

Her heart was pumping so hard she could gasp out no more than a little yelp of outrage. The sudden explosion of terror left her weak and trembling, yet her desire was not gone, but seemed to braid itself into the flame of her anger, the old anger at Kainivilu's obstinate, arbitrary, unfathomable humor. *Hooy*, she hissed, and nestled herself roughly into him, away from the cold sky and the memory of the helicopter. He shook off one mitten, then undid the hemstring of her parka and methodically unzipped and pulled down her padded trousers and underwear. Because of the gathering of his own coat at the waist, only the tip of him entered her at first, in short, vigorous pulses.

He was still growling, a muffled sing-song, as if talking to her in the pure resonance of explanation or apology, even as his movement became stronger and deeper, more organized and rhythmic. She caught her breath, glanced back and the mask was still at her shoulder, the coarse hair against her cheek, the eyes alive. She was startled again in spite of herself – though she knew it was only a crude wooden shell decorated with a bear's skin and muzzle and teeth – and also suddenly pleased, flushed, tickled, in the way of one who has entered, exhilarated, a dangerous passage. She giggled, and let herself go, gliding on his long, solid thrusts.

There was something bizarre and unnerving and tremendously exciting in this. His growls became grunts of pleasure and laughter, and she found herself answering in the same tongue. She felt herself large and solid, a resilience that could contain any power. He was a bear and had made her a bear, they were everything in a world otherwise vast, empty, and cold, and this was somehow as liberating and ecstatic as when the raven flew under her ribs and took her away.

Their spasm when it came was hot and savage and brief, a blind shuddering of nerves that wrung her through and through, and left her feeling at once huge and weightless, like a log floating in an ocean. They had pulled apart, covered themselves again, and fallen asleep immediately, without a word, the mask empty between them.

The next day she had known, by her new, sure instinct, that they would not make love again. Of course they had been too profligate with energy needed to fight against cold and hunger and the hunters who stalked them, but that was not the deepest reason. Something was complete and at rest now between them. She felt gratified, almost serene, and closer to him than before, even though she understood that he was withdrawing now, concentrating himself entirely on this last phase of their journey. She knew, too, that the end of this journey would be their parting, and yet she did not grieve.

By some madness or miracle she was happy, in the mindless and ordinary way people are happy at the sun's touch. She had survived and helped another, an *eyem*, and they were still alive. They were *nymyl'u*. People were trying to kill them and they might freeze, but they had laughed anyway, and made a play of preparing food, of walking carefully in each other's tracks. That was how, she realized, they had always survived.

It was time to go. The gray light of dawn made their safest travel, before glare and shadow. They scooped snow over the scoured head and bones, the empty plastic bags, and put on their crow's feet. Shouldering their baskets, they set off down a long slope, fairly even except for a few large crooked ravines that ended in a wider channel which, they had seen the afternoon before, wound through barren, heaving terrain to join the main channel of the Sugoy.

It was a risk to walk into the sun and toward the river, but they would reach a habitation sooner. However they went, they had to proceed by indirection, keeping to the edges of embankments or just under ridgetops or where the snow had crusted or wrinkled from the wind, so the men in the helicopter would not detect their tracks. But it was apparent these men had already picked up traces and knew where their quarry was headed. In the last two days Satchi had heard the pulsing rotors a dozen times, and they had seen the craft often enough and close enough to know it was the same one: a cargo carrier in the Army's green and black.

They spoke sparingly, and stopped every hundred meters or so to listen and watch the horizon. Satchi was surprised at how much they managed to say with few words. Over the course of these five days he had explained to her how they were related, through Pipik's mother, who lost her husband to a whale and so married his brother, whose son's youngest daughter was Satchi's mother; and therefore how Pipik, as the oldest of the Taigonos tribe, came to try to heal her as a child.

He told her also about his work in the mines. As a youth he had hauled supplies to the worst camps, where prisoners' frozen corpses were stacked like logs. He had stayed long enough to learn how to drive vehicles and speak Russian, because he could see the value of these things. He and his brother had saved their money, bought reindeer and gone beyond the last settlement in the west, toward the Yakut country where there were no mines and no logging camps.

But they could not live there now. They needed too many things. His first wife died of bloody lungs. The children were sick, and when Paqa came she got snow madness. He grew silent for a time, and Satchi knew he was trying not to think of these things, the decisions that they involved, again. Finally he smiled in his sudden way and went on.

When the man came to ask him to freight supplies into the new camp he had said yes. The pay was good. The man knew of his reputation. He made two trips a week in the beginning, from different supply posts – Suksukan, Dukat, Ust – then all the way back to the camp. The men did not want to use their own vehicles, because they did not want anyone to know of their business. All the machines and fuel and tents were there already, brought in he thought by the huge Army copter. He supplied their meat and hauled everything else – jars, cans, soap, oil, cigarettes.

He did not understand the reason for this. They told him he must say nothing to anyone at the settlements when he bought supplies. Nor did they want him to see what they were doing, but he had anyway. It was a machine. It cut the frozen earth in large bricks and stacked them. But it broke down a lot. Perhaps, he had thought, they were ashamed of its failure and were trying to improve it before telling people.

They were also bad men, he had guessed that early. Not the Americans, he had no idea what they were, bad or good; they came only occasionally, smiled and put their hands on him, but it seemed to mean nothing at all, which made him uncomfortable. But the *promyshlenniki* – he knew them. They would cheat you, drink with you, grow angry if you caught them and then shoot you.

Kainivilu said this looking aside at her, and she smiled and frowned at the same time. It still would have been better to tell me, she said. He looked unconvinced. She saw his dilemma: the more she knew the angrier the men would be. And would she have believed him? It made her cheeks warm to remember how she had raged at him, mistrusted him.

'No,' he said now. He growled again deep in his throat and shoved her gently. 'You bite.'

She shoved him back, harder, and they laughed together and stopped just before the crown of a long, low ridge they had been climbing. The sun had just cleared the horizon, rendering the terrain as a series of blazing white islands and peaks in seas of deep shadow. The last snow was light enough that the wind snatched up veils here and there and flung them, undulating, down the slopes. They listened, and heard only the whipping and rustling of these snow scarves. It would be very cold and very bright. They stayed silent a moment longer, and then looked at each other and smiled in joy at what they saw.

Kainivilu lifted one mitten and described a crooked line in the air, showing how they would descend the slight slope and pick up a second, steeper ridge where a series of small slides provided hummocks and plates of packed snow that could serve as cover. This ridge ended at the edge of the floodplain of the frozen river, and he explained quickly how they would skirt that wide, pure sweep until they picked up the first trails into the settlements above Dukat. Now the sun was low, there were many shadows, they should go fast.

They set off, shambling along on their crows' feet, their path always curving and angling to fit as much as possible the contour of the land, so their tracks would be more difficult to see. They continued to stop every few minutes to listen, until they reached the slides along the steeper ridge. There, still in shadow, they felt safer and clambered as swiftly as they could over the jumbled ice and rock.

They had nearly reached the point where the ridge melted into the floodplain, and stopped finally to catch their breath. Satchi had slung down her basket and began to adjust its shoulder strap when Kainivilu lifted his head suddenly and made a slicing motion with his hand. A moment later she heard it too. The helicopter again, far away. They remained still, and the sound grew a little louder. She glanced at Kainivilu, but he made no move. He was listening with intense concentration, and as the pulse of the rotors amplified she realized there was something different about the sound, a lighter and higher hammering.

The sound came from the south and was steady, indicating the copter was flying along the open channel, up the river, rather than stitching back and forth. Kainivilu was moving then, not back toward the slides but angling up the last low rise, the toe of the ridge. Satchi scrambled after, her heart quickened by the realization that Magadan lay to the south of them, that others were likely searching for her, trying to save her . . .

From the embankment they saw the flicker of blades, bright as the sun on water, above the horizon and nearer the opposite bank of the channel. A much smaller craft than the behemoth that had been hunting them, flying higher and apparently on a straight path. In a few moments Satchi could see familiar color in the body of the craft, the vivid orange and green of Dixie's vehicles, machines, and buildings.

'Ai! It is Dixie! Catch them!' She hopped in a kind of dance, forgetting the crow's feet, and tripped herself.

Kainivilu stared at her, his eyes widening in alarm, and seized her by the shoulders. She shook her head, shouting now. 'It's all right! It's good! They come for me!' She pulled away from him and broke into a shambling run down the last few yards of the ridge, trying to wave her arms at the same time.

The helicopter was almost opposite them, whirling along on its same course. She could see the sun glint from the plastic window on its side. 'Stop! Stop! Help!' She could feel the words tearing from her throat, and went down on one knee. She glanced behind her at Kainivilu and screamed, 'Signal them! Stop them!'

She got back up and ran again, at an angle as if to intercept the helicopter. It kept on, a maddening, unvarying thrashing, quite loud now. This time she fell flat, and when she lifted her face from the snow she heard explosions. Behind her Kainivilu was firing the Makarov into the air, and the noise seemed tremendous, echoing out of the sky. He fired again and again and again, and then there was only the hush-hush-hush of the blades, beginning to diminish now.

But even as she shook her head violently to clear away the snow, the sound changed in pitch, then in direction. She blinked and squinted, caught the flash of the blades hooking across the channel, slanted in a turn. She was up and running again, her face lifted bare to the sky. The helicopter was coming back, had seen them! It paused, dropped swiftly and paused again, then eased downward and toward her in a long slant. It was looking for a place to land, she thought, but she did not stop running.

The sound changed again, grew louder, more dissonant, so loud she thought with sudden horror that there would be a crash. The orange metal body was startling as it settled and rocked on its runners, blowing up clouds of white snow. Yet the noise was increasing, a crescendo. She staggered to a stop, bewildered, and a great shadow flickered over her.

The thunder was everywhere, she was inside it, and in panic she spun around to see Kainivilu, a doll-figure on the slope behind her with his arm still raised and in his fist the Makarov, and overhead the other helicopter, green with black blotches, a monstrous insect suspended in a wheel of shimmering light. It swung in a tight circle and then hovered so low she could see the open port on one side, the shape within and the projecting barrel. The barrel jerked rapidly back and forth, and above the hurricane of the great blades she heard a light, staccato slapping, like a hard wooden stick run along a fence.

Kainivilu lurched to one side, fell and rolled over. Then he was moving close to the ground, a dark shape with a dusting of snow. The wooden stick was slapping continuously, and the dark shape lumbered on for a few moments, collapsed, hunched forward once and then was still. She spun again, like a drunk, and saw a figure emerge from the little orange copter whose blades were visible now, rotating slowly. Though she could not see his face she knew who it was.

She turned back and ran toward Kainivilu. The big copter was landing, whipping shrouds of snow over the dark heap, fluttering the wolf fur lining of his hood. She was hardly aware of the whistling, bellowing blades or the stench of fuel, did not look that way. She was concentrated, she was hurtling into her own trajectory, leaving the muzzle of the time cannon again, lifting on the black wings that gave her a terrible freedom.

She seized the back of his coat on either side of the red rip and wrenched him over. His face was caked with coarse snow, except for a pink froth all around his mouth. She could see the bubbles breaking. She cried out his name. One eye blinked, and hastily, softly, she brushed away the snow from his brow and cheeks. His eyes had gone almost black, but she knew he was seeing her. He managed a low, burbling sound, and his arm twitched enough to lift a hand and brush her leg.

She leaned closer, saying his name and calling him *eyem* and saying the names of Pipik and Yayo and all of them – Choti and Euna and Paqa and Navakut and Yina and Tolek and Tatka . . . She had to stop and sob for breath, her face almost touching his, and heard him try to whisper. He flapped one hand against his coat, his eyes shifting, and she opened it swiftly, saw and took the soft skin bag that held the stone and his *kalak*. His lips moved again, bending into a smile. She uttered a deep, strange sob, a compound of agony and horror that also contained a fine thread of fierce exaltation.

Then the smile contracted, and his eyes changed. Satchi felt him go, sudden as a stone dropping into swift water. She was herself weightless on the earth, suspended, the only thing not moving. Then there were hands on her body, pulling her erect, a voice calling her name. A man knelt beside Kainivilu, leaned forward to examine the wound in his chest and to poke at his eyes with a gloved finger.

Kenny's voice, sounding flat and metallic to her. *Satchi! Satchi! Oh my god, baby . . . so glad . . .* The English was strange to her. *God. Glad.* His face was briefly close to hers, and she was startled, recoiled from the sight. The wide mouth working strenuously, the white cheeks with pink blotches of exertion, the eyes glancing, roving, pleading like a dog's. But other men were on either side of her, moving her away. They were Russians, two of them carrying rifles. The wolves who had hunted them.

She heard them saying she was in custody, would be held for questioning. She heard Kenny try to speak to them in Russian, bleating medical attention and go back immediately to Magadan and captive of a dangerous criminal . . . He hurried in a little circle and tried to stand in front of them, but they shoved him aside and she heard one laugh and say maybe it was the other way around.

It occurred to her suddenly that there would be no ceremony, no fire, for Kainivilu. She tried to stop, and when the hands tightened on her shoulders she twisted and crouched, broke free to run half a dozen steps back. Two men were rolling Kainivilu onto a stretcher. She saw they had eviscerated his pack basket and spread his coat beside him. The Makarov had been recovered and lay on the coat, along with the flashlight, his knife and pipe, the fish hooks and line, an old wallet. She dived for him, but someone had her from behind and the two men only looked up, laughing, as she was forced to her knees.

The struggle seemed interminable, dream-like. She was surprised at the strength left in her, and more than once she made one of them grunt or curse. She heard Kenny shouting, telling her not to be afraid, not to say anything, that he was a witness; then a yelp, and a moment later, between the forms jostling around her, she glimpsed him being helped away by two others she had not seen before, apparently his companions.

But inevitably they bore her down and trussed her up tight. One of them jammed his hand inside her parka, squeezed her breast hard and said *pizda* in her ear, his breath hot. Another man with a beard, wearing a red scarf, ran the tip of one gloved finger down her nose, jerked it away just before her teeth snapped together, and laughed uproariously.

They loaded Kainivilu in the helicopter first, then laid her beside him, with more laughter. She heard their gusto, their obscenities, their excitement. When the great motor overhead began its whistling, howling, rhythmic blows, she kept her face turned away and sang the old song that her mother had sung at her bedside long ago, the same song Pipik had sung to the burning child of this son, lying dead now beside his new bride, the black bird.

CHAPTER TWENTY-THREE

'**Y**ou look the Aryan Genghis Fucking Khan,' Peter said, coming out of their awkward hug. 'Completely out of place. But it's good to see you, Swede. And you're early.' He signed the white-jacketed waiter to bring the drink the bartender was already finishing.

'The airline fokked up. Actually arrived on time.' Lafe slung his camera bag on the extra chair at their table and they sat down to regard each other, grinning at the incongruous fortune of this meeting.

They would have a little less than two hours to spend in the lounge of the Hotel Bolívar, with its old, dark wood and elegant chandeliers. Another hour for a quick dinner and then Peter had to pick up his bags and a taxi to catch a night flight to London, and the next day Lafe would be hopping off into the jungle in an old five-passenger Cessna.

'Beard will have to go, mate. It's summer here.'

'I keep it for you to appreciate. Shave it away tonight.' Lafe picked up gingerly the nearest of the two small goblets the waiter had set before them. 'Yesus. Thought I'd never need another drink with ice in it.' He sipped, closed his eyes, and sighed.

Peter watched, amused. This look of an Asiatic Viking intrigued him. Lafe's golden beard was substantial and a touch unkempt, shot with gray; he wore khakis and a plain workshirt and slouched in his chair. One could imagine him with an earring. There was a change, definitely, from the cool, sardonic thinker of three months ago.

For ten minutes they matched airport and hotel and street anecdotes. They were sparring, as they always had, but with circumspection. The big project they had hatched together, the original bond of their comradeship, had come to nothing. One swore, got drunk, and got on with it; the other moved deep into the Siberian winter, pursuing ramifications. But they had stayed in touch.

'Jungle will do you good. Steamy, rank, lots of trees. I gather from your evasive remarks over the phone you're still on the Dixie story, warring on the multinationals.'

'Same story. Different place.'

'Bit obsessive, aren't you, lad? I mean, what did you expect from late capitalism?' Lafe did not answer. He had looked away to a table of tourists across the room.

'Six weeks of Siberia would drive any man to drink. But six weeks in the winter, for a story on spec? Madness. I wondered at you, my friend. Whether my Swede also succumbed to the spell of the little tundra trollop.' Peter had already put on the expression of a salacious schoolboy when Lafe's gaze snapped back. 'A joke, mate, only a fucking joke. Ease off. You know my reputation for even-handed disrespect. I'm sure the young lady Kutznetsova was—'

'You have no fokking idea what she was.'

'Well, excuse me. No idea things had progressed—'

'Just shut the fok up.' Lafe picked up his drink and made the swift gesture of an informal toast. Peter performed an elaborate, vaguely Gallic shrug, returned the salute, and they drank together.

'Sorry.' Lafe's gray eyes were steady, his mouth twisted up at one corner. 'You were put out when the film didn't happen. Lot of work for nothing, from your point of view.'

'Forget it.' Peter fanned out his big hands briefly. 'Money under the bridge. We needed higher quality material. You can't do Beauty and the Beast as a drug epic, now, can you? Anyway, I want to hear what you've got on Dixie.'

'I will tell you. But first I have to set you straight on the drug business. That was a police plant. They wanted to call attention away from that mine experiment.'

'Call attention away from. Hmm. Well put. So they hung it all on the restless native and then shot him. But the last time we talked you told me Carraway and the girl did a little dabbling in the snow, too.'

'True only in a very small way. Kenny gave her coke, but it was nothing much. The police only used that to shut them up, and to squeeze a bit of money from Dixie. They also threatened to tell her father about her using drugs, if she talked to anybody. Any reporters.'

Peter grunted. 'Didn't work, apparently. Sounds like she talked to you.'

'It was all a bluff. Dixie had a narrow window for their big move. They held her for six days, and for another three she was too weak to talk anyway. Also, they misjudged the old man. Tough old bastard. He wouldn't listen to them, no matter what accusations they made. He and I put together that article I sent you. Satchi helped with the English.'

'Really. I'm wondering how the woman survived at all. Why they didn't just—'

'Oh, they would have shot her too, I think, if we hadn't by a miracle flown over them first. When they took my camera I thought they would shoot all of us. They bloodied Kenny's nose very well.'

'They can't be all bad, then.'

Lafe smiled. 'He wasn't as awful as you thought. He lost his girl and his job, but he had guts enough to pass on the pictures from Dixie's files. That was his revenge for being thrown out with no money. I gave my little computer to the Doctor and put him in touch with the Greens in Europe. They've got a very promising little investigation going.'

'Christ, I see now we should have been thinking thriller. They went to all that trouble just to buy a little time?'

'You read what I sent you?'

Peter shifted in his chair, lifted his glass, noted it was empty. 'Got the meat of the thing, more or less. You mean that piece in your international whale-hugger's journal. Gathered it was a stock scheme, a buyout . . .' He waved the glass and the bartender nodded and set to work. 'What did your blokes gouge out of those two Wall Street pirates?'

'Five billion. Stack, the Chairman, and three or four others of the big men got about half of it.'

'Very nice. Very nice indeed. And our friend Pendergast?'

'Not so much. Maybe ten-fifteen million. He was a little fish.'

'You explained it all admirably, but I'm foggy on the details now . . .'

'Well, first thing was a development by a Dixie engineer. A man named Hart. He noticed how, with a few modifications, a machine he built for logging could also cut the frozen ground. They already know of course, that they control leases in the Kolyma country, which is full of gold, but too expensive to mine by the old ways. So they went looking for a reputable mining company, brought in a crew for test work.'

'Ah yes. Homestake. Fucking irony there. You remember that whore in the bar, with the backhoe boyfriend? Had our clue and missed it.'

'Of course I remember. I tell you at that time whores know more than anybody in town. So they begin to develop this new invention, a process especially designed for cold weather—'

He stopped while the waiter presented their piscos with a subtle flourish and picked up the empty goblets.

'*Grassius hamigo.*' Peter nodded the waiter away and went on earnestly. 'It's coming back to me. The laser thingmabob. To quarry the permafrost. Little piece on it in the *Sunday Times*. Frightening idea, I gather, to the whale-huggers. But it was all hype, eh? Gimmicks to inflate the stock, start a bidding war between whatshisname – the Cowboy – and Kravis?'

Lafe pursed his lips and shook his head gently. 'Dobbs. But not all baloney. These men are not stupid. The machine works – up to a point. Someday it will probably make some money. But it was exaggerated. That is why timing was so important. The boom mentality is always transient, and in the age of instant electronic accounting, the whole deal can go down in a matter of seconds. Dixie had to line everything up to make their story convincing: long-term leases from the Russians – Malenky delivered those; the merger with Homestake; then a data bank of tests that would look promising enough, when leaked in the right places. They even circulated rumors – perfectly true – that the logging show was over, in order to drive the stock down a couple of weeks before, which was the bait that brought in Dobbs and Kravis, who are famous for buying carrion, for a takeover, which drove the stock up again so that—'

Peter cowered as at an avalanche. 'Enough, enough. Done your work, very impressive, I don't doubt a word of it. But pardon a workin' man's eye for the main chance. I don't see what I would call a crime. Hard evidence.'

Lafe allowed a pause. The tourists across the room laughed at something. 'True,' he said finally. And then, as if an afterthought, 'Malenky.'

'A cunt, I grant you. Our old friend the inspector – what happened to him, by the way?'

'Sokhalov?' Lafe's mouth became a tight line. 'He came back, but they had removed his spine.'

'Ah. Too bad. He was a rather clever fellow. Not good enough at hiding it, apparently. Anyway, before I left he'd already figured out Malenky was the connection to the Army, had pried the helicopter off them, and had brought in the narcopolice for muscle. No question they were a nasty bunch. But as far as connecting Dixie directly to all that . . .'

'Without Dixie none of it would happen.' Lafe was leaning across the table now on his elbows, his eyes clear and cold.

'One point of view. Unfortunately, it's a little like what I pick up from some of the Maoists here, the would-be bombers. As they have it, it's the North American fascist consumer ideology that is really responsible for Peru's suffering. They blow up the local bourgeoisie because they can't reach the real evil, those spoiled middle-class Americans who want their cocaine and coffee.' Peter opened his hands again, as if releasing a puff of gas. 'Come on, mate. They're all in it. So are we. We're the scribes. We suck scandal. I'm here to feed on the terrorists, and you want to get your fangs into Dixie's Amazon operation. It's all a scam, as the Yanks say.'

'A bloody scam. They shot the man down like a dog. I saw. Would have shot her too.'

'But Dixie would never . . .'

'Oh fokyew, man. Five billion. Dixie didn't care what Malenky did. What are you thinking? What has happened to you?'

Peter leaned across the table too, his grin wide and white and close. They were both aware that their voices had carried; the room had gone quieter and no more laughter came from the table of tourists. 'You cut me off,' he said softly. 'I was about to say that Dixie wouldn't have done anything so stupid on its own. I wager they hired Malenky to keep their little project quiet and well supplied, and then found themselves in a shitbog with a gang of dangerous psychopaths. Okay? Seems to me, mate, that something has happened to *you*. You're on a bloody crusade. D'ya mind my askin' you why?'

Lafe looked down at one of his hands lying still on the tabletop, made a fist and raised it an inch before striking the polished wood with a soft, soundless blow. He seemed to be concentrating, forming an answer. He lifted and dropped the fist again. Then he looked up and began to speak rapidly, quietly.

'There is a very small village, not so far from where all this happened, where we found Satchi, where the man called Bear Ear was killed. Near Suksukan, on the Kolyma. Maybe two hundred people there. A few buildings, couple generators, a lot of tents of reindeer skins. Just two years ago the road came in and they build a school. For the native children – Yakut, Koryak, and Chukchi. You know who is signing on as the new teacher, at what works out to about forty English pounds a month?'

Peter cocked his head on one side, then the other, looking steadily into Lafe's eyes, which were quite nearly the color, he thought abruptly, of the Siberian landscape he remembered. 'I think I do,' he said.

'And you are thinking, but she doesn't have to do this, they could move to Krasnoyarsk or Irkutsk or even Moscow, she could sell her story – not for the big bucks we thought, but something respectable at least – or she could get a job translating or tutoring.' He stopped, waiting.

'Did cross my mind.'

'In this school many children are orphans or got left by their families because there was no food. Two of these children belong to a brother of Bear Ear, and this brother and one uncle disappeared coming back from the Dixie camp. Then there is a medical post in Strelka, for the Koryak, run by Indigenous Affairs – Malenky's people. There is an old man there who sings and beats a little drum all day long. He pisses on himself and nobody cleans him up. I was there, I saw him. He was the other uncle of these two brothers.

Now, you remember the agent who was shot, one of Malenky's boys at the Dixie camp? The police say that Bear Ear killed him with Satchi's gun, but Satchi told me it was this old man. Very old man, a stick who pisses on himself. He shot this agent because he was trying to rape Satchi.

'These are the last ones to come in, Bear Ear's people. They didn't adapt, you see. Couldn't escape. Had nothing but a few skeleton reindeer, old guns, skins for clothes, some baskets. Bear Ear, the last one of the last ones. And he came in because of her, because of Satchi. She had tried to help his boy, a boy of about five years, who died of fever. They burn up his body in front of her. And he knows what Malenky's boys would do to her, so he tries to take her back himself. They go three days with dogs, four days on foot, the helicopter hunting them all the time. Very cold, very little food.'

Lafe is looking up at Peter this time, the gray eyes colder still, freezing even, and the fist comes down solidly enough to make a sound. 'And we fly over, and they shoot off their gun and we see them and they think they are free and she runs to us, and just then the Army helicopter slides over the hill behind, and they shoot him. And you think that is it. That's the end. You think you see. No, no, don't nod. You don't see. I didn't see, we don't know a fokking thing.'

Peter licks his lips, not used to having nothing to say. He is saved by a distraction; the tourists are leaving, not looking in their direction. He watches their retreating backs and then gets out one syllable, almost whispered. 'Shit.' He looks back to Lafe again, peers more closely. 'There's more.'

'She was pregnant.'

'Ah. Ah, so . . .' Peter tries a grin and discards it, hunches his shoulders as if in an invisible rain. 'So it goes. That asshole. Now that qualifies as tragedy. What—'

'No, no.' Lafe shakes his head. 'Not Kenny. The Bear. She laughs when she says that. It is mental stress, I think at first. But it was curious how light she was about it. She tells me everything, all I have told you, and then says this was her education; she learns everything from a bear in the mask of a man. This bear lost everything: his children, his family, and he goes on anyway. Finds food, finds shelter, finds a big black bird for his mate and plays with her. Gives her cubs, you see? And then dies with a smile. How many people, she asks me, could do this?' Lafe himself smiles faintly, embarrassed and defiant. 'And she answers her own question. No people I know, she says. Only bears.'

Peter is watching Lafe's hand, unclenched from the fist, and sees it is trembling. He sighs and grimaces, looks up at the ceiling and then back to Lafe. He squints. 'Mate,' he says, 'I think you're a bit too close to it. I respect what you're doin', I hate the bastards too, and they've fucked over the natives – Christ knows the poor buggers in the bush are getting it stuffed to them everywhere – and what happened to the Kutznetsova girl is a bloody shame – talented, beautiful young woman – but you can't let it eat you alive. The world does what it does, man, and we just keep the books. Get the story. That's all. We—' He stops, seeing Lafe's smile. 'All right. So you know this.'

'I have to make you see something. Beautiful young woman wants to go live with these hopeless ones. Live with these old men and lost children. Teach them, read them books in a little shack in the mud. Have her cubs. Be the widow of a bear. She wants to. *Wants* to. And you know why?' He is smiling fiercely now.

Peter has recoiled slightly and looks sober. After the first sip, his pisco has gone untouched, but he picks it up now and drinks with concentration. When he is done there is a light mustache of white foam on his upper lip. 'Was about to say no, but maybe I do have an inklin'. She's *not* doing it to make somebody's movie. If that's what you mean.'

Lafe regards him with a level interest, almost surprise. 'Yes. Very close. Good.' He takes a deep breath, then another. 'To die with a smile. That is why. With a smile. And that is more than just a story, Peter.'

There is a pause. Peter finishes his drink, sets down the goblet and they look at each other, then away. 'All right.' Peter purses his lips. 'That's something. I grant that, mate.'

Another silence. Then Lafe plants his elbows on the table and rubs his temples with both hands. 'Was a long flight. Maybe I am thinking about this too much.'

Peter recovers a little of his grin. 'Well, you know me. I'm one of those who will die with a jeer on his lips, but I've enough blood in me veins to see your Satchi was a rare one. Her old man too. And I hope you kick their asses – Stack and Pendergast and the lot. So forgive the vulgar remarks, and . . .' He glances at his watch. 'What say you finish that drink and we take a stroll to catch a bit of Lima's foul air, before we find ourselves a *chifa* for an early dinner?'

Lafe considers, gives his friend a swift, rueful smile. Then he drinks his goblet and reaches for the camera bag. They rise and go to the bar, where Peter pays their check with a twenty dollar bill, indicating with a lifted finger that the change is all tip. The huge, ancient door of dark hardwood with iron fittings is ajar, and they step through it.

Except for one couple at a window table, talking in an intense whisper, the bar is now empty. The two waiters are at rest near the bartender. They have watched the two men leave, and now exchange a look. The bartender lifts his eyes briefly heavenward, an ambiguous comment. Then their eyes return to the very small television on a shelf beneath the bar. There a beautiful young woman is emerging from her bath, to a music just at the threshold of audibility, and looking back at them over a smooth, golden shoulder.

CHAPTER TWENTY-FOUR

A n egg this morning, and her father had prepared it for
Satchi in the old silver cup. He had also cleared his papers
and books from the main table in the salon and set out
bread, a heel of cheese, the tea things, and a single silk rose in a
slender vase of yellowed cut glass.

'The tea is hot,' he said when she came in, though he did not
look up from his desk. The screen of his little computer was full
of lines and figures. His voice was taut, rougher than he meant it
to be, she knew. She was touched at the hint of formal ceremony.
Her bags were packed and already set by the door, and this would
be their last breakfast together for many weeks. She was aware the
egg and the rose also marked other, more profound changes.

She took a cup and filled it from the small brass samovar they
used for breakfast, then sat in the chair nearest him. When he had
finished scribbling down a note from the screen, she said, 'You
look happy. Have you found something?'

He glanced at her, frowning. 'What?' He shook his head
impatiently. 'We find plenty of material, that is not the problem.
Happy? I do not know what you mean.'

She laughed before she could stop herself, holding the teacup
precariously. Her father was a man who could not bear to realize
his own happiness, who preferred to nurse it like a habitual,
unconscious cough.

'You look interested.'

'It is appalling. They – I speak of three or four men – made
almost four billion dollars. Ruining others. And our best revenge
is likely to be that we *embarrass* them.'

'At least you have smelled them out. With your Swedish ally.'
She tilted her head at the little computer. 'Do you want me to
look over the English?'

'Later, if there is time. The taxi is coming at eleven.'

She sipped reflectively. 'I told him, you know.'

He regarded her, and for a fraction of time she felt shame. She was being defensive, and that was foolish.

'You may tell whomever you wish. I tell no one.'

They were silent for several moments. Satchi glanced again at the computer. 'There is a telephone at the school in Galimyy. Perhaps I can call every week and help with any problems in translation.'

'As you wish.' He fiddled with a pencil, prepared to write again, and then set the pencil down. 'You know my feelings on this.'

She sighed and then got up, conscious of her heaviness, even a little defiant in the firm way she set her feet down. 'Come,' she said, 'eat breakfast with me.'

He stood and moved to hold her chair from the table, an ancient and automatic courtier. She waited for him to pour the tea, then smiled across the table as she picked at the egg with a small, ivory-handled spoon. In spite of himself, glowering at her from beneath his white brows, he smiled back, the ferocious little smile that she, as a child, and her mother had so often teased and tormented him into yielding.

'That's better,' she said.

'You,' he said. 'You are feeling well? It is a bumpy ride.'

'We are fine,' she said. A tear came magically, from nowhere, and ran down her cheek. 'Now please eat.'

Embarrassed, he became preoccupied with buttering his bread. Turning and scraping the knife against the crust, he said, without looking at her, 'You must rest every day. In these provincial schools they will try to give you everything to do. You must make clear—'

'Hush, Papa.'

He looked up then, and she saw in his gaunt face a bewildered suffering, deeper than grief and anger. He did not understand her; and he was a man for whom understanding was the only redeeming good, the only salvation.

'I will be fine, Papa. You must not worry. Some of my new relatives are there to help out. I know you do not see why I have chosen as I have. I wish I could explain.' She was calm, despite a heart full of sadness. She did not bother to lift her napkin to wipe away the glistening tears on her face. 'Perhaps it is like your feelings for the prisoners in the camps. Or for your hawks and cranes and mice and frogs.'

The comparison sounded lame even to her, and the Doctor's cheeks were tinged a pale rose. Without meaning to, she had stung him.

'I did not join the prisoners, or go to live with mice,' he said stiffly.

You married a fox, she thought in a flash, but held her tongue.

'I would know one thing,' he said. 'Whether you loved this man.'

She heard the tremor in his voice and did not answer right away. She ate with care, her eyes lowered. She had thought of this word often, in various languages – *amare, amour, Liebe, love* – and had rejected them all. 'Not as you mean it,' she said finally.

'Do not try to guess what I mean. I only want to know if you cared. If you were at least half in love, as you said of Kenny once.'

Now she felt a rush of blood to her face. 'I did not love Kenny. Ever. Whatever I said then.'

Her father looked away and his mouth drew into an ugly little smile. 'A woman is no loaf of bread one man can eat.'

She sat stunned. His eyes came back to her, furtive and already anxious. It was an old, vulgar proverb, and she understood finally how deeply she had hurt him.

He had opened his mouth to apologize, but she jammed her spoon into the egg cup and spoke rapidly, softly, and with merciless clarity. 'I am not anyone's loaf of bread, papa, and I do not belong to anyone, not to you either, and love is a word I do not use anymore. It is a name that attempts to control and make acceptable what is not manageable or nice or fair or sensible or anything else.

'So. This match I can tell you. At the time we were together we had no one but each other, and we had nothing else. Not even hope. And in those circumstances you see into people, all the way, and what I saw was an *ayem* – what they call a strong man, a leader – and the only man I've ever seen who was truly at peace with himself, who was truly beyond fearing death, or horrors worse than death. And this man gave what was left of his life to me. So I am giving back.'

She stopped and closed her eyes, because she was remembering now the way he had bent and stalked on the clumsy snowshoes, cocking his head so like a bird, absurdly convincing even though his bulky, ragged shape was that of a bear. She had laughed like a child, even while the deadly shadow was wheeling through the sky, hunting them everywhere.

'And something else.' She opened her eyes. Her father lifted his head to look at her fully. 'I told you that the old woman, the mother of Bear Ear, was probably the one who came to heal me when I was very young, who gave me the little charm. She knew our Yayo, said we were of the same clan, the whale people. She told me I was very, very ill. Is that true?'

'That is true,' Doctor Kutznetsov said hoarsely. 'But listen, I – I did not mean—'

'I know. It does not matter. I know what people will say, what they think, and I am sorry it hurts you. But I am curious to know why you brought this old woman – her name is Pipik – to my bedside. You, a doctor, let her work her spells – her mumbo-jumbo, as you surely thought of it – on your own daughter.'

He put one hand to his forehead, the long, knobby fingers spread as if to fence in some restive memory. After a moment he said, 'I did not think you would live. I thought it was a dust-fungus at first, then asthma, then pneumonia. I tried sulfa, penicillin – nothing worked. You could not breathe, you would not eat. You could take in nothing, and were wasting away. Your mother . . . well, she sent out word somehow to her people, without telling me, and this woman, this Pipik—'

'Mouse,' Satchi said with a swift smile.

'– this woman came with her drum and her charms, and a powdered plant-stuff of some kind. I knew I would be ridiculed, or even taken in for questioning, if they found out I permitted these ceremonies. But I had tried everything I could think of. I thought you might leave us at any moment. You were five years old and could not . . .' He was no longer able to speak and the muffled sound he made would have been a sob, but for his tremendous effort.

She resisted the impulse to reach across the table and touch him, for she knew he would be embarrassed and ultimately resentful.

'And so you took a chance. And here I am.' She smiled fleetingly again. 'Still bedeviling you. Though of course – you are about to say – I might have lived anyway.'

'I cannot know that.' Doctor Kutznetsov had recovered his voice, still hoarse but now almost a whisper. 'I do not pretend that our modern and scientific system explains every mystery. I do not know to this day what was the matter with you, and in the same circumstances I would call this old woman with her powder and drum again.'

'You took the same chance with mother.'

'She was dying. Of course I did whatever she asked. It was cancer, and I had no doubt of that, but in every disease there is a psychological factor, whose somatic effects can be very significant.'

'Ah. So are you saying that sometimes – in certain dire circumstances – the spirit has dominion over the flesh? And we may somehow go beyond ourselves?'

He gave her a small grimace of amusement. 'You imagine I am an old stick without imagination or dreams. You believe I am only a rationalist, with a heart the size of a bean, and as hard, but that is not so. I loved your mother very much, and I respected her beliefs, however different from mine. And yes, as for the foxes and mice and hawks and so forth, I hold them sacred, too, in my own way. They are certainly forms of life more benign and enlightened than our own. But we are human, we are part of the monstrosity of civilization. We must recognize that and use our talents to—'

'Wait! Wait, Papa!' She interrupted him with her voice, her hands, and eyes that flashed into his with an imperious plea. 'Go back to this respect you say you have. Respect? Beliefs are not a matter of respect. To hell with respect! What if I believe Yayo is alive still, a spirit who is with us here? What if I told you that she spoke to me, as clearly as you hear me speak now? What if I said she guided me into this reindeer herder's bed, so she could have grandchildren?'

He stared at her. His face had once more taken on a faint flush. The silence between them was filled by the muttering of the gas heater and the distant rumble of a plane taking off from the airport at the edge of the city. The six hours of light for this winter day had begun, and in less than two hours Satchi would embark on her own journey in a much smaller craft.

'You . . . you believe this? You have converted then, to the pagan religion of your mother's people?' Doctor Kutznetsov shook his head, as if at some bothersome buzzing sound. 'You abandon your studies, the hope for a scholarship in England, and go to a remote native village to teach and to bear a dead man's child – because you heard your mother's ghost?'

'Not a ghost. *My mother*. She is a spirit that I carry within myself. And Kainivilu is another. I see them and hear them every day, and they are telling me I belong with the *nymyl'u* now, and my children belong there.'

'*Children?*'

'Yes. There are two. Boys.'

'But you do not—'

'Yes I do. Without any examination. I know. I will not attempt to explain how I know but I do.'

He was pink with exasperation and shock, and she burst into laughter. 'I *am* sorry, Papa. You have had the misfortune to be surrounded by illogical women. And now with no warning you are twice a grandfather. Ah, yes. Perhaps that makes you unhappy . . .'

'Of course not! I am . . . that is, I have always wished . . . but—'

'But not in this foolish and irresponsible way? Would it have pleased you more if I had married Kenny? Or Malenky's boy – he's very rich now, you know—'

'Stop! You insult me!' Her father pushed back from the table, his gnarled hands gripping its edge. 'That was unjust. I detest the Malenkys, father and son. I care absolutely nothing for their dirty money. Yet I went to him on my belly, begging. I swallowed my revulsion . . . all in hopes of getting help to find you . . .'

He was trembling with indignation – she felt it through her forearms resting on the table – and her heart contracted. 'Oh Papa. That was unfair, you are right. I always knew that you were doing everything to bring me home, and it was a great comfort to me, right up until the very end. Until then I *did* want to go back. Desperately, desperately! Until Yina – the little boy – died. And then – you see, Papa, everything can change with something like that. You see that your own life is selfish and small – most lives are – that we are all prisoners behind invisible bars . . .'

The tears ran freely now, dripping from her chin, but her voice remained clear and urgent. 'I was being cruel – I don't know why – and now I'm not making very good sense. But it was my chance to change, to break out of my prison, to be valuable to someone – this bear-man – the same way you took a chance in marrying a fox and calling on a mouse to save your child! I felt like a black bird with great wings, and did not care what storms or cliffs might be ahead. If we had made it to a village and escaped the police, I would have stayed with him, you know. With his people.'

He contemplated her. His frown relaxed into puzzlement. 'Yes? You would not have come back here anyway?'

'Only to say goodbye.' She smiled again through her tears. 'To hand in my resignation as a station attendant.'

'But I have been retired! I would not—' He stopped, uttered an explosive sigh at having been caught by her teasing again. He picked up his teacup, examined it, and then tilted it to drink. Setting it down again, he said, 'My grandchildren, you say. In what sense? Since they will apparently be raised as reindeer herders.'

Her smile broadened into a grin. 'They will be scientific herders. They will speak four languages, at least. And you can tutor them in biology. When they are big enough and strong enough we shall take them to visit England. They will be famous curiosities, like the wild men of America and Samoa and Tasmania, who were shown off to royalty—'

'You are not serious. God in Heaven, Satchi, suppose this intuition of yours is correct – you will have two sons to care for! Have you any idea? What future can they have in the Taigonos? There is nothing there. Nothing. Why—'

'Of course I am not quite serious, but more so than you think.' Satchi laughed, conscious of how startling was her merriment in this context. 'I *do* want your services as tutor, when the time comes. I do intend to educate them well, but not only in science and languages. There are other kinds of knowledge, Papa. In the Taigonos old men and women know things we cannot easily conceive.' There was another pause, during which she saw his expression change. 'You think I am mad.'

'No, I do not think that. A delusion would be treatable. You are a more difficult case.'

'And what is that?'

'You are a recent convert. You believe in transcendence through penance and suffering. Perhaps you think of yourself as chosen for martyrdom. Perhaps—'

'Oh Papa, please!' She was gasping with the effort of containing her mirth. 'Nothing so grand. It is very simple.' She held up a hand to forestall any more speculation, and after a moment was sober enough to go on. 'I only realized – no, best make it even simpler – I mated with a bear. An old bear who merely happened to have taken a man's form. That is how Kainivilu viewed himself, I believe, and I myself discovered that I became one of Big Raven's daughters, on certain occasions. I know you think these are only charming, primitive metaphors, or perhaps hallucinations, but I prefer them to dead facts. I believe that metaphor is the only dimension the spirit can move in.'

She spoke lightly, but with a certain finality, and Doctor Kutznetsov did not reply immediately. He wagged his head in mild wonderment. They heard another plane rising into its trajectory above the city, and the light behind their drawn curtains was growing brighter.

'We are different,' he said finally. 'But I see you have thought a good deal about this sort of thing. Even as a child, I remember, you read a few books on your mother's ancestors. Romantic accounts of migrations, and so forth. But I had not realized how deeply it went. Or that you would forsake your other interests.'

'Nor I,' Satchi said. 'I did not realize many things.'

He understood her immediately. 'You are not a child now. You found a . . . a mate, as you say, and then lost him. My dear . . .'

'I saw him shot down in the snow.'

He looked at her, then down at his hands. 'Yes,' he said quietly.

'We are actually more alike now, Papa. You lost your mate, too. And you came here and made your way when this was a savage place, when millions were dying, in order to advance your country – as you understood it then. But you could have taken a comfortable post in the West, or you might have emigrated after the Union disintegrated, but you stayed. And not just, I think, to care for the hawks and the mice. We love Siberia, Papa, in our own way, is it not so?'

He paused, then gave her the fierce little smile. 'Not as you mean love.'

She laughed, and then they heard the vehicle turn the corner outside and together they stood and walked around the table to embrace. They were both murmuring simple and ordinary words, not aware of their meaning, only feeling the rending in their hearts at this parting, so soon after the exhausting miracle of finding each other again. She could feel his bones through his old housecoat, the tremor in his spare frame.

When they heard the horn they pulled apart, and the Doctor insisted on taking her heaviest bag. He was saying something to her about time, about how it left one no time.

'Time is the great prison,' Satchi said. She was wriggling into her coat. 'I learned that from a bad book, and from children.' When he looked intrigued, frowning slightly, she said, 'It's only a little story. I'll save it for you. Now you shouldn't go out, in that old housecoat . . .'

'I am a Siberian,' he said with affected brusqueness, 'I enjoy it.'

She smiled at this, for it was as close as the Doctor got to humor. She picked up her toilet bag and book bag and went before him through the door to the little roofed porch. It was a typical midwinter day, bright and still and very cold. The driver got out of the taxi as soon as he saw them and approached to carry her luggage.

'I did not mean what I—'

'I know, Papa. Do not think about it. Think about how you are going to embarrass Dixie. I want to see you soon.' She greeted the driver and gave him the toilet bag, which he shouldered before relieving the Doctor of the large suitcase.

'I will come,' he said. It was the first time he had made such an assertion. 'Perhaps I shall bring a few things, to show your pupils.'

'Papa . . . now you will make me cry again. You go inside, before you get a chill. I will hold you to this, however. When the weather is better, and we have a little more light.' She kissed him swiftly on both cheeks and turned and walked away after the driver.

But Doctor Kutznetsov did not go inside. He watched his daughter going away from him, her bearing already more stately, her gait measured. She turned once, with one leg already in the taxi, and waved with a little frown of reproach, biting her lower lip at the same time. The driver had closed the trunk and got in behind the wheel after one glance. The motor gunned once and then the vehicle pulled away, slithering a little on a patch of old, dirty snow.

The Doctor stood motionless after the taxi was gone around the corner and out of sight. He did not notice the cold or the deep, incandescent blue of the sky. He was remembering how as a young man he had boarded the train for Omsk, where he would begin his training for the post at the Kolyma mines. Only his mother had come to see him off, for the rest of the family thought him foolish or possibly mad to have volunteered for such work. Possibly he had been. He remembered only the wild joy of seeing the steppes lift to a horizon that went on and on, of believing that he was riding into adventure, into a future beyond his imagination. He was young then, and perhaps the young were always mad fools. He had thought this of Satchi, when she told him she was with child, and would keep it . . . or them. And now she believed her children were half bear. He wished all at once, with an intensity that caused him to fumble for the door handle in order to support himself, that he were young again, that he were going with his daughter to this remote, outlandish village of herders. To see if impossible things could be true.

He took a long breath and looked up finally, into that sky, deeper and colder and brighter than any other. This land was a place where impossible things were at least believed. He had once believed Stalin was a good man. A smile twitched on his face. That was more incredible than having bear cubs for grandchildren. Let it be a benign delusion, then. Let Yayo have it her way, at last. Wooden charms, sacrificed dogs, endless songs – whatever the method, she had come back from the dead to give them grandchildren. And if these twin boys had the souls of bears, then he would go along with the fantasy. Their father was, at least, a rare man, who had by choice lived the old way and been slain for it. By the likes of Dixie and Malenky.

With this thought he remembered the article he was preparing, and became conscious of the chill, shivering for the first time. So be it. He would fight in his way. Satchi in hers. He would teach these boys what he knew, and the *nymyl'u* would train them in their sort of knowledge. He clutched his robe around him and opened the door. Perhaps that was the only hope for justice. Passionate young biologists, with the souls of big, angry bears. He grunted aloud, pleased, and the noise surprised him. He was smiling the fierce smile, to himself, when he closed the door on the winter outside.